A Master Passion

The story of Alexander and Elizabeth Hamilton

by

Juliet Waldron

Print ISBN 978-1-77145-674-6

Books We Love, Ltd.
Calgary, Alberta
Canada

Dedication

How I Met Alexander Hamilton

In a sepia shadowed bookshop,
Where an imperious charcoal
Cat with yellow eyes glared from
A fly-specked window,
I found you.

You—
Ecstatic, thin, fair head thrown back,
Face shining, 1776 on fire!
No wonder your friends,
Fellow aides-de-camp to the great
George Washington, nicknamed
You "Little Lion."

Across time
We held hands,
Wandered brown-sugar sands,
Watched waves rise and
Toss wild white manes against the reef,
Brother and sister—
We were alike,
Children in peril.

Part One
Love and Liberty

Chapter One ~ West Indies

Sharing a sick feeling, Alex and Jamie Hamilton stood on barefoot tiptoe and peeked through flimsy wooden louvers, all that separated the rooms of their small West Indian house. Both boys were red-heads, but there the resemblance ended. Eleven year old James was well-grown and strong. Alexander, seven in January, was delicate, fast-moving and nervous, like a freckled bird.

"An idiot would have known not to trust him." The beautiful dark eyes of their mother flashed. Rachel faced her husband, a slight man of aristocratic feature, who wore a white linen suit. Like him, it had seen better days. His wife's tone was challenging, her arms akimbo. Her stays, containing a generous bosom, rose and fell.

"I—I—took him for a gentleman." Father sputtered, attempting to fall back upon a long ago mislaid dignity. "He gave me his word."

"His word!? Which means bloody nothing! How many times did I tell you what was going to happen? How many times?"

"Shut your mouth, woman!"

A sharp crack sounded as he slapped her. Rachel, hair spilling from beneath her cap, staggered backwards. From the kitchen came the fearful keening of Esther, their mother's oldest slave.

"There's naught canna be dune noo!" James Hamilton, his long face flushed, roared the words. Scots surfaced whenever he was angry.

"Yes, nothing to be done. As usual." A livid mark glowed upon Rachel's face, but she, with absolute disregard for consequences, righted herself and finished what she had to say.

"This time Lytton's going to let you go. And if you can't even manage to hold a job with my kinfolk, where will you get another? What are we supposed to live on? Air?"

In spite of the fact that it was winter on the island, the best weather of the entire year, Alexander shuddered. Distilled fear slid along his spine.

How many times in his short life had he watched this scene replayed? Listened to Mama shout Papa's failures, watched as his father, humiliated and enraged, used his fists to silence her?

A business deal gone bad! Money lost....

Will we move again?

Every change of residence, from Alexander's birthplace on cloudy Nevis, to St. Kitts, and from there to St. Croix, had carried them to smaller houses and meaner streets. The carriage, the two bay horses and the slaves who tended them, were only a memory.

Mama was shrieking now, about loans and due dates, things which she declared "any fool" could understand. Frozen, knowing what would surely come, Alexander watched as his father, crossing the room in two quick strides, caught his mother by the shoulders.

With the strength of rage, he threw her like a rag doll. She struck the wall so violently the flimsy house shook. Small emerald lizards stalking the mosquitoes drawn by candlelight, vanished into shadow.

Silenced at last, Rachel crumpled to the floor, sobbing. Her once gay calico dress, muted by many, many launderings, lapped her. The under-shift, always scrubbed to a sea-foam white, drifted from beneath.

James Hamilton, breathing hard, blind with rage, tore open the door and strode past his cowering, terrified sons. For the last time, Alexander saw his beloved father's face, a sweating mask of fear.

* * *

"Come on, boys. Out of there."

6

A candle shone in the balmy West Indies night. The voice wasn't unkind, just drunk and hurried. From outside came the bell-chorus of an untold host of peepers.

Alex and Jamie, in shirts too ragged to wear during the day, had been asleep in the only bed. There was a mattress filled with palm fronds in the next room upon the floor, but this time of year scorpions came in. When Mama hadn't returned, they'd decided to sleep in the greater safety of her bed.

Jamie groaned, sat up and rubbed the sleep out of his eyes. The Captain of the Guards, Mr. Egan, leaned over. He breathed rum and seemed unsteady. Behind him, supporting herself on the door frame, was Mama. She was, Alexander noted with a thrill of disgust, bare-shouldered, her cap removed, her shining dark hair loosened.

"Out, boys," she echoed. "Esther said she'd beat your mattress and lay it out after supper. What are you doing in here?"

Neither boy replied. She didn't want an answer. What she wanted was for them to leave. Tomorrow she'd give them a scolding, but not tonight. At the moment there were other, more important things on her mind.

"Here, young fellow." Egan, muscles rippling beneath his shirt, handed Jamie the candle. Obediently, Jamie took it. Their rooms were, after all, rented space in the front of his house.

"Use this to look if you're worried something's in your bed. Your Ma and I won't be needing it."

He threw a grin at Rachel, who was restlessly tossing a dark curl over a pale shoulder. Mrs. Lavien or Mrs. Hamilton—whichever name she used now that she was living alone with her sons on St. Croix—was almost thirty, but she still turned heads whenever she passed along Christiansted's bustling main street. Anticipation caused the captain to deliver a slap on the rear to speed the smaller boy along.

"Don't you touch me!" Alex spun and glared, his thin face white under coppery curls.

Jamie grabbed a handful of his brother's shirt. "Oh, come on, Alex!" He dragged his slight brother through the door. "The captain didn't mean anything."

Alexander was wide awake now, his eyes blazing blue fire. The distant echo of surf, the sighing palms, the intoxicating fragrance of Lady of the Night that climbed in profusion over the house, held no power to still his pounding heart.

Grinning, Egan stepped back, threw an arm that was infuriatingly proprietary around his mother.

"Yes. Don't start," Rachel cautioned. "Just mind your own business and go back to sleep." Her dark eyes turned toward Egan. One hand moved easily across his chest, taking in the feel of hard flesh beneath. Alexander wanted to kill them both.

"If you and Jamie slept where you were supposed to, this wouldn't happen."

"Come on, woman." Egan terminated the conversation, pulling her playfully through the door into the darkness.

"The little brats." Their mother was heard to sigh when the door closed. "I swear they do it on purpose."

In the next room, the boys busied themselves in a thorough inspection of their mattress. Satisfied at last about the absence of scorpions, they extinguished the candle and lay down together. From over the transom came whispered laughter and the sound of the captain's boots dropping to the floor.

In the soft darkness, beside his now stolidly motionless brother, Alexander crammed fingers tightly into his ears. Tears pooled against his cheek.

"Oh, Papa," he whispered into the night. "Papa, please come back."

* * *

"You aren't bastards, you know, no matter how many say it." In their room over the store, Rachel sipped at her glass of rum and gazed out the window.

8

Jamie rolled his eyes at Alex. Here it came, the nightly monologue. And what difference did their innocence make, anyway? Jamie knew there was no escape.

"My mother made me marry this rich Dane. Anyway, *she* thought he was rich." Rachel began as she always did. "A wretched worm, that Lavien! I was about your age, Jamie, when she gave me to him. The fool was even worse at business than your father. It only took him a year to lose my dowry."

Rachel smiled crookedly, drained her glass. The man she'd been expecting hadn't appeared. It had left her melancholy.

"Lavien got crazy drunk and beat me. I hear he beats the donkey he's got for a wife these days, too. One night, in fear for my life, I ran away. That cowardly, spotted caitiff went to the magistrate and said I was unfaithful, that the man I'd run to for protection was my lover. He had me locked in prison for adultery."

Rachel frowned, stared at the ceiling and twirled a dark curl meditatively. By now, Alex knew mother was already very, very drunk. Inwardly, he shrank.

Fat bugs circled the oil lamp, creating a dizzy pattern of light and shadow. The space held their mother's bed, a wardrobe, a hulking sea chest, a table and three chairs. Sometimes it was a pleasant place to be, for the high windows of the room caught the prevailing breeze. In this part of Christiansted, though, where there were taverns and whorehouses, it was best to be above street level at night.

A roaring sea shanty began in the inn a few doors down. Jamie's head swiveled toward the sound in a gesture of impatience. He wanted to be away, out on the street with his friends, but Rachel was still busy with recollection.

"Captain Egan got me out of jail and sent me back to Nevis, to my Mama. I carried a child, but as soon as he was born, Mama gave him to a nurse and sent them back to Saint Croix. I never suckled the ugly little brute, not once. Lavien got a divorce, but what justice is there for a woman in this world? Bloody none, I'll tell you. The law, the Danish Law," Rachel twisted the words, twisted them so

9

that they became a sneer, "says that because I'd run away from a man who'd threatened to kill me, I was no better than a whore, and that I could never marry again."

Into the pause that followed, tree frogs shouted. The relief their neutral chorus provided was broken by drunken laughter from the street below. Inwardly, Alexander damned those sailors. They seemed to mock his mother's painful story, the one she couldn't stop retelling.

Across the table, his older brother maintained an expression of studied disinterest. He'd heard it a thousand times. Alex knew that Jamie had plans to meet his forbidden friends, that "bad company" he just naturally seemed to prefer.

"Still," Rachel's gaze fixed upon the intent face of her youngest, "When I met James Hamilton on Nevis, he said he didn't care a fig for any stupid Danish law. We were married, too, married by a clergyman."

She leaned across the table to stroke Alexander's thin cheek. "So, these Danes may call you bastards, but you aren't. And," she added, sitting back and splashing a drop more rum into her glass, "they may call me whore, but I'm not that, either. Not that we wouldn't live better...."

For a blessed moment, the tree frogs sang unaccompanied. Then his mother concluded as she always did. "If your father had been half the man I thought he was, we'd be rich now and no one would dare talk to us like they do. Hear me, boys! In this rotten world, money is the salve that soothes every sore."

* * *

"And a couple of pounds of salt pork too, young fella."

Alex tugged open the cask, then picked up a knife, excised a chunk of the hard gray stuff, and weighed it on the balance scale. As he neatly wrapped this in a piece of newspaper, he said, "You owe us six shillin's, Mr. Inness. We could use some on account. Today, if you please, sir."

The red-necked customer scowled, but Alexander held the package tightly to his skinny chest and stared up steadily at the man towering over him. He was only ten, and small for his age, but there was not so much as a flicker of fear in his blue eyes.

The money was due. The money was for Mama.

There was a grumbling pause, then the purse came out and a few coins were counted down. "Well, Alex, 'course, ahem, I cain't give you all, but will that hold you for a while?"

"Yes, sir—for today, sir. But we can't keep your account open all the time because we have to pay Mr. Cruger on thirty day terms. That's how you get everything for less here than over at McIntyre's."

Alexander toted the difference and handed over a receipt.

"Thank you, Mr. Inness, sir. I'll look forward to the rest on Friday." His manner was differential, but his tone was not.

When the customer left, muttering and shaking his head about being pushed by a child, Alexander went straight to the ledger. No new customer came, so he climbed onto the high stool and began working at the figures.

Jamie had slipped out earlier. He was probably down at the docks by this time, hanging around with the thieving, gambling idlers he called friends. Alexander routinely covered for his absences. He didn't miss his brother. Jamie was a nuisance. He gabbed too much with the customers, never asked for money and never wrote things down.

* * *

Some months passed. Jamie was apprenticed to a carpenter on the other side of the island "for his own good." Just after, a fever swept through Christiansted. Rachel caught it first, then Alexander.

In their upstairs room, Mother and son tossed on the same bed, tended feebly by old Esther, the only slave not rented out. The surgeon came, bled Rachel, and gave her medicine. Two days flowed by in a throbbing, aching blur.

Both patients were drenched in sweat, always thirsty, skin on fire.

Alex didn't know how long it was that he and his mother lay in that bed. The passing of a day was signaled by the reappearance of the surgeon to bleed Mama, the hours by Esther. Humming softly, whispering prayers to the many gods she knew, Esther would sit beside the bed and patiently spoon chicken broth or some cold, bitter herb tea into their parched mouths.

Day and night spiraled; the doctor appeared to give Rachel an emetic. For the first time, he bled Alex, too.

Mama had been tossing and moaning, but, after a long spell of vomiting, she'd grown quieter. A kind of rattling came with each breath. Alexander, aching and shivering, drifting in and out, didn't mark the moment when the sound stopped.

In his fever, unable to move or speak, the pool of urine in which they lay felt strangely good, comforting. Esther's withered, weeping black face materialized for a time and then disappeared.

Next, the doctor and two Danish officials arrived. They began poking around, picking up ledgers and opening drawers. Alex tried to protest, to order them out, but only a kind of murmuring came. The fever sat like a giant on his chest.

"Ask Mrs. McDonnell to come and lay her out."

They took things—Mama's things…!

Alexander struggled to rise, but he couldn't.

"Esther." He whispered to the old woman who rocked and wept beside the bed. "What de doin'?"

"Takin' your Mama's things for de Court, Masta Alex. Soon de goin' to take me, too. Oh, what'll become of poor Esther? Your sweet Mama knowed I could'n work n' more."

Alexander tried to push himself upright, but everything disappeared as soon as he lifted his shoulders from the pillow.

Mama is dead.

The pale yellow room and everything in it flowed. The pain in his joints, in his head, was shattering. Alexander now had an idea that he, too, would die.

"Not much left of the boy." Apparently attracted by his struggles, a fat face peered down. "Hey, you, Hector! Put him over there, away from the body."

The black obediently gathered Alexander up, then, without ceremony, dumped him onto the palm frond mattress on the floor. Movement was agony. Blackness rushed him again.

"Don't look like he goin' to last." The same fat, unsympathetic face stared down, a face familiar, although Alex couldn't summon the name.

"Leave the old N'gress stay. She can tell us when he dies."

"Too bad 'bout him. He a real sharp little fella, a big help to his Mama."

"Well, that's as may be," said fat face, "but I never seen a whore's get amount to a damn."

Afterwards, Alexander believed it providential, the flash of rage which coursed through every fiber of his weakened being. Fury pulled him back from the brink.

* * *

Alexander gazed at her, now neatly laid out in her best dress on a board set between chairs. She seemed peaceful now, and she had not been that way often. Rachel had been a restless beauty, her last years spent in an almost continual state of helpless rage.

She is quiet now. Nothing can trouble her. There will be no more failure and betrayal.

Alex shuddered. From now on, he must take care of himself. All that was left in the wind of a hot St. Croix afternoon was Mama's pitiful, ripening husk.

Her family buried Rachel in the Lytton family graveyard. Although they—aloof from their black sheep—had done nothing to help when she'd been alive; in death, they reclaimed her. Much of the small estate was used up

13

by the fancy funeral old Uncle Lytton insisted upon, although one useful thing came from it. James and Alexander got the first shoes and stockings they'd had in years.

On the day of the burial, Alexander forced himself to walk, dizzily clinging to his brother's arm. Beneath the pounding sun of an upland plantation, the windy roar of a cane-field ocean in his ears, he and his brother wept.

Beautiful Rachel, who had rocked them, who had taught them, who had loved them and shamed them—Rachel was gone.

* * *

His mother's first husband, Mr. Lavien, returned to Christiansted, as the devil she'd always claimed him to be. With the Court's blessing, he took all that she'd worked so hard to earn, both money and slaves, every bit of property that Alex and Jamie had helped her earn at their little store. Lavien took it for that half-brother, a child Rachel had never wanted, a child she'd "never once put to my breast."

When Alexander learned what the court had ordered, he ran through the crowded streets of the town, past the pastels of the stucco stores, past the colonnade. Weaving like a madman, he ran across the paths of carriages and around erect, brown women carrying baskets on their heads.

Bare feet down the road! Slaves, sweating, glossy blue-black, turned their heads beneath wide-brimmed straw hats as he plunged past a chain gang on the road. Finally, he crashed into the palm fringe of the beach, startling the mulatto women who rested in company with a crowd of goats and children in the slanting shade.

At last, feet stinging from the cuts sustained on the road, Alex hit the burning, too soft sand of the upper beach. He twisted an ankle, but he didn't stop. Reaching the harder wet stuff where the waves came and went, he resumed a quick stride. Only when his chest was on fire, and when he felt certain no white person would see him, did he fall to his knees in the sugary wetness.

There was a fierce onshore wind. Breakers exploded over the reef. At last he could cry as loudly as he wanted, in a place where his helplessness, his weakness, would only be witnessed by the thundering sea.

"Everything Mama and I worked so hard for, every coin we struggled to make! This devil out of her past appears and the court hands it all to him. To a son she gave away!" Long tongues of sea licked the beach. As the wind rose, it started to rasp an ever-deepening gully into the gravel. Although now at the edge of the trench, sun burning his fair skin, Alexander did not move. He almost wished a big rogue wave would roar in and carry him away.

"Oh, Mama, you were right! There is law, but there is no justice. I swear to God, I'll never trust, never rely, never believe in anything but myself, not ever again."

The air filled with flying spray and driven sand. Alexander's hair stiffened with salt. Each gust threw a prickling handful of grit into his tear-stained, sweating face.

* * *

Alexander carefully closed the heavy ledger. Though he was barely half finished, it had already been a long, long day. Numbers swam before his eyes. He rested his head, those tight fine curls, upon it.

Louvers were angled against the sun, but the heat of a heavy, thunderous summer afternoon invaded the room. No one would come into Mr. Cruger's Store for some time. It was after dinner, siesta for the Spanish and Portuguese— and for anyone else with half a brain.

His gut was puffed with breadfruit and fresh fried flying fish—a delicious dinner for the staff today—and he had stuffed in as much in as he could hold. Tomorrow, it would be back to the usual gooey salt pork plopped onto yams or rice. Now, the effort of eating so much, the work that had begun for him before dawn and the muggy heat of tropical August weighed him down.

15

Part of a long row of two story pink stucco buildings flanking the Christiansted square, the store had a high ceiling, a verandah beneath a colonnade and tall windows. It stayed fairly cool in the morning. Nevertheless, by 2:00 p.m. the room was almost as hot—and far stuffier—than the sun-blistered sand outside.

Beyond the door, nothing moved. No immense casks rolled by sweating blacks, no oxen, heads swaying, pulling an endless train of high sided, lumbering wagons. No planters in carriages with their ladies—fancy and otherwise—no heart-rending lamentations from the slave pens or shrieks from the public whipping post. No drunken sailors and their whores, seeking shelter for negotiations in the shade.

Only gulls stirred, wheeling and shrieking, making an incredible din. Alex knew they swarmed behind the building, fighting over refuse the cook threw out.

The sea, always moving, rising and falling, dangerous and alluring, could be smelt and heard, the fence that kept him in. Perhaps, someday, it might become a highway to the greater world, a world of which he continually dreamed.

His work area was a tall desk with a decided slant. The ledger rested on a narrow tray at the bottom; the wood was ink stained and grimy. Readjusting himself so that he could secure his seat at the high stool, Alexander looked down at his own bare calves and feet, dangling high above the broad, saw-dusted planks of the floor.

On every side, crammed in around him and around the counter, were casks and barrels of every size. Some contained Irish butter, some salt pork or salt cod. Others contained flour, keg bread, cornmeal or rice. Bohes and Congo tea sat in canisters. Yard goods, a rainbow of color, were piled on one counter or laid away in long pigeon holes which occupied most of a wall. Kitchen utensils and jars of green or blue containing medicinals occupied another shelf.

Pipes of Madeira, hams and barrels of Virginia tobacco shouldered in the cool, constant temperature of the stone

16

cellar below. In a long warehouse area at the back of the store was stacked white pine from Albany, Georgia pitch pine, white and red oak staves and headings, along with casks of hinges, hooks, and spouts.

Behind the counter, another servant lay sleeping, his snores practically rattling the lids from the apothecary jars. Alexander knew he should be taking advantage of this time and resting, too, but he was too skinny to risk the floor and the irate toe of a rum-soaked planter's boot if he overslept. The last time that had happened, his ribs had ached for weeks.

Someday, he thought, I shall sail away from here. I shall make my fortune and live like a gentleman. I shall have silk stockings and shoes with silver buckles, and ivory buttons on my vest and upon my knee breeches. As I go about my business, people will politely and respectfully lift their hats to me, the way they once greeted my father, in that long ago time when our family lived at Nevis.

* * *

His friend, Ned Stevens, at whose house he sometimes slept, sailed away from St. Croix, to King's College in New York City, to begin the study of medicine. To him, Alexander wrote:

Ned, my Ambition is prevalent that I condemn the grov'ling and condition of a Clerk or the like, to which My Fortune etc. condemns me and would willingly risk my life tho' not my Character to exalt my station. I'm confident, Ned that my Youth excludes me from any hopes of immediate Preferment nor do I desire it, but I mean to prepare the way for futurity. I'm no Philosopher you see and may be justly said to Build Castles in the Air. My Folly makes me asham'd and beg you'll Conceal it, yet, Neddy, we have seen such Schemes successful when the Projector is Constant. I shall Conclude saying, I wish there was a War.

17

* * *

He did not want to remember how it had advanced over weeks, over months. Slowly, one by one, things happened, subtly hemming him in. He was burned—as indelibly as the red hot brands with which they seared the flesh of slaves and the Puerto Rican mules penned behind the store.

He had not believed such a thing could happen. He had trusted, taken the kindness, the generosity, at face value— as Christian Charity—such as they spoke of in church. But this "Charity" proved a fiction. It was all exactly as his mother had said, those many nights when she'd raved and wept into her cups.

Goodness is never its own reward, Alex. Something is always expected in return.

Ah, yes, the bill had at last been presented, and he'd been forced to pay.

"Who in hell do you think you are, you ungrateful little bastard? Why, if I hadn't taken you in, you'd be on the street, begging every poxy sailor with sixpence. I warn you, boy, you could find yourself on the quay tomorrow."

There had been pain, shame, and the choking tears he had striven not to shed, the grotesque finale enacted amid his sobs. Senses reeling in the darkness, a spark stayed desperately aware, waited his opportunity. Drunken sleep came to his master, and Alex crept away. Sliding out of the bed, intent on escape, he held his breath. His knees shook with each creak of the floor. He found his breeches and left with them in hand, letting himself out through a verandah door.

There was a humiliating pause in which he'd stepped back into them. Outside, cool slates touched his feet. Rosy bougainvillea lapped the moonlit walls. At first, he wanted to go straight to the quay that extended into the harbor and leap into the ocean. The sharks which cruised there looking for dead slaves would put an end to his wretched existence....

18

How can I hold my head up again with this filthy name pinned upon me—and by a man I trusted? Flesh—so defiled, so utterly disgraced—is fit only for those ferocious watery scavengers. After this, nothing is left. Father and mother are gone. My inheritance—and now, my honor, too.

He'd been used with the same nonchalant rapacity with which planters used their bondsmen.

On the street, in the soft, sweet darkness, the mortifying ache let him know he could not bear to walk much further. Falling to his knees upon the warm pavement, he retched a scalding slurry of beef and wine—the fine dinner he'd first been treated to—into the gutter.

Standing, he groped his way along, leaning on the still warm stucco walls, damning his weakness. It was a weakness he'd tried and tried to destroy, one that compelled him to believe in people, to hunger for guidance and praise.

I should have known better. I'm twelve, after all.

He thought of himself as grown—he had to—but still the fatal frailty reappeared, this pitiful, childish wish to have a father, to be within a circle of family affection.

And now, once again, he'd been betrayed, brought down by this pitiful desire, deceived by a man he'd trusted, and brought to the depths. He wanted revenge, to settle the score. To return to that room with a knife, and plunge it deep into that pale, exposed throat. For a joyful moment he imagined a swift slashing blow, the dark eyes opening helplessly, the monster gargling on his own blood. An ocean of red might just wash his shame away.

And yet—yet—Oh God! I would still rather live than make a certain end upon the gallows…

Alexander stumbled into a storeroom. It was locked, but he, trusted by his Master, knew the location of an outside key. In this muggy refuge, smelling of a recent American shipment of cornmeal and pine, he would lie upon a heap of discarded sacks.

Sugaring time was coming, where work never stopped, hardly even for sleep. At least, tomorrow was Sunday, and he would not have to face the man who had abused his trust—the man he depended upon for survival. The man he now utterly despised.

At dawn, he could slink down to the sea, strip, and let the salt water wash away whatever it could. For one day, he had a reprieve, did not have to serve in the store, did not have to bow and smile on cue and say to all and sundry, "Yes, sir! Right away, sir!"

What's your pleasure, sir?

Now, he knew.

Oh, God help me! There is no one else....

* * *

"Cut if off," Alexander said. He sat on an empty barrel in the barren yard. "Cut it all off."

The old black barber hesitated, scissors in hand. Around them, a crowd of curious, naked black children gathered. Nearby their mothers, dressed in patched shifts, tied bundles of laundry. Squatting, one of them was making a neat coil of the oily rag she used to cushion her head from the load.

"Got lice, Masta Elicks?"

"Yes. Cut it close. Close as ever you can."

A little while later, like the petals of some alien northern flower, the ginger curls lay all around his bare feet in the sand. Alexander felt the morning breeze touch his scalp. The sensation was strange, but it seemed apt.

I am naked now, stripped, almost to bone.

"You don't have no lice. What ya wan' me cut da kine hair?" Shaking his graying head, the barber held up a mirror. It was ancient, of polished metal. Alexander stared into the gray surface, and saw himself: pale thin face, freckles, deeply shadowed eyes, long head. Here and there little fuzzy licks of red stuck out, as the tight curl began to reassert itself.

That's me. I'm not even the smallest half-step better now than a nigger.

20

***

He developed a sense of when it was coming, rather like his mother's rages, fierce and sudden as a mast-snapping squall bearing in from the eastern sea. For a few days, he would warily manage to side-step, but in the end, one way or another, he'd be trapped again.

Master Nick would drink too much and general disaffection would settle in: "Why am I the one stuck on this god-forsaken, plague-ridden island? Why wasn't I posted to London, instead of Peter?"

And later, after the threats and beating, after violation, smothered in sweaty linen, crushed against the bed, as he wept with helpless rage, the voice over his shoulder would become self-pitying.

"Goddamn you! You've always got to fight, don't you?"

Next, would come drunken justification: "A little of this won't hurt you, 'cause you ain't a man yet. Never changed me, after all."

* * *

Gulls blew over the harbor in dazzling morning light. The sea was an element Alexander could taste in the back of his mouth, like blood or sweat. He stood on a ship tied at the quay and watched as two more high-masted ships tacked towards Christiansted. He carried a ledger, the servant's deferential step behind his lanky, pockmarked master. These days the book seemed to almost be a part of his body, dragged everywhere, the way he'd seen insects carry egg sacks.

Around him, sailors with tattered shirts scrubbed the planks and painted, pounded, sewed at sails, the thousand tasks of men whose ship is ashore after a long journey. Accompanied by the captains, Nick Cruger would look over his merchandise.

There were cargoes of timber, barrel staves, flour, and corn meal from America. Sometimes, with the smell of

21

death and feces so penetrating Alexander feared he'd faint, he stood on the decks of ships where below, groaning, weeping Africans were chained and stacked like wood. As bad a stench came from those as from the ships filled with listless, half-dead Spanish mules, imported in bulk from the Main.

No matter what the ship contained, no matter what else attracted his attention as he stood on those gently swaying decks, Alexander listened, listened as he had never listened before.

This is what my father couldn't learn. This business of shoveling flesh, bone, wood and metal into the maw of an island sugar factory. I will learn my way out of hell.

Timing the market was the thing, whether the merchandise was a hold full of suffering blacks, or half-starved, staggering mules. He heard how excise taxes in the North America trade could be avoided, the names of officers in various ports who could be "tipped" to overlook the fact that the barrels were full of something which differed from the bill of lading, the strategies of loading and unloading so that high duty items would escape the Harbor Master's eye.

He listened to the captains—grim, bitter men, hard as the oak planks of their ships—when they spoke of sailing the routes where pirates and privateers lurked. He heard tales of bloody encounters. He watched as Nick Cruger acquired cannon for his ships, and looked on as the captains recruited the kind of men who knew how to use them.

Alexander also went with his master when he journeyed to ride the plantations. To prosper, a merchant in the import trade had to make an educated guess about the harvest. As peak ripening approached, the island hummed like a gigantic hive preparing to swarm.

Then, the store was jammed with everything from firewood, to barrel staves and brass fittings, to codfish and cornmeal. The pens bulged with slaves and mules.

Sales went on day and night. The harbor became a dense, bobbing thicket of masts. The normally sleepy

22

streets of Christiansted would be crowded with gangs of slaves and laborers, endlessly loading and unloading. Sailors and whores conducted their business in the shade of the alleys, while the taverns played host to drunks and gamblers.

Crimes were committed: theft and murder, brawls over games of chance and women. Slaves displeased their owners. There were daily hangings, whippings, and brandings on the parade ground outside the fort, blood spilled and flesh seared, by the brightly uniformed Danish military. All of this went on just a stone's throw from where Alexander worked, red-eyed and sleepless at the store's counter or seated at a high desk, toiling over a ledger.

Occasionally, some of the ladies from his mother's family would appear, ostensibly to shop for fabric, but actually to look Alexander over. He always bowed and chatted, as if shoeless and in ragged pants, he could still claim membership in a Plantation family.

Nick Cruger watched these performances with a cynical eye, but one of these ladies, Mrs. Venton, decided that this child of her wayward Cousin Rachel was charming. She began to invite Alex for supper, and then, one day, although she was hard pressed for money herself, she took her young relative to a tailor.

When Alexander started for church in a new suit of white linen, wearing fine black stockings and black shoes with pewter buckles, Adam, the biggest of Cruger's house negroes, gave him a huge grin.

"Goin' courtin', Masta Elicks? I swear, de gals in church won' be able to sit still when de sees yah!"

Alexander held his head a touch higher than usual as he entered the square stone church, squatting in the languid shade of tamarind trees. Although sunburned and freckled—he had just come in from a stint of riding the cane—he was confident in the knowledge he looked every inch the gentleman he wanted the world to see.

* * *

Alexander clung to religion. He prayed night and morning, aloud, and down on his knees. Instead of slipping off to fish and swim with other boys on Sunday morning, he attended church.

Surely the God that made me as I am had a purpose!

Besides, church was where the men of influence and power could be seen. To assist his survival, his plan for escape, he knew he must be noticed. These days, he sat beside his new friend, kind Mrs. Venton, and listened with solemn attention to the invigorating oratory of the island's newly arrived Presbyterian preacher, Reverend Hugh Knox.

Knox was a genuine scholar, a rarity in the West Indies. As was customary, besides preaching, he taught the children of local gentry. Mr. Stevens, the father of the beloved and absent Neddy, decided to ask Reverend Knox if he'd mind seeing another student at "odd hours."

At first, the Reverend was lukewarm. He said he'd have to judge whether the boy was worth the trouble. After the first lesson, however, he was all enthusiasm.

"A boy who wants to learn is rare enough at his age, but the way he soaks it up! It'll be my pleasure to teach such an exceptional young fellow."

"I'm glad to hear you say so, Reverend," Mr. Stevens replied. "The boy's born out of wedlock. His mother is dead. His father's run off. The family he's got left are too lost in their own troubles to be of any assistance. It's a real shame, for Alex is as smart as a whip. I confess I've often wished my Ned had half his desire to get on."

Reverend Knox soon formed a plan for his newest pupil, a plan that involved getting Alexander to college in America, perhaps to his own Alma Mater, the young college of Princeton in the wilds of New Jersey. The Reverend wasn't sure how the money could be raised, but he had a powerful confidence that Providence would intervene on behalf of such deserving.

He gave Alexander permission to come to his house and read his own collection of books. Besides this, he started

24

him on several courses of study necessary to college preparation, Latin, Greek and Algebra.

* * *

When Nick Cruger went to New York to recoup his health after a debilitating bout of the West Indies fever, he left fourteen year old Alexander Hamilton in charge of the store. For an entire winter, Alexander handled the St. Croix trade for his penultimate employers—Cruger & Sons of New York City.

He knew what to do and how to do it, but the responsibility was immense. Skinny and small, he had to boss men three times his age, ferocious sea captains and rough plantation bailiffs.

St. Croix
Oct. 21, 1771

Captain Newton:
You know it is intended that you shall go from thence to the Main for a load of Mules & I beg if you do, you'll be very choice in Quality of your Mules and bring as many as your vessel can conveniently contain. By all means take in a large supply of provender. Remember you are to make three trips this Season & unless you are very diligent, you will be too late as our Crops will be early in.
— A. Hamilton

There were letters to keep Master Nick and his family in New York informed. On his fifteenth birthday—a work day, like any other—Alexander wrote:

To Nicholas Cruger
Via Merryland & Philadelphia
From St. Croix Jan 11th 1772

Dear Sir: The 101 barrels superfine Flour From Philadelphia are just landed, about 40, of which I have already sold at 11 1/2 pieces of eight/bbl but as probably there will be much less imported than I expected I intend to insist on 12 for the rest. Capt. Napper is arrivd and dl'd everything agreeable to his Bill Lading. He landed all at the Westend. The Beer I beg'd Mr. Herbert to sell there. The plate stockings etc. are deposited in Miss Nancy De Nully's hands, and the Cheeses in #4 are disposed of thus: two, Mr. Beekman kept, and the other two I sent on to Mrs. De Nully.

I called upon Mr. Heyns to Day with the Bill on Capt. Hunter but he was at the Westend so that I can say nothing of that matter. (Mr Heyns I am told is Capt Hunters Attorney.)

Capt Gibbs is landing as fast as possible and you may depend I will give him all the dispatch in my power but I will not undertake to determine precisely when he will Sail as he tells me his cargo is Stow'd very inconveniently and the St. Croix part of it rather undermost. If so he could be detained longer than cou'd otherwise be expected. His Cargo will turn out pritty well. Lumber is high, 18 pounds, and most of the other Articles in Demand enough. But as I am a good deal hurried just now I beg you'll accept this instead of a more minute detail of these matters which I shall send by the Next conveyance. I have not time to write your father.

I shall do as you desire concerning the Brig Nancys accounts.

Capt. Wells Cargo consisted of Lumber, Spermaceti Candles, Codfish and Ale Wives. All the Hoops he brought were sold immediately to Mr. Bignall at 70 pieces of eight/M and the Spermaceti Candles to different persons at 6 Spanish Reals per pound. We are selling the Codfish at ps. 6 1/2 Per hundredweight and the Ale Wives at 5 & 6 pieces of eight per Barrel. He will return in about 10 days with Sugar and Cotton.

This is all I have time to say now and if I have neglected anything material I beg you'll excuse it being with the closest attention to your Interest.

26

Your most obt Servt: Alexander Hamilton
I shall provide Rum and Sugar for Capt. Gibb; the price
of rum is now 2/9.

* * *

Every week of his Master's absence, Alexander measured himself against a doorsill in the back of his store, marking his height with a penknife. He was at last growing, and the change heartened him.

No matter how long the day before him, every morning he went into the back to direct the slaves who moved the stock around. He began to help with the physical labor. It seemed the easiest way to show the men how he wanted things, but there was another motive, too.

Alex had observed the muscles on those black arms. It seemed apparent to him that, just like book learning, even his skinny, boyish body could be taught. When Nick Cruger returned, Alexander had determined he would no longer be a helpless boy.

There came, in the course of things, the inevitable day when, as Alex stood tall as he could behind that mahogany counter, a bailiff he'd never liked called him a liar. Those who witnessed the event always laughed when retelling the story, saying that the fight had been like a small orange tomcat leaping on a mastiff.

Surprise and rage, combined with a couple of speedy, head punches, left the bailiff on his back, bleeding and, briefly, unconscious. Alexander got off the man's chest and coolly directed his slaves to carry his adversary outside and dump him in the sandy street.

Later, sucking on his aching, bleeding knuckles, once more behind the counter—the best place to hide his shaking knees—Alexander saw that the slaves, even the other gentleman in the store, looked different. A huge, drunken sensation swelled, and for a lingering instant he had the dizzy sensation that he was so tall that his head pressed right against the ceiling.

27

* * *

When Nick Cruger returned to St. Croix, he had his health back. More than this, his father in New York had provided Master Nick with a bride, a woman with the proper mercantile connections. When one of the house slaves regaled him with the tale of Alexander's fight, Cruger nodded. Then, after a sideways glance, he said something about how much Alexander had grown.

As they worked alone together, Alexander sometimes glimpsed the old lewdness on his master's face, but it was now papered over with an assumed disinterest. Nevertheless, Alexander took no chances. These days, his nights were spent either in the house of Mr. Stevens, or with his teacher, Reverend Knox.

* * *

When Cruger resumed control of the business, life, for Alex, slowed to a crawl. Accustomed to running from dawn to dusk, standing tall and making every decision, he was a clerk again, to say "Yes, sir" and "No, sir" on cue. He was only fifteen, but independence felt further away than ever.

He took up his studies with Reverend Knox with a vengeance, but after so much hard work and real responsibility, school seemed like child's play.

When, Alexander wondered, as he lay, waiting for sleep in a room filled with the snoring of the Reverend and his black servant, am I ever going to escape this grov'ling condition which fate has ordered up for me?

* * *

The sea was azure, the tide low, the wind light. The swell lapped a throaty gurgle as it ran against a reef that meandered close to the beach. In the shallow water behind, tiny brilliant fish, as well as a hundred other forms of stranger life, rippled, crawled and darted.

28

Alexander walked barefoot, splashing along, enjoying the feel of sand and cool sea. He'd left his straw hat behind, today not caring that the sun was freckling and reddening him. Terns skittered, keeping just ahead, doing their dance of attack and retreat before the water, probing the bubbling sand with slender bills. Over his head, gulls wheeled and cried.

From above the shell and weedy litter, across the blistering white expanse where a shelter of salt-drinking mangroves began, came giggles. Sun-blinded, it was hard to see, but at last his blue eyes fastened upon the source of the sound.

Lithe young women, dark eyes, white flashing teeth— a group of brown sugar concubines, chatted and lazed together under the palms. He knew most of them from the days in his mother's little store, where he had sold them trinkets, needles, bright calico and small blue bottles of laudanum for their women's complaints.

"Masta Ham! Masta Alexander! Come 'n visit!"

They were coaxing him, laughing asides. Thinking of things about which the Reverend Knox repeatedly cautioned, he pretended not to hear.

Wind gusted. At once the responsive sea bounced, a thousand mirrors sparkling. Alexander knew the girls were joking about him, were daring each other.

The child inside still longed for caresses, but there was another impulse, too, burning within his maturing, work-hard body. It shouted at him to go back, to explore whatever possibilities the girls offered. To walk away was harder than swimming against the tide.

* * *

"You goddamned puffed-up little nobody!" The planter had Alex by the shirt.

Ordinarily, he would have defended himself, but this was an important customer, so, instead, he only twisted and ducked. The ham fist struck his back, almost knocking the breath out of him as he wrenched free.

29

"I'll teach you to talk back!"

It had not been because of anything, really, but simply because the fellow was in a foul mood. He'd entered the store in a rage and passed it along in the casual fashion a man might kick a cur in the street. Mr. Cruger watched from the back, but made no move to interfere.

The customer is always right. Especially this son-of-a bitch! And Cruger's absolute indifference to right or wrong, is the best the filthy snake can do....

At quitting time, Alexander was off down the beach. He hated his life and everyone in it.

"God help me, or even the Devil." He spoke aloud, feeling supremely daring. "When the next war comes, I shall jump ship and run straight to it."

There was a special place to which Alexander went whenever he wanted to be alone. It was a rough trek through a forbidding grove of twisted manchineel and then up a brush-covered headland. After a slow ledge-to-ledge descent down the cliff face, he'd reach an outcrop a mere twenty feet above high tide, but hidden from anyone above. Today, all he wanted was to stretch out, to listen to the boom of the waves. He anticipated a rare moment of fantasy, one that involved sailing away, maybe to some distant war, or maybe to America to see his friend Ned Stevens.

To his chagrin, however, a girl sat cross-legged in the hidden place, a slim, brown girl, wearing a thin white dress. She regarded him balefully, sullen, grass-green eyes flashing. Her silver collar gleamed in the sun.

They had a shared history. Diana had been purchased by a slaver named Collins soon after Alex's father had gone away. Prior to that she'd had a good master, had been reared in what Reverend Knox termed "a Christian home." Alexander, a youthful cynic, deemed it nothing less than the inevitable way of the world when the kind master went bankrupt. It had been an incidental part of that good Christian's wreck of fortune that Diana, aged ten, had been sold to the debased Collins.

After breaking the girl in, it sometimes amused her new master to give her coins to spend on cloth and trinkets. Like other maroon concubines, she'd come with these coins to Rachel's little store, for not only did "Miz Rachel" stock the prettiest calicos, but a certain sympathy hung in the air between his mother and these beautiful victims.

Years ago, Alex had gone so far as to sit behind the counter with Diana, backed against a barrel of cornmeal, and had patiently explained the value of the coins, so she wouldn't be cheated. Slavery had only been an ordinary part of life, until he'd seen, up close, what had happened to this girl, so near his own age. Alex would never have admitted it to anyone, but thereafter he'd felt a bond between them. They had both been left, mere children, to be devoured by the Evil that—clearly—ruled this wicked world.

"What are you doing way out here?"

"Stayin' away from dem all, Masta Ham."

With heroic disregard, she went back to staring out to sea. After a moment, Alex sat down crossed-legged beside her. He was dressed in his usual workday white shirt and plain brown knee breeches. Although he owned a pair of shoes and stockings these days, he'd stored them beneath a shelf before making the angry tramp down the beach.

Diana was dressed scantily, but not shabbily. Her brown arms jangled with bracelets, Collins' largess. A red silk scarf had been braided into her brown, crinkly hair.

"How did you get way out here?"

"It'twas easy. De pig and his frien's dead drunk. I go back when I good 'n' rea-dy."

In those three sentences, a thousand rules were violated. Slaves were whipped bloody for the slightest insubordination.

"Won't he beat you?"

"He don' wan'ta damage his propertee, but I don' gi'e a damn if he do."

"There are lots of ways to hurt that don't leave marks."

"Tink I don' know?" She gave her head a ferocious toss. "I kin take care ah' m-sef."

"If you say so."

"I do. Say, Masta Ham, dis is one good place to hide. Do ya be here of-ten?"

"Yes. Whenever I'd like to kill them all."

Her smile, a beautiful flash, appeared. "So! Even clever two-shoes white boys gots trouble. What's de mat-tah, din' you kiss ass quick 'nouf for Masta Nick?"

Black to white, she was way over the line, but in the next heartbeat, a bitter laugh broke from his lips.

"Yes. Damn his rotten soul to hell."

Diana drew up her long brown legs beneath her skirt, hugged them, and stared out to sea. In the silence which followed, she thoughtfully chewed the tip of one delicate finger. Alexander aimlessly flicked pebbles over the edge and tried not to stare.

After a few minutes, as a soft wind blew off the bay and ruffled her thin white dress, Diana said, "You won' tell any-one I was here, will ya, Masta Ham?"

"No, 'pon my honor." Solemnly, he met her lime-green eyes.

She gave him a sharp, humorous look, as if she'd been ready to laugh at the idea that a poor bastard clerk could have any claim to 'honor,' but she didn't.

* * *

After that, Alexander found her there often. They talked in this lonely spot, putting aside the distinctions that would have kept them apart in any other place.

Here in Christiansted she and I are both nothing, Alex mused, dirt under everyone's feet. But I have a chance to escape because I'm a man and because I'm white. There are ways out for me, but for her, a woman of color—a slave—there are none....

"Collins wants to sell you to St. Thomas the next time Captain Harken comes through."

For months, Collins had hemmed and hawed about what to do with his increasingly unruly possession. It seemed he was more attached to Diana than he wanted anyone, particularly the girl herself, to know.

"Well, at least I'll be gone from stinkin' St. Croix." Diana twisted a ribboned braid.

"Is Marcus so bad?" asked Hamilton. He knew that since Collins had purchased a new girl and begun her "education," Diana was being given to a favorite house servant at night.

"A black pig instead of a white one." Diana was briefly dismissive. "Another old man! Collins say if I don' breed wi' Marcus, he' sell me away. Could be worse. He could gi'e me to a mob o' field niggers."

Diana gave an inadvertent shudder at the image she had conjured up. She had as strong a fear of the brutalized field hands as any white person.

"Marcus isn't so old."

"An' you jus' a man. What you know?"

"I—I know." Alexander tried to keep his voice even, but in those two words he'd breached his own bottomless shame. It had been several years now—*since*—but the shame didn't go away. A quiver he couldn't suppress visibly shook him.

"I'm sorry, Diana. Anything that son-of-a-bitch orders up must be hell."

Diana, utterly worldly, seemed to understand all of it, both said and unsaid. He blushed beneath the long measuring look which followed, but after a minute, she reached to stroke his jaw. Just this morning, he'd shaved away the sparse blonde whiskers that now grew there.

"Ah'm sick o' stinkin' ol' men. Ah tink Ah'd like to do it wi' a pretty young fella, Masta Ham."

* * *

It was a muggy night at the start of rainy season. Alexander had been trying to sleep on a camp cot at Stevens' house, currently empty of anyone but him and a few slaves for the Stevens family often visited a relative's upland plantation during the summer heat. The darkness was saturated with the heavy perfume of Lady of the Night, but an overhanging frangipani was in bloom too, and the green and sugar scent of the tree struck a clashing chord. Inside a stifling but indispensable mosquito net, his skin alert to the delights of the slightest breeze, Alex sweated. Our at sea, a storm sent down fiery bolts, but not a breath of air relieved sweltering Christiansted.

Perhaps he'd slept, for at first Alex thought the presence under the mosquito netting was a wonderful dream. After all, he'd been imagining it for weeks. Then those slightly moist satin hands took hold in a way which awoke him up completely. It was moonless, but the spice of her told him exactly who was, even now, sliding a leg across him.

Later, skin slippery with love, Diana mused thoughtfully into Alexander's ear, "You know, you de firs' man I lie wi' who smell good."

* * *

"It's not much, but it's all I can give. Maybe you can save and buy your freedom."

"Free-dom? You crazy? Ah couldn'a keep it. Anywhere ah go, some white son-of-a-bitch would just know from de color o' mah hide, ah do belong to him!"

"But there are free maroons...."

"Damn you, bastard red-neck fool! Ain' whorin' wi' you!"

Alexander swallowed hard, fought back the red mist a certain word always raised.

"I don't want to be like Collins."

"Ah'm pleasin' m'sef wi' you, white boy, an' don' you forget't."

* * *

Sometimes, brain rattling from a tremendous box dealt by her displeasure, he'd sit back, dumbly shaking his head.

34

"Ignorant!" Her eyes sparkled with laughter and malice. She'd lean back, in the siesta glow seeping through the lattices to tempt his touch again.

"You men so clumsy, so rough! Pay 'tention now. I show you what de woman wan'."

She was Love—her crinkly braids, the salt and spice of her sandy skin when they were lost in lust and ecstasy on the nighttime beach. It took all their combined cunning to achieve a rendezvous, but they had both learned patience and subtlety. Still, they were very young, rebelling against every rule of their brutal world. In the twilight shadows of the Manchineel, just above the moon-glittering surf, chances were taken.

* * *

Alexander was hard at work in the store, trying to reconcile some figures that a new clerk had thoroughly deranged, when something caused him to look up. Through the louvers tipped against the fierce afternoon sun, he spied a sailor leading a jenny. On the animal's back sat a slender mulatto girl wearing a thin white dress. She wore a broad brimmed hat and rode astride, beautiful bare brown legs dangling.

Around her ankle silver gleamed; a long chain was now attached to her silver collar. As they passed the store, the girl turned a proud, expressionless face toward the windows. Alexander threw down his quill and began to open the shutter, ready to jump out and run after her, but before he could get it done, a rough hand landed on his shoulder and spun him around.

"Stop right where you are, Hamilton."

"Who bought her?" Alexander, fearless, twisted away from Cruger to get a last glimpse.

"One Mrs. Yard, whose famous establishment is at St. Thomas. Collins says he got a nice price."

Alexander swallowed hard, tried to fight back the tears. The pain of loss instantly merged with the horror of imagining her in such a place.

"Cheer up, boy," Cruger said. "You're gettin' off lucky."

"What?" After being called "boy," Alexander left off the "sir."

"Watch yourself, boy! You better believe Collins was plenty pissed when he found out, but he finally agreed to overlook your trespassing. He did say something about not expecting any better from an uppity yellow bitch and a whore's son."

Without an instant's hesitation, Alexander swung at his master's narrow, pock-marked face. Nick Cruger, knowing exactly what his words would elicit, struck first.

There was an explosion—pain and stars—followed by a roaring blackness. When the world returned, Alexander found himself lying on his back on the floor, his employer squatting beside him.

The expression on Cruger's lean, pitted face was ironic. Beyond, other interested faces, both white and black, crowded the doorway.

"Collins said I ought to horsewhip you, but the nice shiner you're going to have tomorrow will have to do. Now, Hamilton—" He pulled Alexander, whose head felt as if it were going to shatter, into a sitting position, "Where's your good sense got to? Do you want the French disease? The way Collins let that slut wander around, who knows who else she was tupping?"

Alexander's soul yearned to defend Diana, to throw another punch at that smug, scarred face, but instead he ground his teeth and said nothing. The strain of prudent inaction was so agonizing that for one rushing moment he thought he was going to lose consciousness again.

"Have you been so busy following your cock around that you don't know old Knox is on the verge of convincing some of his rich friends to help you get to New York, to go to college with Ned Stevens? Let me tell you, Collins was ready to tell the good Reverend about your whoring, but he finally agreed with me that boys will be boys."

36

Cruger got to his feet, roughly pulling his clerk up after him. Alexander shook with anger, but he was still so dizzy he was forced to accept help to stand. The confiding growl went on.

"Discretion is the word with women, be they whores, or be they ladies. No more fooling around, at least, till you're where Reverend Knox won't know. Black ass—even so fine a piece—ain't worth losing your chance over."

* * *

For days an oily calm lay upon the ocean. The temperature rose suddenly, a full ten degrees. In the northeast, the sky was color of metal. Next, a succession of increasingly violent squalls rushed in and drenched the port.

Captains, knowing and fearing, unloaded in record time. From the porch of Cruger's store, Alexander thought the quays looked like a struggling insect overwhelmed by ants. Some ships simply put to sea without unloading, setting their sails toward other islands. After anxious hours, the tall ships fled, leaving only a few small local traders still heaving at anchor.

Alexander stood at the docks. Wind scoured his flesh as he watched the monster approach. Black clouds reared above the surf now biting into the beach. The northeast sky was a terrible army of lightning-shattered, roiling thunderheads. He had boarded windows, worked with the slaves at shifting stock from the floor onto high shelves, and loading the most precious articles into wagons, now gone to the inland warehouses. In fact, Alex should have departed along with the last of it, but he hadn't. Instead, he and many others ventured down to the quays.

Alexander had been in hurricanes before. More than once he'd shared an anxious watch, standing on the shore beside merchants and sailors, staring as the giant anvils moved in from the northeast, sailing over a strangely muddy sea. Those storms had grazed St. Croix's shore twice during his younger days, bringing deadly lightning

37

and flooding rains that swept soil, men and animals into the ocean, even as it flattened the precious cane. Over all had been the voice of the wind, keening like an injured animal, the sound itself able to tear down buildings and windmills, to crush ships to kindling.

A darkness more terrible than night flowed out of the north. Lighting gored glowing wounds in the sable sides of clouds. The water, casting itself upon the beach, was mountainous, a dirty white. The ground beneath Alexander's feet shook.

"Headin' right for us!" A mulatto freeman made commentary to anyone within range.

"'Twill be deep water sweepin' the streets afore this blow is past." Agreement came from Jack, a scarred and crippled sailor who was spending his final years roosting and begging in various places around the square, baking his aches and pains.

* * *

Alexander shivered inside his sodden shirt, and shielded his eyes from a slicing wind. The fury bearing down on this hateful island filled him with terror—and a weird, joyful elation. What he saw in the sky, what he felt in the agitation of his companions, sent his imagination careening wildly, like the gulls hurtling down the wind.

"*...This tempest will not give me leave to ponder on things would hurt me more...*"

It was six weeks and three days since Diana had been sold to St. Thomas. Every instant, his body—his mind—burned with anguish.

Rain beat upon his skinny frame. He stood, closing his eyes, letting it hammer him, barely aware that, one by one, his companions had left the dangerous, thunderous beach.

"Young Master?"

A weathered hand rested upon his arm. He turned, and through the pelting rain saw Jack.

"Do you think I could lay out the blow in back of yon store? I won't take nothin'."

Alexander knew Jack lived in a hut close by the water. It was no doubt already gone, carried away by the waves now chewing through the beach.

"...*Why, thou wert better in thy grave than to answer with thy uncovered body this extremity of the skies....*"

"Come along, then, father." Alexander shouted his answer against the wind. He offered the old man the dignity of polite address as well as his arm. "We'd better get inside before we wash away."

* * *

The wind hammered against the hurricane shutters till it broke in, a howling giant loose in the room. Alexander had crawled beneath a shelf and turned his face to the wall. He was silent, even while others around him were screaming and calling upon God in many languages. There was nothing but pandemonium; he didn't dare open his eyes. In a cracking rush which popped his ears, the roof lifted and blew away.

Icy rain beat against his back. Men sobbed and prayed. He began to pray, too, for the rising water in which he lay tasted of salt.

* * *

Christiansted, September 6, 1772
From the Royal Danish American Gazette—
By Alexander Hamilton
"I take up my pen to give you an imperfect account of one of the most dreadful Hurricanes that memory or any records whatever can trace, which happened here on the 31st of August at night. It began about dusk, at North, and raged very violently till ten o'clock. Then ensued a sudden and unexpected interval, which lasted about an hour. Meanwhile the wind was shifting round to the South West

39

point, from whence it returned with redoubled fury and continued so 'till near three o'clock in the morning.

Good God! What horror and destruction! It is impossible for me to describe or you to form any idea of it. It seemed as if a total dissolution of nature was taking place. The roaring of the sea and wind, fiery meteors flying about it in the air, the prodigious glare of almost perpetual lightning, the crash of falling houses, and the ear-piercing shrieks of the distressed, were sufficient to strike astonishment into Angels.

A great part of the buildings throughout the Island are levelled to the ground, almost all the rest very shattered; several persons killed and numbers utterly ruined; whole families running about the streets, unknowing where to find a place of shelter; the sick exposed to the keenness of water and air without a bed to lie upon, or a dry covering to their bodies; and our harbours entirely bare...."

* * *

"Yes. It has come to my attention that Cruger's clerk wrote this."

"Indeed, Your Excellency," Hugh Knox replied. "Young Hamilton's native intelligence is a text upon which I've been long preaching."

Knox, his lean black-stocking calves patiently crossed, had waited many days for an audience, off and on, in the Governor's outer rooms. Since the hurricane, there was plenty to occupy the man, but one must, Knox thought, strike while the iron is hot.

The walls of the waiting room were decorated with a bristling circular display of muskets with bayonets attached and an array of swords, appropriate panoply for a colonial governor. Among the businessmen, planters, and soldiers, Reverend Knox had humbly waited to be summoned by the sallow, officious secretary. He would only have a few minutes, for the Governor was an administrator, one still coping with a monumental disaster.

40

Now, the moment is come. Though Hugh Knox was a man secure in himself and used to men of power, there was an instant of absolute fear, as he faced this pale, eagle-beaked Dane enthroned behind his mahogany desk.

"'Tis uncommon to discover such originality of thought and facility of expression in one so young."

"The piece is handsomely written. His sentiments are most apt and pious," Knox said. "Master Hamilton has had little formal schooling, and so it is quite astonishing to see how far he has come. One must concede this is not the natural inclination of youth, especially one who must labor under such conspicuous disadvantages."

"It was remarkable how well the boy did with Nick Cruger's business while he was away. The literary arts are one thing," and here the Governor tossed the newspaper aside, "but the sort of address and decision which are needed to manage a business is quite another."

"Yes, indeed, your Excellency. I most heartily concur." Reverend Knox, an accomplished preacher, dared a pause. Then he spoke the words he'd been rehearsing ever since the plan had formed in his mind.

"I have often wondered, your Excellency, what might become of such a deserving youth if he were to receive the benefit of an education at an institution of higher learning, perhaps one of those now established in the American Colonies...."

* * *

The island looks so small, a green bead set on a long white thread of surf....

Legs braced against the swaying deck, Alexander shaded his eyes with a tilt of his hat.

So many times I have dreamt of this! So many times!

Sails billowed, full bellies of gray and white. The British tricolor galloped from the main. Gulls drifted in their wake, gliding and crying plaintively. The world looked sharp-edged and bright. Alexander heard the whisper in his head

41

as he watched the shocking green of that coral-encrusted jewel recede.

You will never see me again.

Turning, he put his back to the island and walked to the bow. Here, he faced an expanse of waves, nothing ahead but ocean. He blinked against the sharp breeze and the sting of salt spray. The wind here was cold and hard, blowing straight from the north.

Chapter Two ~ The Pastures, Albany, NY

The girls had strayed too deep into the old pasture to run back to the red brick pile of their house, so they hid. Angelica grabbed little Peggy and together they crouched inside a big hole within the trunk of one of the squat, ancient fruit trees, one that Papa said had been brought as rootstock by the very first Dutch settlers.

When they'd first spied the Indians, Betsy had been climbing to pick apples. It was too late to climb down, so she tucked long skirts over her knees and made herself into a small bundle, hugging the trunk and praying the leaves would cover her. As the party passed directly beneath her, she froze and tried not to think of the old war stories the servants told, about how Indians had killed her Uncle 'Bram—shot dead right on his Saratoga doorstep.

These intruders were wearing buckskin trousers, homespun shirts and hats with foxtails and feathers. The European touches were a good sign, for this was the way Indians dressed when making a formal visit to Albany.

There was a woman, too, walking very erect. Beside her marched a boy. He must have recently joined the men's lodge, for his head was newly plucked, pale as a butchered hog on either side of the bristling strip of hair. He looked straight up, met her eyes, and then, without a word, continued on with his elders.

Betsy knew these Indians were Mohawks, a tribe with whom her father was on good terms. Nevertheless, trained, as all frontier children were, to hide from strangers, she didn't twitch.

Today's Indians must have had a claim on Papa, for they went directly to the wing of the imposing brick house which contained his study. A few minutes later, in the distance, she saw father come out to greet them.

Sometimes, if Chiefs arrived in rain or snow, they would be invited in to sit cross-legged in the downstairs great room with Papa. Here they dipped their dinner out of three-legged pots carried in from the kitchen. Betsy and her sisters would slip out of their room, down the staircase, and try to get a peek through the door which led into the study wing. Here, if they were lucky, they'd see warriors sitting-crossed legged on the carpet, solemnly gazing around at the French panoramic wallpaper and up to the crystal chandelier.

Relieved that these were only visitors, Betsy climbed down to join her sisters. They collected their dolls and walked slowly back to the house, Betsy holding Margaret's sticky little hand. They met slaves already carrying out carpets and furs for their guests.

"Let's sit here." Angelica, the oldest, and always the leader, took a seat on one of the long benches along the study wing. "We can watch."

Peggy, however, was done with outside. She wanted to go in, and began to complain. They were close to the kitchen now, and the smell coming from there made her think of the treats she could wheedle from the kitchen maids.

"I want a *koekje!*"

Peggy strained at Betsy's hand, and, after a little pulling, Betsy gave up and simply let her go. One of the house slaves at work there would certainly take charge of her little sister. Peggy went charging away, as fast as her short legs would carry her, toward the kitchen door.

While they watched, a pavilion arose beneath the biggest maple, and a fire made. Tables and carpets came out, and an entire joint of beef was carried out, hot from the oven.

Then, a commotion began. Mama was at the center of it, although this was a surprise. Their Mama rarely lost her temper. She came out of the kitchen door, hauling Ruby, one of the slave girls, by the arm. She had a hazel switch in hand.

44

"Ruby, if I set you to watch my girls, you are not to let them out of your sight!" Mama switched Ruby's legs, and poor Ruby hopped up and down in her short skirts, shrieking.

"Why is Mama so cross?" Angelica asked, as Mrs. Ross, their plump Scots governess, herded them away into the house and upstairs.

Something was very wrong. Mama never lost her temper.

* * *

Darkness came. Papa sat outside with his visitors. The rest of the family—the children, the governess, and Mama—had supper as usual at the walnut table, laid with East India Company blue-and-white china.

"Who is the Mohawk lady who looks so grand?" Angelica dared to ask the question on everyone else's mind.

"She is Mary Hill," her mother said. "The daughter of a Clan Mother."

"And who is the boy, Mama?"

"Her son, I suppose."

"What have they come to see Papa for?"

"Gifts! What else do Indians ever want? Now," Catherine Schuyler said, "finish your supper. You are going to bed early tonight."

Betsy watched in disbelief as Angelica's rosy mouth dared to frame a "why," but then the strangest thing of all happened. Papa sent in his servant, tall, black Prince, to invite them out. The expression on Mama's face led Betsy to imagine that she would refuse, but instead she rose with a brisk rustle of linen and silk.

"Come along, girls. Mrs. Ross, you as well."

Looking apprehensive, Mrs. Ross lifted Peggy. As Mrs. Schuyler's long, warm fingers came to enclose Betsy's, Angelica sprang up and raced toward the door, chestnut curls bouncing.

"Angelica!" Their mother spoke sharply. "Walk—and stay beside me."

As they approached the pavilion, Betsy caught the smoky smell of the visitors. Nervously, she tightened her grip upon her mother's hand.

"Do not be afraid." Mrs. Schuyler leaned to whisper softly. "Remember who you are, Elizabeth."

Betsy obediently straightened. *I must be brave. On both sides I am descended from the first Patroon, Killian van Rensselaer.* Still, it was a struggle to put away the nightmare images of so many oft-told tales—*the bloody scalping knife—flesh in the fire!*

Quivering, Betsy stared at them. She saw strong berry-brown faces, aquiline noses, delicate spirals of tattooing, and black eyes. Mary Hill sat beside Papa, but at the appearance of Mrs. Schuyler, she gracefully arose.

The Indian woman's hair was gathered into a shiny knot at the nape of her neck. She wore a fine white blouse, red calamanco skirt and jacket and a pile of necklaces—gold chains and silver, trade beads and shells, bones and feathers—all jumbled together.

Mohawk or not, Mary Hill was beautiful.

The two grown women gazed at each other in a cool measuring way, something Betsy had observed ladies do at parties. Overhead, the pavilion flapped and scarlet leaves whispered. These two women—one dark, one fair—were both tall, handsome—and so proud!

Mary Hill's wise eyes met Betsy's. Brown fingers reached to touch the single black curl which trailed below her cap. The woman gestured to her companions, half turned to speak in her own language. The men were unreadable, but whatever she'd said caused the boy to stare.

Betsy couldn't help herself. She stared back. His brown skin, his tattoos and newly plucked scalp made him strange, but his face, now that she truly considered it, seemed as familiar as any of her cousins.

Mary Hill said, "Three fine strong daughters are a blessing, but a Chief needs sons. This will help." Searching

46

among the mass of necklaces, brown fingers sought and removed one. Betsy saw it, made of tiny bones, bird's claws, bear's teeth and dainty feather tufts.

Her face a mask, Catherine Schuyler accepted the necklace and very slowly and ceremoniously, put it around her neck. Then she removed the locket she wore, one hung upon a satin ribbon. Inside, the girls knew, was a likeness of Papa.

"This is dear to me and mine. Look upon it and think well of Philip of the Pastures."

The Mohawk woman received the locket and solemnly added it to those she already wore. Blue eyes gazed steadfastly into black. Betsy thought she saw a secret there, something between great ladies.

From her father came a kind of sigh. Relief—satisfaction—it was impossible to tell.

"Your son will be a strong arm to his clan." Mama spoke again, in a gracious tone.

Betsy could feel Angelica shifting beside her, no doubt bursting with questions, but suddenly Papa made an expansive gesture that took in the entire group and said, "I give many presents in honor of your son's manhood and Bear Clan."

A line of slaves came out of the darkness. They carried blankets, rifles, bright knives and kettles. Last, a beautiful green silk petticoat and an armload of calico were presented to Mary Hill.

While their guests crowded close, their dark eyes and brown fingers investigating the treasure, Mrs. Schuyler motioned to the governess. With Betsy by one hand and Angelica by the other, she walked back to the house.

* * *

Later, after the girls had on their nightgowns, they ignored Mrs. Ross' protests and trotted away to peep through the upstairs great room window one more time. Below they saw points of light—pipes glowing around the fire.

"Papa has given them horses, too." Betsy pointed them out for little Peggy.

"She must be terribly important." Angelica added her own estimation.

Three white-capped heads leaned close together. The girls could easily identify their father's square body, now seated on a camp stool beside the relaxed squatting form of black Prince.

* * *

The next morning the girls awoke to bird song. In the low bed set beside the one they shared, Mrs. Ross snored softly, her braid of silver and brown trailing across the pillow.

She sleeps hard. The girls' eyes met. They knew that slipping from the room would bring no rebuke—especially if they returned before she awoke.

A few steps later, once more gathered on the window seat, peering into a misty dawn, the girls watched the Indian boy as he stroked the neck of the gift horse. Others were awake, too, cutting meat from the remains of the joint and loading packs. Yawning and shivering, the sisters huddled close.

Horses loaded, tumplines set on foreheads, burdens shouldered, the Mohawk retreated, a silent line that vanished into autumnal mist. Only a blackened spot at the foot of the maple and the dew-heavy pavilion remained to prove that any of it had happened.

* * *

"Why did the Indians go away so soon?"

Until Angelica spoke, breakfast had been quieter than church.

"They got what they wanted," Mrs. Schuyler said.

"But they usually stay for days."

48

"Only when they don't get what they want. Now, no more prattle about Mohawks, Angelica."

* * *

In long coat and planter's hat, while Prince held his horse, Philip Schuyler mounted. This morning he was off to oversee the northern farm. Betsy watched as her Papa, with unusual humility, bowed low over Mama's long, elegant fingers. Catherine Schuyler received his ceremonious attention with an expression of cool abstraction.

In the upstairs great room, the two older girls and three young maids were set to the tedious task of sewing shifts for the slaves. They were cut, some already pin-pieced, so after their Mother got them started, the girls sighed and threaded their needles. Ice in their mother's eyes clearly signaled the dangers of complaint. As they began to work, Mama gave the order "no chattering," then she and her own maids went to the other side of the room where small spinning wheels were set. They began to work upon the contents of a basket loaded with hanks of flax.

Sensing her mother's upset, Betsy couldn't concentrate. Soon, there were consequences.

"Good heavens, Miss! You've sewn the wrong pieces together."

Betsy flushed, embarrassed.

An entire seam must now be snipped apart.

"Perhaps reading aloud will clear your head. Go and fetch Reverend Vanderdonk's red book."

Betsy's heart sank. The book had been written by a famous Divinity Teacher, "for the moral instruction of children." Not only was it written in Dutch, but it was most dreadfully dull.

"Yes, Mama." Dutifully rising and dropping a curtsy, Betsy started for her parent's bedroom. She walked upstairs slowly, hand trailing along the curves of the banister, watching the room below appear to shift and change at each ascending step.

49

She crossed the upper great hall, lifted a latch and went in to her parent's bedroom. Since the war with the French was over, Papa had finished the interior of their house. Men from New York had come and installed green brocade wall paper—a design of yellow birds and trees set on a lime background. The background colors matched those of the bed curtains. A magnificent wall-to-wall carpet, also green, was the finishing touch. This had been woven in Amsterdam, made especially for this room.

Betsy used a step-stool to reach the shelf where the red book was kept, picking it out from among the others: geographies, surveyors' studies, histories, Shakespeare and several Bibles. She sighed as she stepped down again, but as she began toward the door, Betsy's eye caught the twinkle of something new pinned to the head curtains of the parental bed.

Crossing the room to get a better look, she recognized the Indian necklace, bird's feet, bear teeth, beads, and tiny bones dangling. Holding that book of stern Calvinist dogma in her bosom, surrounded on every side by all the fashion and luxury Europe could provide, Betsy stood stock still, studying it.

* * *

During her fourteenth winter, Angelica was sent to visit Livingston kinfolk in New York City. She went from Albany with her head high, without an ounce of anything but anticipation.

Down the green lawn from the house, standing on their father's quay where his river schooners loaded and unloaded, Betsy and Peggy cried while Angelica and her slave, Pearl, went on board. Angelica said good-bye to them tenderly, but she didn't shed a tear. She was full of confidence, like a newly-fledged goose winging on its first flight to a far land it has never seen.

All winter, Betsy sorely missed her sister. Nothing seemed as much fun; all games grew stale. In the spring,

50

after the ice had gone roaring like a white mountain down the Hudson, her beloved sister came home at last.

Betsy was overjoyed, but within hours she understood that everything which set Angelica apart had been enhanced by a winter in New York. From the British officialdom that set the tone, Angelica had learned the word "Provincial." Within five minutes of landing she used it—with just the proper disdainful curl of a rosy lip.

She returned with new dresses in the English fashion, with new dances to teach her sisters, and a freedom in speaking to her elders that would have shocked her Granddams to the core.

A harpsichord and a Huguenot music master arrived as well. The poor fellow wore a flowing black wig and much lace at his neck and wrists. He stood goggling on the Schuyler's quay as if he half-expected a savage to leap out of the brush and hack off his scalp then and there.

Catherine Schuyler took one look at the elegant little lady who arrived wearing rouge on lip and cheek and chattering about balls and "the charming Major Smith" and "the most engaging Lieutenant Jones" and knew her little girl was gone forever. The big bed that the three girls had shared since childhood wouldn't do anymore. Betsy and Peggy were both sad when Angelica moved into a room by herself, along with Pearl and the brand new harpsichord.

Even Pearl had acquired airs in New York City. When Pearl's mother, her temper stretched to the breaking point, finally took a strap to her, it set off a near riot. Pearl had refused what she haughtily termed "common nigger's chores" in her mother's garden plot, but when she refused to lift a finger in the kitchen, too, it had been the last straw.

"How dare she whip my Pearl!"

Angelica swept into the upstairs great room where her mother sat embroidering in the light of the long front windows. The drama of her entrance was somewhat diminished by the fact that she'd had to race all the way from the kitchen wing to the main house and then up the steep staircase. The tight lacing she insisted upon had left her seriously short of breath.

"Pearl is mine!" Her face was scarlet with rage and exertion. "Her only work is the work I set!"

Betsy, who had been sewing, stared with a dropped jaw. *How did Angelica dare talk to Mama like that?*

Catherine Schuyler lifted her level hazel gaze from the day's hand-work, completely serene.

"Pearl is still a child, Angelica, and so are you. Her Mama and I took turns rocking you both together in the same cradle, so let me tell you that in this house, both of you—my woman's child and my child—do what they are told. If her Mama requires her help, it is her duty to give it. If she refuses, it is her mother's right and her mother's duty to whip her. Pearl is yours, true, but as long as she lives here, she has duties to her mother as well. No mother's wishes will be defied in my house."

Within hours of that uproar, Mrs. Schuyler thought it proper to deliver a lecture to all three of her daughters.

"It is no shame to be in the kitchen, girls. That silly notion is why the English gentry often have such bad food. Their servants cheat them at the market and then cook the cheap stuff they get carelessly. The surest way to have things as you want them is to learn to do everything yourself. How, I ask, are you to teach a cook to produce what you desire, if you don't know how to do it?"

Despite of the lecture, neither Angelica nor Pearl spent much time in the kitchen after that. Angelica could hardly be prevailed upon to sew an inch of anything now except embroidery. Her days were spent practicing music, studying French and reading poetry—or, that other plague that had come home with her—English romances.

Sitting with his wife before the evening fire, a bottle of Madeira open on the shining surface of a walnut table and set conveniently close by Prince, his gouty leg propped upon a pillow, Philip Schuyler was frequently heard to sigh, "Thank heaven we didn't leave her at the Livingston's for one minute longer."

Angelica talked endlessly about life in the sophisticated city. Her favorite story was about Governor Moore's daughter, who had climbed out the window into the strong arms of "a wonderfully handsome Captain."

"You see, they had to run away because her parents refused to allow the marriage—even though—by breeding, her Captain was most suitable. Really, the only thing he lacked was money."

Understandably, Major and Mrs. Schuyler found this tale not at all to their taste. Angelica had just turned fifteen, Betsy was fourteen and Peggy thirteen—all of marriageable age. Dutch mothers were not slow in telling their daughters where babies came from.

"And what if the rogue hadn't married her as he'd promised, but simply carried her off somewhere and made use of her?" Papa was outraged. "Regrettably, in this day and age, such things are not uncommon. Then what? She'd be ruined, disgraced for the rest of her life, nothing but a burden to her family. In Roman times she would have had no alternative but to open her veins. It might be better if that were still the fashion."

Mama Schuyler lifted a chestnut eyebrow slightly, but when she spoke again, it was simply to agree.

"Understand that what is fashionable is rarely moral. Of course, here in Albany, no young man would dare such a trespass. Even if a young woman committed an indiscretion before marriage, her suitor would never dare to abandon her. If her young man dared that, why he—and his family, too—would be ostracized."

"Far be it from me to contradict, but times change everywhere, Mrs. Schuyler, even in Albany. My dear daughters, please understand that an elopement is a positive danger that a young woman should never, under any circumstances, undertake. How can you forget," he turned to his wife, "that English officer who dishonored our cousin, sailing away and leaving the foolish trusting child with a bastard?"

The girls had already heard this tale. During the French War, officers had been quartered in the town. One of them had seduced and abandoned a girl from a good family, even though her parents had offered to settle upon him every inch of their not inconsiderable property.

"Yet the City folk are shocked when I tell of the fun we have with our House outings and parties. They think us compromised because we are seldom, if ever, chaperoned." Angelica, jutting her jaw, dared to argue.

"Chaperones are unnecessary when you are with your House friends, whether they are Blue, Green or Red. Among Van Rensselaers, Schuylers, Livingstons, Ten Broecks and Van Cortlandts, good manners and a high standard of conduct may always be relied upon."

"Let the city folk say what they will." Their father shook out a newspaper, preparing to retreat behind it, "but your honor is far safer at a House berrying party than it will ever be at any New York Governor's ball."

Soon after that conversation, Angelica was dispatched to a strict finishing school for Young Ladies in Poughkeepsie. Betsy and Peggy stayed in Albany and continued to read histories, Shakespeare and the Bible with Mrs. Ross. There were still eggs to be gathered, fowl to be tended, bread to bake, hams to cure, clothes to sew, the endless business of house and garden.

And the Mohawk charm did its work. More babies were born—boys at last—John Bradstreet, Philip Jeremiah and Rensselaer.

Around the growing Schuyler family, the bustle of a successful and wealthy northern plantation went on. Papa's schooners carried foodstuffs and lumber to the port of New York and sailed back with the manufactured items that, by law, had to be imported from England. When Betsy's father wasn't in his study receiving rents, writing contracts with his attorney, or negotiating land deals with other moneyed men, he rode about his vast holdings, advising his tenant farmers and instructing his overseers.

Mills and tanneries were erected all across the Schuyler holdings with the help of immigrants for whom Papa usually paid passage. He wanted artisans: weavers, smiths and mechanics, all of whom were needed, "to people and civilize this New World."

* * *

Today was a berrying party for Blue and Red Houses, a Dutch tradition that insured marriage among the right families. Occasionally these outings without chaperones had consequences: autumn weddings followed by winter births. Still, it was a time-tested way to hasten settling down. On this bright day the young people were headed down the Hudson to an enormous patch of berries growing on the eastern shore.

The revolution against England had begun, but since the decisive defeat last year of Burgoyne at Saratoga, things had returned to something close to normal around Albany, though there were still reports of bloody fighting to the west along the Mohawk. At last, after several turbulent years, it was again safe enough for a berrying party. Nevertheless, each boat carried a complement of arms.

Although she did not have a beau, Betsy was in happy anticipation. Occasionally she trailed one hand in the cold green water as she watched ducks, busy with their families, dabbling in the shallows. She had been feeling penned up in the house, trapped between mother and siblings, between the eternal sewing, childcare and the kitchen.

They came ashore across a rare, gravel bottomed bay. The girls collected firewood while the boys bent saplings for bowers. In the shade, blankets were arranged and the food they'd brought stored. As always, a flask or two of strong spirits had slipped in among the provisions, and these were now making their way into game bags to be consumed at a discreet distance from the ladies.

Betsy and Peggy gathered lidded baskets and prepared to go with the others. Once home, some blackberries would be pounded with dried meat for winter journeys, just as the Indians did, but the best were for conserves and pies.

Not all the boys would go picking. A few, those not courting, would go to hunt small game or climb down among the rocks to fish.

"Miss Peggy!" It was 'Bram Cuyler, a square, broad faced cousin. "Allow me to accompany you."

Peggy gave him a warm smile, but just as 'Bram was collecting the baskets, sixteen year old Stephen van Rensselaer stepped up beside him.

"I believe I'm the one Miss Peggy asked to escort her." Slender Stephen spoke with all the calm dignity of a man.

'Bram flushed. Stephen might be the next van Rensselaer Patroon, but he was also one of the youngest members of this group.

Didn't the serious intent of twenty-one take precedence?

"Oh dear, I did promise, didn't I?" Peggy appeared embarrassed and confused, but Betsy was sure that her sister had engineered the difficulty.

"Well, why don't you both come along? There are two of us, after all." There was nothing forward in Betsy's proposal. They were all Blues, companions from childhood, and everyone knew she was a girl who spoke her mind.

The others accepted her suggestion while Betsy had a flash of irritation. Peg was growing more and more like Angelica with each passing day. She had no doubt that after the picking, Peggy would disappear with whichever of the two pleased her most. Betsy would be left to soothe the hurt feelings of the loser.

In this case, duty wasn't an absolute hardship. 'Bram was a good fellow and easy going. Stephen was bright and charming, even if he was younger.

Besides, ever since Angelica had run away with the dashing Jack Church to the van Rensselaer mansion, Stephen had been forbidden to visit them. Betsy and Peggy both missed him and were glad for House gatherings like this which allowed them time with him.

As for Peggy's choice today, in a few weeks, at the next dance or boating party, everything might change. Just like

Angelica, Peggy was not only pretty and lively, but absolutely capricious.

"Walk with me, Cousin." Betsy extended an arm towards slim, fair Stephen. She was sure the young Patroon was fated to be this afternoon's loser.

Stephen sent a regretful look after curvaceous Peggy, now supported on 'Bram's big arm, but he collected his share of the baskets with a show of good humor. The tramp to the bushes and back was not yet done. Time would tell whether all was lost.

Around them a similar good natured jostling had begun, but eventually they set off. A few stayed behind, the girls chatting and sewing in the shade of the bowers, the boys down by the river, fishing.

The way to the bushes began with a climb through a pine woods. Peggy and Betsy and a good many of the others wore moccasins, which allowed them to scramble easily up the hill, despite stays and petticoats. Finally, emerging from the shade, they began a steep, brushy descent to a hollow which held a great patch of blackberries.

Finery had been left at home. The girls wore rough brown skirts, rolled shirt sleeves, and leather stays. Hair that was teased and powdered for dances was today braided, coiled, and covered with a cap in the plain fashion of their grandmothers.

This particular June day had dawned overcast, but as the sky cleared, the air grew hot. There was an audible murmur of complaint before they'd covered half the distance. Betsy paused, set down her basket and then took a few minutes to get a straw bonnet settled on her head.

The patch came in view and Betsy joined the others, now shouting and clapping. The hunters fired off shots. Shrieks followed, for a small brown bear and her cub made a brief crashing appearance on the far side of the brambles before loping away.

Feeling safer now, the young people spread out, carefully moving in among the tangle. Soon the only sounds were birds, crickets and a gentle wind.

Betsy pushed through to a place where the berries hung thick and shiny black. She would be twenty-two this summer, but she still took her 'Blue House' duties seriously. Blue was today pitted against Red for baskets filled. Peggy, 'Bram and Stephen were also Blues, but playing character-building games—especially those devised by one's teachers—was no longer very interesting.

First, Peggy stabbed her finger on a thorn and the men argued over which of them should be the one to bandage it. Her dress became entangled and she tore it freeing herself. Next, a gust of wind carried her straw hat away and 'Bram and Stephen had to coordinate an expedition into the worst of the patch to retrieve it.

Finally, she stepped into a hole, fell, and spilled most of what she'd picked. Sitting on the ground, rubbing an ankle, Peggy looked fragile and helpless. The heat had turned her fair face pink.

"Oh, Betsy! This is awful, no fun at all. Look, our two dear men are covered with scratches, my dress is torn, and now my ankle's certainly sprained. It hurts most dreadfully."

Betsy inwardly sighed. She knew what would come next, and, of course, it did.

"I can carry you back, Miss Peggy." 'Bram's blue eyes gleamed.

"You will do nothing of the sort." Betsy was stern. Although Peggy was dainty and 'Bram had a wonderful compliment of muscle he clearly longed to show off, it was a steep, rough way up the hill.

"Stephen will have to help," said Betsy. "Peggy can go between with an arm around each of you."

"Yes. That'll be best." Stephen, naturally, was prompt to endorse.

"But, Betsy," Peggy said, "what about the berries? If I don't bring mine back, the Reds will be sure to win. And what about you? What if a Tory comes out of the woods? Or what if the bear comes back?"

"Bear?"

58

They all turned toward the newcomer. Out of the brush appeared one of General Gates' aides, one Caleb Starke, the son of a New England General. A shy, gangly young man, he'd been among the hunters. He was an interloper at a House event, but the powers who decided such things determined that he was permitted to make up the war-time deficit of young men.

Apparently Starke had caught the end of the conversation. He stood awkwardly before them, squirrel tails drooping from his game bag.

"No bear, Major Starke," 'Bram replied. "Miss Peggy has twisted her ankle and it's going to take both van Rensselaer and me to get her back to the boats."

"These gentlemen don't wish to leave my sister," Peggy said, "and we have all these berries as well."

Caleb Starke raised his eyes to the bright sky. There was a halleluiah look in them, as if, for some queer Yankee reason, he should bless his Maker.

"I shall be honored to assist Miss Betsy in any way I can." Starke bowed. He'd been to dinner at the Schuyler house with his father. Betsy had been seated beside him each time, although she hadn't thought much about it. She was often set to putting shy people at ease.

She must have done an especially good job because the ordinarily silent Yankee had bubbled over like a newly dug well. He'd begun by responding to her queries about younger siblings and then gone on to tell about the troubles he was having with his new horse and finally about peculiar errands upon which he was sometimes sent by General Gates—the same odious person who had stolen Philip Schuyler's command from him last year, just before the great victory at Saratoga.

Not long after Starke's arrival, Peggy, supported by her suitors, was helped up the slope. The area, so full of talk and laughter only an hour ago grew quiet as everyone headed back to the boats. Betsy knelt to save what she could of the spilled berries.

This is the first time I've given up two *men to a sister!*

"Swantie and her beau picked gallons, I'm sure. Even if I get these back, I fear we'll lose to the Reds."

"We could pick more, Miss Schuyler."

"Well, yes, but how will we carry them? You've got your gun and those squirrels and now two baskets as well. What's here will have to do." Betsy smiled encouragement. "Come, sir. Set down your rifle and help."

Starke fairly hurled his game bag to the ground and fell to his knees.

"Oh dear, look at you!" Betsy noticed her companion had gotten into burdock. The burrs were stuck in a line down the back of his tan hunting coat.

At the touch of her hands, his ears—about all she could see of him—turned red. Though she noted it, Betsy wasn't sure exactly why.

Yankees — unaccountable creatures!

Betsy tried to get Caleb to talk about his hunt, but his replies were so short and grudging that finally she gave up and continued in silence. All at once she was hot, tired, hungry, and annoyed by black flies. On top of it all, this odd fellow would not say one word.

Suddenly she was roaringly cross with Peggy, not to mention her cousins, who, instead of thinking of the honor of Blue House, had only wanted an excuse to put their arms around her sister. It was a curse to always have to live up to a reputation for being "the best tempered girl in the world."

When she started to get up, Major Starke scrambled to assist her. In doing so he tipped his basket and spilled the precious berries all over again.

"Just leave them! They aren't fit for anything now!"

He made no defense, bantering or otherwise.

What was the matter with the man, anyway?

Was this her reward for coaxing him out during that interminable dinner? He was no better company than a scarecrow! For his part, Caleb looked as if he wanted to bolt into the forest.

"I'm sorry, Miss Betsy." He was lean and wiry, with a long New Englander's face, big ears, and solemn eyes.

How he managed to handle a rifle and fight as expertly as she'd heard she couldn't imagine, for he looked to be the clumsiest man God ever made. At table last week, he'd spilled his wine.

"How many shots did you get?"

"Six shots, Miss, and four squirrels fit to keep."

"You must have good aim."

Hitting squirrels neatly in the head required a steady hand, but was there any other evidence he owned such a thing?

All around was silence, broken only by bird calls and an occasional breeze. Their progress uphill through the brush was slow. Betsy ascended the steep parts like an Indian, scrambling on all fours. When Caleb attempted to assist, she refused.

"Thank you, but I'm sure-footed. Just mind you don't spill those." She nodded towards his dangerously tilted basket.

The top of the hill was welcome for more than one reason. Besides shade, a blanket of fragrant needles under the ridgepole pines had smothered the underbrush. The rest of their way would be easy. Again, below, Betsy could see the wide Hudson. A little further on and the shore-side shelters of the party would appear. Singing wafted up, as well as the smell of fires and cooking.

"Not much further now."

Betsy set her baskets down to give her arms a rest. She felt apologetic for snapping at him.

"Would you like me to make pies out of your squirrels? I'll have them sent over to you...."

Her speech trailed away into astonished silence, for his pale eyes were now crowded with tears. Lowering his head to hide them, Caleb hurriedly dropped all his burdens— berry baskets, long rifle, engraved powder horn and game bag, too.

"Miss Schuyler, I have something to say. I didn't dare ask to walk with you, especially after I saw you take the young Patroon's arm. Now fortune has given me time alone with you, but I'm such a fool that I've not said what I meant to."

Surprised, Betsy gazed up at him. The poor man trembled, but even as he did so, he caught her hand in his.

"I'm no good at speeches, Miss. Please don't be offended!"

Feverish kisses rained down upon her fingers. Betsy was so astonished she accepted them.

"There is no impropriety, Miss Schuyler! I have your father's permission to speak. Give me a little time, just a little time to plead my case. I—I love you."

* * *

Peggy sat on a stool, cane resting nearby. Her foot was in a pan of icy spring water. The ankle was not much better after three days. It had come as something of a surprise to Betsy that her sister was genuinely injured.

They were in the summer kitchen, where copper pans, drying fruit and herbs hung from the rafters. Black children sat by the windows slicing early apples while on the stoop their dark mother labored, her strong arms making a steady thump-thump at the churn.

The doors and windows were open, although the day was chilly. A big thunderstorm had come in and dropped the temperature some twenty degrees, nothing unusual in an Albany summer.

Black hair tucked under a cap, an apron over her dress, Betsy first measured blackberries, and then grated a sticky West Indies sugar cone into a pot. Her mother was nearby, ladling already cooked conserve into thick jars. One of the slaves trotted back and forth between the fire and the jars with ladles of liquid beeswax.

"Betsy won't have to marry Major Starke if she doesn't want to, will she?"

Peggy broached the horrible subject.

"Don't be foolish, Margaret," Mrs. Schuyler said. "But, I must say, Major Starke is a fine young fellow who knows

62

how to behave like a gentleman, even if he is a New Hampshire man."

Betsy stared into the iron pot. Had she grated three cones or two? She couldn't remember.

Mama Schuyler called for more wax. Later today, pieces of fresh bladder from butchering would be stretched over the jar tops to complete the mouse-proof seal.

"I think you should give Major Starke a chance, dear."

"Caleb Starke falls over his own feet." Peggy giggled. "He mumbles. That is when he can find two words to say. He's a dreadful dancer."

"New Englanders don't believe in dancing or chit-chat. He's been brought up to be shy around women. Papa says he cuts a fine figure with his troops and that he's a crack shot and an excellent horseman, quite bold enough there. General Starke says that admiration for our Eliza has knocked the brains right out of his poor boy." Their mother interrupted herself to wave a servant over to heft Betsy's pot of fruit and sugar onto a crane over the fire.

"Only fifteen jars of Blackberry, and Papa loves it so." Mrs. Schuyler was regretful. "We'll have to organize another expedition before the bears get them all. Major Starke must come too."

There was a limit to her endurance. Picking up her skirts, Betsy fled the kitchen, dashing through the stable yard and out into her sanctuary, the windswept orchard.

* * *

September came. A great expedition was mounted against the Seneca and Cayuga. When young Starke had ridden out with them, Betsy had worried about him.

Obedient to her parents' wishes, she'd accepted Major Starke's courtship. They walked together on lazy afternoons. They picked more berries, all alone in the small patch close to the Schuyler house. Caleb rowed her on the river while she read aloud. Caleb kissed her, too, and while he had been tender, it hadn't been very exciting, even to look back upon.

Betsy thought he did cut a handsome figure on horseback. His blue and buff uniform lent dignity. Talking with other soldiers, Starke seemed to grow, to have opinions and presence, but with her or Peggy, he remained painfully shy. He couldn't bear a joke and he almost never laughed.

How different from her Albany cousins! They teased and delighted in being teased in return. They drank rum, rowed the sisters wildly around the river, fell out of the boat and then climbed back soaking wet, insisting they were still fit to be kissed.

* * *

One warm afternoon, a few young people, Schuylers, Cuylers, Stephen van Rensselaer, his sister Elizabeth, and Henry Livingston, too, were lounging by the river.

"You, I hear," Livingston said with a grin, "are being officially courted by that hopeless stick of a New Englander."

In this new military world, Cousin Henry was "Lieutenant." At the moment, however, he'd shed decorum. Leaning against a wide sycamore close by the water, jacket unbuttoned, shirt open like some country boor, he was drunk. The cause was Peggy. Lately, she'd been kissing Henry at dances as well as 'Bram and Cousin Stephen. Each man was crazy jealous of the others.

Just now, Peggy had disappeared, supposedly to answer the call of nature, and utterly vanished. Disappearances were something that she, like Angelica before her, excelled at. When heads were counted, it was known by everyone that Stephen van R was missing, too. Peggy, Miss Cuyler said as the boats pushed off, must have decided to take the young Patroon seriously!

"It's astonishing, your Papa letting a damned *Jannke* dolt court you, Betsy. One of us would have eventually gotten 'round to it."

"Why should I bother with any of you, sir?" Betsy underlined her words, flinging a dusty sycamore seed at him, which he, slow because of all the rum he'd swallowed, caught on the cheek. "I shall certainly marry none of you. And as for Major Starke, well, I don't think you should talk about him that way. Not only are you speaking in as uncouth a manner as those you mock, but the gentleman outranks you."

"Gentleman? Starke? A cabinet maker's son? Rude and rank be damned, Betsy Schuyler! You're spending so much time with that pitiful bumpkin you hardly have a moment to comfort your poor cousins anymore, no time to give sisterly advice when they confide woeful tales of love gone wrong. We're all missing you, Little Saint."

"Don't be stupid, Henry."

Undeterred by the severity of her tone, he rolled over onto his stomach, seized her small hand and pressed a kiss upon it.

"I demand sympathy. Right this minute! Your devil of a sister is off somewhere kissing that snot-nosed boy."

"At the next dance, you shall be restored to her favor, of that I'm certain." She tried to disengage him. "And as for her being with Stephen, you don't know that."

"Oh, don't I? And it's not just sympathy I'm after today, Betsy Black Eyes!" With that, Henry threw his arms around her and dragged her close. The kiss he gave tasted strongly of rum.

"Leave off." Betsy pushed him hard and then scrambled to her feet.

"Oh, good! Let's play!" Henry stumbled upright and came after her.

There was a thrill of danger. Henry was young, strong, and, just at this moment, focused.

"Angelica always loved to be chased and caught. Peggy does, too!"

"I'm not them." Betsy backed up, but he lunged, this time catching her around the waist. The blonde, plump face so close to hers was a stranger's, flushed and hard in the bright reflection from the river.

"Don't you ever get tired of being our little saint?"

She pushed, but to no avail. Rummy breathing engulfed her.

"Shouldn't we—second-fiddle sister—poor discarded Henry—shouldn't we have a little fun? Don't you want to know what you're missing?"

"Dolt!"

Betsy cuffed his ear as hard as she could. Henry cursed but let go. In a whirl of petticoat, Betsy ran up the hill toward the house.

* * *

Rubbing his ear and much subdued, Colonel Livingston cursed once more and then subsided against the sycamore.

"She's too brown anyway."

Taking out his flask, he took a long drink of consolation.

* * *

"Oh, Mama, Caleb will be so hurt. He's such a good fellow, really. It's just that I can't love him. I've tried and I can't."

"You've hugged him and kissed him, and you still don't like him?" Mrs. Schuyler knew caresses were powerful persuaders to young flesh.

"It made him so happy, but I didn't like it." Betsy paused to sigh. "I hope Papa won't be disappointed."

"If you don't like his kisses, you can't love him. Do what your heart tells you."

* * *

"You won't reconsider?" Major Starke stood perfectly still, gazing away from her, out the window.

"I don't want to hurt you, sir. You will always have my friendship, if you want such a poor thing." Betsy hoped she sounded determined. It was time for him to march away, and therefore time for a decision.

He turned, cleared his throat and straightened his shoulders.

"Then it's good-bye, Miss Schuyler." As he bowed formally over her hand, Betsy felt a tear drop.

"Think of me sometimes." His farewell was barely audible.

She pitied his hopeless loving, but she feared it, too. She knew she must stand firm now, or be tied forever by ropes of religion, by knots of pity, to a man she didn't love.

* * *

Her twenty-third birthday came. It was a warm, star-glowing August night, spent with her cousins. They danced in the great room upstairs, and big blonde 'Bram Cuyler made an affectionate toast to "Our Little Saint Betsy to whom all the boys confess," while Henry Livingston glowered from a corner.

"How shall I," she confided to her mother as they prepared for bed, "ever get a husband? Men like me, but only as a friend. Peggy's beaux dance with me, take me for drives and boat rides and then sigh about her. I don't mind, but if every man I meet treats me like a sister...."

"Maybe," Catherine Schuyler replied, stroking her daughter's shiny hair, "maybe one of these fellows will surprise you. Marriage is harder than romance. Sometimes, after a flirt breaks a man's heart, he turns to a constant friend. Friends often make far better husbands than lovers."

"But you and Papa had romance. Everyone knows it! I want someone who loves me, someone who tells me I'm beautiful, even if it's not true."

"Hush! You are beautiful and it will happen, my darling, never fear.

Chapter Three ~ Revolution

Hamilton shivered, shivers so bone-shaking they threatened to knock him off his aching feet, but he kept trudging along. It was just before dawn on Christmas morning. A howling wind blasted the marching column of men with sleet.

He could barely lift his arms, for ice had frozen over his coat like a suit of glassy armor. His companions in what remained of the New York Artillery Company tramped along before and behind. Men and officers alike were exhausted, but somehow they kept moving, pushing their aged cannon along the rutted track.

The entire patriot army had just performed a maneuver of dubious sanity: crossing the ice-filled Delaware. They had just marched through the night to attack the enemy, now snug in warm beds in the little river town of Trenton.

Alexander stumbled, steadied himself against the nearest cannon. He'd come to love—and fear—these relics. Until General Washington's campaign, most of these ancient pieces had not been discharged since the French and Indian War. Each shot fired put the lives of the soldiers at risk. In New York, at the very beginning, two of his men had been killed when one venerable weapon had burst. Alexander was now familiar with the idiosyncrasies of those that remained.

After their first runaway battles around New York City, he'd emerged with a black powdered face and ears that rang for days, but otherwise none the worse for wear. His men, who had been dubious about having a slender, bookish collegian for a captain, had begun to take him seriously. Not only had he faced death alongside them, but "the boy" hit what he aimed at.

So long since summer, the bloody and nearly fatal farce that had been the Battle of White Plains, where militia companies, one after the other, had run without firing a shot! For a moment, Hamilton let his mind wander back to that day. His still handsomely outfitted provincial artillery had been pale with fear, but had kept good discipline and held their posts—the last to be overrun—among the woods and sunny meadows of Manhattan.

Henry Knox, last year a Boston bookseller, now Artillery Commander of Washington's army, had come with the news that an American retreat had been cut off. Despite their apparently hopeless position, a command was given to turn all cannon to protect the infantry. They had resolved to defend to the last their post at Bayard's Hill.

Then, with redcoats closing around them, and Hamilton readying himself to die, one of General Putnam's aides, Colonel Aaron Burr, had come dashing up, his horse in a lather. The image of this gallant youth had stuck in his mind, perhaps because Burr was as small and elegantly made as Hamilton himself, like a dark-haired, dark-eyed twin. He'd shouted there was one path still open—and that he'd lead them to it, across country.

Following Burr, who had spent years hunting through these woods, they'd escaped the closing jaws. The company had rout-marched, dragging their cannon and baggage nine miles through brush and onto the road to Harlem Heights. Once with the main force of the army, the discipline of his men had continued and they'd followed his order to dig emplacements and throw up earthworks before setting watch.

That night Hamilton had been exhausted, physically and emotionally stretched almost to the breaking of his own formidable will. He'd been warm, then.

Today, he was somewhere in Jersey, in the middle of the war he'd once imagined he'd wanted. So far, it had been a war without glory or advancement. In fact, as time went on, it seemed increasingly likely that they would all be hanged. Under the command of General Washington, the army had lost and retreated, lost and retreated.

In between defeats and running, the Continentals had sickened and starved. Out of the well-drilled and brightly

69

uniformed hundred that had left New York City with Captain Hamilton, only thirty-six were left. Although he'd tried to be a good leader, using every strategy he could think of to get the pay and supplies to which the men were entitled from the scarce stock available, there had been desertion. Some had died fighting; more had died of camp fever. Worse, a lot of fellows had, when their time was up, simply gone back to their farms.

Summer soldiers, the pamphleteer Tom Paine called them. Alexander could not blame the men who'd left, feeling deep in his heart that they were guilty of nothing more reprehensible than pragmatism. Along with his men, the young captain endured the pangs of hunger. His body had been stripped of all excess—nothing left these days but a frame of bone held together by sparse, hard muscle.

The raggedy thirty-six were thoroughly disheartened. So was Alexander. His college money, charitably dedicated to his education, he'd spent in supplying his company. The future he'd hoped to seize in this rich and rebellious colony had never seemed further away.

The Continental army had been pushed by General Howe straight across New Jersey, and had, up until a few hours ago, been hiding behind the narrow barrier of the Delaware River. They'd managed to commandeer or destroy all the large boats on the east side before they'd crossed into Pennsylvania. It was one small thing that had gone right.

"Thompson," Alexander asked the sergeant now wading through the crusted snow beside him, "have you got any idea how much farther?"

"No, Captain," was the provincial's half-expected reply. "Never been west of the Hudson 'til the run we just took 'cross Jersey."

"I hope we get there soon." Hamilton muttered inside his frozen, sodden muffler. He was giddy with misery, suffering a terrible catarrh. His head and chest ached. His hands, feet and face stung and burned. He tried to rouse his strength by focusing upon the upcoming battle.

70

Once again we'll fight the British. Fight them—by God—after all this running!

Nevertheless, the pumping thrill of anticipation he'd felt as they'd met the enemy in summer was nearly impossible to muster, a dead horse incapable of being flogged to life. It was as if his mind was as frozen as his feet.

We will fight—eventually. We will be killed—or not be killed—eventually.

In the meantime, they were on an endless march in an icy hell, putting one aching, numb foot in front of the other.

"If it goes on sleeting like this, I won't be able to lift my arms."

There was a grunt from the stalwart sergeant. The company, as he scanned what he could see in the muffled lantern light, looked like a troop of snowmen. The cannon were glazed and dripping, metal encased in ice.

How hungry I am!

But what had there been for the last few weeks? Gritty flat cornmeal cake—or mush—the kind of slop they fed slaves.

It seemed a very long time since Thomas had caught the goose. Hamilton had been far too hungry to scruple about exactly where it had come from. After all, Jersey was full of burned out farms and straying livestock.

He'd heard the men joking. "Killed a Hissian, did ya?"

"Yes, with my bare hands, by Christ!"

"Always knew you fer a bold warrior, Davy!"

When Alexander had asked what they were talking about, they'd explained, canny peasant faces smiling, that a "Hissian" was not one of those fierce and dreaded Hessian troopers. Toothless Davy held up the big limp body of the goose by the neck, and Hamilton saw it was one of those bravado-deriding, run-away-as-fast-as-you-can American soldier jokes.

A few months ago he would have taken them to task, even though the owner of the goose was doubtless long fled. On that day, he'd helped pluck it.

With a scavenged pot and some tired turnips and potatoes discovered in the root cellar of a ruined house, they had eaten. Not much, but a greasy mouthful of something savory.

His stomach growled, begging in response to memory. Sternly, Alexander tried to put the goose out of his mind.

Shuffling along on pins and needles feet, he thanked heaven that he'd had the cannon stuffed with straw. When they got to wherever it was His Excellency George Washington was leading them, the weapons might be of some use.

Finally, in the paltry light of a dripping winter dawn, they saw a small whitewashed town, smoke rising from the chimneys. Someone must have seen them coming, for in the street below there were a few men staggering about, trying to get organized. A guttural shout of alarm rose through the frigid air.

Der Feind! Der Feind! Heraus! Heraus!

As the Americans began to ready their cannon, a smart barrage of musketry fire sent balls whistling past his ears. At last, Hamilton's blood rushed. The battle had begun, and he must sight and adjust, shout commands, while his men rushed around serving the cannon, all while surrounded by flying balls and ever greater clouds of blinding black powder. He sent a quick prayer to his severe Presbyterian God to keep the cannon intact.

Peering through smoke and snow, he tried to gauge where his first shots had gone. Fire was returned, and though he noted the balls, their flight, even so close, did not shake his concentration. Another roar, and this time he was rewarded by the sight of tall metal helmets going over, a falling row of tin soldiers.

Under covering musketry fire of their own troops, they hauled the cannon forward. He and his men were moving with the front line to take a stand on the upper part of the main street. The reloading frenzy repeated, while volley after volley went screaming past. Something almost knocked Alexander's tricorn from his head, even though he'd tied it against the wind with a scarf. There was neither pain nor a gush of blood into his eyes, so he forgot it.

72

Eight horses emerged from a side street, pulling a pair of cannon. Hessians stumbled around, frantic to set up. Hamilton was hoarse from shouting, tugging at the ropes, urging his men on. At this range, whichever side fired first would be the ones left standing. Slipping and sliding in the ice-covered snow, he adjusted the range.

Cannon spoke at the same instant, and soldiers fell face down. Balls roared past. Flying metal and frozen dirt stabbed and pelted.

"Got 'em, Captain!" his men shouted, scrambling back to their feet, rushing like wild men to once more serve the cannon. In the street below, enemy artillery was surrounded by milling soldiers, not a one of them in a complete uniform. Their snow was now splashed red.

"Grape!" Hamilton shouted. Heedless of the shriek of balls from what remained of the ragged line below, the grape was stuffed and sent on its way.

After that smoke cleared, he saw Hessian infantry running, retreating into a side street, cannon abandoned. The American infantry charged, whooping like Indians. Captain Hamilton's cannon were swabbed and dragged forward again, but another order to fire was not forthcoming.

Pushing the nearest weapon, catching welcome heat from the bore, Alexander shook in every limb. His ears rang painfully; his head felt as if it might explode. Still, it seemed that he'd not only survived the night in the ice and wind, but the battle for the little town of Trenton. He went on giving orders in a voice cracking with illness and strain, trying to keep his men together, to make out if anyone was wounded—and, if so, how badly.

"Hey! Yer one lucky fella, Captain," his sergeant cried. When Hamilton gave him a blank look, he added, "Check yer hat."

Not wanting to expose his head to the wind, Hamilton tugged the brim forward and rolled up his eyes. Against the gray sky he saw a half-moon shape bitten into the felt, the hole where a ball had passed. For a moment, he fingered the rough edge, realizing it had missed his skull by a bare inch.

Six months ago this would have occasioned a nervous overflow of chatter and graveyard humor. This morning it was hardly worth thinking about. There was far greater matter in being cold, sick, and stomach-twistingly hungry.

Meanwhile, the American infantry broke line, running into the white clapboard town waving their guns and whooping. The artillery continued to march as a unit, towing, pushing and tugging the gun carriages. As they struggled along, faces blackened and streaked, an imposing figure mounted on a huge steel gray horse came alongside.

As Alexander gazed into the snow-dappled sky, the tall officer called, "What company is this?"

Hamilton stepped outside his column and attempted, although his ice-covered coat now seemed to weigh at least 400 pounds, to make a smart salute.

"New York Artillery, sir; Captain Alexander Hamilton, at your service, and proud to have the honor, Your Excellency."

The face beneath the tricorn was pockmarked and severe, as if carved from pitted marble. "And I am proud to have such brave and resolute soldiers. Your men kept good order, Captain." There was a nod of approval as George Washington surveyed the ill-clad, sooty-faced company, now standing irregularly at attention in the snow.

Washington tapped the sides of his horse and was immediately swept up by a mounted contingent of green-sashed aides de camp. The glorious moment with the commander-in-chief was over. Captain Hamilton fell into the straggling tail of his own company.

A couple of his men had been hurt, but not seriously. Their comrades helped them hobble along.

"What'd His Excellency say?" Sergeant Thomas asked. Hamilton suddenly wondered if he looked like Thomas: a powder-blackened face with two bright blue eyes.

"General Washington says we did a good job, and that we should be proud!" Hamilton called this out as loudly as he could, hoping these loyal sufferers would hear and take heart. Then, in a softer voice, spoken just for Thomas' ears, he said, "But I confess I'm too damned cold and too damned hungry to feel a sensation as subtle as pride." He didn't mention sick, although now that the engagement was over, he was both dizzy and nauseated.

"Amen to that, sir."

They continued forward, wading through a leg-lacerating drift. Nearby, Continental infantry herded captured Hessians into a group in the middle of the square. From somewhere close, a renewed chorus of happy cheers arose. Although his ears still rang and roared, Alexander thought he recognized the particular joy of soldiers who have discovered a cache of rum.

The front end of his line, about fifteen men, broke and stumbled toward a cask that was even now rolling out into the street with the assistance of the Continental infantry, directly into their path.

Alexander quickened his pace. They'd been so obedient, so brave, had won in the middle of this frozen hell—but—by God! What if they got drunk and the British sent a flying cavalry over from Princeton? Aching in every limb, he shook ice from his shoulders and then hurried forward, to see if he could keep them in good order.

* * *

The smell of America, Hamilton thought, wrinkling his long nose. Head pounding, he found consciousness.

For two years, he had slept on the ground with his men, or on some dusty barn floor beneath the acrid muzzles of cannon. Now, he awoke as Aide de Camp to a commanding general. He slept under roof and bundled in a camp cot, but he still woke bone tired.

Since joining George Washington's household, Hamilton, a newly promoted Lieutenant Colonel, spent the hours between midnight and five indoors, but lodged in a situation guaranteed to give him whatever illness was presently loose upon the others. As many aides as possible

75

bedded down in a single room in some unfortunate citizen's home, all of them unbathed, all of them snoring exhaustion, and discharging from last night's heavy, onion-laden supper. The other smell was wet wool and soaked leather—boots, bags and saddles—saturated with the interminable ice and snow of this ninth circle of hell Americans called 'winter'.

Hamilton's head ached because he was recovering from a cold, and because he'd barely had six hours of sleep. Hunched over His Excellency George Washington's paperwork in the light of a single candle all day and half the night, drafting letters to merchants the army could not pay until his fingers ached and invention failed.

By God, this was no way to run a business—or found a nation. Those jackasses in the Continental Congress, quarreling over their little private kingdoms, willfully ignorant of what was necessary! Most were so unschooled they imagined that printing money by the bushel, without an ounce of gold to back it, would solve their problems.

Congress *was* the problem, and Hamilton, as he often did, awoke in a rage of frustration, for this would be the matter of his day. Congress was unable to agree on anything, certainly not upon an incendiary topic like taxation. This meant it could not find the money to buy what was needed to wage a successful war: shoes, clothes, arms, and gunpowder. When they did raise a little money, most of it slipped into someone's pocket at the commissary. Someone, needless to say, ensconced at a safe distance from the fighting.

It didn't make sense when every man on the American side was about a quarter of an inch from having his neck permanently stretched by His Britannic Majesty! Hamilton knew the English newspapers daily trumpeted: "Such divisions will be the downfall of the rebellion. These Americans are a race of mongrels, all bark, bark, bark—and no bite. As soon as they get a good look at their master with a stick in his hand, all you will see is backsides."

Last winter, after riding the length of the Hudson on a hopeless mission to secure troops from General Gates, he'd developed a raging fever. His lungs had bubbled like a cauldron of back-country stew. Alone, except for his Sergeant, he'd lain, almost dead, in a hovel by the frozen river.

Hamilton hadn't been able to secure the reinforcements Washington needed. Not from that smug intriguer Gates, sitting comfortably in Albany with General Schuyler's stolen Saratoga laurels on his brow. He had not succeeded in moving the regiment that wily old Putnam, dug in at West Point, had first promised and then refused to release. Sick as the proverbial dog, it almost seemed easier to go to an early grave than return to Valley Forge to face the brunt of Washington's powerless rage.

In the end, he'd survived both the winter and Washington's black mood. Spring had come to Pennsylvania. Shad ran up the Schuylkill and the army ate again.

Washington worked Hamilton hard, for he was better trained than the sons of the American gentry. He'd learned that Alexander had clerked for a living, and that by the age of fourteen he'd been writing most of the letters and running the day-to-day operation of an enterprise which did business with every part of the globe.

Today, encamped at Morristown, snowed in by the heaviest storm yet, Hamilton tested the frostbite scab on the elegant bridge of his nose. It was about to fall off, which was a good thing, because one bit of cheer was soon to be had.

In a few days, the first of the winter's social gatherings would be held at the house known locally as "Ford's Mansion." The French officers, naturally, sneered at the attribution. However, in this plain but commodious residence, young ladies of good family would arrive to dance with the gentlemen of General Washington's military family. In this time of blizzards, opposing armies were immobilized, but not adventurous American ladies.

The British likewise held winter courts, theirs in the snug comfort of Philadelphia and New York. The Americans huddled in rural Morristown and danced with the daughters of the most radical and daring local patriots, girls sufficiently brave to hazard long, perilous sleigh rides in a frozen land at war.

As well as the Hudson, this winter the ocean had turned to ice. The Atlantic supported raiding horsemen from Staten Island all the way down the Jersey shore. This might have been an item of purely military interest, but the hard freeze had transformed the waters into smooth causeways, perfect for civilian travel, too.

Hamilton owned nothing beyond his wits, so he'd decided long ago that a good marriage was a necessity. Besides, as the Reverend Knox had often counseled, it was better to marry than to burn. He did burn, too, for the delirium that lay between the lovely legs of the fair sex.

Hamilton hoped to combine pleasure and practicality in a marriage, but, thus far, the Field of Venus remained as unyielding to Hamilton's will as had the Field of Mars. Still, winter brought dancing, bright eyes and banter, soft hands and sweet lips, things unavailable during the alarms and marches of summer.

It had been months since he'd had his last easy country lass. Now, dry as tinder, he was hot for a spark. True, he had tried and failed to gain the hand of lovely Peggy Lott, but there would be others.

I will dance, dare, and flirt until one of these rich papa's darlings imagines she's made a conquest she must keep....

An instant before the sentry knocked, Hamilton pushed back the blankets. It was a trick he'd learned long ago, setting an internal clock. The cot creaked as he rose. He shivered as soon as his feet struck the frigid floor. He was, as always, the first aide out of bed.

Up with the slaves and out in the kitchen, yawning, bare feet planted on the rungs of a stool, waiting for the water to heat, for that first cup of tea that he would serve his master in a St. Croix dawn....

"His Excellency wants you as soon as possible, Colonel Hamilton."

A soldier, lighting candles, passed the word. Apparently, Washington's slow mind had turned all night on some matter, and a conclusion had been reached. Action would now be taken without delay.

"Thank you, Roberts."

In his shirt, Hamilton walked across the room to add wood to the banked fire. The soldier joined him, grabbing the poker to encourage the remaining coals. In the other cots, beneath the blankets, the rest of the aide-de-camps shifted unhappily.

"Bad night, Corporal?" By the feeble light, Hamilton noted the man's face was drained as a corpse.

"Yes, sir, Colonel. It's cold as Hell's tit out there again." His breath hung in the air.

Hamilton shivered and nodded. They worked in silence, encouraging the fire.

"Are you off duty now?"

"As soon as I go back down, sir."

"Take yourself off at once, Roberts."

As the young man—no older than himself—saluted and turned, Hamilton thought: *Yes, by God, I'm a Colonel now, a free man in a free country, no longer a bastard son of St. Croix.*

Chapter Four ~ Morristown

Soon after coming down to Morristown, Betsy went sleighing with her Aunt Trude and her Uncle Cochran, the army surgeon, to the encampment at Jockey Hollow. At her feet sat two big kettles, one filled with a posset of wine, sugar and crackers, and the other with a slurry of skimmed broth, vegetables and bread.

"No grease, just what those poor sick fellows can digest," explained Aunt Gertrude.

On that frigid first day, Betsy saw the woods devastated. Of the forest, only thousands of low stumps remained. Every tree in Jockey Hollow had been turned either into huts or smoke. When Betsy wondered aloud where all the wild creatures—even the birds—had gone, her Uncle said they'd been used by the army as well.

"All gone into their bellies, Bess."

And the Continental soldiers—ragged scarecrows, some wrapped in nothing more substantial than a blanket, dashing from hut to hut or to the necessaries which stood stinking, even in the bitter cold.

So many! So much dirt and suffering!

Betsy had gone to the farms of tenants, to slave cabins to tend the sick. She'd seen many hard things and smelled many bad ones, but none of it prepared her for the military hospital. The rows of patients, shivering and shaking on pitiful heaps of straw under thin blankets, was a daunting sight.

At the door of the big cabin that served as a hospital, Surgeon Cochran watched his niece turn pale, and then said, "A bit more than you bargained for, eh, Miss?" He hadn't been very keen when she'd asked to come along.

"I—I've never seen so much trouble, Uncle."

"Well, stick with your Aunt. She'll show you what to do."

The tattered 'women of the army' knew Mrs. Cochran, and came rushing up to the wagon, chorusing a greeting. The first task was to get the pails of posset and broth ladled out. Betsy helped her Aunt with the task.

Mrs. Cochran, she noted, addressed each ragged woman with great politeness.

"This is for you, Mrs. Perkins. This is for you, Mrs. Sullivan." Out of a basket, she produced knit stockings and mittens.

"For your friend," she said to one woman. "For your husband," she said to another.

These women were here with their men—a husband, a brother, a lover.

Betsy soon found herself kneeling by a soldier, supporting his head so that he could swallow the thick posset. After he'd taken in what he could, she sponged his face and hands in vinegared water and dried them. The poor fellow was abashed in front of this fine lady, but Betsy's shyness had passed. Once she began to work, one on one, it was just nursing. That she understood.

The next man, despite the cold, sweated. When she began to unwrap his injured foot in order to give it a clean dressing, she smelled the trouble before she'd finished unwinding the stained cloth. Though she was careful, he could barely endure the touch of her hands. The blackened foot stank.

"Don't tell the surgeon."

Betsy nodded silently, but she knew gangrene, knew that she'd have to tell her uncle if the fellow was to have a chance to live.

On the way out, Mrs. Cochran had explained that in winter, frostbite was the soldier's chief enemy, coming on during raids or foraging or simply from standing sentinel with almost shoeless feet. Sometimes it mortified, and then amputation was the only option.

Betsy had never seen a "cutting," and found the prospect terrifying. She knew, however, that her Aunt Gertrude had assisted her husband for years. Her Aunt and Uncle had met for the first time during the French & Indian War; it was a famous love story. Everyone else being occupied, Gertrude had assisted in the emergency amputation of a crushed leg.

The operation had taken place on Philip Schuyler's dining table. Surgeon Cochran had been not only grateful for Miss Gertrude's help, but impressed by the way she had kept her head during the bloody baptism. After shucking off his gore-soaked leather apron and wiping his hands, John Cochran had asked Gertrude to go for a tranquilizing walk with him in the orchard behind the house. Philip Schuyler said that he had always known his sister to be a hard-headed woman, but this was, without a doubt, one of the most unusual courtships ever.

"He can get a leg off in a blink and stop the blood just as fast. He's a fine surgeon and the proof is that his patients live to thank him." Aunt Gertrude remained proud of her husband's skill with a knife.

After a few trips to the Hollow Hospital, Betsy grew accustomed to the dirt, the smell, and the crowding. She even assisted, without faintness, while her uncle used a forceps to open wounds and drain pus.

Some days she'd only spoon posset or broth into sick men. If things were quiet, she took dictation from them, many of whom could not read or write. Betsy took the money to send their letters out of her own pocket.

Some days, Aunt Cochran did not go to the Hollow. Instead, she'd take Betsy to visit the local gentry. In scattered farmhouses, Betsy would sit by the fire with other genteel New Jersey ladies and they'd get to know each other over cups of sassafras tea—this being the only patriotic drink during the on-going boycott.

The visit might be social, but their hands were never unoccupied. As they talked, they knitted mittens, caps and stockings for the soldiers, or spun new thread out of the ravelings of old. For an army badly supplied, this work was a gratefully received necessity. During these social visits,

Aunt Gertrude collected charity baskets of things needed at the Hospital: soap, thread, or scraps for patching and bandages.

Although other gentlewomen occasionally came to the hospital, the companion with whom Betsy and her Aunt traveled most frequently was Mrs. Washington, who had joined her husband at Morristown. One day, returning home in Mrs. Washington's sleigh, Betsy received a compliment.

"You are the most faithful angel of mercy among our maiden ladies. The others might nurse officers," and here Lady Washington's periwinkle eyes twinkled, "but hardly the poor men."

"I wish to help, Lady Washington."

The rosy face of Martha momentarily brightened. Then she said, "But how sad you are today, Miss Schuyler."

Betsy shivered, cold to the bone. Outside, the drifts were on the move before a lashing wind. Although the road to the Hollow was continuously traveled, there were places where the horses labored, almost chest deep. The weather was bad, but the day had been worse. One of the men had died, a man Betsy had known well. When she'd gone to him this morning, he'd been deep in delirium, muttering and chattering, his mates around him. While Betsy had soothed his forehead with vinegar water, he'd died, going out just like that, leaving nothing behind but a wisp of white, a last exhalation which had lingered briefly in the chill air.

"I'm accustomed to helping our tenants or the slaves when somebody falls ill, Lady Washington, but this is so different. So many poor soldiers here without any help at all! Those Congressmen should be made to see this hospital, see how their stupidity has made these brave fellows suffer. There's so little food, so little clothing! I never saw so much misery packed into one place. It feels as if all we're doing is pouring water into a bucket with a hole in it."

"Yes, dear. We all feel like that. Angry, and sad, too."

Aunt Cochran's gloved fingers clasped hers.

"If we can comfort a few of those poor fellows, even a little," Lady Washington said, "I believe we've done something worthwhile."

"And Mr. Pond lost his foot after all."

"Yes, a pity. A farmer, with a young family at home."

"And it was poor Mr. Hushman who died today as I sat beside him."

The older women were philosophic, murmuring about "God's will."

"Poor Mr. Hushman," Aunt Cochran said. "That catarrh just wore him out. God rest his soul."

"And cutting is terrible, but it might save Mr. Pond's life. Your uncle is an excellent surgeon, Miss Schuyler. I truly believe that Mr. Pond will live and return to his family." After a pause, Martha Washington reached to pat Betsy's blanketed knee. "Perhaps, my dear, you should take some time away. You've been out to the hospital pretty regularly."

"Just what I've been saying." Mrs. Cochran nodded. "My dear, you must not dwell too much on what happens there. It's the only way you'll find the strength to return."

"Your aunt is right, Elizabeth. Instead of going to the Hollow tomorrow, I shall dispatch you to Mrs. Lott's tea."

"Oh, um...." The Lott girls were close to Betsy's age, and pleasant enough, but sitting in a warm parlor seemed— after the sacrifice of Mr. Hushman and Mr. Pond—the act of a craven.

"In two days, we shall have our first dancing assembly." Aunt Gertrude touched her shoulder. "And, Bess, have you forgotten? Your Cousin Kitty is already down from Basking Ridge. This drifting will certainly keep her—and Lord Stirling's girls, too—here."

Betsy inwardly groaned and settled deeper back beneath the blanket.

Listening to Kitty Livingston bewail the loss of the New York society!

Widow Ford's big white house appeared through the windows of the Washington's covered sleigh. It was full to

84

bursting nowadays, for besides the wealthy Widow, her two young sons, and servants, His Excellency George Washington and his official family of aides de camp and servants were also in residence.

"Silas!" Lady Washington rapped on the roof and called to the coachman. "Go on down to Surgeon Cochran's first."

"Another blizzard coming for sure." Lady Washington settled back into her seat and fixed her attention upon Betsy. "Well, Miss Schuyler, are you ready for the assembly? The General's aides really are charming young men, so hard-working. They deserve some pleasant evenings in the company of patriotic young ladies. And dancing is so good for young people."

"Will Colonel Tilghman be there?" Betsy noted the sparkle that kindled Martha's bright eyes, so added hastily, "Colonel Tilghman visited us in Albany when he was up for a parley with the Indians. He is the only one of His Excellency's aides to whom I have been previously introduced."

"Colonel Tilghman will certainly attend. Do you know, he's been with General Washington ever since this war started? He is not only one of our most well-educated, genteel young officers, but from one of the finest families in Maryland."

"Well, aren't you a sly boots, Betsy," said Aunt Cochran. "I didn't know you were acquainted with any of the aides de camp. Do I detect a method to this madness of a winter visit to your dull old Aunt and Uncle?"

"Miss Schuyler, I promise that I shall not allow the General to keep a single bachelor away from the assembly, no matter how much work there is to do, most especially Mr. Tilghman."

After thanking Mrs. Washington for driving them home, Betsy and her aunt stepped from the carriage and walked down the narrow path between piles of snow to the kitchen door. The house the Cochrans had rented, a five-over-four farmhouse, stood about a quarter mile from the Ford mansion.

Inside, they doffed their outer dresses of plain brown Duffield and the aprons which they'd worn to the Hollow. Then, still shivering, in front of a hearty fire, they stood in their shifts and washed before redressing in a manner suitable to gentlewomen at home. In the depths of a miserable winter, this meant heavily quilted petticoats and long, brightly colored caraco jackets. A serving girl came to assist, leaving the pot she'd been tending to bubble over the fire.

"Lady Washington is right, Niece. No more of the Hollow for you. I don't want you to take sick."

* * *

Kitty Livingston and Betsy Schuyler dressed in the bedroom at Surgeon Cochran's farmhouse. The windows were etched with frost. Chimneys spewed thin hardwood smoke into a broken sky. Ruby, the black maid who had come with Betsy from Albany, helped her mistress into a new pink dress. With a silken hiss, it slipped over the tightly drawn stays and covered her quilted winter petticoat.

The party dress was cut in a form fitting style called *a la Anglaise*. It had recently completed a long journey from Paris to Philadelphia, then, by special messenger to Albany, and, just recently, by sleigh to Morristown. The rose pink set off Betsy's olive skin and black hair. The style drew attention to her slender waist, and away from her small bosom.

The stays were intended as a remedy. After shaking them out of the box, Betsy, dismayed at what she saw, had brought them to her mother.

"Look, Mama! The wretched shop has sent the padded ones!"

"It's chest protection, my dear, as it's so dreadfully cold this winter, the worst anyone can remember. And you are about to take that long journey to New Jersey."

86

"Mama, if a gentleman ever does put his hand inside, the poor fellow will be bitterly disappointed." Since she'd refused Major Starke, her parents had taken up doing little things that let her know they were becoming concerned about her prospects.

"Elizabeth! Such talk! The padding is to give your figure some balance. All the Philadelphia girls are said to be wearing them."

Although Betsy had pointedly not packed the offending stays, they had mysteriously made their way inside her traveling trunk. Tonight, in front of her worldly Cousin Kitty, a belle who had danced in New York City before the war, Betsy had to swallow her distaste when Ruby produced them.

"Your mama said you was to wear 'em at dances." When Betsy made a face, Ruby whispered, "You know your mama will have her way."

Cousin Kitty had commandeered the mirror, where she was busy studying her thin, pretty features.

"If we ever do win this interminable war, General Washington's aides will find themselves at the pinnacle of society."

She leaned forward to better examine the effect of the rouge she'd artfully applied to her cheeks. "Papa says that brains, ambition, and good connections will often take a man farther than an inheritance." Pleased at last by what she saw, she turned to her cousin. "If you won't powder, do put on some of this." She tapped the rouge pot with an elegant, long finger. "You *are* going to get yourself a husband this winter, aren't you?"

"I believe your need is far more pressing than mine." Betsy might be twenty-three and unmarried, but Kitty, still single, had reached the advanced age of twenty-six.

Kitty turned, more than a little surprised by her country cousin's barb.

"Do forgive me." Betsy moved away toward the blurry, frosty window. "I am always nervous before dances, especially ones where I hardly know anybody. Not to mention that I'm on pins and needles about meeting Colonel Tilghman again."

"Well, indeed! To be so unkind isn't a bit like you, Our Little Saint to whom all the boys confess."

"All their sins, but never their love."

"It's more than you deserve, but I shall share some intelligence. My spies tell me that Colonel Tilghman has been singing your praises ever since he heard you were joining us. He is telling everyone that you are not only charming, but 'the best-tempered girl in the world,' a thing he claims to value highly."

"Indeed?"

"Yes, my dear. The rattle at Headquarters is that you are the one destined to finally mend Tench Tilghman's singularly tiresome broken heart. Why, imagine! It must be five years since his Jenny ran off with George Carroll."

When Kitty retreated downstairs, Betsy did not immediately follow. Instead, she leaned against the sill. Here, where cold was tangible, she breathed upon the pane until she'd melted a circle through the lacy frost.

She did not know what to make of Kitty's news. She knew the chaste kiss Tench Tilghman had given her those long years ago had certainly not changed his resolve to remain true to his lost love. On their solitary walk, he had offered his broken heart as an excuse for his lack of gallantry. He'd been yet another man who saw her only as a confidant.

Cross that day, she'd tossed a barb about something he thought was a secret—his recent adventure with an Oneida girl. She almost wished she hadn't, because it revealed she liked him enough to be jealous, but temper had got the better of her. She'd told him that toying with a woman's heart was unkind, whether the owner was white, black or brown. Men, it seemed, despite the vaunted superiority of their intellect, seemed to use it mostly to justify their pleasures.

Then, when he'd turned red and been so utterly abashed, she'd relented. To try to make up for embarrassing him, she'd given a little speech to the effect that she was extremely sorry that his Maryland sweetheart had treated him so cruelly. They had resumed their tramp down the steep path together, a quick march now driven by gravity and chagrin, weaving between rocks and around the knotty toes of pines.

"Allow me to prophecy for you." As their companions had come into view, Tilghman had attempted to renew their earlier playfulness. "Soon, Miss Schuyler, a knight in shining armor will come, a gentleman who will kiss you exactly as you deserve to be kissed. I only hope that he will be sensible of the high honor you do him." Equilibrium regained, he'd smiled at her in a way that had made her feel every bit of eighteen in the presence of a worldly twenty-six.

Betsy knew the whole embarrassing situation had happened because she'd been trying to be something she was not. She was not a born coquette like her sisters, but that day she'd flirted with Tilghman, played the tease, tried to get a kiss just to see if she could. She was not that kind of girl, not really.

Tonight, at this assembly ball, being who I am will have to do.

* * *

"Mrs. Washington has a mottled orange tom-cat (which she calls, in a complimentary way, 'Hamilton') with thirteen stripes around the tail, and its flaunting suggested to congress the thirteen stripes for the flag."—Rivington's Gazette, New York

The ladies entered a long, rectangular room with a high ceiling and broad board floors. The scene was lit by candles set in reflective sconces and already crowded with party-goes. Slender-limbed chairs lined the walls. Betsy noted with pleasure the fine panoramic wallpaper, a scene of Grecian temples, rather like what they had at home.

89

"There they are." Kitty whispered as they shed their cloaks into the hands of servants, "His Excellency's famous redheads."

In every shade from auburn to common ginger they stood, resplendent in their blue and buff, a group of young men as handsome and well-knit as any Betsy had ever seen. As she gazed at them, she knew perfectly well they were discussing her—the newcomer.

"Who is that? The one the others are listening to?" The young man in question, rosy-cheeked and animated, was a center of attention.

"Oh, that's Alexander Hamilton, exercising his powers of oratory, as usual."

"One of the Philadelphia Hamiltons?"

"No one we know." The wave of Kitty's fan indicated a certain disdain. "He's from St. Croix in the West Indies."

Hamilton was shorter and more delicately framed than the other aides. Betsy noted his grace. In an extreme of military correctness, his head was closely cropped. A thin, tightly braided rat's tail trailing down the back of his jacket was a single nod to fashion.

"Just look at all these pretty fellows. Not a dreary cousin among them. This winter, mark my words, Betsy, you will have love letters and as many kisses as you desire."

"Kitty! Hush." Betsy cast a worried look over her shoulder, hoping her aunt hadn't heard. She was relieved to discover Gertrude Cochran busy chatting with a small, plump lady in plum velvet—Martha Washington.

"Don't be such a prig. And I advise you to watch out for that Colonel Hamilton."

"Why, pray tell?"

"Beneath all that charm, Colonel Hamilton is something of a rogue."

Betsy was surprised at her cousin's vehemence. Expressing a contrary opinion would certainly annoy Kitty, but she knew it was as quick a way as any to get pertinent information.

"He's rather attractive, though, isn't he?"

"Humph! If you think he's pretty now," Kitty replied, "you should have seen what an angel he was when he stayed with the Boudinots before the war. Why, those eyes of his! Really, it's not fair for a man to have such eyes. I tell you in strictest confidence, Betsy, he kissed me, he kissed Suki, and he even kissed Sarah—after she was engaged to Mr. Jay! Somehow he always made it seem as if there was no harm in it. Both my Papa and Mr. Boudinot dote upon him. It makes my brother Brock madly jealous, but Hamilton simply requires that everyone spoil him. Perhaps we should, for he hasn't so much as a penny with which to bless himself."

Betsy was intrigued, but conversation hidden behind fans ended there, for the time to pay respects to their elders had arrived. She and Kitty advanced among the patriot gentry to make formal curtsies to Lady Washington and her imposing husband. General Washington wore a civilian suit of black. His massive, silver head was higher than any other in the room.

The first dance, the customary minuet, was announced, and Colonel Tilghman approached. He was, Betsy noted, broader and more mature than he had been those summers ago in Albany. Tilghman saluted both ladies gallantly, but it was Betsy he asked to dance.

She flushed at the touch of him, and then suffered agonies of embarrassment when pale Tilghman began to blush, too. He did seem uncommonly pleased to see her. For an instant, she wondered if—for once—Kitty knew what she was talking about. As her cousin passed on the arm of Colonel Webb, she poked Betsy with her fan, a clear "I told you so." When the fiddlers struck up, Betsy had the awful sensation that every eye in the room was upon her. Silently, she thanked heaven—*and dear Papa*—for the dress from Paris.

"Such a pleasure to see you again, Miss Schuyler." Tilghman was formal as he turned her around.

"And you, Colonel."

The minuet was repetitive and stately. Everyone, old or young, could dance it in their sleep, which made it an excellent choice for those who wished to talk.

The most uncomfortable part was the first procession, which was made in pairs across the center of the room. After all the dancers achieved the floor, the slow graceful figures allowed for extensive eye contact and conversation.

"I've come upon a friend's errand, Miss, to advise you before any other gentleman in His Excellency's service offers to dance. I hope you will not think me presumptuous."

"If you are, nothing will have changed." After Kitty's heated speculation, his opening gambit was something of a disappointment.

"Nevertheless," Tilghman said, "as one who considers himself your friend, I must speak. My companions are good fellows, the best in the world, but they work too hard and don't have the company of ladies as often as young men should. As a result, they are—impetuous."

"And what about yourself, Colonel Tilghman? Has hard work and no play made you impetuous?"

Betsy smiled as she spoke, for she could sense his admiration. It was plain from the way his eyes followed her, from the way color remained in his cheeks.

"Some of my brother officers are downright dangerous, Miss. Take them all with a grain of salt."

After this tantalizing prelude, small talk followed. The Colonel discussed the weather and asked polite questions about her father's health. When he relinquished her at the end, she felt relief, for, just as she'd suspected, nothing between them had changed. His caution, however, left a prickle of anticipation.

In the next dance, one in which couples worked through figures while passing down a line of the opposite sex, Betsy went out on the arm of the portly Baron von Steuben. The Baron had visited her father at Albany, and the family had enjoyed his company. Dancing with him was something of an adventure for he was too stout to be nimble. Betsy knew no German, so they spoke Dutch together.

As the ladies passed hand-to-hand down the line of men, Betsy gazed straight into face after intelligent young face. The aides, she noted, looked weary, but happy to be dancing, happy to be, as much as the business of war allowed, "in society."

While some were shy and others uninterested, Colonel Hamilton frankly looked her up and down with a pair of opulently blue eyes. The boldness of his appraisal was so startling that she nearly missed the outstretched hand which her next partner, freckled Colonel McHenry, extended.

* * *

"For the past few months, Colonel Hamilton's been paying court to Peggy Lott." There was a pause in the music, and Kitty was again at her side. "Don't they make a pretty pair?"

The question was rhetorical. Shapely, brunette Peggy complimented Hamilton's slender fairness to perfection.

"What a couple they'd make!" Kitty's eyes brightened as she watched them in the midst of a laughing circle. "But, as I said, Hamilton hasn't a penny, and I heard that Peggy's father has warned him off."

"Simply for lack of money?" Betsy didn't consider herself a belle, but she knew a member of the privileged sisterhood to which she belonged could break the rules. With sufficient spirit—and a rich father under her thumb— a determined girl could marry any man she wanted.

"Well, I shouldn't repeat this, but while it is said that Colonel Hamilton's grandfather was a Scots Laird, the poor fellow was born on the wrong side of the blanket." Kitty clearly relished the widening this brought to her cousin's eyes. "Papa himself told me."

When it was time to choose partners for the next dance, the handsome subject of her gossip approached. The first bow he made, playfully profound, was to Kitty.

"Miss Livingston, how delightful to see you again." A dazzling smile appeared. "Pardon me, dear lady, but I must have an introduction to your companion." Under long, coppery lashes sparkled the bluest eyes Betsy had ever seen.

"I should have known you'd present yourself, Colonel Impudence. As I'm certain you know full well, this lady is Miss Elizabeth Schuyler. She's journeyed all the way from dull, dreary, snowbound Albany to cheer us in equally dull, dreary snowbound Morristown." To emphasize, Kitty playfully tapped Colonel Hamilton on his blue and buff chest with her fan.

An instant later, he'd captured Betsy's gloved hand. As he bowed over it, Kitty made a joking introduction.

"Allow me to introduce Alexander Hamilton, by way of Elizabethtown Academy and Kings College, previously Captain of The Thirty-Second Company of New York Artillery and now Lieutenant Colonel and Aide de Camp to his Excellency George Washington."

"I regret, Miss Schuyler, that you were not at home when I had the honor to visit your father last year. I didn't, until this moment, have any understanding of the loss I suffered in not making your acquaintance." His eyes shone with confidence and good humor.

"Do you always begin with a salvo, sir?" Betsy gently withdrew her hand.

"Don't let it go to your head," said Kitty. "Colonel Hamilton can't help himself. He stayed at King's College just long enough to become thoroughly acquainted with Ovid's naughty *Amores* before plumping for our cause and the life of a soldier. But beware, Cousin! This gentleman carries hearts at his belt just the way one of your wild Mohawks carries scalps."

"That's devilishly unfair, Miss Livingston, especially when you've taken a few such trophies yourself." Hamilton winked.

Playing at anger, Kitty flourished her fan.

"Truth will out, Miss Livingston." Hamilton smiled, and Betsy saw a spark leap between her companions.

Something still burns there—and that is why Kitty is so cruel....

"I must confess, Miss Schuyler," Hamilton said, immediately confirming her suspicion. "Your lovely cousin once dealt me a nearly fatal blow."

"Impertinent!" Despite what Kitty said it was clear she enjoyed bantering with him, teetering precariously—and ever so fashionably—along the edge of impropriety.

"I beg the honor of a *tête-à-tête* with you later, My Divinity." Hamilton bowed, hands at his sides, inclining his head with playful humility.

Even as he spoke to Kitty, his hand had recaptured Betsy's. It was lean and strong, exactly like the rest of him. With her cousin's warning sounding in her head, Betsy's heart began to race.

"Now, Miss Schuyler, shall we dance?"

The answer was a foregone conclusion, even though from the elegant prelude the French fiddler was making, Betsy knew it would be another minuet. As off balance as she felt, that initial lonely procession across the floor would be a thousand times worse than it had been with Tilghman.

Alexander seemed to sense Betsy's apprehension, for at first, he didn't say much, and simply confined himself to dancing. Nevertheless, Betsy was profoundly aware of his body, of strength and good reflexes. She was so self-conscious that she even started to go wrong, but the pressure of his hands smoothly corrected. After a while, she relinquished herself to his guidance. How graceful he made her feel!

As soon as she relaxed into his care, Hamilton began to talk. Had her sleigh ride from the North been eventful? When she answered that the journey had been without incident—except for the sleigh upsetting twice and throwing her out into drifts—Hamilton had smiled.

"The last few winters are said to have been unusually fierce, but as I grew up on Saint Croix, I haven't seen enough to compare. To me all winters are wretched. I fear I'll never find a good reason for snow."

"If you hate a New Jersey winter, sir, you would most certainly loathe an Albany one."

"Yes, I saw your formidable mountains of white when I was up to twist General Gates's arm for reinforcements for our southern army. Still, I must say, the frozen river made a fine highway for my ride home."

"Perhaps it's because I don't suffer any hardship, but I like snow. When it comes, it changes everything. The Mohawks say that winter is a mighty white panther hissing and howling as it crouches over its prey."

"I had heard the savages were natural poets, Miss Schuyler, and from what I have seen of your north country, the sentiment is apt. Certainly," Hamilton handed her smoothly around, "even a bitter Albany winter would be endurable if it were warmed by the fire of a great love. A lady as lovely as you are surely starts many such blazes."

The sudden twist into flirtation caught Betsy off-guard. "Oh, no, Colonel," she replied. "I have no beaux."

Embarrassed by the attraction she felt and also by the implications of what she'd said, Betsy lowered her lashes and sent a prayer to the Goddess of Coquetry for a clever remark.

"I warn you here and now, Miss Schuyler, I'm severe with ladies who trifle with me." Hamilton waited, apparently expecting a suitably coquettish reply.

"No," Betsy said, feeling strangely hot all over. "I assure you."

"Then the men of Albany are blind. I hasten to assure you, Miss Schuyler, I am not." Hamilton smiled his beautiful smile and did not miss a beat.

His daring, expressed not only in words, but in his lingering touch, his gaze, snatched her breath away. Blushing mightily, mind scrambling, Betsy finally found inspiration.

"Your friend Colonel Tilghman has just cautioned me that his brother aides are dangerous fellows. But truly, until now, I deemed him guilty of slander."

"Dangerous? Why, whatever could dear Tilghman mean?" The impossibly blue eyes widened. "If I am guilty of anything, Miss Schuyler, it is of plain candor."

"Do you think it proper to be so forward, sir, upon five minutes' acquaintance?"

"I may be rash, but I am also an enemy of falsehood," he replied. "As to the briefness of our acquaintance, I do, in fact, know a little about you. All I have heard, I assure you, is laudatory."

There was now a peacock circling, a deep curtsy and an answering bow. When it was done, the dancers began an elegant repetition.

"For instance," Hamilton said, "I know that you have often gone with Surgeon and Mrs. Cochran to the Hollow. We in the General's family stand in admiration of your bravery and patriotic spirit. It takes not only compassion, but a strong stomach to assist at the hospital."

"I always go with my mother to help our tenants when they are ill. Mama says it is a duty for those of us who have been especially blessed to help the less fortunate. But, really, sir," Betsy rushed on, "I only do small things. Aunt Cochran and I knit stockings, mittens and caps, and brew pails of posset. I don't assist my uncle in surgery like Aunt Trudi does, though I've learned to stitch wounds. Sometimes I feed poor fellows who can't hold their heads up, or write letters home for those who don't know how."

"But those aren't small things. The sad fact is that most people are better at lip service than at actually doing anything. It seems to me, Miss Schuyler," and Betsy saw her mercurial companion grow serious, "you have achieved a triumph over human nature, which is lazy, selfish, and highly inclined to overlook the suffering of others."

"You have a poor opinion of humanity."

"I do. I've seen little in life to make me revise the opinion." The flirtatious manner was as absent now as if it had never existed. His fantastic eyes grew solemn.

"I do hope, Miss Schuyler, you will be staying in Morristown for a while."

"I may go to see my sister, Mrs. Church, who is in Easton, but nothing is fixed yet. And, of course, this unceasing bad weather...."

"I have had the honor of meeting your sister and her husband. Perhaps Mrs. Church might be persuaded to visit you here and shed her illumination upon our poor society. We would be fortunate indeed to have both of you."

"Well, that depends upon Mr. Church's business with the army. I do miss my sister very much since she's married, and so, one way or another, I hope to spend time with her before they return to Boston." Betsy began to feel more relaxed now that he had acknowledged Angelica's blazing star. If he was fascinated by her sister, it put his behavior into a familiar frame. Betsy wondered if he had only been leading up to his real interest.

"It has been a very great pleasure, Miss Schuyler." Hamilton made a final bow as the dance ended.

Betsy blushed as he lifted her hand. When she felt the daring brush of his lips against her glove, she felt quite breathless.

"Allow me to hope that you'll be in Morristown for many weeks more, Miss Schuyler, doing good at the Hollow and ornamenting our dances."

One by one, handsome aides took Betsy dancing: stolid McHenry, gentle James Meade, blunt Gibbs, dumpy, shy "old Secretary" Harrison. General Washington scared her to death when he presented himself, declaring, "Mrs. Washington informs me that I've been negligent, Miss Schuyler."

He made her feel like a doll on the arm of a giant, but Washington was a stately, utterly correct partner who walked her through the figures.

"Tell me," he inquired, "how is your good father this winter? Is he well, not too much troubled with rheumatism? I've written to him, asking him to come down if he's able, so that he may advise me on some matters pertaining to the

98

commissary. I believe there's not a man in America who knows more about such matters." In spite of his formality, Washington's conversation was kind and attentive, belying his glacial manner.

Although she did not expect it, Hamilton came for another dance, a lively country one with many changes of partner. Not much could be said, but excitement flowed from his fingertips and his eyes shone. He was a wonderful partner, and they flew back and forth, until they were laughing and breathless.

All too soon, at least for the young people, the clock struck eleven. As Betsy prepared to leave with Kitty and her aunt and uncle, Colonel Tilghman appeared.

"Dear Miss Schuyler," he said, taking her cloak from the hands of the servant, "allow me to assist you." Hand on her arm, he drew her out of the chatting crowd, ostensibly to get room to toss the cloak around her.

"Now that we have a little distance between us and your Cousin Kitty, I shall speak." Tilghman settled the cloak around Betsy's shoulders. "It seems a certain brash young Colonel already has you in his sights."

Betsy smiled up at Tilghman in the best imitation of Angelica she could muster. "Do you mean the gentleman who is courting Miss Lott?"

Tilghman focused upon fastening the frog beneath her chin. "Cupid delights in turning our dear Hamilton around like a weather cock at least twice a week."

His eyes, sincere gray transparencies, rose to meet hers. "I foresee kisses for you very soon, Miss Schuyler," he said softly, "just as hot as you deserve, but exactly—and I give you fair warning—exactly like those Miss Lott has already had. I want you to promise me that you'll take care of your gentle heart."

Standing there, as shocked as if he had shoved a handful of snow down her back, Betsy felt every eye upon them. A blush beat hotly in her cheeks, while, neutral as a brother, Tilghman bowed his auburn head over her small, gloved hand.

* * *

"In spite of myself, I liked that Schuyler gal." Gibbs'
northern twang grated on Hamilton's ear. "What a dance
we galloped! She's nothing like the rest of those stuck-up
New Yorkers."

"Far too brown for my taste," Sam Webb remarked, a
touch of disdain. "Indian pudding in that exalted Dutch
lineage, if you ask me."

"Nonsense!" The words were out before Hamilton could
stop himself. "Why, she's just a perfect 'Nut Brown Maid,'
like the old song."

McHenry sided, as he usually did, with Hamilton.

"Rude Yankee!" He playfully squared off against Webb.
"The fellow's blind."

"But, my dear Hammie, that little Dutch miss can't hold
a candle to Miss Lott. I'm sorry if the truth offends you."

"That's not just rude. It's damned rude." The remark had
come from an unlikely corner. For Caleb Gibbs to even
recognize "rude" was so far out of character that there was
a pause while everyone recovered from astonishment. The
remark pleased Hamilton until Gibbs added, "Miss
Schuyler is no Aphrodite like her sister Mrs. Church, but,
as Tilghman says, she's a friendly, jolly girl."

"Well," McHenry said, "I grant you, there's more good
nature there than beauty."

"Enough!" Hamilton said. "Are we speaking of a heifer,
or are we speaking of a lady?" For some reason—he wasn't
sure why—he was on fire to vindicate his taste.

"During the country dances, didn't I see a beautiful
ankle, the beautiful ankle which leads to a higher beauty,
exactly as our friend Tilghman has so observantly
remarked?" McHenry apparently intended his jest to
hamstring the dispute, but when the others laughed,
Hamilton felt even angrier than before. The strength of his
reaction left him momentarily speechless.

"Miss Schuyler did look pretty on your arm, Hammie."
Just in time, Jamie Meade's meditative Virginia drawl

100

wandered into the conversation. Ordinarily, Meade existed in a daze, love letters burning in his pocket. He was head over heels for a beautiful Maryland widow.

"And Hammie knew it, too. Why, he never stopped pouring on the charm."

"The sight of Hamilton writhing in the toils of a new passion is always entertaining." Webb yanked out a chair and leapt upon it.

"He who could bow to every shrine;
And swear the last the most divine;
Like Hudibrass all subjects bend,
Had Ovid at his finger's end;
Now feels the inexorable dart,
And yields Brown Betsy all his heart!"

McHenry, usually a reliable ally, threw an arm around Alexander's shoulder.

"Confide in us, Great Alexander! Has a new divinity descended from heaven?"

Webb's boots hit the floor with a thud as he hopped down.

"And, further, may I now lay a siege of my own to the fair Miss Lott?"

"What I want to know, damn it, is why I am so unfairly singled out?" A shift to the offensive, Hamilton decided, might be useful. "I am simply defending a young lady who is both handsome and uncommonly agreeable, as anyone with two proper eyes can attest. The fact that I took pleasure in Miss Schuyler's company does not mean I have abandoned Miss Lott. And, as for the rest of it—you, Gibbs, and you, McHenry—not to mention the blind man from Connecticut—have chased a few skirts before."

He began to list places where the army had rested and the girls who had brightened their off-hours. As each adventure was described, the subject squirmed and protested. The others, notwithstanding the fact that theirs had been the last exploit held up for scrutiny—or that theirs would be next—took temporary refuge in laughter.

"Ah, who can forget that buxom Quaker lass?" Hamilton had saved this escapade for last. "McHenry got her alone in the cow shed, there with all that fresh, new hay, and he expects us to believe he only kissed her? Expects us to believe that instead of making love to her, he told her to 'beware of young officers, more dangerous than the whole war to a beautiful girl'?"

"Another word from you, Alexander Hamilton," said McHenry, freckled face glowing, "and we shall, in unison, break your neck."

At that moment, the door opened and Tilghman, wearing an on-duty expression, entered.

"His Excellency wants you, Hamilton. He says you've been in correspondence with one Mr. van Pelt and that you probably know more about the matter than he does."

"The rum consignment! We'll have a mutiny if that doesn't arrive."

"In which we shall all join," shouted his friends, pelting him with the ever-present wads of crumpled paper.

Buttoning his jacket, Hamilton rushed down the stairs to the front room where he knew George Washington would be waiting. Knocking at the General's door, he felt a chill that didn't come from outside.

If anything has gone wrong with the rum consignment, I am about to catch hell.

"Your Excellency." Hamilton saluted and stepped close to the commander's desk.

"Ah, Colonel Hamilton." Confronted by that weary, wintry face, Hamilton feared the worst. "I have here a letter full of conundrums from Mr. van Pelt."

The letter was passed. Hamilton speedily scanned it, and thanked his lucky stars. As irksome as this new problem was, it was apothecary supplies, not the all-important rum consignment.

Standing tall, Hamilton summarized in a few brief sentences the recent transactions he'd had with van Pelt so the General could fully understand where the matter stood. Washington nodded his gray head, listening.

102

While he talked, Hamilton's mind darted to a possible solution. This allowed him to conclude with a suggestion. He was relieved when the commander nodded.

"Try it, Colonel. Still, it's damned hard to do business with our Congress promising—but never quite delivering—the money."

Hamilton nodded emphatically. Lack of funds was the distilled essence of the Continental Army's troubles.

"Write me a letter to this refractory gentleman. Intimate we'll have what we need one way or another. Twist his tail a little. We'll send it off under my signature, first thing in the morning."

Hamilton seated himself at a nearby writing desk and found paper. Washington appeared grimmer than usual. It had been a long day, and the added strain of socializing with the patriot gentry had made it even longer.

If you were an ordinary man, George Washington, you would yawn and stretch, lean back in your chair and close your eyes.

Instead, the General picked up another piece of correspondence and proceeded to study it, grave as a monument. Hamilton tapped his quill on the edge of the inkwell and searched for the words to prod Mr. van Pelt.

Embers of blue and rose glowed upon the hearth, illuminating blackened logs. A winter wind, like a starving dog, snuffled around the corners of the house.

After half an hour, Hamilton had crafted a letter. While he stood at attention, anxious and weary, Washington read it, nodded, and then signed with a flourish.

"Excellent, Colonel Hamilton. As much and as little as needs to be said. That last sentence, which could be construed as a threat, will probably elicit some action."

A cold, slight smile of approval curved the General's lips as he dried the ink with a sprinkle of sand. As Hamilton inwardly heaved a sigh of relief, Washington spoke again.

"One last matter, Colonel."

Now what? Every muscle in his body begged to go upstairs, to fall into his narrow camp bed, and plummet into unconsciousness.

With precision, Washington folded the letter. He fired wax and let it drip onto the crease, setting his seal precisely. As this went on, there was silence, nothing but wind and crinkling coals. Hamilton was motionless. Washington was a ponderous thinker, and long pauses were common. What the General finally articulated, however, was neither about the commissary or the war.

"You could do far worse, you know, Colonel Hamilton."

"Sir?"

Washington lifted his head and regarded him levelly. "Than a little winter campaigning, my boy, directed toward capturing the heart of a certain charming newcomer to our assembly."

With alarm, Hamilton recognized amusement in those cold blue eyes. The "my boy" had signaled that the usually distant Washington intended their conversation to be intimate.

Alexander knew, of course, that he had gone after pretty, shy Miss Schuyler with all the subtlety of a puppy chasing a squirrel. After a weak start, he had managed to defend his dignity among his peers, but here, now, all he felt capable of was sinking into the floor.

"As I'm certain you understand," Washington said, "a connection with the Schuylers would be an asset for any gentleman. Particularly for an—ah—enterprising— gentleman like yourself, one who hopes to be of future service to his country."

Alexander knew His Excellency spoke from experience. George Washington, born as a younger son into a family of middle rank, had scaled the heights of Virginia society when he'd married Martha, the colony's richest widow.

Swallowing hard, Hamilton took refuge in formula. "Be assured, Your Excellency," he said with a slight bow, "that your advice is most highly regarded."

"They say a word to the wise is sufficient."

Was there a smile lurking in those icy eyes? Before Hamilton could quite discern, the august head tilted to gloomily regard the remaining stack of paper on the desk.

"Dismissed, Colonel Hamilton."

It took all of Alexander's self-control not to dash from the room like a boy after a thrashing. Still, as he entered the now darkened room where the other aides lay, he knew he'd been blessed by the highest authority. General Washington and Major General Schuyler were peers, great planters, and they were friends as well. The attraction he'd felt toward Miss Schuyler might be, he thought, sitting on his cot and tugging at his stock, more important to his future than anything he'd achieved so far risking life and limb in the army.

* * *

It was another assembly at the Mansion in the long upstairs hallway, and the impertinent Colonel Hamilton had made his way to Betsy's side again. Precious candles burned, illuminating the punchbowl and the walnut sideboard upon which it stood, but he'd walked her away from the cheerful group now gathered around it.

"You talk the most outrageous nonsense, you know." Betsy raised her fan in an attempt to hide. She felt a hot flush in her cheeks.

"Yes, I'm afraid I do. It's a stratagem, you see. I'm really a bit afraid of you ladies."

"The truth, Colonel Hamilton, is quite the other way around. It is the ladies who ought to be afraid of you."

The bright smile that followed Betsy's thrust was nothing less than an admission.

"Well, if my conversation doesn't please," Alexander replied, "perhaps my dancing will. Give me your hand, won't you, Miss Schuyler? We'll go out for the reel."

From nearby, the lovely Lott sisters looked daggers, but Hamilton put his back to them.

"Haven't you heard that a man never knows what a woman is really like until he dances a reel with her?" His eyes sparkled with anticipation.

"I've heard it said, but I've never understood what it meant. I'm not certain I ought to dance again with a gentleman who has an inconstant heart, Colonel Hamilton. Miss Lott, to whom you are said to belong, thinks so, too."

"Belong?" Alexander arched a sandy brow. "Until a certain treaty has been signed, the word is without justification. There's nothing so serious between the lovely Miss Lott and myself. You see before you nothing but a poor, hard-working soldier, wild as a boy let out of school after hours of flogging and Latin. I'm full of high spirits. I want to play."

"An artful speech, Colonel. In spite of it, I think I shall dance with you. But only because Colonel Tilghman has just come to your rescue."

Peggy Lott, with a toss of her head and a defiant sidelong glance in their direction, was at this very moment going out on Tilghman's arm.

Before he led her to join one of the forming sets, Alexander raised Betsy's small gloved hand to his lips. "I'm deeply sensible of every honor you do me, Miss Schuyler." He smiled into her eyes and thought that after tonight, he owed Tilghman a hundred favors.

There were two musicians tonight, the Widow Ford's slave, Pompey, and a young valet who belonged to one of the French officers. Neither musician spoke the other's language, but they'd been getting along pretty well, the boyish Frenchman and that bent old man. Pompey had watched, listened, and then begun to softly accompany the Frenchman during a minuet. On the next dance, the Frenchman had returned the favor, sawing his instrument to achieve the wail proper for a country dance. Admiration, musician to musician, had been growing steadily all evening. McHenry brought tipple, and the musicians were happily toasting one another. Well inspired, they now proceeded to improvise the wildest, longest, strangest reel on Yankee Doodle ever heard.

The slave played country style. The Frenchman proved he was a master of his instrument, playing higher than a piccolo, plucking and bowing in every scale. Their joy set wings upon the heels of the dancers. Before it was over, almost everyone in the room was up. The General and his lady presided from the high table. Plump, rosy Martha fairly beamed. His Excellency, for once wearing an expression that seemed to impinge upon cheer, beat time on the table.

The young Ford boys swung each other around in imitation of the grownups. Worn out before it was over, older dancers staggered, panting, back to the chairs, but the young ones, Alexander and Betsy among them, flew all the way to the end.

When the music stopped, everyone whooped and cheered. All dignity forgotten, some gasped for breath while others laughed. The hair of several ladies had come cascading down and they were forced to retire for repairs.

"To *Yankee Doodle* and Our Right!" Glasses raised in a patriotic toast. With a flourish, McHenry splashed another generous shot into the fiddlers' glasses.

"Well, Colonel Hamilton," Betsy said, gasping for breath. "Did you fathom the mystery?" She reached up to test the security of her hair.

"Miss Schuyler, this splendid reel has only convinced me there's more about you that I must discover."

"And how, sir, do you propose to do that?"

"Ah, that I may not tell, but I give you fair warning—be on your guard."

* * *

As it was the first ball at which Alexander did not dance more than once with Miss Lott, the gossip was intense. There was even more a few days later, when Colonel Hamilton and Miss Lott quarreled. Kitty Livingston brought Mrs. Cochran's maid, Nancy, upstairs to retell what she'd seen.

"I was on the way to my mother's house and happened upon them. Begging your pardon, ladies; I couldn't help but see, as it was right in my path. Miss Peggy smacked Colonel Hamilton hard as ever she could and then ran inside. I was astonished, yes I was, when he got on his little black horse and went off with a smile."

Kitty was quite annoyed when Betsy showed little interest in the tale, simply continued winding yarn. Her efforts to get this done were continually frustrated by the spirited attacks of a leggy ginger kitten, who kept attacking the yarn and tangling himself in it. For some reason, Betsy seemed far more interested in playing with him than in commenting upon Nancy's story.

"Well," sniffed Kitty, after dispatching the maid to fetch tea, "If he's got Peggy to dismiss him, I'm sure the rogue will be presenting himself to you at once. What do you think of your winter conquest, Betsy? He certainly is an amusing fellow, even if he isn't one of us."

Betsy didn't respond. Instead she dangled yarn, encouraged the kitten. When he responded with a leap, she pulled it away and then tried to grab him. He, ringed tail extended, beat a scrabbling retreat under the skirts of the sofa.

"Betsy Schuyler, stop fooling with that little brute and talk to me. This is serious. Two winters ago, the brazen fellow had the temerity to write a love letter to *me!* I confess, even if he did live in our house for a year, and even if Papa is fond of him, I could not believe his presumption."

Betsy said nothing. She moved onto the floor, and then, head down, dark braid trailing, rolled the ball of yarn back and forth beside the sofa.

"Come out, kitty-kitty-kitty!"

A paw emerged and struck a dozen blazing strokes. Betsy simply went on with her game until he stormed out and tackled the ball, hugging it in a full-bodied embrace.

An orgy of biting and vicious back-leg kicking followed, until the ball was thoroughly ragged. Smiling, Betsy sat up.

"Are you sorry you didn't write Colonel Hamilton some sweet nonsense in return?"

Kitty's jaw dropped.

"Uncle Cochran says Colonel Hamilton's a real patriot, more so than plenty of Americans he could name. And the last time I was at the hospital, Lady Washington told me His Excellency thinks the world of Colonel Hamilton. You know there is not a man on this earth who is harder to please."

"Except for your father!" Kitty had recovered, at least enough to give the warning she'd intended. "Angelica told me all about the hell he put her and that handsome Mr. Church through. If Hamilton asks to marry, your papa will never give his permission."

"Marry? Who said anything about that? All I can see is that just as you said, I'm going to have some fun this winter."

Kitty opened her mouth and then closed it. Betsy returned her attention to the kitten. He, hoping for a resumption of the game, had rolled languidly over, displaying a round, cream-colored belly.

Scooping him up Betsy first held him high, then slowly lowered him. Initially, her whispers of "pretty boy" and eye contact held him in check, but then, abruptly, an orange paw made a lightning swipe at her nose, one she barely managed to evade.

"You ginger devil!" She squeezed the squirming, scratching kitten tightly and dared a kiss on the top of his head. "I shall tame you—and a certain saucy Colonel—into the bargain."

* * *

Outside the Cochran's house, the night was frigid. The young guests were by the hearth roasting chestnuts. There were shrieks when one exploded after being set injudiciously close to the fire.

Tilghman, McHenry and tall William Colfax from the General's personal life guard had been flirting with a triad of patriot beauties who tonight included Caty and Mary Stirling as well as Kitty Livingston. From a stool in the corner, pretty, fourteen year old Susan Boudinot watched and listened, all big-eyed interest. In the dining room adjoining, Aunt and Uncle Cochran, and their guests, General and Mrs. Stirling, were still at table, sipping Madeira, cracking walnuts and chatting.

Betsy had gone to peep out the farthest window at a small fire in the back yard. The bitterness of the night had driven all except the unfortunate pickets inside the kitchen wing. There was a sudden thrill when she saw Alexander's reflection appear behind her.

"What else besides how well I dance the reel would you like to know, Colonel?" Turning and leaning against the chilly sill, Betsy attacked before he could.

"What else?"

"Why, yes. I've been thinking about what you said at the assembly. Surely you can't learn everything about a person from a reel?"

"Well, of course, every clue helps." Alexander drew close, his lips curving into a boyish smile. "Sleigh rides and tea parties are also most instructive. My curiosity regarding you, Miss, remains far from satisfied."

"Well, ask what you would like to know. I fear I'm quite ordinary." From under the lace trim of a white cap she gazed up at him.

"Ah, Miss Schuyler!" Alexander leaned closer, "Your wish for me to know you better fills my mind with a hundred pretty notions. I'm deeply sensible of the honor you do me."

"As you should be, sir."

* * *

Alexander smiled. He had seen the metamorphoses many times, how the plainest woman slipped into beauty

110

when she flirted. Elizabeth Schuyler was no goddess, but her skin, roses blooming beneath brown satin, told him everything. If this was a barmaid instead of a General's daughter, he would simply take her in his arms right now and start tasting, set free the shiny dark hair hidden so demurely beneath her cap, with every expectation of an eventual, delicious surrender.

"If you'll allow me to say so," Alexander murmured, struggling valiantly with his inclination, "I've learned of one small thing, which, if executed properly, is a short cut through a long march of flippant chat, a thing which instantly unlocks the deepest mystery of the most circumspect lady more thoroughly than fifty reels."

"One small thing? Whatever could that be, sir?"

"Well, I'd certainly like more than one, but one, well executed, may tell all."

Laughter gusted from the fireside; a ruddy glow rippled across the ceiling. Snow hissed against the thick panes.

Miss Schuyler rested her hand on the rough wool of his uniform jacket, fingertips just touching the brass buttons. She lifted her chin, demurely lowered her black lashes and waited.

* * *

His eyes, bright with daring, blazed like the noonday Caribbean. When his mouth touched hers, first brushing and then taking a delicate, ever so thirsty sip, Betsy felt herself go weak. She saw the flush of his fair skin, heard his sharp intake of breath.

How perfect this is!

A loud bang, followed by laughter, came from the fireplace. Startled, they spun to face the others, but it was immediately clear that the merry pandemonium didn't have anything to do with them. Another chestnut had exploded, sending burning fragments upon the skirts of those seated closest to the hearth.

"Just as I suspected," Alexander said softly. "One tells all." He stepped behind her, drew her hand into his.

111

Holding it at her back, where no one could see, his fingers took up a tender tracery of her palm.

"Dear heaven, Miss Schuyler." He whispered, as she, trembling at his touch, leaned against him, "I pray that you have a merciful—no—generous—nature. I fear that even a hundred of those won't be sufficient."

* * *

Betsy sat before an embroidery stand set in the cozy Cochran parlor. The very picture of genteel domesticity, she worked at a new circular fire screen for her Aunt. The ginger kitten, sleepy and quiet, curled in the cozy shelter of Betsy's skirts. Her father, the General, had sleighed down from Albany to talk with Washington, so he, too, was present.

She struggled to keep her mind on what she was doing. It would be a disaster to make a mistake and ruin a mile of scarce imported thread, but she kept interrupting herself to steal a look at Colonel Hamilton. His attention, however, was tonight concentrated upon her uncle and her father and the nuts scattered upon the table cloth. Only occasionally their eyes met. The last time it had happened, he'd flashed the sauciest wink. She'd blushed and quickly looked away.

"Another ten cases of barrel fever at the hospital." Uncle Cochran shook his head while stuffing tobacco into his pipe. "Barrel fever" was a not uncommon affliction among the soldiers. It came from an overdose of rum followed by a brawl, leaving its victims sore and sick.

"Our Continentals are such a disgraceful rabble." Aunt Cochran took up her knitting. "All those fellows ever seem to do is knock each other on the head. Too bad these New Yorkers and New Jersey men aren't as feisty with the British as they are with Connecticut Yankees."

"Well, Sister," said Philip Schuyler, "the poor fellows don't have much to keep them occupied now, shut up in those huts in this damnable weather."

"Exactly." Dr. Cochran twisted a paper spill for his pipe.

"In fact, Mrs. Cochran, we're lucky the rum ration arrived when it did, or we'd have had a mutiny on our hands," said Hamilton. "The rum helps them forget how rarely they get any meat, poor devils."

While the two older men talked, he'd cracked nuts, his long fingers busy. The meats were rarely eaten, simply left in a neat pile on the cloth, where they could be collected and put to use in Mrs. Cochran's kitchen.

"Another fellow died today of catarrh," the doctor said. "Of course, they've all got colds, but at least this devilish winter has shut down the camp fever. That's a blessing, because I'm out of everything I need to treat it."

"Doctor Rush is attempting to secure supplies for your hospital," Betsy's father reminded his brother-in-law, "but our merchant friends are far more inclined to take specie than Continental paper. The way things are with our weak-kneed Congress, I can't say I blame them."

"True, sir," Hamilton agreed, "but, if I may speak freely, I believe the fundamental defect is a want of power in Congress. The Articles of Confederation are drawn in such a way as to leave the government hamstrung, neither fit for war nor peace."

"Correct, Colonel," Schuyler replied, nodding his heavy bewigged head. "And it's no wonder that our paper currency is worthless. There is no power of taxation to back it."

"That is certainly the worst defect of our Confederation. As each state considers itself sovereign, that defeats any power given to Congress. There is no effective executive branch in our government because of these sectional jealousies."

Schuyler nodded vigorously, and so Alexander did not pause for breath.

"Of course, it is natural for men to look after their own interest. It would be easier to stop the sun in its course than to change that! Every businessman knows the Confederation does not have the means to clothe or feed the troops and therefore wants his pay in British silver rather than our worthless specie. Still, when I'm begging for something that has been promised months ago, something we can't do without, like shoes or beef or flour, and I'm lied to and let down over and over again because the politicians have reneged and the state levies have not been paid, I believe those ragged fellows out at Jockey Hollow are better men and greater patriots than most of our gentlemen suppliers."

"I agree, sir. The common soldiers, men whose names no one will remember, are some of our greatest patriots," her uncle said. "The indignity and neglect those stout fellows have suffered! Yet, somehow, they hang on."

"What we need is some way to restore the value of our currency."

Betsy watched a flush flow over Hamilton's pale face. It was clear how deeply the subject roused him.

"All we need is a simple form of taxation everyone can agree upon. If we could supply our army properly, I think we could drive the British out in short order."

"What about those who argue that taxation was what started this in the first place?" Drawing deeply on his pipe, her uncle played Devil's Advocate.

"Well, we've begun a war for liberty and should have the discipline to support the means to carry it on," her father said. "And I couldn't agree with you more, Colonel, about this Congress of which I am a member. 'Tis a hydra with a hundred heads, each intent upon satisfying a special interest."

"Power without revenue is a bubble," Hamilton said, and the summation drew an answering flash of approval from beneath Schuyler's bushy brows.

"Why is it so difficult for people to understand that without funding we can't pay the soldiers, and that without them, we can't win the war? This country is rich. Americans are an ingenious people! I'm certain we could produce—and manufacture—all we need."

"Sound ideas, Colonel Hamilton," the doctor said, "but I've begun to believe the patient would rather die arguing than swallow the cure."

"First, however, the taxes levied to pay for the war must be collected." General Schuyler shifted in his chair. "Every state has reneged at one time or another on its allotment, even those that haven't suffered the same level of destruction as New York or New Jersey. As you have said, Colonel Hamilton, nothing will be accomplished until we have reorganized our Confederation."

Her father and Hamilton leaned closer. Betsy was happy to see her father so engaged.

"Sanctity of contract is the foundation of national character," Hamilton said.

"It is also the foundation of good government. Where the only law is the strongest arm and people aren't safe in their homes and property, flat ruin will follow." The General adjusted his eternally gouty foot.

The talk of finance continued. The two of them went from the pros and cons of paper money to the ways an American bank might be financed. While Betsy didn't understand a great deal, she watched the masculine interchange with interest.

How involved Alexander and Papa are! At first it pleased her, but it was something of a mixed blessing, for as time went on, Hamilton ceased to even glance in her direction. Instead, he focused upon her father, who had begun to detail his experiences with the British commissary and the colonial government during The French and Indian War.

Betsy returned to her embroidery, always a safe haven. Discussion of 'the current troubles' grew theoretical. Hamilton's talk was now studded with references to authors Betsy had never heard of. Malachy Postlethwayt—such a mouthful of a name!—came up repeatedly. Her father held forth for a long time about something called *Lex Mercatoria*.

Dr. Cochran, exhausted after another long cold day at the hospital, fell asleep on the couch. She and her Aunt retired soon after Alexander and her father excused themselves and gone to sit at the secretary on the far side of

115

the room, where Hamilton found paper and ink. They intended to make an estimate of the war debt.

* * *

A few jealous Morristown ladies would have liked to lay the blame for Miss Lott's abandonment at the feet of an outsider, but because the interloper was so generally acknowledged as kind and modest, this was hard to do. It was received wisdom that a penniless but clever young man like Colonel Hamilton was obligated to follow his fortune.

Alexander lost no time in charming Betsy's Aunt. Soon he was visiting every night he could obtain release from his duties. His friends would have been surprised to see him so often silent. He sat beside Betsy on the sofa, holding out his hands for her to wind yarn upon, as domestic and mannerly as the young tomcat that now spent the frigid evenings tending his coat by the fire.

* * *

Only embers glowed. The room was cooling rapidly, but they sat, momentarily alone. Mrs. Cochran had withdrawn to serve supper to her husband, who'd been delayed by a bone setting.

The ribbon encircling Betsy's neck had been enticing Alexander all evening. Now, as soon as he was sure they were alone, he reached for it, his long fingers teasing it lose. Then, slowly trailing it away, holding her eyes, he leaned to bestow a lingering and worshipful kiss upon the pulse in her throat. Her long black lashes closed, her bosom rose and fell with his tribute.

At headquarters, Sam Webb remained disbelieving. To him, Alexander's new infatuation was incomprehensible, except in terms of fortune hunting. "Brown Betsy" was preeminently rich and well born. What other reason could there be?

Alexander couldn't entirely explain it to himself, but he was head over heels. He had written to his best friend, John Laurens, that he was "a gone man." Everything about Betsy excited him, from her melting dark eyes and frank, unaffected manner, to the subtle, singular fragrance of her silky skin.

"My ribbon, sir!" Betsy protested as soon as she'd managed to get her breath back. "Return it at once."

"This ribbon shall be held hostage until you give me another kiss."

He was elated when she promptly leaned against him and yielded her lips. Alexander couldn't remember ever having his ears boxed for kissing, but her response was so delightfully unaffected. Betsy returned his kisses with frank, innocent pleasure. It seemed impossible that a young woman of twenty-three could really be a novice at these "sports of cupid's bower," but the first time he'd slipped his tongue between those sweet lips, she'd pushed him away. The look in her eyes couldn't have been more shocked if he'd put his hand under her dress.

She'd moved away, but only against the back of the sofa, so it was easy to catch her again. As he wordlessly returned, she trembled, blushed. He came slowly, certain she did not really want to escape.

She is caught, this pretty brown bird!

At first, he'd only sipped. Just as she began to weaken, he sat back and felt himself smile at her blind expression. Lips parted, he came for her again, and this time she was ready, her mouth sweet as a mango.

As they kissed, she loosed a burst of fragrance, and then he'd had to restrain himself. What he wanted to do, even at the risk of eternal banishment, would be to carry her palm down upon a part which was even now tugging at his trousers.

It was quite wonderful how far these demure-looking American girls would go.

A dainty hand flew to his, the one that held the ribbon, but he refused to release his trophy. In another moment, she slipped her arms inside his jacket, locked them around his waist and yielded her lips once more, falling into bliss.

He was the one who broke off. Long fingers, coming to rest gently against her lips, forestalled the expected protest. He'd heard something.

"Now that I'm changed, Mrs. Cochran, let's stir up the fire and sit awhile." The voice of her uncle boomed from the hallway.

"Betsy has a caller, my dear."

"I can't imagine who!" The doctor didn't sound pleased. "It's been the same story every other night this week."

As the Cochrans entered the room, the pair shot to their feet. The ribbon disappeared discreetly into Hamilton's pocket.

"Tonight, Colonel Hamilton," said her uncle, not giving either of them a chance to say a word, "you are going to march yourself straight back to headquarters. I've been thinking all the way home of the comforts of my sofa and I intend to avail myself of them."

"Certainly, sir." Hamilton's ears turned red as his face. "I regret if my presence is—or has been—or, ah—an inconvenience."

"No apology required, Colonel."

"Oh, yes!" Betsy joined him in a fierce blush. "Uncle John, we—"

"Hush." Shuffling forward in slippers and heavy dressing gown, Surgeon Cochran seized Hamilton's hand and gave it a hearty pumping.

"Good night, Colonel. Greet His Excellency on my behalf." Pale with weariness, the Doctor sank onto his sofa.

"Betsy, my dear, be a good girl and go up to bed after you've let Colonel Hamilton out."

Under the eyes of the guard at the door, Hamilton was formal, bowing over his lady's slender fingers before stepping out into starry, windswept darkness.

* * *

118

As soon as the door closed Betsy dashed straight upstairs. Once inside her room, she went to the icy window, watched after him for as long as his lantern light could be seen. Stars trembled in the black sky, and she could see her breath against the pane. Her fingers strayed to the spot he had kissed, the warm pulse in her neck. She was shivering all over, not entirely from the cold.

* * *

A frigid wind roared about the Cochran house. Once again, the lovers were ensconced upon the good doctor's sofa. Even embracing in close proximity to a hearty fire, they could barely keep the chill at bay.

"If only I dared to show you all my heart." Firelight glinted on Alexander's ginger head.

"Dare."

Alexander let his hands slide along her arms. Betsy tried not to tremble. She had more than an inkling of what he was going to say. "Miss Schuyler," he said, twining his fingers into hers, "you must know that I have fallen desperately in love with you."

"I had a notion." She knew this sounded bold, but, truthfully, she could hardly meet his eyes.

"However, you see, I must not start there," Alexander continued, urgency rising in his voice. "My circumstances make it—nearly—an impropriety for me to speak of my regard to any gentlewoman."

"I cannot imagine why, Colonel Hamilton."

"You are very generous, Miss, but as I'm sure you have heard, I have no fortune. There is another matter, too, about my family. I must be absolutely candid before I dare to offer you the only object that's clearly in my possession— my heart."

For the first time since she'd met him, Betsy saw shame well within his blue eyes.

"I can't imagine anything, sir, but high intelligence and gentility."

119

Hamilton flushed. "You are very kind, Miss Schuyler. More than you know." Carefully, one at a time, he lifted and kissed her hands. Then, ever so reluctantly, he released them.

"At the risk of fatiguing you with a long story and of forfeiting your esteem, I feel I must begin at the beginning."

He assumed a formal posture. It reminded Betsy of a soldier steeling himself to endure some agony at the hands of her uncle.

"My esteem requires no confidence from you." Betsy replied with equal formality. "If you feel you must speak, Sir, please know that what you say will remain secret, between us alone."

* * *

Wind carried a sharp, birdshot tinkle of ice against the windows. It took time for Alexander to start. He knew that he must begin with his mother's story, about her cruel first husband, about how she'd run away from him and gone back to Nevis where she'd met James Hamilton.

"Miss Schuyler, in the eyes of the law, I am illegitimate." He did not dare to imagine what would happen after he made this confession. He drew a deep breath and began to speak of the past and of things he so much wanted to forget....

* * *

We were born in the same year. All her life, Betsy had been secure and happy, safe in her father's red brick home, wrapped in a warm cocoon of family and privilege. The man before her, by his own admission, had been abandoned, orphaned, insulted, forced to work for his bread while still a child.

"I'm not the least offended, Colonel Hamilton." Betsy gazed into his eyes. "In fact, sir, I have just learnt that you

120

are—the bravest, the most remarkable person I've ever met. But, please…." It was so daring, the thing she was going to say, so daring that her voice seemed to be coming from somewhere else. "Continue—um—with what you were saying earlier about—about—your—heart."

There was a pause, and for a moment Alexander looked so pale, she thought he might faint.

"Miss Elizabeth, if your father gives his permission, will you do me the great honor of becoming my wife?" He swallowed hard.

"I will, Colonel Hamilton."

Just a month ago the idea that he'd propose would have seemed mad, but now the brightest, most exciting man I've ever met, the man with whom I am so deeply in love, has asked me to marry him!

"Dearest Betsy, do you truly understand? I would never want you to be insulted or injured because of my past. The world is very cruel."

"Not the sort of people who matter." Betsy stroked his thin cheek.

"All the fortune I have in this world is in my head, but I'll work hard, so hard! I promise to make you proud."

Their lips met joyfully, and Betsy caressed his face.

The ribbing he must have taken, shaving before coming out tonight!

"Do you think your father will give permission? Mr. Church has told me—"

"Papa would have been jealous of anyone Angelica married, but he knows you better than he ever did Mr. Church, and he likes you. Still, if he makes a fuss, we shall simply do as they did."

"Oh, Betsy, my dearest angel, a poor man has to be even more careful of his honor than a rich one, for honor is all he has. I value my honor above my life and I feel the greatest respect for you and for your family. Only imagine the kind of thing which would be bandied about if we eloped."

"Papa will certainly agree. He admires you, Hamilton. He has told me so."

121

Close in each other's arms, they didn't hear the footsteps until it was too late.

"Colonel Hamilton!" Mrs. Cochran's voice overflowed with reproof. "Is this what you are up to?"

The lovers were on their feet at once.

"Oh, Aunt Gertrude! Colonel Hamilton has asked me to marry him."

"Well, of course he has, dear. Still, that's no reason to let him embrace you. Certainly not before speaking to your father. As for you, Colonel, be off to headquarters at once, audacious young man!"

Suddenly, Betsy was afraid. Between them, everything was simple. Aunt Cochran, standing there, arms akimbo, was the world's first intrusion.

"Upstairs, Miss, and not another word!"

"Please, Mrs. Cochran, Ma'am—before I came here tonight, I prepared a letter for General Schuyler, hoping he would be here, but I understand he has gone up to Basking Ridge. I shall try to call upon him tomorrow."

Quickly, he dropped a kiss on his Betsy's hand.

"Good-night, Miss Elizabeth. And, I give you my word, Mrs. Cochran, I will not call again until I have secured Major General Schuyler's permission to do so."

Mrs. Cochran shook her head as if even that extremity were not sufficient. She stepped back and held the parlor door wide.

"Rest assured, Colonel, I shall wait for my brother's instructions."

* * *

As he threw on his coat in the hallway, Hamilton heard Mrs. Cochran scolding Betsy up the stairs.

"Such shocking behavior, Elizabeth! It's this dreadful war, turning everything upside down."

As he trudged back to headquarters, shivering in the bitter wind, he fretted.

122

Washington likes me well enough to encourage my daring with Miss Schuyler, but what about Major General Schuyler? Even if the proud Dutchman discounts the fact that I am poor as a church mouse, what about the rest...?

As he plodded through the crusted snow, Alexander wondered whether it was rational to expect a haughty patrician like Philip Schuyler to overlook so many defects in a prospective husband. Suddenly, apprehension washed over him.

Then he remembered the way Betsy had blushed, that almost drinkable dusky rose which always made him want to kiss her. Gazing into those doe's eyes brimming with tears of sympathy, he'd seen that she loved him, despite the shameful story he'd told. Nevertheless, it was also clear that she'd never experienced so much as a minute's want or humiliation in her life.

Her talk of elopement had surprised him. For an instant he wondered if he would carry Betsy off against the wishes of her powerful family? The strong, reasoning part of his mind firmly told him he would not be a party to any such trespass.

There are plenty of other fish in this rich American sea.

At the same time, extinguishing prudence, a wild man cried:

I must have her! How she listens, and with what tender, generous charity!

Suddenly, it seemed like another life, the one in which he'd joked with friends about only wooing women who were wealthy and well-connected. The love blazing in his heart would brook no opposition. He'd set a trap and caught—not only the lady—but himself.

He knew that he'd told her only the barest bones of his story, but there was simply no other way. He had fled the islands, fled shame, fled scandal, degradation and disgrace. With his mind, with sheer force of will, he had made a gentleman of himself.

That past was dead; with bare hands, he'd killed it.

* * *

Betsy blew upon the frost-covered window of her bedroom and rubbed it hard with the heel of her hand. In the blurry slick circle, already freezing over again, she saw Hamilton's lantern slowly making its way toward the distant lights of headquarters. Overhead a full moon sailed, a silver face reflected upon the ice-covered snow.

I am brim full, a cup spilling over—with love.

Chapter Five ~ Romance

Betsy was distressed when Alexander, good as his word, disappeared from their society. In fact, he had been sent upon a mission by General Washington, a prisoner exchange. He wrote to her tenderly, but nothing that wasn't suitable for the public eye. Heaven knew how many people, British and American, would read his letter before it reached her.

He was bold enough to call Elizabeth "my dearest" and to say that when the time came for toasts at the officer's mess, his toast was "Miss Schuyler."

She had written to her papa the very next day, pleading their case. Papa Schuyler had returned a letter saying he would be there soon. His first order of business, however, was a meeting with Washington. After dining with the General, he'd come to Cochran's. He said that he'd already had a visit from Colonel Hamilton, but he didn't enlarge.

When her father arrived, shortly after the supper Betsy hadn't been able to eat, she flew straight into his arms.

"Oh, yes, little girl." Philip Schuyler kissed her forehead. "Here's the sugar a father gets when his daughter wants to leave him."

Betsy felt tears prick. She remembered how angry her parents had been with Jack Church, how Angelica, until that moment the precious pet, had cried and stormed to no avail.

What if Papa says no? Hamilton had made it clear that he would abide by whatever decision her father made. As soon as Betsy imagined that, tears spilled.

"Now, Elizabeth." Her father sighed. "Please. None of that."

Together they went to the big wing chair. Betsy shifted a stool so that after he'd settled in, he could prop his sore leg. After that was in place, she dropped to her knees beside him.

"Oh, Papa, I love Colonel Hamilton. And he loves me, too."

"So it seems. As I wrote, your Colonel came to see me. The meeting was brief, but I believe everything necessary was said. His boots were shining, that red head of his was powdered for once and the seat of his pants," her father winked, "neatly patched. He told me all about his honorable intentions and about his situation, which, as he says he has told you, isn't good. He's a poor boy, Betsy, not a penny to his name that isn't charity, no profession except soldier. And, as for his family—well...."

A hard knot formed in Betsy's throat. She rested her head against her father's good knee and hoped that she could hold back the rising sob.

"Now, dear, just let me finish." Her father stroked her shoulder. "Alexander Hamilton may be poor, but in every conversation I've had with him, I've found him smart as a whip and twice as quick. Lord Stirling, Mr. Boudinot and Mr. Livingston all assure me that he's the sharpest young man they've ever met. But what impresses me most about your young Colonel is the way General Washington relies upon him. Why, His Excellency told me that Hamilton can write a letter that steals the words right out of his head. In his opinion, Hamilton is the kind of young man who'll make his fortune or die trying."

Betsy wiped her eyes on her apron, and met her father's dark eyes, so like her own.

"What's more," General Schuyler went on, a slow smile growing as he relished her expression, "I like everything your young man says about finance, too. The other night when we talked about the war debt and remedies for it, I was astonished that someone so young would have so many solid ideas. He cut right to the heart of our troubles."

"Then—then—?"

"I've written to your mama, Betsy, and sent Colonel Hamilton's letter along as well. We'll wait and see what Mrs. Schuyler has to say. She was furious when your sister ran off with that English popinjay." Philip Schuyler loudly cleared his throat, as if Angelica's elopement was still stuck in it.

"In my letter, I explained that while I approve of the match, she must give her approval as well. The final decision will be hers."

Betsy felt blood drain from her cheeks. It seemed her hopes, raised so high, were about to be dashed.

"Mama—is a van Rensselaer."

Under bushy brows, the General's eyes snapped with amusement. "And you believe the van Rensselaers are grander and prouder than the Schuylers? For this instant, I will tolerate the notion, but please never voice such an opinion to anyone else." He patted the hand that lay upon his knee. "Don't you fret. Your mother knows money isn't everything. Your Colonel Hamilton is the brightest, quickest, most personable young man I've had the pleasure to know. His Excellency and I agree that the father-in-law of Alexander Hamilton need have few fears upon his daughter's account."

* * *

Betsy was allowed to write to Alexander while he was away on the prisoner exchange. Looking over that first letter, she felt awful pangs of embarrassment. For the first time ever, she envied Angelica's time at that Hudson Valley finishing school.

Also, for the first time since their courtship had begun, she had misgivings.

How did I ever win this prize away Miss Lott?

Now Peggy Lott wouldn't speak to her, and she and her friends looked so sour all the time. Betsy felt sorry for Peggy, and guilty, too. After all, she'd done nothing to discourage Alexander.

The first letter she penned, Betsy consigned to the fire. She began again. Although this one looked better because the script was neater, she closed thinking uneasily about her rival. She wrote: "I am not deserving your preference."

127

After scattering sand upon the ink, she leaned upon the portable scriptorium. She had pictured herself eventually marrying, in an inevitable way, one of her Dutch cousins, a kindly balding widower, or a plump younger son, someone no one else wanted.

Instead, if Mama approves, I will have this glittering Creole stranger, a man even more dashing and exotic than Angelica's Jack!

* * *

Two weeks of pins and needles later, Mrs. Schuyler's consent arrived. If her husband liked the young man, she said, it was well enough with her. Catherine Schuyler ended by saying that she was looking forward to seeing the couple married at home, Dutch fashion, in front of the hearth.

"But, Papa! That means we shall have to wait until after this summer's campaign is over!"

General Schuyler was once again ensconced in the chair in the Cochran's parlor, his aches today soothed by a dose of willow bark, a drop of laudanum, and proximity to the fire.

"Well, my dear, you've known Colonel Hamilton for all of two months. Mrs. Schuyler and I think an engagement is prudent."

"But I'll have to go back to Albany soon. I shan't see him for months and months! What if—something—happens?"

"Don't start by expecting the worst. Your Colonel is not an artillery captain anymore, but at headquarters. And doesn't His Excellency declare Hamilton to be an inspired penman? Thinking about you will surely stimulate him a great deal more than tracking down a hundred pair of lost shoes."

Betsy tried to smile, but she couldn't. Instead, she put her head against her father's good knee and wept.

"There, there, my Betsy. If it's really love, a summer of waiting won't hurt."

* * *

The Schuyler/Hamilton engagement was a wonder. Every genteel family from Boston to Savannah discussed it. The Tory newspapers made it an item of gossip, saying that Major General Schuyler was willing to sacrifice patrician pride and a daughter in order to secure 'the interest of George Washington's most influential aide.'

Gossiping with the Stirling sisters in their big house at Basking Ridge, Kitty Livingston agreed.

"Betsy is weepy because the wedding is delayed until December, but why I can't think. Colonel Hamilton won't change. He's got what he wanted all along—a rich father-in-law. Honestly, General Schuyler dotes on the upstart fellow quite as much as does His Excellency. It's astonishing."

"Sour grapes, Kitty?"

The younger Stirling girl, Mary, thought it more than high time to ruffle the gossip's feathers. "Colonel Hamilton may be poor, but he's awfully clever and lots of fun. Remember when he had just come up from the Indies, how adorable he was with that funny accent, and what laughs we had teaching him to dance?"

"Of course you'd take his side. He was always kissing you."

Mary's reply was a giggle which denied nothing.

"Well," Kitty said, "I'd help Betsy climb out the window myself, but the truth of the matter is that she needn't risk upsetting her papa. Next Christmas, or even later, Colonel Hamilton will marry her. She is exactly the trophy his red-headed impudence has been so-long-a-hunting."

* * *

129

Betsy looked in the mirror a dozen times a day to see if she was the same person. Every time it surprised her to discover that nothing changed. There were her level, thick brows, her dark eyes, and her sensitive mouth set in a jaw that was a trifle too square.

Were the hurtful words of Cousin Kitty, the ones that had come back through Mary Stirling, true? Was Alexander only marrying her because she was Philip Schuyler's daughter?

* * *

Summer approached. The army would soon march out of winter quarters to meet the enemy, and the Schuylers would retire to the relative safety of Albany.

"Your papa wants us to be certain," said Hamilton, "which is wise and prudent."

They were sitting quite alone on a steamy afternoon, the hottest so far this year. Sweat trickled down their backs. Alexander had ridden to Aunt Cochran's on his little black gelding and when Betsy ran to greet him at the low gate, instead of dismounting, he'd leaned down and seized her around the waist.

Laughing with delight and surprise, Betsy felt herself lifted. As Hamilton urged the horse forward, her foot found his boot in the stirrup. The forward motion shifted her, almost effortlessly, to a seat before him.

As they trotted away, they heard Aunt Gertrude calling. "Elizabeth Schuyler! Colonel Hamilton! Come back here at once!"

They'd ridden a good distance, the knight with strong arms around his lady, in order to be alone. With an army encamped, a private spot was hard to find. Below the short rise on which they finally dismounted, they could see the scarecrow figures of three Continental regulars moving in a desultory fashion, eating berries and occasionally stooping to see if they'd caught any rabbits in the snares they'd set at the edge of the briar patch.

130

Hamilton was in uniform, Betsy in a modest gown of green and white checked muslin, a cap covering her hair. Sitting in the shade, the pesky black flies soon discovered them. These tormentors circled, looking for exposed flesh to bite. The lovers did their best to maintain dignity while slapping them away.

"I shall miss you dreadfully."

Today, their impending separation seemed unbearable. When her tears spilled, Hamilton kissed them.

"I'm worried, too, you know." With a mocking expression, he tilted her chin. "What if one of your eminently more suitable cousins throws himself at your feet, Miss? A rich Hudson Valley beau? Will I get a letter telling me it's over?"

In a few minutes, they were lying, with utter disregard for propriety, on his jacket. Her hair spilled from beneath her cap, while Hamilton kissed her lips apart.

Betsy could feel sweat trickling everywhere, along her back inside the stays and between her breasts. Her sweetheart left off kissing to sip the drops from her throat, calling it "nectar." Their senses were full, of each other, and of blossoming May. Betsy was dizzy with pleasure until she felt his hand slip under her skirt.

"Alexander! No! You mustn't!"

"We're to be married, aren't we?"

He'd gone on caressing as he spoke, although the attack was not entirely direct. The fine lawn of her petticoat lay between that most forbidden, sensitive place and his questing fingers.

I can have her. Have her right in the middle of this patch of dewdrops...I can make her mine, bind this rich prize to her promise! Now, while she is lost to everything but pleasure. She won't be the first girl to become a woman upon a soldier's jacket....

"No!"

He stopped. Up till that moment, he'd not quite believed in her innocence. After all, weren't the Dutch notorious for their unchaperoned courting parties?

Fingers rested upon his lips. Her eyes were deep and dark, the pupils huge.

"We're not married." Betsy whispered, trembling. "You elope, you get married, and then…."

Alexander leaned on his elbow and hungrily kissed her fingertips.

"Lots of fellows would say you've got the last two reversed, Miss. I have promised to marry you, Elizabeth Schuyler, and I shall. Don't you believe me?"

In her eyes the look of alarm grew.

"We mustn't." She spoke, just audibly. "It would be—my dishonor."

Inwardly cursing the powerful trigger she'd so guilelessly pressed, Hamilton released her. Flushed and mussed, she sat up and hastily settled green calico over her legs. Her eyes regarded him with anguish.

He wondered how long it would be before he could bend sufficiently to rise with any dignity.

Women! She might be innocent enough not to understand, but he thought he had made her go—those sighs, the delirious spice of her! For all their prate of modesty, the most delicate female was equipped for twice the capacity of the lustiest man. She had been pleasured, and here he was, left in misery.

"Miss Elizabeth, I only hope a bullet during the coming campaign doesn't make you regret this."

"Don't you dare say that!" Her dusky cheeks were still that wonderful color, but her dark eyes were full of reproach. "You know I love you. You know I do!"

* * *

Loud as anything, a voice inside her head had been crying: *Stop!*

Gazing at him, recognizing his discomfort, she felt twin stabs of fear and regret. Still, she would not let it happen here, where a company of grubby Continentals might suddenly intrude, tramping out of the brush.

"Don't be angry with me, please. I couldn't bear it."

"Hush, darling! Hush. I'm not angry. It's just—hard—for a man to stop. Still, I warn you. You shall not sleep for a single minute the first night we are properly married and in bed together."

On their way back to the Cochran's, he kept his arm around her tightly, but there was no cuddling as there had been on the ride out. Although Alexander assured her that he respected her refusal, when she'd tried to be a little bold and tease him about his sighs, he had heaved an even bigger one and hadn't answered. His silence as he let her down at the gate, as well as the scolding she received from Mrs. Cochran, cast a shadow over their passionate afternoon.

* * *

Her distress forced Alexander to regret not only his cross words, but his attempt to take her. At least, he comforted himself, this was absolute proof that not only was she chaste, but agreeably warm blooded. Of both, all husbands-to-be should be assured!

He trotted his black horse up the lane to headquarters, but as soon as he was out of sight of Cochran's, he turned onto a side path obscured by brush. He needed time alone.

Those delicate shoulders, her sweet small breasts, the storm his love-making had aroused—but what a state I am in! Something will have to be done before I return to headquarters.

Upon reaching the tumbledown shed that was hidden there, he pulled up and hopped down, leaving the reins trailing. The shed was stuffed with hay, but there were other uses besides storage to which it was regularly put.

He headed for the door. *If something else isn't going on in there already....*

As he cautiously entered, he heard a low snicker. A strong arm shot from the dusty twilight; fingers seized the front of his coat and tugged imperiously.

"Well, Colonel! To what do I owe this honor?" The musky smell of the woman, the muscle in her grasp, told him exactly who it was.

"Waiting for someone?" He was surprised, but quickly decided a counter was the best strategy. Behind him, the door sighed and fell shut.

"Maybe you—you rat! Why haven't you asked for so long? All your pretty red-headed friends have, even that bald little Frenchie. And I've been most obliging, most obliging, sir."

As she spoke, she slipped her arms inside his jacket and pressed full breasts against him.

"Don't that make you jealous?"

He didn't reply.

"Wicked, cold-hearted devil, you are; I missed'e."

"Well, ah, I'm honored, Annie, but right now I...."

"What's this?" She interrupted with a throaty laugh.

"Ah! Don't!" She had seized his trouser front, taking hold of the unruly part inside. "I can't pay." He attempted to disengage her.

"Don't be so rude! Such a fine, fine gen'leman don't forget good service. You kin pay later."

In the hot darkness of the shed, he could mostly feel her. She was as tall as he was, "A most magnificent harlot," all his friends agreed. On this hot day, she didn't seem to be wearing much, just a thin petticoat over a thinner shift.

Her fingers had already popped his buttons. "Why, the state of this poor thing!" She fondled what leapt into her welcoming hands. "Them rich virgins always leave you high and dry, don't they?"

"But your friend, uh, the one you're waiting for...."

"He kin wait 'is turn." With a hearty shove, she pushed him backwards into the hay.

* * *

The engaged couple strolled behind the Cochran's house, back and forth in the small garden. A doctor's

134

garden, it held more green simples and brushy herbs than flowers. Now, on a sweet late May evening, Hamilton had come to say good-bye. They knew Mrs. Cochran kept watch at the window. As they walked, Alexander slipped a square of paper into Betsy's palm. When her fingers closed tight around it, he carried the small knot her fist made to his lips.

"Read it before you go to sleep."

Ever so tenderly, he drew her against him for a warm but surprisingly chaste good-bye kiss.

Later, alone in her bedroom, Betsy removed the little square of linen paper from her pocket, opened it, and gazed at Alexander's flowing, secretarial hand.

Answer to the Inquiry Why I Sighed
Before no mortal ever knew
A love like mine so tender, true,
Completely wretched—you away
And but half-blessed e'en while you stay.
If present love turn a cruel face
Deny you to my fond embrace
No joy unmixed my bosom warms
But when my angel's in my arms.

"Half Blessed"? Why, because I denied him!

Heart pounding, Betsy refolded the poem and put it into the copy of *Lord Chesterfield's Letters*, the book she'd begun to read in order to please him.

"No joy unmixed..."

That evening, Betsy sewed a little keepsake purse for his poem. From then on, she wore it over her heart.

Chapter Six ~ Albany

To Eliza, from Colonel Dey's house Bergen County, New Jersey, July 6, 1780:

"Here we are, my love, in a house of great hospitality— in a country of plenty—a buxom girl under the same roof— pleasing expectation of a successful campaign—and everything to make a soldier happy, who is not in love and absent from his mistress. As this is my case I cannot be happy; but it is a maxim of my life to enjoy the present good with the highest relish and to soften the present evil by a hope of future good. I alleviate the pain of absence by looking forward to that delightful period which gives us to each other forever..."

Betsy was at home again, working out-of-doors with Mama and her little brother Rensselaer. Peggy was still within, for she was being "kept close" this summer. Her younger sister had had two offers for her hand, one from 'Bram Ten Broeck and the other from Stephen van Rensselaer. Stephen was only eighteen and still at Harvard, but he'd had the temerity to ask. Philip Schuyler had dismissed him as "too young," although many Dutch marriages were concluded between parties far younger. The fact was that Stephen might be Patroon of Rensselaerwyck, but his Uncle still fumed that it had been in Stephen's parlor that Angelica's runaway wedding to John Church had taken place.

Peggy didn't seem to care much about her father's rejection of Stephen. She was fond of her cousin, but he wasn't an object of passion. On the other hand, she'd been quite upset about 'Bram. He was from a suitable family and had land coming to him, but the problem here was that her father didn't think 'Bram had settled down sufficiently. As

136

an officer in the local militia, 'Bram still managed to spend plenty of time racing, hunting, and drinking with his friends.

This rejection, however, hadn't been absolute. General Schuyler indicated that his position could change if the young man "shows interest in something besides his pleasures."

Because Peggy was confined to the house, Mrs. Schuyler and Betsy were the only ones setting out the strawberry plants. General Schuyler, who'd driven north to the Saratoga plantation with his older sons, John and Philip Jeremiah, had expressed the hope that the womenfolk could get the sets, which had arrived tired and brown, into the ground that very day.

A pony cart held both plants and water and supported a calash, a sail of canvas which could be hoisted to shade the ladies. The Schuyler women wore broad-brimmed hats, gloves, dresses of plain brown and long checked shawls worn crossed over their shoulders and tied down at the waist. Although it was June, this northern day was not particularly warm.

Mrs. Schuyler sat in the cart, holding the reins and supervising. Her weight, as well as another pregnancy, kept her from the physical labor she'd done routinely as a younger woman. Today, slaves did the heavy work of digging deep holes. Then, with gloved hands, trowels and claws, Betsy and Rensselaer crumbled the soil, set the plants at the proper depth, and watered them.

Her brother muttered about having to perform this "dumb dirt farmer's labor," but "all hands to the task" was a Hudson Valley tradition. So far he'd been most useful in lugging the bundled plants from the back of the cart and cutting the packages apart.

"Rensselaer!" Mrs. Schuyler pointed impatiently. "Crumble the dirt finer and be gentle putting those plants in. Spread out the roots." She had set countless bulbs, fruit trees, and strawberries over the years for her husband, but she was no longer shaped for stooping and crawling. Betsy had registered shock when she'd returned home to find her

137

mother expecting. This was, Mrs. Schuyler had explained with pride, her fourteenth pregnancy.

"You aren't any more surprised than your papa and me, Miss." A curiously youthful expression lit her mother's eyes. "It must have been all that billing and cooing at Morristown this winter which inspired Mr. Schuyler."

As Betsy gave the plants a long, slow drink, her mother asked, "Did you finish that letter to Colonel Hamilton?"

"No, Mama. I tore it up."

"Another one? Why?"

Betsy didn't answer. Instead, she slashed the cords that held the bundled plants and began to carefully separate the crowns. "Here," she said to Rensselaer, handing him a bunch. "See if you can do it right, for heaven's sake."

Her brother passed a sulky look, but got down on his knees and began, more or less, to do the work as instructed.

"Your poor Colonel must be desperate to hear from you."

"Oh, Mama. Hamilton is so very hard to write to."

"He doesn't care about your punctuation, dear. He wants a letter which says you love him."

Betsy didn't answer.

"Betsy dear, whatever is the matter?"

"I'm not sure he really cares whether I love him or not." She got to her feet and came to the cart, shaking dirt from her apron.

"Do spit it out, dear." Her mother's round face gazed patiently down.

"Well—um—when Hamilton isn't scolding, he teases. He worries all the time because he's not rich. He says he wants to be sure I can live a simple life. He says if I cannot face that possibility, we should not marry."

That particular letter had been a long one. Alexander had asked Betsy whether she "soberly relished the pleasure of being a poor man's wife?"

"Have you learned to think a homespun preferable to a brocade," he had written, "and the rumbling of a wagon wheel to the musical rattling of a coach and six? Can you

138

be an Aquileia and cheerfully plant turnips with me, if fortune should so order it? If you cannot, my Dear, we are playing a comedy of all in the wrong, and you should correct the mistake before we begin to act the tragedy of the unhappy couple..."

On top of everything else, she'd had to ask her father about Roman history so that she could learn who this "Aquileia" was.

"Rest now." Mrs. Schuyler called to the slaves. The three women cultivating ahead of them obediently squatted, black hands tucking their skirts between their knees. Resting hoes and picks against their shoulders so they could gesticulate, they began to talk among themselves in a rippling patois of English and African.

"I don't believe Colonel Hamilton will actually need you to plant turnips, Betsy. He's a clever young fellow. And, of course, your papa likes him well...."

"Alexander is so proud. He'd never accept anything from Papa."

"Well, be that as it may, I think all his fretting comes from missing you. He probably worries that one of your cousins will change your mind."

"Oh, Mama, why on earth should that be? None of them courted me before."

"Elizabeth Schuyler, after supper you shall sit in the study and not move an inch until you've written your poor fiancé a letter."

Betsy knew a command when she heard it.

"Tell him that you love him and then remind him that you're an Albany girl, not a spoiled southern one. You know how to hoe a straight row, when to put seeds in the ground, how to bake and boil, how to make pickles and preserves, how to sew and how to use a loom for hose and tape."

As the catalog of her virtues continued from above, Betsy, feeling ten years old, stared at the ground.

* * *

139

A chilly wind blew, tossing the trees. The sky was full of rushing gray clouds, a disappointing sort of summer day. Betsy had spent the morning working in the kitchen with her mother, sisters, and the servants. With mountains of West Indies sugar that her father could still command, they made conserves of plums, jellies of wild grapes and jams of berries. Pies browned in the wall ovens. A hot vinegar bath for pickling peaches bubbled pungently over the fire.

Betsy sat peeling and cutting the apples she was to string for drying. She'd been banished to the monotony of slicing because so far this morning her lack of concentration had led her to overturn not one, but two jars of conserve.

"It's a perfect day for putting up." Mrs. Schuyler was in her element. A trickle of sweat ran from beneath her cap and down one plump cheek as she bent to use a length of kindling to push a pot deeper into the fire. "Cold enough outside so that all this hot work feels just fine."

The kitchen hummed like a well ordered hive. At Betsy's feet sat three black children who were shelling pink-spotted beans called "Jacob's Cattle," onto drying trays.

Betsy peeled, sliced apples into neat strips, and fretted. *How did a poor woman do all this work by herself?*

Of course, a poor woman wouldn't be putting up for a plantation, for a steady stream of visitors and for fifty slaves. Nevertheless, the prospect before her appeared ever-more daunting.

* * *

Perched at her father's desk in the long twilight, Betsy stared at the stack of letters she'd brought from her room, all from Alexander. *So many!* They came pell-mell, one after the other.

When Papa hobbled into the room and thrust his craggy head over her shoulder, she'd groaned inwardly at what she'd known would come next.

140

"Look at those inky fingers! Working at another letter to that indefatigable penman you've got for a sweetheart?"

"She has neither finished nor sent a letter to her poor Colonel in three weeks." Her sister Peg lounged stylishly on the sofa, exposing shapely calves in white silk stockings. Betsy knew that one of those elopement-filled and strictly forbidden English romances was concealed inside the covers of the *History of New York* she held. After Alexander had written Peggy an engaging and undeniably flirtatious letter, she was firmly on his side.

"Every letter she starts, she ends by ripping up. Every fire in the house is started with them."

Betsy didn't waste her breath denying. Alexander began all his letters with fretting. Next, he'd scold because she hadn't written. The third paragraph usually hinted at escapades with other women and then he'd conclude by declaring his undying affection. After reading them, she was left hurt and bewildered.

In Morristown it had been so easy to soothe him out of those troublesome black moods. She'd simply put her hand into his, or kissed him. His last letter had ended: "You have had an age for consideration, time enough for *even a woman* to know her mind in. Do you begin to repent or not? If you should be disposed to retract, don't give me the trouble of a journey to Albany."

Hamilton's teasing, a constant between the sexes, was often crueler than mere convention. By the time Betsy's eyes reached the clerical perfection of his signature, she felt as if she'd stepped on a nest of ground bees.

Sometimes she'd sit, letter in her lap, reading and rereading, attempting to sort through the layers of meaning. At the end she'd feel as if she'd partaken of some kind of unpleasant verbal torte, alternating layers of poison and sugar.

"I don't know how to answer him, Papa." Betsy sighed. "Hamilton's so—terribly—clever."

"Don't be such a goose!" Peggy airily interrupted. "Answer all his questions with an I-love-you, and then tell him how much fun you had yesterday boating with

Lieutenant Livingston and Captain Ten Broeck. He'll stop plaguing you at once."

"I believe I should like a little chat alone with your sister, Miss. Out you go, my Marguerite." Peggy smiled, a superior smile she'd copied from Angelica, and swished her long legs down. Carefully holding the books together, she swayed from the room. After all, it would be far safer to read the forbidden book in a window seat upstairs than so close to Papa.

"Now, Eliza, come and tell me all about it." Using his cane, Philip Schuyler settled into his favorite chair and beckoned for Betsy to occupy the stool beside him. She perched obediently, arranging pink skirts neatly, but she didn't speak at once. Her father didn't attempt to hurry her.

"Papa—I'm not sure about Colonel Hamilton."

"Not sure?" Her father's eyes brightened. "From the number of letters arriving from a busy aide-de-camp at a commanding general's headquarters, it seems Hamilton is pressing his suit as ardently as any young woman could desire."

Betsy considered before she spoke again.

"Perhaps what I really mean is that I'm not sure about me. I sometimes wonder if I'm good enough for him."

"Not good enough? What on earth can you mean?" Her father's black brows drew together in disbelief.

"Don't be cross, Papa. You know I'm not good with words."

Her father gathered her hand into his. "I'm not angry, Betsy, but I do want to understand."

"Well, Papa, Colonel Hamilton writes these beautiful letters, like something out of a book. But, sometimes, he says two things at once, one kind and the other—cruel. When he does that, I don't know how to reply. How can he say he loves me and then torment me so?"

The General's expression grew grave. He nodded several times, just as a doctor did when taking note of a meaningful symptom.

"Love is the most peculiar of all emotions. It's an upside down world where young people have the most to do with a power they can't know much about. That's why I don't want just any rogue carrying off my girls." As he spoke, he patted her hand.

"Now, your Hamilton's not only intelligent, but he's thin-skinned, as you surely know. Anyone with a past like his carries fear with him. And fear, as I think you've seen, makes men cruel. Your young man's proud, very proud, and he worries about the continuance of your affection, particularly when you don't write. So, after all is said and done, the first part of Peggy's advice is good. Tell him you miss him and that you wish you were together." The General shifted his perennially aching leg and frowned. "And as for the rest of it—well, any man in America would be honored to have your hand. We've brought you up to be modest, Betsy, but you mustn't forget that on both sides you are grand-daughter to Killian van Rensselaer."

"I couldn't forget that, sir." Betsy lowered her head. "But Colonel Hamilton doesn't want me as I am. He keeps telling me to read and improve myself, and that if I don't, we'll have nothing to talk about after we're married."

"Rude enough to be a Yankee, isn't he?" Philip Schuyler chuckled. "Still, the plain fact is you've always been lazy at your books and he is extremely well-read."

The reproof brought on another long silence. At last Betsy, bravely raising her eyes, said, "You *want* me to marry Colonel Hamilton, don't you, Papa?"

"Ah! Still waters do run deep." Her father smiled. "Well, yes, my clever darling. I do want you to marry him, for I believe that Colonel Hamilton is a rare bird, destined for great things. There's not a young man in America, rich or poor, to whom I'd rather give you. You see, there will be politics, same as always, after this war, and I want Hamilton in my camp. And now that I have been candid, Eliza, why don't you tell me what has happened to the girl who was crying tears of love down in Morristown?"

"Oh, I still love him. So much that it hurts."

Betsy rested her head against the arm of the chair. She couldn't say the rest.

There was such intensity in Alexander. Sometimes, he frightened her.

"Well, my dear, you'd best start that letter."

When Betsy looked up helplessly, he answered the unspoken question with grave patience. "Tell Colonel Hamilton that you wish the campaign were over. You do, don't you?"

When she nodded, her father replied. "Rest assured that the wordy, wild young gentleman will come galloping to marry you at the end of this year's operations. If you were too much alike," he continued, now warming to the subject, "you'd be scratching each other's eyes out at the end of the first year. The best marriages are made when two complementary halves join, and that, I think, describes you and Hamilton. He's brilliant all right, but he needs cosseting and care, and for that there are no women in the world like Dutch women."

"I'm sure it's as you say, Papa." Betsy heaved a great sigh.

"Now, sweetheart, no one will disturb us. Sit and write. Say that you're well, that we're all well and looking forward to his arrival. Tell Colonel Hamilton that love for him made you, for the first time in your life, useless in the kitchen, and," here her father winked and gestured towards the top letter of her pile, "that you intend to inflict severe punishment for all his reckless chat about 'buxom girls' at headquarters."

144

Chapter Seven ~ A War-Time Wedding

Duty had kept him, increasingly restive, with the Army until the very end of November. The day he'd finally ridden for Albany with McHenry and Harrison, Alexander had been surrounded by a whole host of well-wishers, grinning soldiers and servants of headquarters. A dignified farewell to the General had already been made within, so now, after a few handshakes, Alexander availed himself of a servant's cupped hands and flew into the saddle.

Sensing the agitation of the rider, his black gelding tossed his head and stamped. "Mind you don't ride the poor fellow to death," a groom cautioned.

"Or the General's daughter!"

With a chorus of raucous laughter, Alexander turned the horse's head, and, friends beside him, trotted out of camp. He was burning to go faster, but the journey ahead would be long and hard.

Snow began above Newburgh. Half-blinded, they groped along, their horses struggling in rising drifts. Wind tore at their coats. On the third day, when the snow had let up a little, Hamilton's horse threw a shoe and he and McHenry doubled for miles, shivering a little less from shared body heat.

In deepening twilight, they arrived at a group of houses clustered around a smithy. Raiders, who'd claimed to be avenging Tories—but, who, the villagers believed, were nothing more than ordinary bandits—had looted and burned two outlying farms a few weeks ago. In spite of their distress, the people were hospitable enough, even though their houses were full already, crowded with family and now with homeless neighbors.

Plundered and lawless upriver New York was a leveler. The aides tended their horses themselves and spent the night above them in a hay loft. Just as the houses were full, the barn was crowded with animals. Although the air was ripe, it was a good deal warmer than out-of-doors. The aides took watch duties along with their hosts and when it was their turn, slept like stones.

Above Poughkeepsie, the Hudson was clogged with ice. That night it threatened to storm again, but although the wind howled and the skies were leaden, there was no more snow. The embargo had caused shortages. Women passed a single needle from house to house. Men wore leather shirts, trousers and moccasins. There was, however, enough food. At one tumbledown public house where they lodged, there was venison pie and a heap of potatoes and turnips roasting in the ashes, as well as chunks of hot, greasy cornpone. The goodwife offered a ladle of onion-filled gravy to fill the trencher.

Harrison and McHenry accepted with gusto, but Hamilton, who would have liked to indulge in the savory stuff, knew he didn't dare. McHenry, who'd been schooled in medicine, had counseled his friend that the cure for his often distressed gut was to avoid grease. The change from the staples of the tropics—fish, fruit, yams, and rice—was often hard on him.

"Thank you, Ma'am, but no." He refused politely when the dripping ladle was offered. The naked cornpone, a leaden slab of gritty meal and beans, was barely palatable to him when hot, but he was so hungry that tonight, even without gravy, it went right down.

The next day, as the men were mounting up, a boy offered them some delicious Indian jerky, a parting saddlebag gift from his mother. After all, these fine young gentlemen were soldiers, fighting the damned British and risking their necks!

A day later than Hamilton had hoped, they crossed the last steep-sided creek, the horses picking their way carefully among icy rocks. Men and animals were chilled to the bone and aching from days of exposure. The north wind, which had blown against them all the way up the

146

Hudson, seemed particularly sharp today, the sky, ominous. Hamilton's horse had started to favor a leg.

"A long rest for you soon, old fellow." He rubbed the horse's black neck. His fingers were numb, his face stiff, his lips cracked. Just this morning an innkeeper's wife had offered him goose grease for them. McHenry advised him to use it.

"I'm a pale Scot, too, but your skin! Why, tissue is thicker."

This morning, expansive now that the end of the journey was in sight, Hamilton had confessed to his hostess that he was on his way to Albany to marry. The goodwife fairly cooed.

"Let me, young sir." With a gate-toothed smile, she dug her fat fingers into the pot of smelly stuff. Before he could protest, she'd smeared it onto his face, over a week's sandy growth of beard.

"Tell me," she asked, as he, too astonished by her kindly assault to speak, "what's the earthly good of a husband who can't kiss?" For good measure, she rubbed more onto his high forehead where the cold had seared it dry. Today's wind made him glad that he'd submitted to the full extent of her mothering.

* * *

At last they saw trailing smoke, the winter fires of Albany. Directly across the river, on a rise above the flood plain, they could see a manorial brick house backed by a huge barn and flanked by neat groupings of cabins.

"Well done, Alex!" McHenry waved an arm at the stately property of the father-in-law to be.

Waiting for the ferry by the icy river, they stood on a flat expanse, exposed to the wind. Hamilton tightened his scarf across the lower portion of his face. The innkeeper's wife, he thought ruefully, had been right. He could taste blood on his lips.

As they waited, two riders appeared, bringing down a snow-shower from the bank. Their horses were in fine trim, the riders young and well-dressed.

"Ho!" one shouted. "Is this Colonel Hamilton at last? Your bride—my Cousin, sir—is jumpy as a cat."

Introductions all around made clear the newcomers were local gentry, Stephen van Rensselaer and Lieutenant Henry Livingston. As they bantered—a man about to married, after all, must be roundly teased—the fresh strong horses of the Albanians neighed and tossed their heads at the weary steeds of the southern army.

"We're running these devils hard before the really deep snow sets in, or they'll spend the next three months trying to kick their way out of their stalls," said Stephen van R. He slapped the muscular neck of his horse as it snorted, stamped, and noisily champed his icy curb.

"You gentlemen are wanted by the General as soon as possible," Henry Livingston said. "You are to go straight up from the ferry."

"Lucky thing you got here when you did," Mr. van R. added, as he reined his nervous horse around. "A few more days, and ice coming down will make crossing hazardous."

As the Albany boys spurred off, the ferry arrived, low-sided and flat-bottomed. Hamilton, Harrison and McHenry stood beside their horses for the journey across the black Hudson. The ferrymen stayed busy, periodically poling away the substantial chunks of ice that rushed at them.

Then, in his best military posture, Hamilton trotted toward the house. In spite of the cold and his weariness, he was elated.

At the door, they dismounted. They had begun to loosen girths and drop saddlebags on the ground, when the front door opened. Although Albany was on the edge of the frontier, the Blacks who emerged wore bright livery.

"Colonel Hamilton! Welcome to General Schuyler's house, sir."

"Thank you, Prince." Hamilton remembered the tall, distinguished man from his last visit. "Good to see you again."

Prince beamed, pleased by Hamilton's memory and by his politeness.

"Jimmie here will see your horses are blanketed and fed, gentlemen." He extended a hand in graceful welcome. "Please, gentlemen, go straight in to Mrs. Schuyler."

* * *

Upstairs, there was a small commotion. Betsy, who had been sitting for much of every day in a window seat, dutifully sewing her trousseau where she could keep an eye on the snowy road, had seen them approaching. Peggy leapt up, too, and together they scrubbed an open place on the frost-laced window.

It was a shock to actually see him. It had been so long, almost six months, her memory supported by the miniature that young Charles Peale had painted, that, and the beautiful script of his troubling letters.

Hamilton's hat was jammed onto his head. When he'd bent to unsaddle the horse, the same upon which he had carried her off into the Morristown woods, Betsy saw his ginger queue against the back of a faded Continental overcoat.

"Oh! That's him, isn't it?"

Betsy said nothing in reply. A sensation rushed through her, something close to fear.

"Come on!" Peggy exclaimed. "What are you waiting for?"

Betsy wasn't sure why, but she was reluctant. Still, she allowed her sister to tow her out into the frigid center hall, past the panoramic wallpaper and down the stairs. The girls knew that Mrs. Schuyler was in her sitting room below, spinning with her servants. Because Papa was away, that was where Prince would take visitors.

149

"Will you come?" Peggy, impatiently tugged her along. "Why are you dragging?" Carelessly, without knocking, she threw open the door.

Mrs. Schuyler, her pregnancy now advanced, was seated, her feet warmed by a closed footstool comfortingly full of coals. By the fire stood three young officers in travel-stained blue and buff, smelling of horse and cold and wet wool.

Oh, there he was! So thin, and, in spite of the beard, just as Betsy remembered. Bows and curtseys were exchanged. Peggy was presented. Out of the corner of her eye, Betsy could see Mama pressing her lips together, blue eyes twinkling, perhaps at their restraint.

There he stood, the same man who'd written her all those letters, a regular flood of them, from the camp of General Washington! Even through his beard Betsy could see that his fair, faintly freckled skin had taken the cold badly. His hair seemed redder than she'd remembered and his eyes fixed upon her, blazing like a hot weather sky.

Solemnly, blushing, Betsy extended her hand. Alexander bowed over it. His nose was icy. His lips were rough.

"I know I'm not much to look at, Miss Elizabeth," he said. "I should have cleaned up before greeting you."

"Oh, my dear Hamilton!"

She stepped into his arms. A wild joy spilled through her as those cracked lips brushed her forehead, her cheek, and, then, at last, her mouth. The hunger a mere sip conveyed! Betsy felt his lean body pressed to hers, smelled the long winter journey—salty horse sweat, leather, wood smoke, and the rank goose grease. Somehow, it was all intoxicating—even the grease.

There were smiles of satisfaction all around. Peggy was particularly delighted. Her pretty hands flew together, her "How romantic" almost audible. In Betsy's arms Hamilton shivered, a deep involuntary trembling which came from way down deep.

"As we have told your esteemed mama, we are certainly honored to be here." McHenry's voice filled the silence. "We are sorry to look as bad as we do, but we met the young Patroon at the ferry and he told us to come up directly."

"We'll get you clean before supper," Mrs. Schuyler replied. "You can do it by basin, or, if you will risk it, you may bathe. We take those in our laundry house, but we'll make certain it's plenty warm."

* * *

Each day was filled with visiting, with coasting and skating. Every evening was full of dancing, roasting chestnuts and popping corn. The wedding date had been set for less than two weeks away. Nevertheless, after a week of giddy play in the company of friends and relatives, Betsy began, once again, to worry.

She was to marry this man, who by his own admission was poor, whose only fortune was his person—his wit and drive, his charm, his intelligence and good looks. When Betsy gazed into Alexander's radiant eyes, she saw affection and pleasure, but she might, she thought, have seen exactly the same expression if she were Peggy—or Angelica.

Of course, it was understandable. Men had always paid court to her pretty, flirtatious sisters; that was simply the way it was. Now, suddenly, it made her miserable.

Even as bride-to-be, I can't command precedence.

In the midst of the merry whirlwind of sleighing and skating and dining, she sometimes felt as if she had disappeared.

* * *

The wedding took place in the yellow parlor in front of a crackling hearth. The Dutch Reformed minister performed the ceremony and everyone who was anyone for miles around attended. The room was packed with patriot gentry,

151

all turned out in their finest wigs and lace. The young men present were almost universally in blue and buff.

Hamilton had gone to the expense of outfitting himself anew before the trip north and today he looked resplendent in a crisp new uniform. The epaulets of Lieutenant Colonel gleamed on his shoulders; his chest was crossed by the green sash worn by the aides de camp of a commanding general. His hair had been powdered, but not quite enough to extinguish a gingery glitter. Everyone agreed; he looked overwhelmingly handsome.

"If Mama hadn't had all these months to prepare, I'm afraid my little sister would look like a hen pheasant beside that beautiful fellow." Angelica whispered waspishly to the only woman present she considered her peer, tall blonde Arietta van Corlear. Diamond earrings flashed against creamy necks as the belles approvingly surveyed the lithe figure of the groom.

Still, few others present would have agreed. For the ceremony, Betsy had been transformed into a perfect, fashion plate angel. She had submitted to wearing a wig (sent through enemy lines from Philadelphia), which provided her with a tumble of snowy curls. Beneath this, her olive skin, black eyes, and long dark lashes made a magnificent contrast. Mama had insisted upon applying a delicate lamb's wool brush of rouge to her high cheekbones, which hollowed the Dutch fullness. Her dress was a cream-colored sacque trimmed with lace and white satin bows.

When she entered the room upon the arm of her father, a number of Hudson valley cousins suffered unanticipated pangs of regret. Was this radiant bride really their own sweet, plain "Little Saint Bess"?

"They make a lovely couple." Peggy sighed and slipped an arm around the waist of her younger cousin, Eliza van Rensselaer. Peggy had earlier confided to Miss van R. that she herself was secretly "a little in love with that rascal Alexander."

152

The hordes of tow-headed children had been cautioned, and the fire in Mrs. Schuyler's eyes was sufficient to convince the most rambunctious that she meant business.

At the conclusion of the ceremony, a plain gold band, an heirloom from long ago Amsterdam, was slipped onto the bride's delicate finger. The old-fashioned lace veil that had belonged to Grandmother Engeltie Livingston Van Rensselaer was turned back, and Colonel Hamilton, in his blue and buff uniform, gave his lovely blacked-eyed Betsy a worshipful kiss.

Mrs. Schuyler leaned on her husband's arm. She, too, was radiant. Within, the baby she carried stirred restlessly, enlivened by the triumphant emotion which coursed through her mother like the Hudson in full flood. To see her beloved daughter handed properly from father to husband, married in the midst of this sea of relations, was a supreme moment.

By nightfall snow and ice pattered at the windows, another storm roaring in. The Schuyler home, packed full, was a haven of light and warmth.

The guests gorged on a dinner of beef, roast potatoes, dishes of onions and gravy, turnips and hot applesauce. Most of the gentlemen, and even a few of the ladies, drank too much of General Schuyler's excellent whiskey.

In the downstairs great room, fiddlers and dancers grew tired. The female guests, full of chatter and laughter, were on their way up the narrow twisting stair to crowd into large bedrooms floored with mattresses. Betsy was among them, accompanied by Mama, her sisters and her slave, Ruby.

At the door to the little nursery, tonight converted to a bridal chamber, a line of cousins formed. One by one they kissed, teased, and whispered advice along with their goodnights.

The great house glowed. Smoke blew into an angry wind from each of the seven chimneys. Fires had been laid everywhere earlier so that it would be warm, at least while everyone undressed.

Betsy sat before the mirror. Her dark hair had been twisted, coiled, and pinned flat beneath the wig.

"Lord! Why did I ever let you talk me into wearing it? My hair looks smothered." She lifted a limp strand, stared into the mirror with dismay.

Angelica's oval face appeared over her shoulder.

"A hundred strokes will fix it. Isn't that so, Mama?"

"It will. And when one arm tires, another can take over. The men are talking politics. There will be plenty of time to get her pretty."

Angelica giggled. "Especially if Colonel Hamilton gets hold of the bit of discourse. Do you suppose he'll fall so deep in discussion that he'll forget it's his wedding night?"

"Somehow, I doubt there's a man in the world who could do that. Not even that one."

Black Ruby was the first to brush, smiling dreamily into the mirror over her mistress's dark head. Both mistress and maid were glowing with the tender shine of love, for Ruby had a sweetheart, too, a freed man who labored for the Schuylers. Her father said it was an extravagant gesture, one she would soon regret, but before Betsy went away with Hamilton, she intended to free Ruby and see her married.

The brushing went on until sparks flew. Then Black Ruby paused and dabbed a little sweet oil on her palms. After rubbing it in, she began to run strong black fingers through her mistress's hair.

"Don't go on too long," Angelica cautioned. "We still have to get her undressed and into bed."

"Which reminds me. Are the bed ropes tight?" Mrs. Schuyler asked the question, but giggles followed anyway. Black Ruby replied solemnly, "Yes, Mistress. I pulled 'em myself."

Ice tapped the window. Fire crackled. The brushing went on until Betsy's hair was restored to a raven shine. Then Mrs. Schuyler brought out the bed shift she and Betsy had worked. It was of sensible white flannel, but it had been embroidered across the bosom with pink flowers and was closed with tape woven from pink silk thread.

* * *

Hot and crowded, the room was full of men and blue smoke. A whiskey bottle, filled with a powerful home-distilled essence, made circuits of the table.

"It is a great honor and a great pleasure to enjoy your most generous hospitality, sir," Harrison declared to General Schuyler. "It has been out of memory since any of us military men have enjoyed such comfort, or partaken of such a feast."

"Indeed," Hamilton said, "but at the same time, I can't help feeling guilty. I'll swear none of the men we've left behind are sleeping so soundly or eating so well."

"Indeed. 'Tis shameful what has come to pass with our army. No pay, no food, no clothing," said McHenry. "Every day at headquarters we struggle to obtain supplies, written promise our only coin. Meanwhile, Congress occupies itself with trifles. This, while patriots freeze and starve!"

"In my studies, I read it is the way of Republics to feel hostility towards their army, and suspicion, too, no matter how meritorious the army's conduct."

"Well, Colonel Hamilton," said Mr. Yates, an attorney and landowner, "from your studies you must have also learned there are good reasons for this. Many examples may be plucked from history, particularly from the fall of the Greek and Roman Republics."

"Nevertheless, although the provocation furnished to our army has been extreme, we have yet to see a mutiny our Leaders have not been able to quell by plain force of reason. Ingratitude to those who labor appears to be the natural inclination of the human heart."

"Yes, Congress does not seem to believe that it should honor promises made to the army," said McHenry, "Promises made to these men who have given so much."

155

"Yet the states are much put-upon. Have we not suffered losses of crops and trade by the incursion of the British army? What, I ask you, are we supposed to pay taxes with?" One of the Livingston clan protested.

At this juncture, the parson removed his pipe from his mouth to intercede. "Is there no solution then, within the laws of our present Confederation?" He knew they were all republicans, but differences on exactly what kind of a republic they should establish ran deep, especially between the older generation of landowners and the young bloods of the army.

"There is no remedy in the present Constitution, I fear," Hamilton said. "We are thirteen distinct sovereign states, nine of whom must agree upon the necessity of raising revenue. Even after we surmount this hurdle, the delinquencies of every state have grown until the government does not function at all. Each state sets a higher priority upon its own interests and convenience than upon what ought to be the greater interest of the Confederation. One by one, they've withdrawn support from what is a common cause. The result is as we see. An army of patriots without clothes, provisions or pay, one which is learning to scorn the people—and hate the Congress too—for this deplorable neglect."

"I believe the present evil is far more dangerous to the survival of our republic than any evil which is merely projected." The old General tugged at his pipe.

In the far corner, however, there was a small circle of discontent. "Behold a bridegroom who has not yet enjoyed the bride, but finds time to talk politics with old men!" Henry Livingston muttered this scornfully to his neighbor, another cousin. Shaking his head in disbelief, he poured himself another shot of his host's whiskey. The marriage of Cousin Betsy to this "West Indian Upstart" reeked of criminal trespass.

"Which is exactly why he has been granted the hand of a Schuyler daughter." One of Henry's elder relatives made the caution in an undertone. "Now, he's family."

Close to the fire the war talk continued.

"There are those of us in Congress who argue for solid arrangements of finance, but it is a sermon which falls on deaf ears," General Schuyler said. "The mass of our fellow legislators do not seem to comprehend that their prating of liberty is rendered by their neglect, little more than inconsequential rhetoric. By not attending to our finances, we put ourselves in danger from foreigners with an appetite for conquest, and also from the disaffections of our mistreated army."

"You cannot give a body the power to vote taxes and not the power to collect them. It defies all reason." This came from McHenry. His freckled face was red from whiskey and proximity to the fire.

"But isn't that giving too much power away to the Executive?" Edward Westerlo asked. "Is this not the slippery slope? Will we not end by exchanging the tyranny of Parliament for the tyranny of some set of individuals? To a general, perhaps, backed by his army?"

"Any new system of government would have to be established only after deep and careful deliberation," said Schuyler. "I agree with you, sir, there is far too much to lose in rushing to some new arrangement without proper judgment."

"Gentlemen," Hamilton began, "may we not agree that it is our national character which is of prime importance? It has been a system in many states, even before the war, to forget their promises whenever it was inconvenient to keep them. This can only bring Government at home into contempt and must destroy our ability to negotiate with other powers. After all, the arrears on the public debt is growing. We shall need foreign loans in order to continue the war. Moreover, it is unconscionable to ask a man to be a soldier without pay."

"But we are New Yorkers, sir, and you, Colonel—begging your pardon—cannot truly know what it is to be born a citizen of a noble American state." This was Edward van Rijn. "These local powers, and our individuality, must

157

be maintained. They are essential to freedom, to our ancient, common law freedoms."

Hamilton paused, and then said, "We must begin to think continentally, sir. I ask you, is there not something noble in the perspective of a great Federal Republic, closely linked in the pursuit of common interests, for instance, in the establishment of trade? As a man of business, you know we cannot preserve our national character without paying our debts. Moreover, it is quite clear, especially to those of us in the army, that we cannot maintain an effective union without a source of revenue."

"If we are not united under a Federal Government," General Schuyler added, "I believe we will infallibly fall into conflicts with one another, and this will certainly attract European adventurers, eager to build empires upon our backs. The human passions never want for objects of hostility. We must have peace and security, both without and within."

"Congress must have power competent to deal with our emergency. Without sufficient power in an executive branch...." McHenry began.

"'Tis a danger to any republic, sirs," Edward van Rijn interrupted, "to have great power gathered in one place."

"You cannot run a government where no one is in charge, sir," Hamilton replied. "Our troubles are proof of it."

"Ah, but military men are naturally inclined towards obedience to some supreme authority."

"You cannot have a living body which sports thirteen legs and no head, which is the brainless monster we've got now," said McHenry.

A pause followed as each side studied the other.

"Beggin' your pardon, gentlemen." A voice came from a corner of the room, a humble Captain Ackermann whose farm bordered the northern forest. "I'm hearin' quite a bit of theory here. As a plain fightin' man, it seems, sirs, that some of you are kind o' like Indians worryin' about bein' attacked by fantastical flyin' heads, when a whole tribe of

Shawnee is what's really stalkin' ye. With respect, I be'leve it's as Colonel Hamilton says. It plain lacks honor to starve them as have given blood for ye."

Without a word, Hamilton lifted his glass and drank a salute to the humble speaker, who was flushed and abashed at having voiced an opinion among all these gentlemen.

"Now, if you will excuse me, sirs." Hamilton set his glass down with a firm click upon the cherry table. "A certain matter awaits my attention, a matter perhaps unequal to the import of the present discussion. However, I beg that you gentlemen will understand and pardon my leave taking."

"Yes, for God's sake! Stop talking and get thee to thy wife, Hamilton."

Seconded by much laughter, McHenry waved his glass widely in the direction of door.

* **

A gust of cold from the corridor billowed the curtains. From the hearth came an answering tinkle and creak as flames of blue and rose burst from the heart of a fat, ash scalloped log. The bed was not really in the sphere of warmth anymore.

Betsy slept. After a lifetime of sharing a bed, it was neither strange nor alarming when someone got in beside her. Only after he'd stroked her cheek and kissed it, only after she'd caught the scent of man and whiskey, did memory open her eyes.

Alexander was looking down with a tender expression. He'd taken the time to comb all the powder out of his red gold hair, and through the open neck of his shirt she caught a glimpse of a hard, faintly freckled chest. Betsy was thankful she didn't have to watch him undress—at least tonight—before what was to come.

"Sound asleep on your wedding night, Mrs. Hamilton?"

"Yes." She rubbed her eyes.

"A sensible decision, as your father insisted upon adjusting all the troubles of America before I could come to you."

He dropped a kiss upon her nose. There it was again, the smell of Papa's whiskey. A strong, slim body moved against hers. Betsy closed her eyes and let him press her into the pillow with a kiss that was very long and very sweet.

"You do that so well." Alexander sighed as his lips released hers. Purposefully, he brushed off her nightcap, releasing the tide of black silk that had been loosely wound beneath. "My Betsy!" He slipped his fingers through the luxurious darkness. "Oh, my nut-brown maid." He sang the tune as he nuzzled close. "Are you waking up?"

When she solemnly answered "yes," he kissed her again, more hungrily this time.

"Remember what I said last summer?" His fingers began to toy with the silk tape that closed her nightdress. "I'm a man of my word, you know."

There was an edge to this, for a husband's pleasure could be—*anything*. Reality—the grunting couplings she'd stumbled upon in woods and barn—hadn't been very pretty, not much like Mama's simple, mechanical explanation or Angelica's whispered tales of passionate embraces with her handsome Jack, her descriptions purpled with words from romantic novels, like "delirium" and "ecstasy."

"Oh, my Betsy," Hamilton murmured again. "So many times I've dreamed of this."

Then, without further prelude, he caught the hem of her nightgown and drew it up.

* * *

The gentlemen in the downstairs parlor, enjoying yet another round of toasts, fell silent at the sound. Then the Comte d'Manduit, his wig now somewhat askew, arose unsteadily and lifted his glass.

160

"A man and a maid! More eloquent, more moving than the finest aria in the finest opera!"

The Americans weren't too sure about "aria" and "opera," but they caught the gist. D'Manduit's solemn toast, glass raised towards the ceiling, roused the table to a cheerful roar. Everyone who could stand, did, glasses in hand.

"A man and a maid!"

"Good Lord!" McHenry, removed his handkerchief to mop a pale, freckled forehead. The room where the men had gathered was blue with smoke and ferociously hot. More to the point, he'd drunk prodigious amounts of the general's fine home distillation.

"I sincerely hope Ham hasn't rushed the business." No one heard, for beside him plump Harrison was sound asleep, his head down, encircled by a dusting of powder upon the shining surface of the cherry table.

Someone, however, had heard. General Schuyler, seated directly across, stolidly pushed the never empty bottle in his direction. "Another toast, Colonel McHenry," he commanded thickly, "To the start of a fine red-headed grandson."

* * *

The entire plantation slowed to a standstill. New snow had made all work, with the formidable exception of feeding the animals and lugging water and wood, impossible. Besides, the Master, like his guests and servants, was profoundly hung over. Breakfast was a late and mostly masculine affair. There were Betsy's younger brothers, the French officers, a few male cousins and McHenry, Harrison and Major General Schuyler, and they raised a good-humored, teasing cheer when Hamilton appeared at the door.

There was much bluff bluster about the missing females and a good deal of banter directed at the bridegroom. Alexander parried all their thrusts with good humor, although he wasn't an impervious target. The blush he raised gratified his tormentors.

Breakfast was taken in a leisurely fashion straight from the sideboard. The tea and cornbread were fresh and hot, but the rest, the cheese and hunks of cold beef, the cut pumpkin, apple and game pies, were remains of last night's feast.

Alexander loaded his plate and came to sit beside McHenry, who was at the end of the long table, sipping tea and scribbling something.

"It's an epithalamium for you," his friend explained.

Last night I sought her dear retreat
And laid me at the fair one's feet
As thus ye lay the happiest pair,
A rosy scent enriched the air
While to a music softly sounding
Breathing, panting, slow, rebounding
Love arose with powerful spell…

"That's improperly warm." Hamilton interrupted.

"My poem," McHenry replied with dignity, "is most oblique and delicate. 'Tis only yourself, sir, that is improperly warm." He paused, eyed his companion, and broke into a wide grin. "And how is the gentle Mrs. Hamilton this morning? Quite exhausted?"

"Mac!"

"I'm serious, my friend."

Hamilton cocked a sandy brow.

"We in the parlor, in spite of how drunk and noisy we were, noted the initial incursion upon the lady's chastity."

Hamilton flushed to the roots of his hair. McHenry chuckled.

"I see you're proud of yourself. And perhaps you should be. You stirred up such a tempest that there wasn't a willing female in this house, old or young, black or white, who lacked a partner last night. By the way, the Comte de Manduit gave you an accolade. He felt sure you had French

162

ancestry. Although it ruffled our British and Dutch feathers, he insisted that only a Frenchman would possess so much stamina."

"As a matter of fact, my mother's family were Huguenot."

An image had formed of a beautiful dark-haired woman, swaying in strong arms, framed against the starry velvet of tropical night. Alexander opened his eyes wide, stared hard at the butter sliding off the hot cornbread onto his plate, suddenly desperate to send that memory back to the underworld from which it had risen.

* * *

Day and night the trees rubbed their icy limbs and groaned. The Dutch called it "The Storm King," the roaring wind now sweeping the land. Sleet enrobed the trees and gave the drifts a shattering, knife-sharp hide. Without snow shoes, the legs of any cross-country traveler would be cut to ribbons. The Iroquois, trapped inside their long lodges, called this time "The Moon of Sore Eyes."

Warmth and comfort held sway inside the Schuyler mansion. More visitors came. Vicomte Chastellux arrived at Christmas, rowed across a Hudson now nearly choked with ice. Then, for hours, Philip Schuyler, Angelica and Alexander sat and chatted with him in French, a rapid flow of which Betsy could catch only a little.

At last the storms subsided, and a clear, shining cold arrived. Wind ripped the snow from the now completely frozen river.

It was time to take a sleighing trip to see the glittering blue-white motionless waterfall at Cohoes. On the way back, the party stopped to skate upon the river.

To Betsy it was strange to be handed into the sleigh, to have a blanket thrown over herself and her husband, to feel his cold hands touch her, to know that everywhere she was his. How different from their drives in Morristown last year, when he had diffidently played with her fingers and worshipfully kissed the tips! Now when his hand moved in

163

that proprietary way beneath the blanket, memories of night came back.

As a girl, Betsy had pondered the business of sex, had been both disgusted and intrigued. She was a participant in the business now, but somehow nothing had changed, except the intensity of emotion. Her cheeks ached from blushing. When sitting in the parlor and feeling the eyes of the Vicomte d'Chastellux fall upon her, she could practically hear his wicked French mind working.

"Let me introduce you, Vicomte, to my bride," Alexander said, pride of ownership ringing in his voice. She groped for understanding as that fierce-eyed veteran made a flourishing bow over her hand. She thought she understood that she "was a lovely blossom that had flowered into fair womanhood amongst the snows."

For the first time in her life, there was no one to confide in. The teasing of her sisters and the whispers of the servants (every one of whom seemed to have fallen in love with the charming and vivacious Alexander) left her feeling quite alone.

It really isn't his fault. She watched her husband chatting so easily with those elegant French officers. For him, this is exactly right. *His manhood is confirmed, the urgings of his body are satisfied; his heart is warmed by possession.*

Hamilton glittered. As beautiful as he'd been to her last winter when he'd been so ardently courting, now, he blazed like a comet. Peggy and Angelica were never done sighing about him.

"Oh, Betsy! Dear Heaven, what a catch!"

"He's so witty! So chivalrous!"

"So handsome and clever! So much fun!"

Betsy knew she was glowing, too, but that was another source of embarrassment.

They all know.

Those Frenchman, Papa, even young John and Philip Jeremiah seemed to know what her husband did with her every night. She wanted to hide, to curl up unnoticed in the

164

bed that she and her sisters had shared as children. Betsy found herself retreating from the company for naps, which, naturally, only brought renewed avalanches of teasing down upon her head.

There were more dances between Christmas and the Epiphany. She blushed and blushed as every friend and relative for miles around took turns teasing her. Blushed and blushed until at last, one evening, she burst into tears and rushed out of the room.

Oh, to be Angelica!

She opened a door, seeking a hiding place in the freezing upstairs.

Angelica can glitter like Alexander does, glitter and glitter, bright as Jupiter on a January night. She laughs and cleverly turns jokes against the jokers....

* * *

When Hamilton found her at last, she was lying on Peggy's bed, breathless from weeping.

"Don't touch me!"

Alexander halted immediately. She sounded desperate and fierce.

"They all know—and I can't stand it!"

There was something wild in her voice. Alexander could see it in the sharp rise and fall of her small shoulders. He set the candle on the trunk that stood at the foot of the bed. Perhaps at a distance he would seem more harmless.

"What do you mean? Everyone is saying how beautiful you are. Everyone wants to congratulate you."

"On what? Because I sweat under you every night like some—some public woman?" The loathing in her voice struck him like a sword.

From below arose the cheerful wail of a fiddle and the thump of dancing feet. In the great room just beyond the door, voices and a fleeting giggle came and went as Peggy, pretending to search for Betsy, but actually taking the opportunity to get lost upstairs with some suitor, passed by.

165

Alexander reached slowly to stroke her cheek, but Betsy recoiled violently.

"No! You'll only start!" She was shaking, teeth chattering in the frigid room. Alexander was growing cold, too, the sweat of dancing freezing on him.

"Don't be afraid. Only tell me what's wrong."

Her dark doe's eyes rolled upward, filled with such terrible anguish that he sprang to throw his arms around her.

"No! No! Don't! Get away!"

She fought like a mad woman, kicking and clawing, but he forced her to accept his body against hers. He didn't do anything else, simply asserted his claim to hold her.

"Tell me what's wrong. Tell me. I love you! You know I do. And you love me too!"

Words! His words! Betsy thought of how he flirted with all the girls, with Angelica and Peggy. That charm of which he was a master!

Does he mean what he says?

The question was more terrible than surrender. She went limp in his arms.

After cradling her for a few minutes, he finally said firmly, "We've got to get warm. Come, let's go to our room. There's a fire."

When she pushed away, he added, "Just to talk. I promise."

* * *

In their bedroom, where a small fire had already been lit, he set about soothing. He desperately wanted to drop kisses on those thin shoulders, but instinct warned him to refrain.

He tried to contain himself, but with each denial he felt angrier.

"Have your way, then! I'll sleep on the floor if that's what you want!"

As soon as the words were out of his mouth, fury took him. Using all his strength, he threw Betsy against the bed, so that she stumbled and fell onto it.

I should slap her!

All at once they were unstoppable, his own tears. Feeling as if he'd gone mad, knowing only that he didn't want to risk hurting her anymore, he ran for the door. His hand was on the latch when she dashed to catch him, arms enclosing his waist.

"Don't be angry! Don't!" Her face had changed, softened, become full of—*pity!*

She knows too much, damn her! Why did I ever confide? Those shame-filled stories about a lost father, a wandering mother—even about a dirty mattress on a scorpion-haunted floor....No wonder she doesn't want me....!

He seized her arms, tried to hurl her away again, but this time she clung with a fierce desperation, like a terrified cat.

"Don't leave! Please!" There was a wild despair in those beautiful dark eyes, a doe savaged by dogs.

Rage, like water from a breached cask, abruptly gushed away. Now, he was sick, dizzy—*afraid.*

"Oh, my dearest Betsy! What have I done?"

Shame, contrition sucked away the last of his strength. Alexander crumpled, fingers still clutching his wife's arms, until they slumped together against the door.

When he drew her close this time, there was no resistance. They wept in each other's arms.

* * *

"I love you, Alexander. I do! I do! But it frightens me, frightens me so much."

It was impossible to say aloud what her fear was, how when they made love and she lost herself....

She recognized experience in his hands. He calculated her response, exactly as her father calculated his next move when he was in the process of harness breaking a reluctant horse. Each time she shared the ecstasy he knew so well how to give, she was bound to him with yet another chain.

167

Hamilton tried to swallow his own tears while rhythmically stroking her small back. "Loving you— frightens me, too."

When she, startled, raised her tear-stained face to look into his eyes, she saw fear, an emotion she'd only seen in him once before, on the fateful night he'd asked for her hand.

"Yes. Oh, Betsy! You see, you must love me. You must! Always!"

He pressed his forehead against hers. For a long time they stayed in place, stiffening legs folded beneath them, holding onto one another, ignoring the freezing draft pouring under the door.

**

One by one, the company at the Schuyler house departed. Just after Epiphany, Hamilton set out down river to rejoin General Washington's winter encampment at New Windsor, his little black horse tapping along the frozen, wind-swept back of the Hudson. Soon after he arrived, he sought and found a room in the village for his bride.

Chapter Eight ~ A Field Command

They hadn't been at Headquarters a month before Hamilton had a furious falling out with General Washington. In a rage, he resigned his duties and then wrote to her father justifying his action. He raved to Betsy, telling her his dignity had been trampled, about how he couldn't support the abuse Washington daily dished out for a minute longer.

"After all the work I've done, the fool's errands I've undertaken, the donkey, the slave I've been to that Virginia tyrant! He dares to insult me, to treat me like his servant—with Lafayette looking on! By God, if anyone else had spoken to me the way he did, I would have called him out."

That His Excellency had a ferocious temper and a lacerating edge to his tongue was no secret. The impossible situation in which Washington had labored for the last five years had effectively shortened an already short temper.

Hamilton's sudden falling out with his staunchest patron was inexplicable. Betsy couldn't understand why he'd suddenly chosen to despise his most important connection. As she saw it, General Washington's good opinion had been instrumental in convincing her papa to allow them to marry. When Washington actually sent an apology through Tench Tilghman, she believed Alexander would relent.

To her astonishment, he haughtily refused. He replied to Tilghman coldly, like a stranger instead of a friend with whom he'd worked for four years. From being a central part of the great General's family, enfolded in the highest prestige of any young man in the Revolutionary Army, he cast himself out, willfully chose a path that left him with neither position nor command.

When Betsy begged him to reconsider, Alexander turned the same stranger's face upon her he'd shown Tilghman.

"You mustn't interfere when it is a matter of my honor."

169

His unrelenting coldness frightened her. She could hear echoes of their winter quarrel, of his now demonstrated capacity for violence.

"Well," Betsy forced herself to say, "What does Papa think?" She knew he'd seized a pen and written a letter to her father almost in the next instant.

"Your good and just father has been most understanding." The reply, just arrived, was handed over. "He is not particularly happy about what I've done, but in his opinion I have committed no impropriety."

Alexander's slim blue-coated figure strode away, marched to stand before the ice-glazed window. "His Excellency must now give me the thing I desire most in the world. A field command."

"A field command?" If he'd slapped her across the face, she couldn't have been more astonished—or more hurt.

"Why, yes. I've spent enough of this war sitting on my ass, playing scribe for His High and Mightyness. My honor requires that I again serve our Cause with arms."

"But His Excellency says you're invaluable to him! Papa says that if he'd had an aide with just half your talent, he'd still be commanding the northern army."

"Why must I repeat, Mrs. Hamilton, that this is a matter which concerns my honor?" In his eyes she saw the warning angry flash.

Betsy sat on the bed, folded her hands and looked down. At home there would have been plenty of retreats, but here there was none. It was clear she was supposed to accept his decision without comment, even though he'd clearly taken leave of his senses. There was not a shred of Alexander's vaunted logic in throwing away his hard-won place at the side of General Washington.

"Oh, Betsy! Don't you understand? You know I entered the war in the line, that I used all my resources for that artillery company. I fought beside my men at New York and White Plains, at Trenton and Princeton. If I don't see action again, people will say that I'm a coward. They'll say

170

I spent this war hiding behind Washington, safe at headquarters."

She was comforted a little. Not so much by his words, but by the fact that he, apparently repenting his sharpness, rejoined her on the bed and put an arm around her.

"Nothing will happen soon. I've promised to stay with His Excellency until Colonel Humphrey comes back from his leave."

And after that? Well, it was impossible to say.

"If everything goes against me, I might just resign my commission and begin studying for the bar."

When she looked up, eyes full of undisguised hope, he chided, "You don't really want that, do you? Surely General Schuyler's daughter is a noble Roman wife, not a selfish American one."

How like him to get on *that* high horse! She knew the answer she was supposed to give, that like the proud women of Sparta, she would rejoice to have him come home dead on his shield. Her eyes filled, but she hid her tears in silence against his shoulder. She couldn't muster the strength for another word.

For the next few weeks, business at headquarters went on with no indication that anything was amiss. His Excellency remained a glacial height that occasionally spilled fire. Alexander was the one who seemed different. He was formal and unsmiling. Without his cheerful ebullience, the atmosphere at headquarters became markedly gloomy.

Washington and his lady took a brief trip to Albany to stand godparents for Betsy's newest baby sister, christened "Catherine" for her mother. Betsy went on doing whatever she could to be useful, making no distinction between whether it was a lady's job or simply a woman's.

She continued Martha's work, knitting heaps of socks and mittens for the men and spinning thread out of ravelings. She sewed for Alex, for Tilghman, McHenry and the other aides, patching and praying over repairs on jackets and pants that had been ridden seatless.

After Martha returned to Virginia to oversee the spring planting, Betsy prepared cakes and poured tea to the approbation of visiting dignitaries. General Washington, in his stiff, courtly fashion, made plain that he appreciated anything she could do to relieve him of time-consuming social duties.

When Hamilton officially left the General's family, the couple followed the army down to De Peyster's Point, where they took a room with a farm family. Her husband was still hoping for that field command, but there seemed to be nothing Washington could or would do for him.

They stayed only a few weeks, while her husband spoke or wrote to everyone who might help him obtain the desired command.

Washington continued to refuse Hamilton's petitions. Granting such a request when Hamilton hadn't been promoted in the routine way, through the Line, would only lead to bad feelings among the regular army. His Excellency refused to make such an exception for anyone.

At the end of April, when the ice had gone rushing down the Hudson in a grinding, mountainous torrent, they boarded one of General Schuyler's sloops and sailed up river to Albany. Philip Schuyler was concerned about his new son-in-law's decision, but he didn't lecture.

Alone with Peggy, Betsy discussed the situation. The sisters agreed that the whole business, from beginning to end, was astonishing, not only Alexander's behavior, but their father's reticence in giving the young man advice.

Release from the constant labor of headquarters only made Hamilton unendurably restless. To fill his time, he wrote a series of pieces for the Fishkill newspaper signed *"The Continentalist."* The series argued for fiscal responsibility and against the various regional prejudices that crippled the war effort. Betsy was asked to help by copying these, and so, for long hours, she sat by his side and performed the task. She didn't know it then, but it was only the first of what was to be twenty years of marriage to

172

a man who fervently believed in the power of his pen to persuade.

"Our whole system is in disorder; our currency depreciated, till in many places it will hardly obtain a circulation at all. Public credit is at its lowest ebb, our army deficient in numbers, and unprovided with everything. The government, in its present condition, unable to command the means to pay, clothe or feed their troops...The great defect of the Confederation is that it gives the United States no property; or, in other words, no revenue, nor the means of acquiring it. And power without revenue, in political society, is a name. While Congress continues altogether dependent on the occasional grants of several states for the means of defraying the expenses of the Federal Government, it can neither have dignity, vigor, nor credit. Credit supposes specific and permanent funds for the punctual payment of interest, with a moral certainty of the final redemption of the principal."

Alexander and Papa had long conversations every night about this. They despaired over the ramshackle Continental Congress, which did little but quarrel. The progress of the war had almost been halted by the inability of the government to raise money to pay and supply the troops.

Then, the spring day came when Alexander received a letter from Tilghman. It sent him racing into the study for a conference with her father.

"What has happened?" Betsy had been on her way to the kitchen wing when she met Hamilton, now heading purposefully upstairs. Prince, a packing case in hand, was behind him.

"Go on up and get started, Mr. Prince," Alexander directed. "I'll be up in a moment." Then, with a sheepish expression, he took her hand. "I'm going down to Dobbs Ferry tomorrow. Tilghman writes that I should."

"Why?" Fear laid on an icy finger.

"Because he believes I can get a field command if I'm on the spot next week."

173

"Hamilton! No!"

"I <u>have</u> to do this. Haven't we discussed it?"

Betsy picked up her skirts and fled the length of the great room back to the parlor where she had been sewing with her mother and sisters. Mrs. Schuyler comforted, but she scolded a little, too.

"Of course you are upset, darling, but Hamilton is a patriot, after all, and this war is far from over. You wouldn't remember, of course, but your papa went away to England for three whole years just after Peggy was born. That was no easy time for me."

"But he wasn't going to war!"

"You know the story, my dear. When the ship's captain died on the high seas, your father had to pilot the ship. Then they were captured by a French man of war and he was almost carried back to France in irons. If that's not being in mortal danger, I don't know what is."

Her mother was just warming to a retelling of the hardships of her past, when a servant put her head in the door and asked Betsy to go the library. When she arrived, Philip Schuyler took his daughter's hand and began to speak of her husband's high sense of duty to the American Cause.

"The wife of such a husband ought to be proud. Hamilton believes that not only his honor, but his duty lies in serving in the Line. I'm sure I don't have to remind you that it is *your* duty to assist your husband."

Eyes bright with tears, Betsy endured. Upstairs, she knew, preparations for her husband's departure went on apace. Before supper, as she tried to ease her mind with sewing, Hamilton came to sit beside her. Although she told him how afraid she was, that she'd die if anything happened to him, he didn't give an inch. How, he said, could she not understand? It was his duty to fight. It was her duty to support his decision.

That night Betsy resolved to sleep with Peggy, but to lose this last night with her husband was simply impossible, no matter how upset she was. When the house had grown

174

quiet, she came on bare feet across the darkened great room to join him.

"Oh, angel," he whispered, opening his arms to receive her. "I'm so glad you came."

In a warm rush he drew her close. "I was just lying here wondering if I dared go to Peggy's room to plead my case."

As he kissed her, Betsy, in a mood of abandon, wrapped herself around him. The eager warmth of the gesture, so unlike her usual shyness, inspired her husband to passion rather than art. Rapture came fast, seized and shook them. When the first thin light returned, Alexander gave Betsy a gentle good morning kiss and then got up, washed in his usual fastidious fashion and started to put on his uniform. Betsy, feeling sick to her stomach and once more nightmarishly distant, watched.

"Will you take breakfast with me, Mrs. Hamilton?" It was a new tack, one that mingled coaxing and formality.

She'd not answered, just shaken her head. After he'd gone down the stairs, Betsy buried her face in the pillow and cried. No matter how much her mother scolded or Peggy begged, she refused to budge. In the end, Hamilton had to return upstairs to say good-bye.

Black hair spilling over her shoulders, she sat up to accept the kiss he offered.

"Godspeed, Colonel Hamilton."

She was frankly glad to see that he too was sad, that no matter what high flown sentiments he expressed, loss and pain weren't hers alone.

"Please don't worry. Everything will be fine. You know I shall miss you terribly. Promise you'll write to me often."

"I shall do my duty as I see it, Colonel, exactly as my husband does."

Hamilton reddened. Betsy felt an angry rush of satisfaction. *Last summer he'd given all those lessons in cruel ambiguity, now let him taste it himself!*

As his footsteps receded, she'd fallen back into their bed, still full of the comforting warmth of his body, and wept again. Nothing anyone said or did helped, for her darling Alexander was gone.

175

About two weeks later, the dreaded letter arrived which confirmed he had secured his field command. She mustn't worry, he'd written. It wasn't likely he'd see any fighting soon.

"Though I know you would be happy to hear that I rejected this proposal, it is a pleasure my reputation would not permit me to afford you."

Heroic equilibrium thoroughly upset by the manner of their parting, Hamilton had ended with a barb:

"I'm lost to all the public and splendid passions and absorbed in you. I'm entirely changed, changed for the worse..."

After reading that, Betsy went back to bed and stayed for two days, inconsolable.

How he hurts me! Me, whose only crime is to love him!

* * *

The sisters gravitated into the same bed, seeking company and long secret chats. Peggy confided to their mother that Betsy was having nightmares almost every night, dreaming that Alexander had been killed.

One night when Peggy was visiting her van Rensselaer grandparents, Betsy had such a terror that it brought Mrs. Schuyler, who'd been up with her new baby, across the great room.

"Eliza, my dear! Whatever is the matter?"

"I dreamed—oh—I dreamed that Hamilton said he'd never loved me! He pushed me away and shouted that loving me brought him nothing but weakness. Oh, Mama! He cannot truly love me. How else can he have gone away?"

"Elizabeth, this must stop." The bed ropes protested while Mrs. Schuyler moved herself in beside her daughter. "I'm too old to be dealing with two babies at once. Kitty is quite enough."

Betsy wiped her eyes. She was ashamed—*yes*—but also she felt so abandoned!

"Now, listen, my darling, it is nothing less than the nature of *that* man to go to *this* war, a cause he carries next to his heart. You must stop being sorry for yourself and admire his courage. You knew who you were marrying, didn't you? I think, Elizabeth, you must be as brave as he is."

Papa's lecture, which Betsy had endured a few days earlier, although with longer words, had been essentially the same. In spite of all this parental advice, any way Betsy looked at it, quitting Washington's service and seeking a field command had been done, not by the wise, brilliant Hamilton everyone so much admired, but by some rash, hot-headed stranger. In the last two months, however, it had become abundantly clear that pointing out his illogic either to Mama or Papa—or, for that matter, to Alexander—was futile.

Betsy sighed. "Oh, Mama, Hamilton is so wrapped up in these noble ideas. I don't always see things as he does. And now I miss him so much and I'm so worried all the time. We've just married but already he's gone again. What if…?"

"If we knew the future, we'd never find the courage to live. Thank God, we don't have to endure foreknowledge, as well as the pain of life itself."

For a few minutes, Mrs. Schuyler rocked her daughter against a milk-full bosom. As Betsy relaxed, her mother whispered, "Now, Mrs. Hamilton, no more fretting about a thing which, please a merciful God, will not come to pass. Let's talk about what's real and right now. You've never been to the rag box once since you've been home. What's the matter, little broody hen, weren't you going to tell anyone, or is it just that you haven't been paying any attention?"

Surprised by the sudden turn in the conversation, Betsy cleared her throat. "Well, it has been three months, but I wasn't sure. You know how I am."

"Betsy" said Mrs. Schuyler, gently pushing back her braid. "As you well know, I can make a baby with little more than a sweet look from your papa. Now don't be such a goose, love, just tell me when your last time was. You know that both your father and your dear husband will be ever so pleased."

* * *

Betsy came downstairs. She'd been sewing in the light of the same window where she had waited for Alexander last winter, but it was August, and the afternoon had grown far too hot. There hadn't been rain in ages and Papa had begun to fret about the crops in the Saratoga patent.

The leaves of the great maples looked silvery, as if they'd turned over. In the branches, cicadas shook their rattles like a thousand tiny Iroquois, but other than that not much was going on. The servants had quit hammering on the new ice house they were building, so that racket had stopped. Mama had put the younger children down for naps and had gone to take one herself.

It was summer at home again, and it felt exactly like so many others. Betsy had the unsettling feeling that the interim, her marriage, the gay, dancing weeks at Christmas, the passionate love making, the terrifying quarrel, the drive down the frozen Hudson, the winter weeks spent playing Colonel's wife in New Windsor where she'd knitted beside Martha Washington and poured tea, had been a dream.

Then Angelica arrived from Boston, an event that contributed to the feeling that nothing had changed—even if her sister did have another big belly on and a toddler in tow. Betsy's first nephew was another Philip, named as a peace offering for his grandfather. Imperious as ever, Angelica had at once ordered up a bath to wash away her ten days journey. She insisted Betsy share it, so they could have a private "married woman's talk."

Betsy was shy, slow undressing. Angelica was cavalier, tossing her clothes into the hands of the latest gift from her

178

wealthy husband, a well-trained exotic-looking slave from the West Indies. Then she stepped into the tub and subsided with a happy sigh into the warm water.

Catherine Schuyler, come to look in on her married daughters, took the opportunity to tease. "See that bump on Mrs. Hamilton's belly, Mrs. Church? Can you tell me what it means?"

Angelica paused in soaping the wash rag, rosy breasts swinging above the water, and stared.

"Oh, how exciting! Why haven't you written? When does my Phil get a Hamilton cousin?"

"Um—ah—Mama says January."

Mrs. Schuyler beamed. "Betsy imagined she could keep it a secret."

"Well," Angelica offered with a cheerful grin, "It simply makes me shiver all over to imagine what you and that adorable Colonel Hamilton have been doing to cause such a thing."

Betsy blushed furiously. Bending over the tub, she struck the water hard, using the side of her hand. Angelica caught the splash right in the face, screamed, and instantly retaliated by kicking.

A water fight as wild as any they'd had in childhood followed. The slave laughed and dodged as tides of water deluged the slate floor. Mrs. Schuyler, after exhorting them "not to act like children" was forced to retreat to her kitchen.

* * *

Angelica was a careful and anxious mother. No one who had the slightest suspicion of a cold was allowed to touch her Philip. She and her father had a running battle over the muskets kept in the downstairs hall. She kept removing them, fearing that her two-year old, who was as active as a monkey and a very devil of invention, would get into them. Papa would remonstrate with her and then have the guards, men from the local militia, put them back.

The guards were at the house because there were rumors of a Tory plot to carry off the General. Papa Schuyler may have lost his military command, but he still maintained a close rapport with local militias and important Indian chiefs, making him a man of significance in the frontier war.

In the growing twilight of the day, Peggy and Betsy took turns fanning each other and reading *The Tempest* aloud. Their father's eyes were closed. The heat kept them downstairs in the great room, where the brick pile of the house kept it relatively cool. A gentle evening breeze now moved between the open front and back doors.

Mrs. Schuyler, Angelica, and Baby Phil retired upstairs to sleep right after supper. The men who were supposed to be guarding the house were lounging under the big maple out front, half asleep in the long slow descent of the summer sun. Heat saturated everything. Even wearing nothing but shift and stays, even without a cap over a knot of hair, Betsy felt sweat trickling. Just as she was wondering about whether she too should simply go to up to bed, Prince suddenly appeared inside their circle of candlelight.

"'Scuse me, Mr. General, sir. There's a man asking to speak to you down at the back gate."

"Who is it?"

"He won't tell me, sir, and I don't know him. Says he's got some kind of trouble and wants to ask for your help. When I asked him inside, he said he was ashamed to do that, 'cause he weren't dressed properly. He asked if you could come out to him."

"That's queer," mused Peggy, putting down her handwork.

"What did he look like, Prince?"

"A big strong fellow, all in buckskin. Spoke like a Scotsman. He were polite, though."

Philip Schuyler considered for a moment and then said, "Peg, Bess! Listen to me. I want you to blow out the candles and then get upstairs to your Mama as fast as you

180

can. Lock yourselves in the bedroom and load my pistols. I'll be right after you."

"What?" Peggy's peaches and cream cheeks turned ashen.

"Do as I say. It's the Tories, come after me. Prince, you go out the front door and see if you can get Mr. Van Tienhoven's attention without a lot of fuss. Try not to get yourself killed."

"I've got to get Kitty," Peggy whispered, heading for the downstairs room in which her baby sister was sleeping. "Go on up, Betsy, and warn Mama and Angelica."

Prince went like a shadow to the front door, opened it, and began to call, but before anything else could happen, screams suddenly issued from the kitchen wing.

"Indians! Indians!"

"Jesus! Get your guns!"

"Peggy!" Betsy turned to go after her sister.

"No!" An arm swept around her, the arm of her father. There was more strength in it than she knew he still had.

"Assist me upstairs!" This was what he said, although, if anything, he was pulling her.

The guards were now in the great room, yanking open doors, falling over each other, and shouting, searching for the muskets. Shots rang out. In the kitchen something shattered. Slaves came tearing out of the kitchen wing, heading for the stairs. In the oncoming tide, Betsy and her father were swept up all the way.

Two of the guardsmen seized chairs to serve as defense and backed up last of all. At the bottom of stairs were— brown faces, buckskin, war paint!

Her father moved faster than he had in years, hobbling to the bedroom where the muskets had at last been found. Betsy couldn't seem to make her feet work. She stayed at the top of the stairs, transfixed by the unfolding scene below.

Her father's men, with no other option, had thrown themselves upon the invaders, fighting hand to hand. As

181

they struggled, a figure in a white dress nimbly skirted the melee. It was Peggy, baby in her arms.

"You, wench! Where's your master?"

"Gone for help." Peggy pounded up the stairs.

A tomahawk, flying from somewhere, bit into the banister as her sister ran like a white streak, the baby a flapping, howling bundle in her arms.

"Stop!" One of the intruders roared. "All we want is the General!"

Musket barrels poked over the railings and Papa Schuyler bellowed, "Damn you, Waltermeyer! I know you! Get out of my house now!" He thrust Betsy behind him.

"Don't make us burn you out, General. Just come of your own accord and we'll leave the house and the womenfolk safe."

"Don't believe 'em, General. Them's Schagticokes."

The general kept his attention focused upon the scene below.

"You're a lying rascal, Waltermyer!" He bellowed over the balcony. "Come and get me."

Everyone ran. As soon as they were inside the bedroom, many hands shoved a massive and ancient wardrobe against the door. Peggy was as white as her dress and still panting from her dash, but by the time Betsy arrived, she was already busy with a powder horn, loading their father's pistols. Mrs. Schuyler was in bed, trying to quiet the little ones. Angelica crouched on the low trundle bed, hugging her son against the big ball of her belly.

Schuyler strode to the window and shouted orders with supreme calm, as if he had a whole troop under his command.

"Load up! Hurry! The downstairs is full of them! That's right, sir! Ready!"

At his direction, a volley of musket fire punched through the back window, aimed at the figures they'd spied beside the kitchen wing. The noise inside the room was terrific. Babies screeched. When the powder cleared, a man could be seen dragging a body to cover.

182

A pepper of fire came back at them, smashing the rest of the window.

"Reload!"

"But, sir! They're in the house!"

"Do it!" cried Schuyler. "Now!"

Everyone got to reloading and another volley went out the windows. From the downstairs came a series of noisy crashes.

"What if they start shooting through the door or the ceiling?"

"We'll do the same."

A third volley was fired. Then, as they were reloading, a man covering the window shouted.

"Hurrah! Here comes the militia!"

* * *

Downstairs was a ruin. A kitchen door was broken and windows were smashed. There were bullet holes and shattered plaster. The silver was gone. Two of their guard had been abducted, but no one in the household had been killed. One of their defenders, a brave man who had raised the alarm and held the kitchen door, had taken a bullet. As the shot hadn't struck vitals or bone, there was reasonable hope he would recover.

Although the heat was still high, teeth chattered. There was a high, wild babble as everyone talked at once about what they'd seen, what they'd done, what they'd thought or felt. The servants were tearful, but Betsy was astonished to see how quickly her mother took charge. Almost at once she was giving orders and bustling about in her shift, candle held high to survey the damage.

Papa spoke with the Militiamen who'd come dashing across the field from Albany. Some of them went to inspect the outbuildings and barns, to see if any Tories still lurked or if any of the slaves or tenants had been injured or carried off. Riders carried messages to Papa's Indian friends among the Oneidas, the Tuscaroras and Cajhnawagas, to ask them to keep an eye out for Waltermeyer's raiders, who, it was supposed, would head north.

Standing in the parlor beside her mother, staring at gaping drawers and overturned furniture, Betsy experienced a weird elation. The war had come straight into her home, but the Schagticokes, merciless demons of so many childhood nightmares, had left without her scalp.

* * *

"Mrs. Hamilton's husband is with General Washington in the south. She's been fretting—haven't you, Betsy?— about her husband seeing action and here a bunch of rascals attack us right in our own home." Philip Schuyler told the tale to the visiting Comte de Manduit.

"Outrageous! But such, I fear, is the nature of this war."

"Indeed, sir. Our trouble here was nothing compared to the terrors the women and children of our settlers endure, but we are bred to alarms, we Americans. Frankly," General Schuyler said, "their effort had the merit of audacity. We were so surprised they could have taken me and any others of us they wanted had they pressed their initial advantage."

"Papa pretended that there were hosts of men with him and set up a musketry fire out the windows which brought the militia from town," Angelica said.

"And you, dear child, have learned not to second guess your father about where the muskets should be stored." Schuyler patted Angelica's hand, while she had the good grace to look embarrassed. It was the only rebuke regarding the episode Betsy ever heard her father utter.

* * *

The bright colors of fall were splashed on all the trees. In the kitchen there were conserves and sausages in the making. In the barn, the harvest was in full flood. A few Indian visitors did similar autumn tasks beside the bark

184

huts they'd thrown up at the far end of the pastures. Bushels of apples were laid by for cider, for drying, for pies and sauce. Peggy was supervising the kitchen today, a cap hiding her chestnut curls. Their mother was busy upstairs today, tending Angelica, who was in labor.

Philip Schuyler had come up, not so much to get news on the progress as to make a suggestion. "About Betsy," he asked his wife when she poked her head out the door, "Do you think she should be there? The child is already half out of her skin with nerves."

"Don't worry, Mr. Schuyler," his wife replied. "I've always thought a girl should have a look at this business before she has to do it. Angelica's making a fuss, but she's almost got it done. In fact, why don't you send one of the boys along to Doctor Stringer and tell him not to bother coming by? That broken leg he's got down at The Flats needs a doctor a great deal more than what we've got here."

Propped up in bed, Angelica looked frail and helpless. The day was cool, but she was sweating, alternately panting and crying. She had plenty of company, her elegant maroon maid, her sister Betsy and Mrs. Schuyler, as well as Mrs. Pieterse, the midwife.

"Oh! Here it comes again," Angelica gasped, writhing and clutching the coverlet. "I'm going to tell John that two babies are plenty. I swear to God! I never want to do this again."

Mrs. Schuyler's expression was disapproving, but she didn't scold. Instead, she wiped Angelica's brow with a damp cloth. Mrs. Pieterse patted Betsy on the back and whispered, "Now, now, Mrs. Hamilton, she don't mean it. Your sister will forget everything as soon as she puts the babe to her breast." Then, with an eye to Mrs. Schuyler, the midwife added, "We poor girls always talk like that, don't we, Mrs. General? And then those men start kissing and sweet talking, and before we know it, we're in the same pickle all over again."

Betsy's mother expressed agreement with a wry smile. Mrs. Pieterse, drawing back the covers, said, "You've about got it done, Mrs. Church."

Betsy had a view of parts unbelievably distended, as well as what was clearly the top of a tiny coral-colored head. She steadied herself by taking a deep breath and placing both hands on either side of her own big belly.

"Betsy!" Mama's voice brought her back. "Sit on the bed and put your arm around your sister. Give her something to lean on. She's almost done, but pushing the baby out is the hardest part."

Betsy did as she was told. As she awkwardly slipped an arm between her sister's sweating back and the bolsters, Angelica groaned.

"Don't mind me, Sis. Mrs. Pieterse is right. But, oh, God!" Her voice began to rise again, "It hurts so much!"

* * *

The following day, General Schuyler wrote a letter to Colonel Hamilton who was now with the southern army at Yorktown. He discussed the upcoming New York State elections. He meditated gloomily upon the ineptitude and factionalism of Congress. He speculated upon the movements of the army, before finally remarking, "Mrs. Church was yesterday delivered of a fine boy. I hope her sister will give me another."

Chapter Nine ~ The Soldier Returns

Alexander rode north in his worn and dirty Continental uniform. Just like last winter, he crossed at the Ferry below Schuyler's, where the gray slate of the river drank twinkling snow. As he trotted towards the lighted windows of the square brick house, he imagined his wife looking out for him, just as she had before.

At the door Prince welcomed him warmly. The only other member of the family there to greet him was Rensselaer.

"Hello, Colonel Hamilton! Papa says you were in a great battle." Rensselaer leapt at him, brandishing a wooden sword. "Did you kill anybody?"

"Hey, soldier! I heard you were in a great battle, too." Hamilton caught the boy and swung him high over his head, but to the bloodthirsty question he made no reply. He had killed, more than he cared to think about, one time with his pistol. The man's head, a bloody pumpkin, had exploded.

Leading the nighttime attack at Yorktown upon an English redoubt, he'd fought hand to hand, driven his spontoon between ribs and into bellies, produced red fountains, all the while slipping on blood and the stinking contents of stomachs and bowels like some inept butcher.

The Battle at Yorktown had been a skyrocket, the warrior's triumph he had once imagined he craved. Now, once more standing in this house, filled with a warm glow he could almost see, he didn't want to recall any of it, especially the dying faces that still came to haunt his nights.

As he set Rensselaer down, Mrs. Schuyler emerged from the front parlor. Little Cornelia followed, dragging a large, limp rag doll by its leg. "Do hush, Rensselaer," Mrs. Schuyler chided as she came billowing across the chilly

187

great room. "Trot to the nursery like a good boy. Colonel Hamilton shouldn't have to listen to your nonsense after his long journey."

"Do as your Mama says, little brother. I'll tell you about the battle later. Right now, I want to see my wife."

"She's sleeping, Colonel Hamilton. It's all she does. That, and cry. She's no fun at all ever since you married her."

"Rensselaer!"

The boy gave his mother an impudent look and ran away, defiantly waving his sword.

"Come on, 'Nelia!" he shouted to his little sister, "Come with me, or redskins will scalp you!"

Cornelia didn't obey her brother's summons. Instead, she gathered up more of her mother's skirt. Sticking a thumb in her mouth, she continued to shyly examine this military stranger, one she couldn't quite remember.

"Ever since that business with the Tories getting into the house, he's been wilder than ever." Mrs. Schuyler sighed and bent to firmly remove the thumb from her daughter's mouth.

She straightened and stretched out her hands.

"Dear Colonel Hamilton, how good to have you here at last! What can we get for you? You look quite worn out."

"Hot water, I guess, Ma'am, so I can wash. Tea, anything that won't be a bother." Hamilton kissed her cheek. "I tired my horse so badly that I left him at Stony Point and came along on one I hired. Dear Mrs. Schuyler! I can't tell you how happy I am to be here."

"Well, we'll get you some water. Then go along upstairs and wake up your wife. I'll have tea and toast sent to you there. She's napping in the room where you became man and wife."

* * *

Betsy slept in the long twilight of a winter afternoon, abetted by gray sky and drawn bed curtains. Hamilton drew

188

these back and sat on the edge of the bed, leaning to drop a kiss on her round winter-pale cheek.

Betsy startled at his touch, then gave a gasp of delight and seized him around the neck, holding on as if she'd never let go. While he sat there, kissing and cradling her, a servant tapped on the door and entered with a tray of buttered toast and fresh tea. A slave child, eyes round with interest, followed with an armload of wood with which to build up the fire.

Betsy clung to her husband, the initial shower quickly reducing to hiccups. Hamilton could feel her small shoulders quiver.

How little he'd known her!

The "finest tempered girl," cheeks glowing, hiking through the snow with the aplomb of an Indian or lying on the ice the better to see a magical frozen kingdom below, had utterly vanished. It was as if making love to her had transformed that sturdy creature into something frail and helpless.

All her tears, all her fears, this sea of emotion in which she'd threatened to drown them both!

She smelled slightly yeasty, like a child roused from a nap. Shyly, he let his hand come to rest upon her belly. More than eight months gone now, the size was considerable.

"Yes." She put her hand over his and pressed. "Oh, feel, dear Hamilton, feel! Our baby's moving."

Alexander felt the rolling sweep through the flannel, beneath the warm mantle of her flesh.

"Oh, my Betsy.

Pierced to the heart, he lowered his head and kissed her belly, blessing her and the small enshrouded being she carried.

* * *

Within a few days of his arrival, Alexander fell sick with an ague. He shook and shivered, coughed and sneezed.

189

Aching, alternately burning and freezing, he lay in bed, almost too ill to rise even for the call of nature.

He felt that terrible northern sickness again, a weight like a huge stone sitting in the middle of his chest, a stone he must cough up, or die. Mrs. Schuyler dosed him with herb teas, as well as bowl after bowl of chicken soup.

The last time he'd been this ill had been the winter Washington sent him north to get men from Putnam and Gates for the southern army, the Valley Forge winter. He'd lain at Peekskill for a week, sweating and coughing, haphazardly tended by the rough sergeant with whom he'd been riding. His faithful soldier had told him later he'd felt Alexander's legs cool, and had, for a few hours, believed he'd soon be digging a grave for General Washington's young favorite.

This time it was different. Betsy, Mrs. Schuyler, and Peggy all tended him, cosseted him. He was fed, dosed, comforted, kept warm and in clean linen. Christmas was subdued. The brightest light was little Kitty, ten months old, fat and active. She went crawling everywhere, trailing a long nightgown and her little black nurse, entrances heralded by the loud thump-thumping of her knees.

Toward the end of January, after the company left, husband and wife were in the same bed again. They'd curled together like two puppies against the fierce cold on the night Betsy's pains started.

She awoke, arms hugging a belly that was contracting, beyond flesh, into rock. It happened again and again, the pains swiftly stronger, but Betsy hesitated to wake her husband. It didn't take long, however, for her shifting and sighing to bring him to consciousness.

"Has it begun?" He rubbed his eyes.

"I think so." Another wave was coming, so she fell silent. Alexander put a hand on her belly, felt the hardening.

"I'll get your mama." He jumped out of bed, reaching for the wool banyan to cover his nightshirt. In the darkness

190

he paused to kiss her forehead. "I'll be right back, sweetheart."

The windows of the great house were soon aglow. Servants were roused. Hot water had to be readied, wood and linen strips carried up, the fire in their room blown awake. Whether Doctor Stringer would be required was discussed. In the end, he was sent for, even though there was no history of birthing trouble in their family. Mrs. Schuyler expelled all her children, even two sets of twins, without the aid of the doctor's extractors, but this was, after all, a first labor.

Hamilton refused to be chased out. He sat in his flowing banyan on the edge of the bed and held Betsy's hand. She alternately thanked him for being there and wept, tossed, and apologized for not being braver.

After the Doctor arrived, he dismissed Alexander.

"She will soon be screaming, Colonel. There isn't any other way for a woman of your wife's temperament. She's afraid you will be ashamed of her and even now it's making her suffer. There's a fire in the library. Why don't you go down?"

Sitting with his father-in-law should have been an easy task, but for Alexander, this was a near impossibility. He prowled the room restlessly. The General's black eyes followed him with amusement.

"Don't worry, Hamilton. The ladies of our family deal with this business very well all by themselves. If not, Stringer's here, as well as Mrs. Pieterse. Take my advice, sir, and pull a chair up by the fire and go back to sleep. It's my experience they'll wake you if and when they want you."

* * *

Birthing is such hard work!

Betsy thought it like trudging for hours through deep snow for it took every ounce of her strength. The fire in the bedroom crackled, the mantel clocked ticked; she sweated and struggled. The cool hands of her mother soothed and

191

endured her squeezing when the pain got bad. She panted so hard and fast she was dizzy. There was no time for fear, only for a brief rest and then a surge to the top of the next agonizing wave. Her body, so responsive to the touch of love, quivered with each ferocious stroke. Finally, she pulled up her knees, and gave a shriek that rang through the house and brought Hamilton rushing up the stairs.

In a great wet rush, the baby came. Betsy fell back into the arms of her mother, sobbing with relief. As the midwife did something between her legs, there was one last contraction. Something hot and watery followed the baby out.

"Good! Very good." The Doctor and her mother nodded together.

"It's all over now, Eliza."

Betsy lay now in a pool of deep peace, while the bustle continued. Mrs. Pieterse cleaned, laying on absorbent cloths and removing bloody wadding. Doctor Stringer, at the foot of the bed, soothed the squalling baby, simply wrapping him in flannel. Betsy relished the pure silence that hummed within.

When she was under covers, Mrs. Pieterse, with a great, gap-toothed grin, laid "the cause of all this trouble" in her arms, so she could see him. There he was, her first born son, with a tattered shock of black hair, perfect tiny fingers and toes.

"Another fine grandson·for the General," said the midwife. "Just as fine, if not finer, than Mrs. Carter's. Aren't you pleased, Colonel?"

Hamilton had just come through the door and was even now looking over the midwife's shoulder.

"I made a boy, just as you wanted." Betsy spoke as her husband, his face shining, bent down to see.

"Of course you did," said Mrs. Schuyler. "She has always been my most obedient child, Colonel."

Formally, Alexander lifted his Betsy's hand and kissed it. Then, unable to stop there, he leaned to press a kiss against her sweaty forehead.

"Are you all right, dearest Betsy?"

"I think so."

"Don't worry, Colonel Hamilton. Everything was natural, smooth as silk," the Doctor said.

Next, eagerly, Hamilton gathered up his son. Betsy thought she'd never seen such a tender expression on his face.

"And what will you name him, Colonel?"

"Oh, he must be another Philip," Hamilton replied, gazing with delight at the baby. "For my wife's kind father."

"And here's a beautiful sunrise." Mrs. Schuyler had caught sight of the glory through a crack in the curtains. As she parted them, a cold draft blew in, but beyond, petals of rose bloomed upon the ice-blue drifts. High above, in the still blue-black, hung a morning star. "Thanks be to God that I've lived to see so many happy days."

"Amen," said Doctor Stringer.

Relinquishing his son to the outstretched hands of his mother-in-law, Hamilton looked on while she helped her daughter get the baby together with a nipple. He felt as if he were floating, as if the core of his being was in bliss. It was a joy such as he'd never imagined.

I'll be the best father a boy has ever had! I will educate, protect, cherish. Philip Hamilton will be secure in the knowledge that he is a gentleman, and that no one—ever— can take that away.

* * *

Hamilton was edgy, insistent upon setting up his own household. In the spring, he, Betsy and the baby moved into a brick row house in town, sharing it with his old friend and roommate from Columbia, Colonel Robert Troup, who was already at the bar.

The narrow peaked house was awash in books and papers. Like all young attorneys of the time, Troup was struggling to find his way through the often contradictory decisions of Colonial and English law.

193

On their first visit to Troup's house, Betsy must have looked around in something like despair, because Alexander had slipped an arm around her and said, "Well, my patient Aquileia, do you think you're ready to plant turnips with me?"

"Turnips would probably grow in here, Alex, if there was a little more light," said Bob. "I'm hoping that Mrs. Hamilton will be able to scare some work out of the servants. They know they have a bachelor at their mercy, and a busy one at that."

"Well, if that's how it is, perhaps Mama will lend me someone for a little."

"Oh, no, Mrs. Hamilton. We're going to manage by ourselves." Alexander was firm. "No more charity from your ever too giving parents."

"Whatever you say, Husband." Betsy sighed and rose on her toes to give him an obedient kiss.

On that very day, she routed out the cook. She enjoyed the look of alarm in the woman's eyes when she recognized that one of Major General Schuyler's daughters was her new mistress. Soon after, sloshing noises from the kitchen indicated that a thorough purge was in progress.

Economy, their slovenly cook already knew. When Alexander stared into his plate on that first night, he saw a mess of Indian beans, cornmeal and tired roots which had been sleeping in the cellar since the previous autumn. A few chunks of stringy meat floated here and there to flavor the gummy mixture. He looked up with an expression of such dismay that Troup began to laugh.

"What's the matter, Alex? Don't you recognize poor man's food, or aren't you really like those noble Romans you've been lecturing your good wife about? Let me assure you that on this very first night, Mrs. Hamilton has made a difference in the quality of my dinner."

Troup paused to ladle a big spoonful into his mouth. "First," he said thickly, "this is hot and fresh, nothing that's spent three days in the bottom of a pot. And look at this

194

bread! Why, it can actually be broken with the hands. Astonishing!"

After that, the food was better. Just as Betsy had suspected, much of Troup's house money had been diverted to other purposes. The cook's husband, she explained, was one of Albany's most notorious drunks.

"I thought I was eating a lot of rabbit and cornpone," said Troup after Betsy explained it to him. "I was beginning to have yearnings to put on war-paint and disappear into the forest."

"Her husband was probably snaring the bunnies so it wasn't costing a penny. I'm afraid that in the last few months you've bought her old man plenty of rum."

"Well, what shall we do? She cooks well enough."

"You, Colonel Troup, have clearly suffered far too long in the army. Dismiss her and I'll cook for you both. That is if I can get someone to help, to butcher and do the scouring, water carrying and to split kindling. I'll borrow someone from Mama until we get this place cleaned up."

"A prospect I look forward to with pleasure, Mrs. Hamilton. I will contribute all I can—I can split kindling—but what about Mr. Hamilton? He seems to have some fixed ideas about making do, and I'm sure you know how stubborn he is."

"I do indeed, but something needs to be done, doesn't it, Mr. Troup?"

Bob sighed and nodded.

"Well, I have a notion." Perhaps, she thought, here was a case where strategy might actually work.

* * *

It was late afternoon when Hamilton came ambling back from Councilor Duane's on the new horse his father-in-law had given him. The animal was walking, flicking his tail and nodding as he strolled along. His new master was sitting erect, but clearly intent upon something other than riding, for his lips moved.

To Betsy's brothers, his choice from the General's stables had been surprising: a placid ten year old gelding. It was, Alexander explained, a horse who took no skill to ride, one who would patiently go on his way, while his master did other things. He dismounted and left the animal at the stables where he was boarded and then, lips still moving, began an abstracted walk down the street of high-gabled Dutch houses. He was thinking over the difficulties of the Confederation, and shaping an article in his mind, something for the newspaper.

There are epochs in human affairs when novelty even is useful. If a general opinion prevails that the old way is bad, whether true or false, and this obstructs the operations of public service, a change is necessary, if it be but for the sake of change. This is exactly the case now. 'Tis universal sentiment that our present system is a bad one, and that things do not go right on this account. The measure of a Convention would revive the hopes of the people and give a new direction to their passions...

America needed a convention. One where state leaders could gather and devise a better form of government than the headless, stumbling establishment they had now.

As he approached the house, Alexander was surprised by the sight of a woman kneeling on the steps, her head covered by a floppy white cap. Rags in hand, a bucket beside her, she was energetically scrubbing.

"Excuse me?"

"Good evening, Mr. Hamilton."

She paused to look up. To say he was shocked was an understatement. On her knees at this most menial of tasks was his very own Betsy, dressed in a stained apron and dress, the kind of things worn by servants.

"What are you doing?" This, of course, was self-evident, but it always took a little time to return from his inner world.

196

"Well, these were a disgrace." Betsy wrung dirty water from the rag. Tossing it down again with a weary slap, she began to scrub the lowest step.

Alexander was well aware, after his years in New York, of the Dutch propensity to clean everything, right out to the front stoop, but this was an extremity he'd never expected.

"Mrs. Hamilton—ah—"

"Good evening, Mrs. Hamilton." A man passing by had paused to doff his hat. "Taking hold of the place, I see."

Betsy looked up. "Good evening, Mr. Loockerman. Yes, high time someone did."

"Good day to you, as well, Colonel." The fellow inclined his head.

"And to you, sir."

Hamilton turned quickly, wishing with all his heart that Mynheer Loockerman would mind his own business. He bent close to Betsy and whispered.

"Mrs. Hamilton! The whole town has seen you."

"And what if they have, sir?"

"Well, this isn't—"

"Why ever not? Someone has to keep the place clean."

"We—I will employ a maid of all work."

"I thought we were down to the bare bones, Mr. Hamilton." Betsy matter-of-factly clambered to her feet, then, with a practiced toss emptied the bucket into the gutter.

"So we are." Numbers went galloping through his head. "But—but—no wife of mine scrubs the steps." He was painfully aware that other neighbors, a good wife and her pipe-smoking man, were leaning over their double door just across the street, unabashedly taking it all in and making, in an undertone, commentary.

"You said we couldn't afford it." The heart-shaped face beneath the white cap turned toward him, weary and stubborn. "I will not live in a pigsty, Mr. Hamilton."

"I don't care if it's the Augean stables!" Humiliated by the thought of all those Albanian eyes that had seen the daughter of its first citizen down on her knees scrubbing— her 'English' husband too mean to hire a maid—Alexander

197

came to a swift decision. Seizing his wife around the waist, he directed her up the stairs.

"Sir! What are you about?"

"Hush, Mrs. Hamilton." As the front door closed, the sound of laughter from the street behind didn't do his temper any good.

Inside, the black and white tiles of the entry way gleamed. This gleam, he saw, by the light pouring through newly scrubbed windows, extended back into the kitchen.

"You've given Albany a tale which will no doubt be down river to New York in time to entertain everyone at dinner tomorrow."

"*You* are the one!"

When she'd begun this task, Betsy had known exactly what would happen when Alexander found her at it, but now she was exhausted. Once she'd started, her housekeeper's sense of propriety had taken over. It had been impossible to stop digging away. Throwing the rag down with a resounding slap at her husband's booted feet, Betsy cried, "If there's any gossip, it will be about you. Hauling me in here like that! I thought I was supposed to make do!"

"My dear Queen Bess, I never imagined—"

"No, you didn't. And now, I suppose," Betsy shouted, the sound an astonishing echo of her father, "you want to know what's for supper?"

"Ahem. Excuse me." The door opened again and there stood Bob, looking singularly cowed after a long day in Court.

"Before you enter, Mr. Troup, you are to remove those muddy boots!" Betsy cried.

Bob, who knew feminine fury when he saw it, backed away as she approached, but Betsy pushed past him and went back out the door.

"Where are you going?" Alexander followed her down the wet steps.

"To get Phil."

"Phil?"

As he walked to the stoop, he saw what he hadn't noticed earlier. From the limb of an old cherry tree that clung to a patch between the house and the mud of what was generally described as "street," he suddenly spied a bark cradle suspended. It swayed gently in the May breeze.

Hamilton had had the strange experience of seeing his son like this before, at his father-in-law's house. While they had still been living with her parents, this cradle had arrived as a gift from a group of Mohawks who had presented themselves at the door. Somewhat to his surprise, his father-in-law had spent most of the afternoon sitting in near silence with them passing a pipe. Phil had speedily fallen asleep on his cradle board, face dappled with the light and shade of the leaves.

Now, as his wife took it down, she cooed. Phil, a gray-eyed papoose, began to smile and wiggle as soon as he saw his mother. Cradleboard in her arms, Betsy turned to face her husband.

"Shall I see if Mama can spare someone?"

Alexander cleared his throat. Every window on every side seemed to sport the white-capped head of a goodwife. Traffic appeared frozen in the street.

"Yes, please, Mrs. Hamilton. Do whatever is necessary for housekeeping."

As he followed his wife into the house, her head high and the cradleboard in her arms, Hamilton shook his head.

This woman knows how to get her way!

* * *

An indefatigable student, Hamilton spent most of his days in Councilor James Duane's fine law library. He'd sit with a great dull book, something with a title like *An Introduction to the Law Relative to Trials at Nisi Prius,* and speed through it, making an outline of what he'd read. When he studied, he behaved strangely.

The first time Betsy wasn't sure what Alexander was doing, walking around and around the dining room table, muttering to himself. She thought he looked very odd.

199

"Alexander?" She called softly. "Alexander?"

Several times he passed by the door where she stood, but he never looked at her, never stopped his pacing. His lips moved constantly.

Suddenly, hands drew her backwards, through the door again.

"Right now," Bob whispered, "Your husband is blind and deaf. Why, the things I could accomplish with you, Mrs. Hamilton."

"Don't play the fool!" Betsy pulled away.

"You're going to see a lot of that from now on." Bob smiled down at her. "At King's, Alex used to take memorizing strolls in the graveyard. At first, we all laughed at him. Then, the masters started to ask us why we weren't 'as quick as that Hamilton.' Soon," Troup was wistful, "he'll have that damned dull tome committed to memory, able to reel if off, head by head, for any judge who demands a precedent."

Sometimes, Betsy felt jealous of Bob. He had spent so much more time with her husband than she had. Still, Troup was good company. He was bright, funny, and personable. With Hamilton in this grimly studious mood, it was nice to have someone to talk to. They often sat by the fire together in the evenings, when her husband was late. The baby, half-asleep in his bed, sucked noisily on the fingers he'd crammed into his mouth. Betsy knitted and rocked the cradle with one foot, a task at which she was learning to excel.

"I'll wager he'll pass the bar faster than anyone. When we were at Kings, people would ask if it made me mad, the way he was, but you know, it never did. I guess I would have been annoyed had he closed his books and gone out to raise hell while I was left slaving. Being faster than the rest of us only meant there was that much more time to learn. He never stopped before I did, although, I swear he learned twice as much."

Betsy came to feel as if Troup were a kind of brother. If Philip squalled, Bob would politely lower his eyes while

200

she lifted her breast over the stay and offered it. More than one evening Alexander returned home to find them sitting by the fire as if they were the married couple.

* * *

Sometimes she had nervous moments, managing that first household, even though she had a lovely London edition of the celebrated Mrs. Raffeld's Cookbook.

"An excellent cookery book, written by a sensible woman." Her mother had made the present. "Although, of course, Mrs. Glasse's book will always be my favorite."

More than cookery, more than anything, Betsy needed to learn more about the ways of babies. There had been all those brothers and sisters, but daily she thanked heaven that Mama wasn't far away. Philip seemed to do a fair amount of crying, and the cause mystified. She'd carry him over her shoulder, pat his little back and hum. Sometimes, when nothing seemed to comfort him, she felt close to panic.

"I've fed you. You're clean and dry. You've burped. I've carried you and rocked you. Whatever is the matter?"

He looked round and rosy, but she began to fear her small breasts didn't hold enough milk, that he was crying from hunger. She began to feed him more frequently, but that wasn't the answer, either. He'd eat and then throw up the excess. Her mother, when consulted, advised Betsy to let the baby suckle one breast only until he fell asleep.

"I think he's one that needs lots of suckling. Don't worry. He's getting plenty. Why, he looks bigger to me than he did just a week ago."

Sometimes Betsy was exhausted after a long day of managing her new servants, of cooking, of sewing and caring for the baby. When he was at home, Hamilton could be helpful. He'd walk the floor with Phil, patting the baby's back steadily—if a little awkwardly—while mumbling law text.

"This stuff puts everyone else to sleep!" He complained one night, raising his fretting son high over his head. "How come it doesn't work with you?"

Many nights Hamilton walked the kitchen floor, talking to his restless son, while Betsy napped. Troup sat nearby, burning the midnight oil as he prepared for an upcoming case. Many afternoons, while Betsy worked in the kitchen, her husband read and rocked the cradle with a stocking foot while Philip, fist stuffed in his mouth, kicked his fat legs and grunted miserably.

The thought occurred that Philip might be teething.

"You stick your finger in the side of their mouth if they bite and that gets them to let go. After he has teeth, I won't be able to let him nurse for so long, but Phil needs lots of suckling. What shall I do?"

Hamilton leaned over his seated wife and admired the easy working of the baby's delicate jaw, the tiny hand that slapped back and forth against his wife's full breast.

"I can't imagine a man anywhere on earth bored while he's got a tit in his mouth, certainly not any son of mine." For the past few months he'd listened to a lot of woman's talk with interest, but even the tenderest husband can be subject to lapses.

"Mr. Hamilton!"

"And while I'm on the subject, those are splendid since you've been in milk, twice the size they used to be."

In order to hide her breast from his less than neutral gaze, Betsy began to stroke Philip's feathery auburn head. "I thought you said I am pretty just the way I am."

"It is the nature of man, rogue that he is, to find stimulation in variety."

Unsettled, Betsy didn't reply, simply looked down upon the downy top of Phil's head and nestled him closer.

202

Chapter Ten ~ Politics

Hamilton made plans with her father, hoping to be elected to the Continental Congress in the fall. Betsy wasn't entirely pleased about it.

After all, didn't that mean that he'd go to Philadelphia, leaving her alone again?

Feeling a little guilty at the trespass, she looked into an open letter which lay on the parlor table. It was addressed to John Laurens, a man she'd never met, but whom she'd heard a great deal about. He'd been a fellow aide to Washington. Hamilton had often talked to her about him— how brilliant Laurens was, how brave he was, how ancient and honorable his Carolina family.

Laurens had fought a duel with General Lee after the Battle of Monmouth. Lee had been accused of cowardice and dereliction of duty and had endured a reprimand on the battlefield, one given by Washington. Lee had, in turn, insulted the reputation of his commanding general.

On behalf of Washington, Laurens had challenged Lee to a duel. Hamilton had stood as second. As Betsy heard the story, the gentlemen had advanced upon each other and fired. After Lee was hit in the side by Lauren's ball, the seconds managed to convince the duelists the affair had been settled with honor.

"The duel," Hamilton recounted, eyes bright with remembrance, "was polite, generous, cool and firm, everything which should mark a transaction of that nature."

There was something about his excitement when he recited this story which angered her. After Yorktown, she thought, he should know better. Elegant ceremony among gentlemen or not, a large caliber ball taken in the flesh was a deadly matter.

Laurens, Betsy knew, was still active in the war, these days fighting bloody skirmishes in his native South

Carolina. Scanning her husband's perfect, copperplate hand she read:

Peace made, my dear friend, a new scene opens. The object then will be to make our independence a blessing. To this we must secure our Union on solid foundations— Herculean task—and to effect which, mountains of prejudice must leveled! It requires all the virtue and all the abilities of the country. Quit your sword, my friend; put on the toga. Come to Congress. We know each other's sentiments; our views are the same. We have fought side by side to make American free; let us hand in hand struggle to make her happy.

Betsy turned away, suddenly cold and sad. Here were great plans for America's future, dreams about Hamilton's and Lauren's part in shaping it. There was not a word of anything she might call personal, not a single regret for leaving his wife and young son behind.

* * *

Occasionally Betsy could detach Hamilton from his studies long enough to get them all away for an afternoon on the Hudson. Peggy came sometimes, but more often Bob was their only companion. In summer the river was full of small boats, some under sail, some rowed, even an occasional birch bark canoe full of little boys, playing at being fur traders.

Today, the sun went in and out as a regal procession of summer clouds marched overhead. Swallows hunted the surface, dusty yellow breasts reflected in the green water. Willows and sycamores overhung the coves while the cattail shallows were alive with fish and the stalking, dabbling water birds.

Betsy knew the best spots along the river to laze and cast a line, and, after borrowing a boat from her father, she guided the men to them. She enjoyed these outings, but didn't like to leave the baby at her mother's for too long, even if there was always some woman in milk who could share. Without Phil, her own breasts ached and leaked.

One fine hot day when the river was crowded with picnickers, they'd ended far down river. At a sandy landing place, the men left shoes and stockings in the boat and jumped out bare-legged, splashing along until they could pull it ashore. Alexander helped Betsy out. Troup carried the basket and a blanket.

The woods were bright with bird song. For Betsy there were memories of picnics with her cousins, most happy, but a few sad, like that of the cousin who had died during the war.

After their boat was secured, the men put on shoes and stockings again. Then, they set off for a spot she knew. The path was narrow, a defile that ran between rocks and over the gnarled, knobby feet of trees.

"Our Indian guide." Hamilton whispered as they watched Betsy scramble up a rocky incline. He and Troup were always amazed at the confident way she simply set off, a Grace in homespun.

"No wonder the Dutch are devoted to picnics." Troup grinned as he watched Betsy's white stockings flash.

After a stiff climb, they reached a hollow, as if a giant had taken a bite out of the cliff face. Grass and patches of wildflower sprang from meager soil. Here, on the height, there was a brisk breeze.

"Albany." Betsy pointed north. Shading their eyes, the men saw it too, a distant smudge of smoke. Sails dotted the gray-green river

They set about spreading the blanket. "Don't bring it too close to that pile of rocks," said Betsy. "There might be copperheads."

"An exhilarating thought." Hamilton took an uncomfortable look around.

"Beer, pickles, cold chicken, and, what's this?" Bob unloaded the basket. "Oh, Lord, no!" He held up a bottle of green glass. "Not Saratoga water!"

"None of us, I believe, desires a purgative. It's from the spring behind Papa's house." Betsy laughed and snatched the bottle from Bob's hand.

"From what cornucopia of delights did this fried chicken come from?" Alexander asked. He was already biting into a leg. "I remember but one chicken in the kitchen yesterday. You said it was destined for pie."

"Ah, this one was still in the yard." Betsy fixed her gaze upon the piece she held.

Bob suppressed a smile as Alexander devoured the leg. He, personally, wasn't above accepting bounty from the Schuylers. He was regularly amused when Betsy smuggled it into the kitchen right under her preoccupied husband's nose.

Today, however, Hamilton guessed. "Wicked woman!" He tossed the bone over the cliff with a flourish. "This is charity chicken! What do you think, Bob? She insists upon feeding us."

"I, for one, am glad of it." Troup reached for another piece.

"The only way I can think to stop it is for us to move as soon as possible to the City. There, if I remember New York correctly, we may starve without anyone's interference."

They ate everything: chicken, bread and butter, sour pickles and ended with apple pie garnished with sharp, white cheddar. When the men began to talk the usual—law and politics—Betsy lay back in the sun and gazed up. White towers rose from the other side of the cliff. As she watched the clouds castle, their talk seemed to drone and fade. She slept.

At last, a rough gust of wind woke her. She sat up and stretched, noting a chill in the air.

"I think we should go back now."

"We bow to your superior knowledge." Troup stood and took a look into the west. "All of a sudden, it does look threatening."

206

"And the wind is up. We're going to have a hard row back."

She wondered why the men hadn't been paying better attention, although, of course, she knew the answer.

Politics, politics! Nothing, Lord help us, is more important.

Still, she knew the weather signs: A too warm—far too early in summer. Now the North scowled and the West jostled with thunderheads.

They were on their way down when Hamilton asked, "Where is the famous trysting place? Didn't you say it was on this bluff?" Grinning, he nudged Bob. "Colonel Troup may yet need to find it."

Betsy rose on her toes and gave Bob's cheek a peck. "You certainly should, for it may hasten the end of your bachelor days. I'll show you, but only if you two promise to row like the navy and return me to Philip before the rain."

Quickly, she left the path, walking into a wilderness of broken rocks and monumental pines. After several twists and turns, a door of light appeared, revealing a passage between two boulders. Ducking between, they found themselves standing on a narrow escarpment about ten feet above the river, rippling with bands of light. Betsy stopped before a curtain of blooming laurel.

"It's through here."

As they entered the thicket, the wind raised its voice. Overhead, the great trees creaked. The laurel shielded a passage just wide enough for single file passage which led to a dell of fairy-green moss. In the middle of the clearing, however, was something which brought Betsy up short. Wind had covered their approach and blown away their voices, or, perhaps, the couple was too heavily engaged to take notice.

They beat a hasty retreat, back the way they'd come. No longer the leader, Betsy clung to her husband's hand.

"Still being used to good advantage," Bob observed.

When they reached the shore they saw that another, smaller boat had landed beside theirs. The river, earlier a placid green mirror, danced now. Gray and restless, it twined the sky.

"Is there any shelter between your dock and here?" Hamilton asked.

"One," Betsy replied. "But maybe we'll make it home."

Even with the men sharing a seat and putting all their strength to the oars, rowing against the wind was difficult. They stayed close to the shore to get what cover they could.

Meanwhile, the sky darkened. Ominous rumbles sounded.

"This damned Albany weather." Troup was red-faced, struggling with his oar.

Hamilton nodded. He couldn't muster breath for speech. Despite of the sudden chill, sweat stained his shirt. Finally, a gust blew them to a stand-still. With it came a huge flash and an ear-splitting clap.

"Where can we go to wait this out?"

"In there, just beyond that fallen sycamore."

Straining against wind and current, the men brought the boat close enough for Betsy to catch an overhanging branch. Alexander stood and pushed at the gravel bottom with his oar while Troup jumped out, rope in hand. He splashed through the shallows, tugging the boat.

A loud hiss came just as they'd finished tying up, and what seemed like buckets of water emptied on their heads. Carrying the blanket, they scrambled up the bank to an overhang. A charred circle and a few stump seats showed that people regularly camped there.

"Another perfect summer's day in Albany!" Troup peered out from beneath the dripping ledge.

"In the Indies I never minded getting rained on," Hamilton said, "but it's always so damnably cold whenever it rains here."

Betsy wondered how long the storm would last. It was past time to feed Philip. Not that he would go hungry, but her breasts were full and aching.

"We're going to blame it all on Betsy and her picnic." Smiling, Hamilton tossed the damp blanket around her shoulders. A blinding flash, followed by a boom, amazed. The cliffs across the river reverberated as if from cannon fire. The lip of the overhang streamed. In spite of how cold and wet she was, Betsy felt elated.

Suddenly, through the drumming beat of rain and the shock of thunder, they heard screams of laughter.

"Good God! Someone's out there!"

In a moment two figures, as wet as if they'd been swimming, came pelting inside. The woman was a goddess. The drenching she'd suffered left little to the imagination. The man was muscular, slim and dark. His pale, streaming face was illuminated by brilliant hazel eyes.

"Colonel Burr?"

"Ah! Colonel and Mrs. Hamilton! Colonel Troup! So that was your boat!" The man spoke as gaily as if they were all met at an assembly ball. "We just ran Jupiter's gauntlet out there."

"Please, Ma'am," said Hamilton. "Share the blanket with my wife."

"Oh, I'll only make Mrs. Hamilton wet," the woman said. "I'm soaked clean through." She had grown subdued as soon as she'd seen Betsy.

"I'm already wet. Come—Jenneke—Mrs. Van Syoc— and sit with me." Betsy spoke firmly. "You'll catch your death."

The beautiful woman was embarrassed, but grateful. Awkwardly, she accepted a share of the blanket. The men huddled into their jackets, pulling the collars up. The women leaned together. Outside, rain fell in sheets.

"So much for a summer's day in Albany." Burr gazed out.

"Just what I was saying," Bob said. "As a native New Yorker I ought to have more loyalty to my state, but the weather this far north is, I believe, devised by some otherworldly lunatic."

"Perhaps this is punishment for my neglect of my studies. The goddess of jurisprudence is a jealous hag." Although Hamilton was pale beneath his freckles, his smile was bright. "My wife's needed an outing and I've been neglecting her shamefully. All of this splendid week I've been promising we'll go out, and *this* is the day I chose."

"To which splendid week do you refer?" Troup spoke dourly. "The four days in a row with no frost? I must apologize to the ladies, but I had my fill of Albany during the war."

"There always used to be wood laid up back there, but I don't see any." Mrs. van Syoc, indicated the spider-web tracery in the darkness behind them.

"No, not a stick," Betsy said. "I looked when we first came."

"Do people usually put back what they've used?" Hamilton asked.

"Yes. At least, they used to."

"That's right," said Mrs. van Syoc. "We often camped here with our cousins at berry time. We always cut more before we left."

"A fine custom which someone has ignored. I suppose it's just common sense if you travel the river regularly."

"Even city people knew to do it."

Bob chuckled. "Even selfish down-river-folk?"

"Yes," Betsy considered her companion under the blanket. "The war has changed everything." It was a gentle admonishment. Mrs. van Syoc looked, for the first time, abashed.

Burr had been watching the interchange laconically, all the time feeling in his pocket. "I have a tinder box." He removed a small, canvas-wrapped square from his coat pocket. "Unfortunately, like me, it's soaked. The women have their blanket, but for us poor fellows there won't even be the comfort of a pipe. Innocents and sinners alike punished by the fury of the storm." He grinned cheerfully.

Betsy looked past him. *You, Colonel Burr, are shameless!*

"Of course, if we really start to freeze, do you suppose all five of us could get under your blanket?"

210

"A thought which instantly makes me warmer, Colonel Burr." Hamilton smiled. "However, where do you propose to put Colonel Troup?"

"Well, in the middle, between the ladies, of course."

"You surprise me! Put an unattached gentleman in such a situation?"

"A man who is unattached will be the coldest of all. He will be able to bask in the glow of our reflected warmth."

"Gentlemen!" Betsy said. "Enough."

"Yes." Bob agreed, winking. "It probably is, although I must confess that Colonel Burr's idea is stimulating."

"You may not have the least particle of my wife's reflected glow, as the Colonel so elegantly phrases it." Hamilton moved to the dripping overhang to study the sky. "If this ever lets up, we can join forces. There is a sculling lock at the stern of our boat."

"A good idea." Burr's slender frame let loose a huge shiver. "The prospect of spending a night here without a fire is not even to be contemplated."

As the men talked it over, Betsy and Jenneke van Syoc huddled close. They were, of course, distantly related. Betsy knew the gossip about Jenneke, plenty of it from the time before her marriage to van Syoc, a well-fixed widower who often traveled on business. If news of this escapade with Colonel Burr got out, there would be trouble. Albany society had a tendency to overlook indiscretion among their own, but not indiscretion with 'outsiders.'

Betsy felt warmth spreading down the front of her dress. For the last hour her breasts had been tingling and now the milk had let down of its own accord.

"Oh, Good Lord, Mrs. Van Syoc, one way or another, I am fated to be soaked today."

"Is your baby with Mrs. General?"

"Yes, thank heaven."

The rain still fell, but not so furiously. Thunder rumbled, but the flashes were now away in the east. There was a yellowish cast to the clouds, as if the setting sun wanted to break through.

211

"I'd be willing to chance it." Burr gazed at the sky. "It's still raining, but Mrs. van Syoc and I can't get any wetter than we are."

"What do you think, ladies?" Alexander reached beneath the blanket to press Betsy's fingers. "You ladies know the most about the temper of the Albany sky gods."

Both women studied the horizon. Betsy modestly kept her arms crossed over her stained bosom.

"There may be more coming, but we might as well take advantage of the lull."

Mrs. van Syoc nodded. "Yes, I agree."

After bailing the larger boat, they launched it, the women inside and the men wading and pushing until at knee depth, they climbed in. Now the current rushed fast.

"We're lucky it hasn't started to flood in earnest," Jenneke said.

"I'll use the sculling lock," said Troup. "You two must be rowing partners."

They'd taken an oar from Burr's boat, but even with Bob sculling furiously, it was an arduous trip. The wind was cold now. On the water, the rain hit harder. The river fought them for every inch.

Betsy and Mrs. van Syoc bailed with gourd cups from the picnic basket while the men strained and pulled. Rain dripped from their noses and eyebrows and coursed through the hair under their caps. Betsy didn't think she'd ever been so wet in her life. When she said so, the men, puffing and panting as they strained at their oars, began to reminisce about the war just passed.

"At least it's not freezing on me, as it did at Trenton," said Hamilton. "After that night march, I was transformed into a knight in armor. My men and I joked that not even a Hessian ball could penetrate the ice that had frozen upon us."

"And I'm not chained in a ship's hold with dirty water pouring through an open hatch, wondering if I was going to be left to drown." After his capture at the Battle of Long Island, Bob Troup had spent a nightmarish eight months, half-starved and lousy, in a rotting hulk afloat in New York harbor which served the British as a prison.

Burr's contribution came last. "Or sitting on a log in the dark with a bunch of Mohawks on the way to that fool's hell in Quebec, all of us freezing and soaked to the skin and still stinking most astonishingly. I was never quite sure I'd still have my scalp in the morning."

When they rounded the last point and saw Schuyler's dock, the men gave a cheer. As they drew closer, they saw a ketch being fitted with a sail. Shrouded in a heavy cape, a familiar figure stood nearby propped by a cane, supervising from the dock.

"It's Papa!" Betsy waved. "Whatever are they doing? Oh, what if something is wrong with Philip?"

"I have a powerful intimation your papa is worried about you." Hamilton strained at his oar.

His was the correct interpretation. The General had been on the point of sending the boat down river to look for them. He was clearly relieved to see them pulling up, but it was also clear he'd been upset.

"It's barely June, you know, sir!" He scolded as Betsy clambered onto the dock. "You ought to have been keeping a weather eye out, Colonel Hamilton. Why, just look at my girl!"

Cloaks were thrown over their shoulders by servants and they were shepherded quickly inside and sent to separate rooms to change.

* * *

"See, Phil? Here's Mama!" Peggy rushed in with the baby.

Philip gnawed his fist. At the sight of his mother, standing naked in front of the fire, small breasts hard with cold and milk, he gave a lusty crow of delight.

"Hist!" Mrs. Schuyler said, "let your sister get her clothes on first."

213

In front of the fire, Mrs. van Syoc sat on a stool naked, toweling her hair. She displayed no modesty and with her figure, there was no reason for it. Peggy pulled up short at the unexpected sight.

"Cousin Jenneke was boating with Colonel Burr. We got caught in the storm and took cover at the Normand Kill," Betsy explained. Mrs. Van Syoc sent a look of gratitude from beneath her towel.

Phil squirmed and made a face when he was set upon his mother's cold lap. A moment later, however, he'd fastened upon a nipple.

"Now, see what you've done. She won't be able to finish dressing. Put a blanket around her."

A blanket in place over her shoulders, Betsy clapped a bit of towel over the other sympathetically leaking breast. Both the hot fire at her back and the relief her son provided were comforting. An earlier swallow of her mother's homemade peach brandy sent heat through her veins.

"He can't really be hungry, the little pig," Peggy said. "He's just glad to see his mama, I think."

"I lost three." Jenneke wistfully studied Phil's chubby legs. "Catarrh, every time, but Doctor Springer says I don't seem to have much milk. Size doesn't seem to have a thing to do with that."

"Too true. You've either got the gift of milk or you don't."

For a time there was silence, except for the crackle of fire and the sound of Philip noisily suckling.

"Mrs. General, Ma'am, I'm much obliged to you. To Mrs. Hamilton, too," said Jenneke. She was busy fastening on an overlarge, dry dress which had been found for her.

When Peggy took Phil again, he tried to protest, but he was too full now to persist. A maid helped Betsy finish dressing.

Mrs. Schuyler wanted to put both Betsy and Philip to bed and have supper sent up to them, but Betsy insisted she would eat downstairs.

"Hamilton can take us home right after supper."

214

"Nonsense! It's rumbling in the west again. You're going to stay overnight, and, *you*, Elizabeth, are going to bed right after supper, that skinny husband of yours with you, if I have anything to say about it."

Betsy sighed, but knew that there was nothing more to be said. In this house, she would always be a child.

* * *

In another room the men also dried off. Except for the contrast in their coloring, Burr and Hamilton were rather alike out of their clothes. Neither was tall, both were slightly made. The years of military service, however, had left what flesh there was, hard.

"Well, Albany provided us with some excitement today, although excitement in Albany usually means being buried in some kind of precipitation," Burr said.

"I never should have gone so far down river." Hamilton spoke softly, half to himself. The general's scolding had gone home. Seeing his wife drenched to the skin, blue-lipped and shivering, had been worrying.

"Don't be silly," Bob said. "Mrs. Hamilton has wanted to show us her picnic spot. And after listening to those two ladies, you know this is not the first time they've been soaked or dodged lightning. Mrs. Hamilton steered us to a safe place. She had no way of knowing how generosity has fallen off. With wood, a night there wouldn't have been the end of the world."

"Yes." Burr sat back down on the bench to carefully dry his narrow feet, "We must rely upon these fair natives for our intelligence. If they can't anticipate, we are lost. Mrs. van Syoc thought it safe enough when we went out. As a matter of fact, she did predict a storm, but only to come in the first hours of evening. Her forecasting was excellent. It was simply a matter of timing."

"Speaking of the fair Mrs. van Syoc, isn't that...?" Hamilton let the sentence hang.

"Well, certainly, I shall take her home at once. Fortunately, your generous in-laws don't espouse the kind of hypocrisy which commonly passes for virtue." Burr's luminous eyes flashed. "And do let me say, Hamilton, that your wife is a great lady. Her natural charity outweighed all other considerations. Let me compliment you upon having made such a happy match."

Hamilton pulled on a shirt. When his tousled fair head emerged again, he was smiling.

"Thank you, sir, for the compliment to my wife, but I do think you should be careful. Captain Van Syoc may be old, but he has the build—and the temper—of a bear."

"And haven't I heard you are set to tie the knot, sir? To the erudite Widow Prevost?"

"Well, yes. After I have made that paragon among women mine, I shall be a model husband, I assure you." Burr reveled in every pleasure, whether anticipated or recently and unrepentantly savored.

"Mrs. Prevost has gone to visit relatives in New Jersey. In the interim this adventure thrust itself upon me. I'm sure you understand. As for the rest, Captain Van Syoc doesn't return for another two weeks. By that time I shall be (a) married, and (b) in New Jersey. Besides, no one present witnessed an impropriety, did they?"

The young men sat together in a row before the fire, pulling on their stockings.

"Certainly not." Hamilton's fingers busied themselves with the breeches' knee buttons to secure his hose. "It would be unconscionable to place Mrs. Van Syoc in such an awkward position."

"Quite a fine position, if you ask me." Troup was wistful, thinking back on what he'd seen.

Burr flashed a cheerful bad boy's wink. "I knew I could rely upon your discretion, gentlemen. After all, what other forms of entertainment are there in this Albanian wilderness?"

* * *

216

Preliminary articles of peace were signed at Paris that year, so Hamilton thought it time to resign his military commission. Just as Bob Troup had predicted, his friend had come to the bar in record time.

Public business, however, kept drawing him away from the law. All through the war he had been in correspondence with various important figures in the Continental Congress, among them Robert Morris, the man known as "financier to the Revolution."

Now, Morris wrote and asked Hamilton to fill the difficult and unrewarding post of receiver of taxes for New York. Getting money from a state which had been as battered by the war as New York was no easy matter, but Alexander tackled the problem with his usual vigor.

He took on another difficult task as well, representing his state in the increasingly factionalized and quarrelsome Continental Congress. He traveled constantly between Philadelphia, New York and Albany. Betsy had never been alone so much in her life, and was heartily glad she was close to her family.

One day, though, when she'd come to help her mama make conserves, just the same as every July of her life, she discovered the house in an uproar. Prince and the other servants were lined up in the great room while her father hobbled back and forth, rapping his cane on the floor and bellowing incoherently.

When Prince discretely signaled a warning, Betsy changed directions. With Phil on her hip, she trudged around the house to the kitchen wing. On her way through the garden, she caught just a glimpse of Rensselaer sliding away among the tall spikes of lavender, going to earth like a fox.

In the kitchen, she found the slaves working silently. In their midst sat her mother, clutching Kitty to her bosom and weeping softly into a fine lawn handkerchief.

"Mama! Whatever is the matter?"

When there was no reply, she set Phil and his toys down, pausing just long enough to be sure that the trailing leading strings on the shoulders of his gown were tied securely to her apron. "What has happened?"

"Oh, it's just dreadful! Shocking!"

Mrs. Schuyler released Kitty. The toddler had begun to wiggle and whine to get down as soon as she'd set eyes on Phil.

"Baby!" Kitty cried happily, trotting over to Philip and his wooden toys.

She crouched down beside him and bestowed several well-meaning but hard pats on the top of his head. Philip squeezed his eyes together while the thumps were delivered, but he recognized her benign intent because he didn't protest. Then he opened his eyes wide to stare and smile at this curly headed aunt who was barely a year older.

"Peggy's eloped." Mrs. Schuyler blew her nose. "It's Angelica all over again! Such folly, such disobedience! Oh! And your father says I—I—haven't raised you girls properly." Mrs. Schuyler dissolved into fresh tears.

"Peggy? Eloped?"

Her mother was incapable of speech for a few minutes, so Betsy concentrated on soothing her, first with an embrace and then by fetching a glass of cherry cordial.

After sipping, her mother finally managed to speak. "With the young Patroon."

"Cousin Stephen? Stephen van R?"

"Yes."

"Is that really so bad?"

Cousin Stephen was four years younger than his bride, but he was rich, well-educated, well-mannered—and a Blue. She had never understood why her father had objected to him in the first place.

"He's just nineteen. He hasn't come into his patrimony yet. Peggy only ran away with him because 'Bram jilted her."

"Hardly jilted, Mama. Everyone knows that 'Bram married Judik de Grood because he'd got her belly full."

"Well, injured pride is no good reason to go running off with the next fellow who asks. And your father is still

218

angry with Stephen for allowing Angelica and Mr. Church to marry at his house. He swore a hundred times that your cousin would never have Peggy."

Betsy hugged her mother, but didn't say another word. That Peggy had married an ardent young suitor to get revenge on 'Bram was unfortunate if true, but that Papa hadn't given his permission was clearly the chief reason for the uproar. Hearing, even at the back of the house, the tempest raging as her father berated the servants for "reckless inattention," she found herself wondering, once again, why he had so easily given her to Alexander.

* * *

When Hamilton set up his own law office in the newly freed City of New York, Betsy took Phil and their sparse furnishings and traveled on one of her father's sloops down river, moving into a narrow three story brick house at 57 Wall Street. The room that abutted the busy thoroughfare was Alexander's office.

Betsy found the new lodgings in New York City noisy, dirty, and a little alarming.

So many people, so close!

The house had a fenced yard behind, but she missed the orchards, pastures, and the moody green Hudson.

The City was hot in summer and always loud. Even at night people roamed through the streets, talking and laughing, discourteous behavior still forbidden in Albany. From the upstairs windows Betsy could see masts of ships in the harbor, a bobbing, flag-and-sail bedecked thicket. Daily their front door was passed by throngs of merchants, sailors, farmers and laborers. She and her servant were never done cleaning up the dust.

Alexander, on the other hand, loved it here. He seemed to thrive on hubbub and bustle, to find it invigorating. After the war, the Tories, many of whom were merchants and businessmen, were persecuted. Many people thought that

219

winning the war entitled them to rob their financially more able neighbors.

Alexander believed it wasn't just. He began to write a series for the newspapers called *Letters from Phocion* defending these beleaguered citizens. The *nom de plume*, Phocion, belonged to a famous Roman General who had always insisted upon mercy for the vanquished.

"If we drive out all the Tories, we are driving out people with money, people with business connections in Europe. In order to survive and start finally paying our army—who have been cheated by the very people they fought for— we've got to return to trading with our natural partners, the British. These businessmen can get the Atlantic trade going again and if they make money, they can pay taxes. The war is past; we're all Americans now."

Not only did he talk and write, but he defended, successfully, too, Tory clients. It was not a popular stand, but it was during those early days in New York that Betsy learned that Hamilton didn't worry about what was "popular," but only about the things he believed to be right. Few attorneys were in a better position to defend Tories, either, than a man who'd been such a prominent patriot.

There was the much more important matter, her husband explained, of establishing the supremacy of law. This was a difficult but necessary task if the nation was not to dissolve into thirteen warring republics. There was no such power in the existing Confederation, and Alexander and his friends regularly discussed ideas for remedying the situation.

As if he weren't sufficiently busy, Alexander also flung himself into the organizing of something entirely novel, a "money bank." This new bank, The Bank of New York, would use specie instead of land for security. As attorney, he drew the constitution, the charter, and the incorporation papers.

The concept of a "money bank" was opposed by the hereditary landowners. Betsy's New York Livingston cousins were among the most vociferous opponents. The owners of great plantations, both north and south, were

220

threatened by anything which made it easier for ordinary folk to make their living away from tenancy.

Hamilton threw himself into his practice. He wrote for the newspapers, talked and argued, his mind full of matters of law and justice, of banks and business. When her sister Angelica and her husband left for England, they gave Hamilton power of attorney and the responsibility of caring for all his brother-in-law's business affairs.

When Hamilton was elected to the Continental Congress and went to Philadelphia to attend, Betsy took Philip and sailed back Albany. She didn't like being alone, and was ready to be out of New York City. Of course, her mother and father welcomed her with open arms.

Letters from Alexander came north, long letters to General Schuyler about the sorry state of Congress. There were letters to Betsy, too, love letters, which made her blush. She should have been used to his absences by now, but she wasn't. Plain and simple, flesh missed flesh.

Still, it was comforting, delightful even, to be in Albany again, surrounded by boisterous brothers and sisters, in a place where everything was familiar and comfortable. She helped, as she always had, but it was very little compared to all the cooking and cleaning she'd had to do in her own home.

Mama seemed to understand. She encouraged Betsy to rest and sent Cornelia to carry off Phil early every morning. It was easy to go back to sleep, to leave the care of him to a fond aunt and the maids. For the first few weeks, Betsy was very lazy, catching up on what felt like months of missed sleep.

She visited Rennselaerwyck across the river. Peggy and her Stephen were content. The estate and grand mansion in which the newest Patroon and his wife lived was a far cry from the Hamilton's little townhouse, but Peggy received her sister happily, seated like a queen, with a six-month-old son at one fair breast. Betsy wept tears of joy at the reunion.

After the first big snow, Alexander sent for Betsy to join him in Philadelphia, but she didn't leave. Instead, as her parents wished, she lingered over Christmas. Papa thought it would be best if she waited and went down with Stephen van R., who had business in Philadelphia in January.

Obligingly, the New Year began with a heavy snow. The entire distance between Albany and Philadelphia could be easily traversed by sleigh. Alexander had insisted that Phil come, and the toddler traveled bundled in furs, like the son of a Mohawk chief. The entire run in Stephen's excellent sleigh was perfect, made without any upsets or really dangerous storms. Both mother and son arrived in Philadelphia without colds.

The rooms where Betsy found Alexander lodging were small, but clean and warm enough.

"You were having a good time at Albany?"

They lay in bed, whispering. Phil was asleep at last, his bed made in a drawer.

"Yes. It was wonderful to be home again."

A pause followed. Calling Albany "home" always made her husband cross.

"You certainly didn't hurry to get here. Didn't you miss me at all?"

"Of course I did, but I had to wait for Stephen." It was an excuse, and they both knew it. "And, besides, Papa didn't want to let me go. He fretted about us making a journey in this weather. I had to argue myself hoarse in order to bring Phil. Papa was determined to keep him in Albany."

"Your father!" Alexander sighed. "Mr. van R. and I had quite a chat on *that* subject."

While Betsy had been getting Phil to sleep, the men had stayed downstairs, sipping wine and talking over family business and politics. "I hear there was not a civil word passed between The Pastures and Rensselaerwyck until they made a suitable peace offering in the form of a grandson."

"Well, Papa has his ways."

"And you, I'm beginning to suspect, have yours, Mrs. Hamilton. Don't you know it's most unwise for a wife to

222

stay away from her husband for so long? I hope you're prepared to pay the price of my long frustration." His eyes were bright with purpose.

"Mr. Hamilton!"

"It's more than high time you did your duty with your husband. Just as I have been doing mine in this damned doltish Congress."

"What about Phil?"

He kissed her throat. "Phil's very much on my mind, and I've determined,"—his lips continued a relentless traverse along her neck—"that it's time we started a brother for him. Now," he whispered, moving over her, "do your part, my love."

Chapter Eleven ~ New York

The baby was howling again, but Betsy had a way to soothe her. She rocked while crooning in a sweet, husky voice. *"Engeltie*, Angelica, my pretty Angel."

After a few minutes of this, Angelica changed her cries so that they were just this side of shrieks. Large blue eyes fixed upon her mother. Named for her aunt and a whole line of Dutch grandmothers, she was deciding whether or not she really wanted to stop.

Alexander had returned to the City after six weeks of traveling the court circuit upstate. In his absence, his new daughter had grown. Her head, bald at first, was now covered with a fledging of orange fuzz which matched the outrageous color of her long and indisputably feminine eyelashes.

Betsy sang on while Alexander took off his overcoat. He gave his wife a kiss on the forehead and then got wash water from the pitcher in the kitchen.

"Where's Phil?" He picked up a towel. It was always the first question.

"Napping. There's a fire lit, so Nancy's with him. I've set her to sewing the new bed curtains."

"Is he over his cold?" Alexander pulled a chair beside his wife's and presented a finger to Angelica, who made a face while pushing it away.

"Nearly, thank heaven." Betsy turned her daughter across her shoulder and thumped her back.

"You sound hoarse. Have you caught it?"

"No, but I've been singing for hours. I think our Angel is teething, and it's the only thing which quiets her. With her hardly sleeping, and Phil's being sick, I haven't had

224

much rest. Those big eyes of hers just shine and shine all night. She sets up a howl as soon as I try to set her down."

"Well, hand that girl over and let her papa sing for a bit. I need to get acquainted with this troublesome Miss some time before she elopes. Just look at all the hair that's sprouted since I went upstate. What a color!"

Betsy smiled. "Do you suppose yours was like that?"

"Perhaps. Why don't you get some tea, sweetheart, or lie down a bit? I think she's going to let me hold her."

"Well, if she yells, I want her back directly. She mustn't wake Phil."

"Agreed, but I'm quite confident that Angel will like my songs."

Angelica, who had gone from her mother with reluctance, now stared at her father uncertainly. As Betsy got up, she stretched out her arms and whined. Hamilton didn't appear concerned. Instead he bobbed her gently and then began to sing a song which had been on the lips of all patriots during the Revolution:

"'Twas in the merry month of May,
When bees flower to flower did hum,
Soldiers through the town marched gay,
The village flew to the sound of the drum.

The clergyman sat in his study within
Devising new ways to battle with sin:
A knock was heard at the parsonage door,
And the Sergeant's sword clanged on the floor.
'We're going to war, and when we die
We'll want a man of God nearby.
So bring your Bible and follow the drum,
Follow the drum!'

Angelica stared at her father, eyes wide, rosy mouth trembling. For a moment Betsy paused at the door, but Alexander went on singing in a pleasant tenor, bobbing his daughter up and down. Emotions flitted in quick succession across Angel's mobile face, but finally she broke into a

225

glorious, open-mouthed, gummy baby smile. Planting one dainty, moist hand on her father's long nose, she pronounced, "Ah-ooo! Ah-goo!" Alexander serenely accepted the nose pulling and responded to his daughter with conversational noises of his own.

Betsy smiled as she closed the door behind her.

Was there was a woman on earth who could resist that man?

* * *

Betsy bent over the fire. Phil and Angel dozed together in the cradle, the two of them completely filling it. They were being rocked by a little black girl who was to go to Mrs. Livingston's house when that lady returned from a visit to kin in Maryland. Una was supposed to be learning something about cookery, but today she was happily rocking the cradle and singing.

Betsy had nothing to complain about though, for Una had been a big help earlier chopping meat and vegetables, and now she was keeping the little ones quiet.

"Where's Mrs. O'Rourke?" Hamilton tossed his tricorn onto a chair.

"Sick, her boy came to say."

"Drunk, more likely."

Hamilton felt it beneath his wife to cook, but he was always impressed when he saw her at it. Sometimes he'd find her seated upon a low stool, frying sausages over a circle of hot coals she'd scraped onto the hearth, sometimes loading a tray of loaves into the wall oven.

"Well, for whatever reason, she isn't here, and we're having company for dinner," Betsy replied, pushing a straying strand of dark hair back under her cap. She was red-faced from the fire, which she'd built up higher than usual in order to get the wall oven hot for baking.

"Well, you don't have to do all this. We'll have cold mutton and potatoes. All our guests have eaten worse than that before. And there's that head-splitting cider your papa

226

sent down last week. After a mug of that they won't even know what they are eating."

"Attorney Morris will most certainly notice if he is fed cold mutton at Attorney Hamilton's. Why, the story would be all the way to Philadelphia in two days." Betsy used a piece of kindling to push the crane that held a pot of calves' feet into the hottest fire. "Mrs. O'Rourke didn't cook these, although I asked her to do it yesterday. Now it's got to be done before they spoil."

Betsy saw her husband's eyes sweeping, with a growing expression of dismay, over the table where she'd marshalled an army of ingredients. Two basins, one filled with apples, currants and sugar, the other with cooked meat, sausage and onion, both dusted with flour and spices, stood on the kitchen table. A broad sheet of dough was already rolled out.

"You're going to be exhausted and fall asleep over your plate."

"Well, I'm sure I can stay awake to preside, at least until you all start to talk politics. Then you won't need me anyway."

"Now, now, Queen Bess—"

"Never mind, Mr. Hamilton, I'm too far in to stop. As long as Nancy comes in to serve and wash up, it should be all right. Everything is tidy."

"And how else could it be with my Dutch wife?"

"We'll manage. Una will mind Phil and Angel while I put the pie together. Won't you, Una?"

"Yes, Mistress." The girl's round, dark face was attentive.

Hamilton sighed. "I've got a brief to work on, but I can do a little around the children. It's too bad Angel doesn't seem to enjoy listening to legal arguments the way Phil used to, but I guess it is to be expected that a daughter would rather be hugged and told she is beautiful."

Betsy straightened, pushing her knuckles into her waist and stretching her back, to survey the scene. A pot of greens sat on the edge of the fire, simmering with a bit of salt-back. She'd cook the calves' feet fast, and then skim

227

the pot and set the bones to cooling. As soon as she could handle them, she'd pick the meat. Then she'd thicken the broth and season it up with onions, garlic, lemon rind, sherry and a little more flour, and there'd be the soup. Not particularly fancy, but it would have to do. There would be a roast with turnips around it, a meat pie and one of apples and currants, the bread, and the greens.

"I don't know if I'll have time to make a sweet." Arms akimbo, she reflected upon the table.

"I have an idea," Hamilton said. "You are always wanting to help the less fortunate. Today, in a small way, we shall. I will go to the French baker, Monsieur Haumont down the street, and get something from him."

Betsy was about to protest, but to forestall any objections, Hamilton put his arms around her.

"We shall have confection from one of my noble comrades in arms." He drew her close. "I don't want you coming to the table in deep fatigue—not to mention that apron! Everyone will say I'm a terrible provider, and I shall suffer from their opinion—even if it is true."

"Hardly, sir." The denial came automatically. They got along, but her life was far from the servant-buffered comfort of Angelica or Peggy, neither of whom ever had to so much as peek into their kitchens if they didn't feel like it. The fact was that Alexander just couldn't seem to concentrate upon his private practice. Some public calling always seemed to take him away, tasks which "*must* be performed for the common weal." This work, however, earned him at least as many foes as friends, and very little cash.

Betsy pondered as she rested her head against her husband's jacket.

It *would* make tonight easier if she only had to finish what she'd already started.

"What could Monsieur Haumont have left at this time of day? Will it be expensive?"

He dropped a kiss on her nose. "Never fear, Mrs. Hamilton. I shall deliver my request in French and we shall reminisce about the war. After that, I shall undoubtedly receive his best at a reasonable price."

Interruption from the cradle came in a thin moan. "Miss Angelica be waking up, Missus." Una's voice was a bare whisper.

"She needs her milk, I suppose."

"Yes," said Betsy. "And, sir, you no doubt require something as well."

"Well, Mrs. Hamilton, let us compromise. You feed Angelica and I shall feed the rest of us. A woman can't nurse a baby, cook, and not eat for herself. What's in here?" He'd already stepped away to look into the pantry. "Ah! The makings of a meal any poor soldier would be lucky to get."

Una continued humming and rocking the cradle, but now Philip could be heard as well.

"You mean the pork pudding?"

"God, no! One more bite of Mrs. O'Rourke's pork pudding will deliver me to an early grave. In fact, why don't you give it to her if she shows up again? I don't think my gut—to mix a metaphor—can face it even one more time."

"Then, what, sir, do you propose to feed us?"

"I shall make a rabbit. A Scots' rabbit, of course."

"I accept your offer with pleasure, Mr. Hamilton." Betsy smiled. Her man's hard upbringing had given him some unlikely talents.

The thin complaint of Angel was sufficient to start her leaking. Betsy picked up her daughter carefully, trying not to disturb Phil, although it was next to impossible. As usual he had his arms wound around her, as if she were an adored doll. .

Alexander pulled a chair close to the fire for his wife. While she untied her neck kerchief, Una fetched a clean cloth.

"Here, Missus."

"Thank you, Una. You're a good girl to know I wanted that." Betsy gave the child's satiny cheek a stroke.

Angel was a year old now, in that half-awake state where babies are notably grumpy. She knew the breast was coming, but had to cry for it anyway.

By this time, Una had Phil in her arms, comforting. Betsy planned to tell Mary Livingston what a wonderful knack this girl had with babies. Of course, girls of that age often did, willing to play with them and oblige them endlessly. She would be sorry to send Una away, and although Mama would have cheerfully given her the girl, Hamilton didn't believe it right to own other human beings.

She watched, as Alexander brought things from pantry to the table. Taking a knife, he cut thick slices of bread and then buttered them.

He really is going to make a rabbit! He hadn't done that since they'd lived with Bob Troup. Typical of male cookery, it required several pieces of equipment, dexterity, and ended by producing with a meal of utter simplicity.

The bread was impaled on the toaster and a bed of coals scraped out of the fire to surround it. While that browned, he cut thick slices of cheddar and laid them on a low grill which he'd earlier moved over the coal bed. When the cheese darkened and bubbled, the sticky side was then rolled with a fork onto the bread and then left in place until it all melted.

"Here Una." Alexander forked the first hot rabbit onto a plate, "Let it cool a little and then give the corner I'm cutting to Phil. Tuck in a napkin so he doesn't make a mess and don't let him have it too soon and burn his tongue, please. The rest is for you." He looked at his wife and then added, "I'll put the next one beside you, if you think you can manage it, Ma'am."

Soon they were eating Scotch rabbit by the fire. Betsy had been ravenous, almost faint. She decided to give Angel a piece of apple to gnaw after the breast emptied. Later, when the pies and bread were in the oven, she'd reheat some cornmeal sup'pawn left over from breakfast for the babies.

"That O'Rourke woman is going to have to go."

"But Alex, perhaps she is sick. She doesn't seem well and all those children of hers—poor creature!"

"Yes, I know, I know. I'm sorry for her trouble, too, but you shouldn't have to be in the kitchen like this."

"I prefer my own cooking."

"So do I." Then, he surprised her. "I suppose I could get a slave for you, someone from your mama's."

"What?" Though she had grown up with slaves as an accepted part of her childhood, this surprised her. Her husband had spent a great deal of time during the last few months working with friends to found The New York Society for Promoting the Manumission of Slaves. On his desk lay a register which contained the names of owners who had freed their slaves, as well as the name and a description of the men and women involved so that they would "be better enabled to detect attempts to deprive such manumitted persons of their liberty."

* * *

As Betsy nursed, their daughter's small white hand stroking the warm flesh of the maternal breast. Her husband felt admiration and concern mingle. His wife had looked smaller than ever, laboring before the cavernous opening of the hearth.

"My opinion hasn't changed, but the institution *is* with us. Whether or not you and I keep a slave or two probably wouldn't be so bad, for we'd treat them well. And we're keeping Una with us now. Are we splitting hairs?"

"Why are you suddenly arguing the other side of the issue, Mr. Attorney?"

"Because you need help, Mrs. Hamilton." Hamilton stretched and sighed, then noticed that Una had been following their discussion. As soon as she saw his eyes upon her, her dark face went blank, like a candle suddenly pinched out.

Alexander recognized—and hated—the fear which lay behind the girl's swift assumption of the mask.

231

Coffee-and-cream colored skin, eyes green as the angry sea that bit into the beach that night, kisses of fire, the first he'd ever had.... She's probably dead now. That brave, strong soul snuffed out, her beautiful, rebellious body used up by violence or disease....

"What do you think, Miss Una?"

Una almost dropped her bread. She did let go of Phil, who slipped off her lap and made a bee-line for his mother. As he trotted past, Alexander scooped him up and set him on his knee.

"No! No, Papa! I wan' Mama! I wan' Ain-jell!"

"Mama's lap is full. You stay with me—and hush."

Phil, catching his father's tone, subsided. Instead of fussing, he put his thumb in his mouth and meekly laid his curly dark head back against Alexander's waistcoat. Mama's lap was best, but Papa's was a good place, too.

"And now, Miss Una," Alexander handed Phil a chunk of apple. "I asked you—what do you think?"

"Masta?" The empty expression was replaced by one of alarm. "What I t'ink?"

Hamilton smiled grimly. She wasn't going to escape like that.

"Yes. Do you think you should be free?"

The blank expression struggled to stay in place. "'Tis God's will, Masta."

This was the reply of a docile Dutch slave. Alexander knew, from his own bitter childhood experience of service, that when she looked down, it was not acceptance, but hiding her true feelings from view.

"That it is God's Will, I do not believe." He tried to keep the anger he felt out of his voice. "And you don't believe it, either, do you?"

No answer, he knew, would be forthcoming.

"You are a good girl, Una," He spoke again, hoping to soothe her. "Good to my babies, good to my wife. It means a great deal to me."

She must be given something tangible, a present, before she was sent to Livingston's. There would be no eating

232

with the master and mistress in that house. No Scots' rabbit prepared by the master's hands. She would be going from her more egalitarian Dutch masters to a harder slavery, more like the kind he'd seen in his boyhood. She was sable black, nothing but the blood of Africa in her veins. A few years in the south, would her "increase" be lighter?

"Una, we shall give you a gift before you go to Mrs. Livingston's, something just for you. And you, Mrs. Hamilton, are right, as usual. There shall be no slaves in our house."

* * *

Betsy awoke. The newest baby, Alexander, grumbled in bed beside her, but her husband was gone. She knew he was not far, though, for she could sense him nearby. Lifting her head, she saw his outline against the moonlit window.

He was thinking aloud. Or, more properly, trying out a speech. Like the Iroquois, he often composed orations in this way, creating without benefit of pen and paper.

"Congress stands in a very embarrassing situation," Alexander spoke into the darkness. "On the one hand they are blamed for not doing what they have no means of doing; on the other, their attempts are branded as encroachments and lust for power. It is the duty of all those who have the welfare of the community at heart to direct the attention of the people to the true source of the public disorders—the want of efficient government—and to impress upon them that the States must have a stronger bond of Union, one capable of drawing forth the resources of the country. This will be a more worthwhile occupation than complaining about a weakness which is built into the current constitution."

He turned towards her, having somehow divined that she was listening.

"I shall go to the Annapolis Convention after all. Something could happen, something that could finally pull this country together. We can't leave untried any possibility."

He returned to their bed, and took a seat beside her.

"My Betsy." He stroked her hair, "I shall soon be leaving you again."

She slipped her hand through the open nightshirt to touch his chest. It was hard not to be cross. He seemed happy when he was home with her and the little ones, but he was also gone a great deal; he arranged his life that way. She had a premonition that like his tenure in the Continental Congress, he'd return to her from this latest Convention in a state of rage, boiling over, like a neglected kettle.

"The more I see, the more I find reason for those who love this country to weep over its blindness."

The convention at Annapolis would be a forum for like-minded gentlemen from several states to discuss the problems of the Confederation. However, many powerful people in New York—Governor Clinton among them—didn't really want anything to change.

George Clinton was more interested in setting up New York as a private enterprise which would be run by him and his cronies, an "Empire State," which, with bustling port and rich hinterlands, wouldn't need membership in any closer "Union." The governor's backers were farmers and frontiersmen who feared that a strong central government would force the payment of debts to Tories, or dislodge them from the Indian land where they were already squatting, or force the payment of back taxes.

The spectacle of thirteen states, creating trade barriers, warring over boundaries, with differing currencies and laws, all while the Continental army remained unpaid and with a huge war debt coming due, was not one which inspired confidence in either foreign lenders or in America's more thoughtful citizens. Hamilton and his father-in-law agreed that without a central government which paid its debts and soldiers, they were sure to come to grief. Some land-grabbing European power could easily appear on the scene to fragment and then gobble up the weak, separate states.

"You haven't said anything." His voice broke in upon her reverie, as his fingers trailed along the length of her braid.

"You will go, Mr. Hamilton, no matter what I say."

"Oh, Eliza." It did not sound like a protest. In fact, he seemed contrite. She did not quibble when he kissed her forehead and then drew her silently down into the bed, to settle in for sleep. Baby Alex snuffled, gurgled and pressed small sharp feet against her stomach, while her husband lay, spoon fashion, behind.

* * *

The little house at 56 Wall was crowded, for Alexander had brought home two newly manumitted, but now indentured, black servants.

"It will be tight to house them with us, but now you won't have to work so hard."

"Mr. Hamilton, you never cease to astonish me. What, by the way, has happened to that wretched Aquilaea and her equally wretched turnips?"

Hamilton arched a sandy brow.

"My dear, it's the surest way I know to get you some reliable help. I hate to see you sewing from dawn to dusk or struggling in the kitchen with Alex tied to your apron strings and both of you in grave danger of falling into the fire. You'll be pleased with them, I'm sure. It's our Miss Una and a young friend of hers who can split kindling, lug water, scrub the steps, and take care of my horse."

Two years later, Una had blossomed, making a quick change from child to woman. She was shy at first, but Betsy had a feeling she was glad to be with them again. The downcast, sullen boy was about the same age, but as is often true with boys, he hadn't begun to grow.

"This is Davie. He wasn't getting along at Livingston's, but things are going to be better here."

The boy wouldn't look up, just continued to glower at the ground. He's been treated badly, Betsy thought. She

235

wondered, with a sudden sinking feeling, whether she could manage him.

"Hamilton," she said, when they were alone, "I think Davie is going to run away. He looks so—wrathful."

"He is, but he'll stay."

"Will he? Papa always said the look Davie's got in his eye meant running."

"Not in this case, because Davie's in love with Una. As long as she stays, he'll stay."

"That boy?"

"Not so little. He's fourteen, which, if I remember correctly, is quite old enough for a grand passion."

"Don't joke."

"I'm not." He exhibited so much touchy dignity that Betsy thought it best to let it pass.

There would always be so much about her husband she'd never know.

"Um, well, how did you find that out?"

"They both worked in the kitchen at Livingston's. I had a chat with the cook."

"I don't want to seem ungrateful, but you know very well that, dependent upon us they may be, they may also be just as troublesome as day servants."

"Yes, that's true, but I think Una will be content. She remembers how she was treated here. As for Davie, well, she's not in love with him, at least not yet. If it comes to pass, we'll do the decent thing and see them married. When they can care for themselves, they can stay or go as they wish." Alexander slipped an arm around his wife's slim waist. "In the meantime, patient Aquilaea will have some help."

* * *

With her husband's erratic earnings—sometimes feast and sometimes famine—and what came down river from Albany, Betsy managed her household. Now there were two indentured servants and a family of five to feed and clothe. Then, out of the blue, they acquired another child—a little girl of two, an orphan.

Alexander had gone to a meeting of The Cincinnati, a society for officers of the American Army to which every prominent man of their circle belonged. He returned from this monthly gathering with a bare-legged, raw-boned frontier woman sitting astride behind him. The bundle in her arms turned out to be a tiny, sickly blonde baby.

"This is Fanny, the daughter of Colonel Antil, who was in a Northern regiment. He was ruined by his devotion to his country. He got a piece of land in the Genesee valley, but you know how that is. His wife died of the hardship, and now he's sick, too. He's come, with his last bit of strength, to ask for our help. The poor man collapsed at the tavern. We're seeing he is cared for properly, but when we carried him back to his lodgings, we discovered he had these two ladies with him as well."

The woman hopped off the horse by herself. Dressed in rough brown cloth and none too clean, she bobbed a clumsy curtsy.

"Pleased to meet you, Mar'm."

"Gussie Muldoon is the nurse," Alexander said. "I promised Colonel Antil we'd take care of his daughter and his servant until he got better."

Betsy nodded. They were cramped in the house already, but the first sight of that tiny, sickly baby girl and the sad-faced country woman tugged at her heart strings.

Colonel Antil died a few days later. Although they searched for relatives, none could be found. Fanny Antil remained in their care, and Gussie, who was devoted to her, stayed on, becoming a valued extra pair of hands.

Chapter Twelve ~ The Philadelphia Convention

Alexander tended his law practice in New York. It was profitable and would have been more so if he had stuck with it, but a desire to be a part of various legislatures, from the Continental Congress to the New York Assembly, interfered. The Assembly met far up river at Poughkeepsie. When he wasn't riding the circuit, other obligations kept him out of town for long stretches.

Hamilton had corresponded for years with Betsy's father, James Duane, and other influential New Yorkers. After the Annapolis Convention, another friend was added to the list, one James Madison of Virginia, a neighbor of George Washington.

"Madison is a bachelor, a scholar, spilling over with lectures upon the Greek Republics, but he has some practical ideas too. We both are of the opinion that the Confederation should be scrapped and a new plan drawn up. It was gratifying to discuss the Resolution to Summon a Convention which I wrote during the '83 Congress with someone who actually agrees."

"Scrap the Confederation?" Betsy wondered if she would ever grow accustomed to living in a republic. When men, not Gods or Kings, made the laws, things could, apparently, change with astonishing suddenness.

"Yes. Here is a copy of the letter we sent to the legislatures of Virginian, Delaware, Pennsylvania, New Jersey and New York."

Dutifully, Betsy accepted it and began to read.

"...Your commissioners, beg leave to suggest their unanimous conviction, that it may tend to advance the interests of the Union, if the States, by whom they have been respectively delegated, would use their endeavors to procure the concurrence of the other States in the appointment of Commissioners to meet at Philadelphia on the second Monday in May next, to take into consideration the situation of the United States, to devise such further provisions as shall appear to them necessary to render the Constitution of the Federal Government adequate the exigencies of the Union; and to report such an Act for that purpose to the United States in Congress assembled..."

"Another Convention?"

"This time, perhaps, influential gentlemen from every state can be persuaded to attend. If they do, something useful may actually come out of it."

* * *

In May, Hamilton interrupted his law practice again. Leaving Troup to handle his cases, he rode to Philadelphia to attend what was being called a "Constitutional Convention." He knew he was going to a fight, for the other New York State delegates, Yates and Lansing, were Governor Clinton's men. Like their patron, they were dead set against any plan which would lead to any sort of closer union among the states.

For weeks Betsy as well as the rest of American world knew nothing, for the members had agreed to conduct meetings in secrecy. She received an occasional brief note from Alexander, in which he sent his love and asked about her health and that of the children, but said little more.

* * *

As Hamilton predicted, the new servants settled in. Una had learned cookery at Livingston's and it was wonderful to be able to have regular help in the kitchen as well as with the children. Davie was short, but he could scrub pots and split kindling. After a time, he did his chores without being asked, fetching in water early every morning. Before the horse had gone with its master to Philadelphia, he'd enjoyed taking care of him, too. Davie, it seemed, liked the horse best. He had a real knack with animals.

"Mizz, you could keep some chickens here. I kin hammer up de boxes."

Betsy thought it a good idea. She lost no time in sending upriver for layers and a couple of geese. Davie actually smiled, the first smile she'd seen, as he knocked together lumber scrap for nesting boxes.

Fowl were kept by every good Dutch housewife. Here, amid the unfriendly hustle of New York, it cheered Betsy to see them scratching and muttering in her backyard and down the alley behind. It didn't take long for the geese to settle in and consider the property theirs. They were better lookouts than any dog.

One day while Gussie minded Alex and Fanny, Betsy went to the shed with Phil and Angel to look for eggs. Sometimes a real search was required. One hen, desperate for chicks, kept hiding hers in all sorts of clever places.

At the sound of a horse blowing and snorting outside, the geese screeched and flapped their wings. The children dashed to peer into the alley.

"Papa! Papa! It's Papa!" Phil pelted out to greet the slim man dismounting. The horse was covered with sweat, a heavy spindle of froth dangling from the bit, which surprised Betsy. She'd rarely seen Hamilton ride his horse to lather.

"I didn't expect you." Betsy called over the children's squeals.

"I never sent word, Mrs. Hamilton."

Betsy had a distinct foreboding, for Alexander appeared not only hot and tired, but depressed. As he led the bay gelding inside, the fowl, having set up housekeeping without either horse or husband, flew about squawking. One of the geese came swaggering, wings raised in threat.

Understandably, the horse balked. Hamilton waved his hat at the truculent goose, but it took Davie soothing and shooing to get her to back down and move away.

"Where'd all this come from?"

"From Grandma," Angel explained.

"Davie made the boxes." Phil had watched in fascination the day Davie had constructed them.

"Oh." Hamilton appeared unsure. "They aren't a nuisance, are they?"

"No, Mr. Hamilton. Davie and I can manage them."

"Ah, my Albany goodwife! But if they don't behave themselves any better than that lady there, they shall end as my dinner." He indicated the goose who continued to honk and strut threateningly nearby.

"No! Papa!" Angel's thin face puckered. She was constitutionally incapable of recognizing teasing. "You mustn't eat 'Lady Mary'! She's the mother!"

"Sir, the geese just don't know you and Sergeant." Phil hurried to explain.

"Don't fret, either of you." Hamilton swung Angel up into his arms. "I'm joking. I would never eat Queen Bess's fine Albany geese."

As he embraced the children, Davie took charge of the horse.

"Hello, Davie."

"Sah." Davie inclined his curly head.

"I've brought old Sergeant back to give you more work around here. But, mind now, he's hot as a firecracker."

"Ah'm washen him down an' walken him, sah, a'fore he gits drink." His black hand came to stroke the horse's sweating neck. "He bin goin' plen'y hard." With Sergeant, Davie showed all the initiative anyone could wish.

"I rely on you, Davie, and you're correct. I've ridden the poor fellow halfway 'cross New Jersey today."

They left Davie busily removing tack and soothing the horse. The children danced around their father, full of chatter.

"Is the great Convention over, Papa?"

"No, Phil, not yet."

"Then why are you home?"

"Yes," Betsy said. "What has happened? We've all had such hopes, what with so many gentlemen of stature, like General Washington, there."

241

"Yes. Well, in spite of His Excellency's august presence, nothing much has happened, except argument. And there wasn't much I could do with Lansing and Yates strung around my neck like millstones. Just as Governor Clinton wants, they vote me down every time. It was damned aggravating to sit there and politely listen to so much folly. Talk is no substitute for action. Frankly, I couldn't endure being there for a moment longer. Besides, I got a letter from Troup about a client of mine who needs attention at once."

"Will—will you go back?"

"I haven't made up my mind. So far it's been a complete waste of time. There were entire days I spent pacing the back of the room. I thought I'd suffer apoplexy while listening to them. Your father, God bless him, would have. The petty squabbling among the states, the posturing, the theorizing! All nonsense when the country is bankrupt, when we have lost both credit and honor! I'm entirely worn out with trying to be a good citizen of this benighted republic. It's an exercise similar to repeatedly running headfirst against a stone wall. Perhaps I'll just stay here and put money in my own pocket instead of wasting my time building American sand castles."

Betsy recognized his mood. She hoped that Alexander wouldn't be overflowing with his peculiar brand of restive gloom.

At supper, when he'd calmed down and eaten some of the fish and potato pie she'd made, he began to talk about what seemed hopeful to him. This was mostly about his new friend, James Madison of Virginia. He talked about Madison's erudition, his patience, and the careful notes he was making on the convention.

Betsy thought Alexander would spend the evening writing letters or maybe calling upon Bob Troup or the troubled client, but just about the time she tucked the children into bed, he slipped up behind her and put his arms around her waist. Lips grazed the back of her neck, sipped at the ever-present July perspiration.

242

"Is everyone in bed?"

"Yes."

"Good." Smiling, he turned her around. "Do you think, Mrs. Hamilton, that you might be persuaded to offer some wifely comfort to a man severely disappointed by politics?"

Betsy blushed. She had, of course, been anticipating this too, but she had imagined it later, in the warm secrecy of the summer darkness, with the candle snuffed out. "I'd planned to finish sewing a new frock for Alex this evening." It was still light, after all, and she had so much work. "It's impossible to get much done during the day between the children and everything else."

Instead of arguing, Hamilton simply picked her up. Then, smothering her protests with kisses, he carried her away. Knowing that the marital bed would be filled with drowsy children, he set a course for his study.

Once inside, he set her on the low daybed and then went back to bolt the door. It was impulsive and romantic, but Betsy found her thoughts returning to the children, the servants, the possibility of visitors, the unfinished frock. How typical of him to arrive and turn all her plans upside down!

With a possessive manner, he sat down behind her and set about unhooking her stays.

"What if one of your friends comes to talk politics?" She tried to squirm away. "Hamilton! Heavens! The sun isn't down."

"A poor defense will not save you." Kisses fell, tingling the back of her neck. "Gussie has been instructed to tell everyone you're indisposed. Besides, I'm sworn to secrecy about the Convention, though, God knows, there's nothing to tell. Ah! Victory!" He had come, triumphantly, to the end of the stay loops.

Betsy clasped them to her bosom, refused to let them fall.

"Even if Bob Troup pounds on the door?"

"We are indisposed, even to our old comrade."

Because she was clutching the stays so valiantly, he began an attack on another front, pulling off her cap and

243

setting loose her matronly braids. "Mmmm." He lifted one and kissed it. "You have no idea how many times I lay awake in Philadelphia longing for the touch of my nut-brown maid."

"What if the children cry?"

"Gussie or Una will see to them. Hush, my Betsy, and give me a kiss. And let go of those damned stays."

"Alex is teething. He's bound to wake up."

"It's so hot tonight." His lips repeatedly and tantalizingly grazed the back of her neck, "I think we should play Adam and Eve. You know, Mrs. Hamilton, that I will have my way."

Kneeling beside the divan, he slipped a hand beneath her skirt to loosen the knee garters. Then, one after the other, he pulled off her stockings.

* * *

Outside the narrow house, the evening bustle was in full flood. Empty wagons rattled by, goods now delivered. Up and down the street there were shouts, laughter and conversation. Sailors, traders, slaves, apprentices and servants, lawyers and doctors, fishmongers and coopers, tailors and candle-makers, were closing shop, another work day done. Gulls wheeled and called over the low brick houses. A welcome breeze blew from a choppy sea. Ships rode low tide easily, bright flags fluttering in a bobbing forest of masts.

The salt tang on the wind reminded Hamilton of another time, another place, of a similar sensual, sweaty interlude—of bliss and satin. Once his wife's perennial modesty was put to flight, the deliciously responsive woman might have been from the Island time. Still, the sweet sighs, the beautiful dark eyes in which tears of pleasure gathered, were undeniably those of his Albany princess.

* * *

244

Writing to Washington a few days later, Hamilton said: "In my passage through the Jerseys, and since my arrival here, I have taken pains to discover the public sentiment, and I am more and more convinced that this is the critical opportunity for establishing the prosperity of this country on a solid foundation.

"The prevailing apprehension among thinking men is that the Convention, from the fear of shocking the popular opinion, will not go far enough. They seem to be convinced that a strong, well-mounted government will better suit the popular palate than one of a different complexion. Men in office are indeed taking all possible pains to give an unfavorable impression of the Convention, but the current seems to be moving strongly the other way. This serves to prove that we ought not allow too much weight to objections drawn from the supposed repugnance of the people to an efficient constitution.

"I own it to you, Sir, I am seriously and deeply distressed at the aspect of the counsels which prevailed when I left Philadelphia. I fear that we shall let slip the golden opportunity of rescuing the American empire from disunion, anarchy, and misery."

Hamilton watched the ink slowly sink into the humid paper. Either these American gentlemen looked reality in the face or they didn't. He couldn't roll the stone uphill by himself. And there, as usual, in the middle of it, sat George Washington.

He doesn't have the luxury of walking out when he starts to go mad. Of course, he doesn't go mad as quickly as I do....

A smile came, thinking of his old commander stuck in that oven of a building with that incompatible collection of ivory tower philosophers and state-minded factionalists yanking each other back and forth. Hamilton had spoken his mind from the floor, saying "We are now to decide forever the fate of Republican government. If we do not give to that form due stability and wisdom, it will be disgraced and lost to mankind forever. I am as zealous an advocate for liberty as any man, and would cheerfully

245

become a martyr to it. But real liberty is neither found in despotism nor the extremes of democracy, but in moderate governments."

After that day, he had stayed silent and listened to Americans-born. He'd seconded motions for increased representation in the House, and for a "popular branch" laid on a broad foundation, to balance the proposals for a more exclusive and less numerous Senate. He had also supported a strong executive with veto power. He had pointed out that a nation needed a national judiciary, and some kind of supreme tribunal as a final court of resort, when lower courts disagreed.

He had supported election of all representatives directly by the people rather than by legislature as essential to the democratic rights of the larger community. The nation could rest on no more solid basis than the consent of the people.

"National power ought to flow immediately from that pure, original fountain of all legitimate authority."

He smiled to himself, remembering old Ben Franklin's suggestion that prayers be offered at the beginning of each session, for debate had grown progressively more personal. In passing, he'd joked to Jonathan Dayton that he hoped their Convention could "transact the business entrusted to its care without the necessity of calling in foreign aid."

* * *

Hamilton tended his law practice, but, typically, soon became involved in something more dramatic, second in a duel. This meant letters and secret meetings with his opposing second. As was customary, the men tried to keep it a secret, but Betsy knew and feared the signs. After days of anxiety, "extremities" were prevented. The matter was settled peacefully.

She understood that Alexander had given and received challenges during the war. None of these had reached the actual "interview." She knew her husband had been second

246

for his dear friend John Laurens and that he'd witnessed, with vast approval, his duel with General Lee. After Lee had been wounded, the seconds declared honor satisfied and forced a conclusion, although Lee, with blood running down his side, had wanted to have another go at Laurens.

It was the kind of military story recited after the ladies had withdrawn, but Betsy had more than once overheard. Every word was colored with lethal meaning: "explanation," "satisfaction," "insolence," "gentleman," and loudest of the warrior's litany: "Honor." She feared it.

Across America political tempers ran high over the proposed Constitution. In fact, the fight just averted had been started by a member of George Clinton's faction who'd been loud about his intention to "get Hamilton, once and for all, out of the way."

When a new and tearful bride, her husband had gone to risk his life in the line, she'd come to know the ferocity of his pride, his total devotion to the gentleman's code. Betsy knew he'd accept a challenge in a heartbeat.

Then, one day, a letter came from Washington, asking Hamilton to return to Philadelphia. It was brief, a note saying: "I am sorry you went away. I wish you were back."

Unable to ignore a summons from his old commander, Alexander mounted Sergeant and took the blistering, dusty August road back to Philadelphia.

* * *

When he returned at the beginning of September, a copy of a proposed new constitution came along in his saddle bag.

"No one's ideas were farther from this than mine, but I believe this concoction has sufficient vigor to last—for a time, anyway. The system of checks and balances should prevent things from getting too far away from the center. After Yates and Lansing left, I signed it. It was an empty gesture without them, but who knows?"

"Will you be able to stay with us now?" Betsy put a hand on his arm and braved the words. If it weren't for bounty coming down river from Albany, she wasn't sure what they would have eaten for the last month.

Alexander slipped an arm around her waist. "I'm afraid this Convention has just been the beginning. The real battle will be fought in the State legislatures. Everyone who signed now has to lobby in his own state to get it ratified. Success depends upon every state joining. Here in New York, George Clinton and half of your Livingston cousins are against it. Your father and I have got our work cut out. I'll be writing pamphlets, corresponding with federalists in other states and working to get elected to the State legislature. I must be elected to congress, so that I can argue for the Constitution here. I'm afraid I anticipate months of debating."

"Hamilton...."

At last his eyes focused upon her.

"I have not forgotten that it is my duty to keep his family fed."

He put his arms around her, gathered her close. Betsy sighed, rested her head against his chest, listened to his heart steadily beating. All her needs and news—particularly about the new life his summer visit home had started—would wait. For the moment, it must be enough to hold this restless man, however briefly, in her arms.

* * *

The Schuyler women had been sitting, peacefully shelling beans on the lawn, watching the ancient willows finger the green surface of the Hudson. Angel and Phil were playing among the rocks in the care of two little black maids. They hadn't been gone long when Angel began to scream, blood curdling shrieks.

Dropping beans without ceremony into her mother's lap, Betsy ran as fast as she could to the sound. She discovered Angel standing stiffly erect. She held her head between her hands and let out shriek after piercing shriek. Her nursemaid kept trying to pick her up.

"Hush, Miss Angelica! Hush!"

The other girl had her arms around Phil, who was silent. A rag, streaked with red, was pressed to his forehead.

"Oh, Missus! Masta Phil was playin' an' he slip an' fall an' Miss Angelica pitched a fit. Dere ain' a mark on 'er!"

"Don't worry, Mama. I'm all right." Philip spoke up bravely. Then he added, in his sternest grown-up voice, "Angelica Hamilton, you stop that noise at once!"

A crowd of servants came in Betsy's wake. Both children were carried back to the house. Pandemonium followed, someone crying that the little nurses should be paddled for not taking care of Mrs. Hamilton's babies. Betsy wouldn't allow it.

"It would have happened no matter who was there."

It was decided that Phil should wait in bed until Doctor Stringer could be summoned. After he had examined his small patient, the Doctor pronounced no lasting damage had been done, but stitching was required.

Angelica, white and shivering, though without a mark on her, lay beside her brother, who she'd insisted upon joining in bed. The moment she saw the needle being threaded, she began to screech, so Betsy picked her up and carried her to a chair in the great room.

With Grandpa Schuyler in attendance, Phil was a soldier. He didn't make a sound. Outside, however, Angelica shrieked and held her forehead. Betsy rocked her and gently reprimanded, saying she was making it harder for Phil, who was so brave.

After that, Angel clenched her teeth and didn't make another sound, although so many tears welled up in her gray eyes that they ran down her cheeks. Finally, to her mother's dismay, she fainted. The Doctor had to examine her, too.

"What's the matter, Miss?" Stringer was gruff, running his hands over her. "Are you hurt too? Some place we can't see?"

A shudder shook Angelica's thin frame. "My head hurts!" She rubbed her temple.

Carefully, the Doctor inspected the part she indicated.

"And when did that start?"

"When Philip hit his head and then after you stitched." Angelica appeared surprised that the Doctor would ask such a question.

"It started when Phil hit his head?"

"Yes, Doctor."

"And what does stitching feel like, Miss?"

Angelica pondered and then she said, "Stitching is like bee stings, but all in a line."

After a moment's thought, Stringer asked, "Do you always hurt when Phil does?"

"Yes, Doctor Stringer."

Betsy was dumbfounded. Angel was known for a vivid imagination, but she was not given to telling tales.

The Doctor looked her over a little more, asked some other questions and finally prescribed a compound. As well as ordinary simples, things like hops which Mrs. Schuyler grew, there were a few ingredients needed from the apothecary.

"A word with you, Mrs. Hamilton."

When the Doctor motioned, Angel was shifted into the ample arms of her grandmother. They went to confer at the top of the steep stairwell.

"I don't understand this, Doctor. I have never heard her tell a lie."

"I don't think she is." Stringer looked at the floor thoughtfully before speaking again. "She screamed at each stitch, exactly when the needle went through her brother's flesh. It is a curious phenomenon, but I have seen it before, although only between twins. A sort of mental connection exists."

Betsy was silent, thinking of all the times Angel and Phil had been sick together, of the way Angel wept upon those rare occasions when Phil received a swat on the backside.

"At any rate," Doctor Springer said, "it bears watching. I suggest plenty of exercise and fresh air, and other playmates. Separate them more and send him off to school early. Mark my words, they won't take kindly to separation, but it's the only way I know to end what could become a most unhealthy connection."

With a queer down-spiraling sensation, Betsy saw the doctor out. When she returned upstairs, Angel and Phil were in bed together again, heads resting on the same pillow. Phil seemed to be dozing, but Angel lay on her side, those curiously pale eyes of hers open, fixed anxiously upon her brother's bandaged head.

"She wouldn't be still any other way," her mother explained. "What a pair of angels! When I think of how Rensselaer and Cornelia quarrel all the time...."

"Mama, Doctor Stringer told me he doesn't think it's good for them to spend so much time together."

"With all due respect to the good doctor, they'll grow out of it. Phil's seven and she's but four. I know they seem big to you, Elizabeth, but believe me, they're still just babies."

Looking at them lying together, two pretty cherubs taking comfort in each other, Betsy decided her mama was right. Besides, because the children appeared so upset, it did not seem the best time to start something new.

* * *

Betsy arose from patting the toddler's back. Alex Jr. squiggled slightly, but he did not wake up. He was teething again, getting his two year molars, and was not happy about it.

Betsy had promised she would help her husband with copying the beginning of another piece for the newspapers. Alexander had declared (or perhaps cautioned?) this would be "the longest and most important work he'd ever done." His essays in defense of the new Constitution were to be written under yet another *nom de plume*, this time, "Publius." Hamilton had initiated the project, with assistance promised by John Jay and James Madison.

Betsy found him pen in hand, fair hair glinting in the candlelight, quill scratching. When he heard her enter, he stopped to smile up at her.

"How is our boy?"

"Asleep at last. I only hope he stays that way."

"Yes, so do I. Although he probably thinks he has first claim upon his mother, I am in desperate need of you. Please sit, Mrs. Hamilton." He stood and offered her a chair. After she'd taken the seat, he moved over and pulled a neat pile of paper close.

"This is the first of it."

As he returned to his side of the table, Betsy surveyed the stack. Hamilton was off to a good start. It was already longer than the longest brief she'd ever seen.

To the People of the State of New York:

After an unequivocal experience of the inefficacy of the subsisting Federal Government, you are called upon to deliberate on a new Constitution for the United States of America. The subject speaks its own importance; ...nothing less than the existence of the UNION, the safety and welfare of the parts of which it is composed, the fate of an empire in many respects the most interesting in the world. It has been frequently remarked, that it seems to have been reserved to the people of this country, by their conduct and example, to decide the important question, whether societies of men are really capable or not, of establishing good government from reflection and choice, or whether they are forever destined to depend, for their political constitutions, on accident and force....

Among the most formidable of the obstacles which the new Constitution will have to encounter...the obvious interest of a certain class of men in every State to resist all changes which may hazard a diminution of the power and consequence of the offices they hold under the State establishments....

Ambition, avarice, personal animosity, party opposition and many other motives...are apt to operate...nothing

252

could be more ill-judged than that intolerant spirit which has, at times, characterized political parties. For in politics, as in religion, it is equally absurd to aim at making proselytes by fire and sword....

History will teach us that...of those men who have overturned the liberties of republics, the greatest number have begun their career by paying an obsequious court to the people; commencing demagogues, and ending tyrants....

"Poor Mrs. Hamilton." When Alexander saw her nodding, he threw down his pen. A moment later, he'd lifted her chin and kissed her nose.

"You are to go to bed at once, my dear. I'll finish."

Betsy lay under covers and watched the light under the door. In the darkness, his small, dozing namesake lay beside her. She was tired, but she couldn't seem to go to sleep.

Outside, her husband's quill scratched vigorously. How familiar that sound after eight years! If it wasn't a brief, he was working away at a piece for the newspapers, a piece which would, he hoped, sway opinion in the direction he— and her father—desired. Endless persuasion, so many words pouring from his restless pen!

* * *

Mr. Jay fell ill and Mr. Madison was engaged in the ferocious struggle for ratification going on in Virginia, leaving Alexander to finish the task of "Publius" alone. He didn't seem to mind.

"The Cause of America is greater than my need for sleep."

Or, so he claimed each hollow-eyed morning.

Betsy linked each baby she'd had with some momentous event in their lives. Philip had been born after Yorktown. Angelica had been born the year Alexander had argued *Rutgers v. Waddington,* one of the first cases to test the supremacy of Federal law over State law, in defense of a

253

persecuted Tory. Alexander Junior had been born the year his father had become a member of the New York Assembly, the same year he and his friends had, at Annapolis, managed to arouse sufficient interest for another constitutional convention.

Perhaps this baby she carried would be born at the very moment when the country would adopt this new constitution, one which would provide the "effective government" that all the men in her world wished for.

How Alexander had labored for this new constitution, even if he didn't have much faith in it. He often quoted Alexander Pope:

"For Forms of Government let fools contest:
Whate'er is best administered is best...."

* * *

Then the baby kicked, causing Betsy to shift in bed uncomfortably. She was certain it was another boy, and sincerely hoped it was. There was something about the child's eternal activity and the way she carried up high, just as she had with Alex and Phil, which made her believe it.

Fanny Antil and Angel were such a lot of trouble compared to the boys, so demanding, so emotional! The little girls followed her around all day, wanting attention.

Fanny was a dear little thing, but she had a permanently runny nose. After her rough start in life, susceptibility was to be expected. Angel was physically well enough, a pretty creature with a halo of fine auburn curls, talkative and bright, but she was exhaustingly high-strung, given to bouts of night-terrors.

The boys slept like stones, were sturdy, affectionate, and easily distracted. They were content to busy themselves with toys, even just a mess of spoons and cups. This allowed her time in which to cook, sew or clean.

Yes, I hope this sturdy kicker is another boy. They had already decided upon James, after Alexander's father. Girl's names were harder. When she suggested using his

254

mother's, Alexander had smiled wryly and said they had already flaunted Dutch tradition once by naming Angelica for Betsy's adored sister, instead of Catherine for her grandmother.

"If we call her 'Rachel,' your papa will stop sending us those quarters of beef, bushels of potatoes and fine cheeses and then we'll starve. Besides," he added, a shadow crossing his face, "it might be ill-omened. I would not wish a single instance of my mother's myriad sorrows upon a child." The words were spoken with an uncharacteristic nod to superstition which Betsy divined he didn't genuinely feel.

"But why ever not? Haven't you said that your Mama was very beautiful, that she taught you to read, to speak French and to keep a ledger, that she read Shakespeare and Mr. Pope's poems to you, that you were her favorite?"

"Well, yes. All true."

Betsy fell silent. She recognized tension in him, knew this discussion touched one of his secrets, something to do with the darkness surrounding his past. There was something boyish in the urgent way he drew her close, in the caresses he lavished upon her full and moving belly.

"As your sister Angelica has already given the world a "Kitty," ours could be a "Katy." Either way, I'd pray that any daughter of ours would grow to be as full of virtues as the lady who raised my excellent wife."

Betsy's time was nearing. Every joint ached. This baby was night-restless and wakeful, drumming her ribs. She had reached the heavily gravid stage, and needed extra pillows in bed. While she wondered about his reaction, there was no energy to pursue the matter.

* * *

Betsy stood on the high stoop, her dark hair covered. In the city, she wore it so summer and winter, to keep it free of the dust constant traffic stirred up. Two-year-old Alex rode her hip, and together they watched Hamilton trot away

255

with his fellow nationalists, her cousin Bob Livingston and the elegant John Jay.

Alexander's ginger queue, trailing down the back of a gray traveling coat, made a bright line under the chilly spring sun. Phil and Angel stood beside her, both teary as they waved good-bye to their adored and adoring papa.

As the horses' burnished rumps swayed out of sight among the incessant carter's traffic on Wall Street, Betsy herded the children inside. She felt drained, as she always did when he left. Alexander was gone, and along with him went a great deal of his contagious energy.

This new constitution! What dread she felt, what fear for its fate, almost as if it was one of her children. After listening nightly to the men, after copying those long pieces for the newspapers, Betsy felt she knew as much about the dangers which faced America and this proposed new form of government as any man in the country.

* * *

Una, pink palms up, arrived to take Alex. Betsy relinquished him with a grateful nod. From the well-used cradle, resting at this moment in the parlor, the newest Hamilton, Jamie, now a month old, could be heard waking up.

"I'll nurse him and then I'll take him upstairs and maybe we can both rest a bit. All of a sudden I don't feel very well."

"Do you need some raspberry, Missus, or ma'be Chamomile?"

"Chamomile, I think, is best. Bring it up as soon as it's steeped."

Una carried the protesting Alex away, those sturdy toddler legs kicking from under his skirts. Betsy turned to her two older children.

"Go up and play quietly. Don't, for heaven's sake, wake Fannie."

Her foster child was suffering through yet another cold and had just had a morning of fussing and tears extinguished by sleep.

"Yes, Mama." Phil was obedient, but Angel, in a wispy voice, asked, "When is Papa coming home?"

"Oh, it will be a long time, darling, just as Papa said. He's got to go up the river to Poughkeepsie, almost all the way to Grandpa's house." Betsy, seeing tears gathering in her daughter's gray eyes, knelt to hug. "Papa's got to win a very big, important argument with some very angry, very stubborn, very proud men, and it's going to take weeks and weeks."

"Well, it's very bad of them not to listen to Papa."

Betsy smiled. "Papa—and your Grandfather, too—don't know why these gentlemen can't see what's best for our country, Angel, but that's the way it is."

"Yes," Phil gravely chimed in, "Papa told me all about it. Don't worry, Angelica. Come on, we'll go up and I will show you an easy way I've just learnt to draw horses." He sent a swift sidelong glance at his mother.

With a free arm, Betsy collected him close and squeezed. Every day she thanked God for giving her such a treasure.

"Yes, darling, go along with your brother. I've got to feed Jamie." Betsy kissed Angelica's pale forehead encouragingly.

Taking his sister's hand in his, Phil led her up the narrow stairs. Betsy watched, wondering how on earth she'd be able to handle Angel's constant neediness without him.

The whining from the next room suddenly grew to a wail. James, when his first grumbling summons hadn't been answered, was angry now. With a sweep of skirts, Betsy marched into the room, scooped her howling son from his cradle and plumped herself down in a comfortable wing chair. Her mother would never have undertaken such a task in the good parlor. After all, with a new baby, the risks of spills from one end and leaks from the other were high, but Betsy couldn't bring herself to walk another step.

257

As a piece of insurance, however, she snatched up his flannel wrap.

Unbuttoning her dress, she got bellowing Jamie in place, experienced the sharp tug and the answering flesh gone-to-sleep prickle of the let-down. Then, one end of the cloth pressed to stem the flow from the neglected breast and the rest tucked strategically around James, she watched her newest son's jaw work as he mastered the initial tide. He was round and fair, even balder than Angelica had been, but a similar halo of red fluff had begun to rise upon his pink skull. As different in some ways as the children were, there was a certain sameness in the general outline: gray eyes, long heads, a kiss of red in their hair.

Betsy leaned back, relaxing into the comforts of nursing, when she heard a knock at the door.

"Davie!" When she called out, James startled. "Una! Gussie! The door!"

In stretching for the bell on the end table, she dislodged James and he promptly set up a renewed cry at this sudden, rude interruption of his dinner.

"Temper, temper!" Betsy rubbed his open mouth—and the yell—against the nipple. She noticed, with amusement, that his bald head instantly became scarlet with rage.

She decided to ignore whoever it was. If they wanted in badly enough, they'd go around to the kitchen. Then she heard rapid footsteps in the hallway, the sound of Davie running, followed by voices. Soon, the parlor door opened and Peggy poked her head in.

"May I?"

"Of course, Peg. Heavens! I didn't know you were in town."

"It was spur-of-the-moment. Stephen is having trouble with Mr. Beekman and decided to come down and straighten it out face to face. I thought I'd come too and see what's in the shops. The first of the London fashions are arriving."

During this speech, her sister settled on the facing sofa. She was very much the lady of leisure, in a gown of peach

258

satin layered over an ivory petticoat upon which hundreds of tiny birds in flight had been painted. As she removed the long pins which held her broad-brimmed straw hat, she revealed a wealth of chestnut hair.

"Davie says I just missed Colonel Hamilton."

"Yes. Not half an hour since he rode off with John Jay and Cousin Bob Livingston. I confess I'm worried about what will happen in the legislature. There are only nineteen men who are for the new Constitution against the forty-six who are against."

"I am concerned, too, though I've never really understood politics. Still, we've all had an education in the science of government. Papa, for one, is absolutely relentless on the subject."

"Yes, that's all Alexander ever talks about, too, either to me or anyone else."

"Well, thank heaven there are women to keep the day to day world going 'round."

Peggy moved closer to get a good look at the new baby, happily gulping again.

"What a big strong fellow! I swear, Sis, you're as good at this as Mama ever was."

Although their eighth anniversary wouldn't come until Christmas, James made the fourth little Hamilton. Peggy, on the other hand, had carried only one, the precious son and heir to the ancient line of van Rensselaers. There had been nothing afterward but a sad string of miscarriages.

Mindful of her sister's feelings, Betsy simply said, "Thank you, Sis." She sat Jamie up and patted his back. As he slumped into her hand, his big eyes goggled.

"That one is going to take after Mr. Hamilton for sure. Look at those blue eyes."

"Well, perhaps. But our babies seem to come fair and then darken up, all except for our Angelica."

"Are she and Phil upstairs?"

"Yes."

"Well, in a minute send one of your girls to bring the darlings down to their adoring aunt."

Tea came in, with Una's thoughtful addition of some fine English sweet biscuits that had recently arrived from London, sent by Angelica Church.

"Shall I take James, Missus?"

"No, he's quiet and you've got enough going on. Where is Alex?"

"He be watchin' Gussie scrub."

"I'll take care of Jamie," Betsy said, "but if you hear Fanny squawk, let me know."

Peggy poured tea while Betsy laid the flannel upon the upholstered sofa and then proceeded to quickly change James atop it.

"You are a lucky girl, you know."

Betsy looked up from wiping a pasty yellow smear from Jamie's cherub's bottom.

Peggy giggled. "Why, I mean Alexander the Great, of course. He's a kind of knight of the round table in our benighted modern age. Papa is quite tiresome on the subject."

"True, but being the wife of Alexander the Great isn't easy. I mean, look." Betsy gestured at the little parlor with its few furnishings.

"Money isn't everything."

"Only to those who have enough." Betsy wrapped the diaper up carefully before setting it on the floor. "And I don't think I shall ever get used to living in this city. There are times when I do so envy you. Your husband is with you almost all the time instead of riding off on crusades. Even when Hamilton is at home, half the time he's tied up in knots and might as well not be here at all. Day and night are the same to him when he's working. This whole winter and spring it's been nothing but those Federalist Papers, then letters to Mr. Madison and Mr. Jay and all the others who are in it with him. Then there's earning a living, which means more writing, visiting clients and riding the circuit. Mr. Church's business is also in his lap since they've gone back to England. And, as if that isn't enough, he gets involved in setting up a money bank which most of the Livingstons are dead set against."

Betsy paused to pick up James. The long speech had come as something of a surprise, even to her.

"My Stephen's for the bank."

"Thank God! You know, Hamilton is actually gone for so much of the time that I get over missing him and begin to organize my life—the children's and mine—without him, and then, suddenly, here he is again, riding back from wherever. He walks in the door as if he's never been gone, and there he is, my dearest husband, but as soon as I begin to enjoy having him around again, he's off again, to some whole new battle."

"Well, Betsy, that's who he is. I'll never forget what you went through the first year you were married. I remember thinking Hamilton was noble and charming and a wonderful playmate at a dance or a sledding party, but after a while, I was certainly glad he wasn't mine."

"You know Angelica calls him "Don Quixote, incorrigible tilter at windmills."

Peggy laughed. "Does she say it to his face?"

"She does."

"And how does our hero respond?"

"Well, he blushes, and then he says, 'You will excuse me, Mrs. Church, but the giants I raise my lance against are very real. Anarchy and weakness are the most dangerous of monsters.'"

"Well, of course they are." Peggy rose in a rustle and joined her sister on the sofa. She slipped an arm around Betsy's shoulder. "Perhaps what I really meant to say is that we all stand in awe of you, too, my dear. Mama and I recently decided that you are every one of those dauntless Roman matrons Hamilton is always extolling all rolled into one. I don't know if he knows—what husband ever does?—but Alexander Hamilton could never be half so great without his paragon of a Schuyler wife."

"Oh, stop!" Betsy felt a prickle in her eyes when her sister hugged her. "I'm afraid that any sympathy now, when I don't know what is going to happen or how long he'll be gone will only make me cry."

* * *

Phil and Angelica jumped up and down, squealing with delight. Gussie held Fanny, whose big dark eyes looked ready to pop. Alex clung to his mother's skirt, uncertain amidst the shouting. Betsy held Jamie, who blinked and gaped at each roar from the crowd, but did not cry. They stood upon the freshly scrubbed front steps while a grand Fourth of July parade wound past on Wall Street. People cheered for her husband; they tipped their hats and bowed as they passed the door.

The whole city of New York, even the Anti-Constitution people, had turned out for the big parade. There were bands and horse drawn floats, the most imposing of which was the "Federal Ship, Hamilton" drawn by ten white draft horses. Built by the naval carpenters' guild as their contribution to the festivities, the "Hamilton" had a seven foot keel and a ten foot beam. It was completely rigged, equipped with real guns and manned by uniformed sailors and officers. An actual salute fired by those guns had started the parade off at 10 o'clock. The carters and sailors carried a banner which declared:

Behold the federal ship of fame;
The Hamilton we call her name;
To every craft she gives employ;
Sure teamsters have their share of joy.

Artisans, merchants, mechanics, shopkeepers, lawyers, academics, clerics, law students and judges all marched together. More than 5,000 strong they wound toward the sweeping green lawn at William Bayard's house. Here, on the sloping banks of the Hudson, an enormous canopy of canvas covered a feast of roast oxen, of mutton and ham, enough for all.

262

Although the parade was a celebration of "Union," New York State had not yet ratified the new constitution. Hamilton was still in Poughkeepsie attempting to persuade the opposition. It had been going on ever since May, speech piled upon speech in the assembly. The galleries were packed, throngs listening to what was lauded far and wide as the finest oratory ever heard on this side of the water. Each night fights followed the debates in the packed taverns as opposing sides asserted their beliefs with bottles and fists.

Hamilton was winning adherents. One newspaper had dubbed him "...the political porcupine...armed at all points, and brandishing a shaft to every opposer. A shaft, powerful to repel, and keen to wound." Those original nineteen Federalists had steadily gained converts. Meanwhile, news of ratification came posting in from other states. Hamilton, General Schuyler, Robert Livingston and John Jay paid the messengers out of their own pockets. As state after state ratified, public opinion shifted.

On July 24, weeks after the great illumination and feast in the City, the State of New York at last ratified, without condition, the Philadelphia Constitution. Hamilton, unable to contain himself, came hell-for-leather from Poughkeepsie, riding as he hadn't ridden since he'd been an aide to Washington, hurtling like a highwayman down the road to New York.

Chapter Thirteen ~ A New Nation

When Alexander's friends visited in the evenings, Betsy would sit, almost invisible by the hearth at her sewing. She'd listen while the men rambled on, in the unique vocabulary of politics.

At the end of April 1789, Washington arrived in New York and took the oath as first president. The next months were spent forming the new government. Alexander waited, a thing he did very badly, for his appointment. The position he wanted was one no one else did—Secretary of the Treasury. His mind already seethed with ideas.

He'd prepared himself for the last decade, reading everything on the subject, from Adam Smith to the great French financier and statesman, Jacques Neckar. Neckar, had he not been destroyed by court intrigue, had been on the verge of performing the nearly impossible task of returning the improvident French monarchy to solvency.

Typically, as soon as he received his appointment, September 11, 1789, Hamilton lost no time getting down to business. He set to work the same day his appointment was approved by the new Congress.

The next house over from his was rented for the use of the Treasury Department. On tables made of doors and sawhorses, with a bare-legged manservant, the first Secretary of the Treasury organized the pertinent papers.

So much to do! Treasury would soon have five hundred employees for him to supervise, compared to twelve at State and six at The Department of War. The job required administrative and fiscal ability from top to bottom. Every task cried for priority.

The first order of business was a report on public credit, a series of recommendations for funding the looming war debt, which Hamilton would soon present to Congress. The need was desperate. State bonds stood between two and twenty cents on the dollar. Their paper money was worthless; The United States was bankrupt.

* * *

The ocean tossed white froth against the walls of the Battery. Hamilton had walked here as a college student, watching the ships and memorizing lessons. How well he remembered his first winter, the onshore wind searing the skin right down to his aching bones. Only a few years later, he'd been captain of a brand new company of artillery, had paraded and drilled here in that first summer of rebellion, before the Americans had lost New York.

He'd been Captain Hamilton, full of hope and fantasies of adventure, entering a war which he believed would make his fortune. He'd traveled a long hard way since those naïve days, through the beyond-despair crossing of the Delaware, to the ice of Trenton, to the rising from a sick bed to begin the endless administrative and clerical labor at Washington's headquarters. Now, he was a key member of the first democracy since the days of the Greeks.

Along the battery this evening, women, and boys, too, leaned against the wall, just as they had in his college days. They looked to see if he was 'looking,' this slim, blue-eyed gentleman in a suit of businessman's black. Hamilton was not. He simply liked to smell salt and hear the slap of waves while he worked things through in his mind.

Something about the rank smell of sea and the sight of ships, of casks upon the wharves, of the sailors and long-shore-men, always made his heart pump faster. The life blood of America coursed daily through this swarming port.

One hundred and ten days, that was the time in which he, Secretary of the Treasury of an impoverished new-born republic, had to formulate a workable solution, a plan which would keep European armies from cutting the country up like an unguarded pie.

Wily old fox Robert Morris, who had spent the war years making credit appear out of thin air, hadn't wanted the job. "Treasury is a young man's job," Morris had said. "You are probably quixotic to think you can persuade Congress to accept an agreement about the debt. I wish you good luck, sir, and I fervently thank God there is someone else willing to take on the task. After the Revolution, I tell you truly, I have not the stomach left for any such matter."

Hamilton had listened, only praying that he knew the obstacles as well as Morris did. Financial matters inspired "the warmest feelings in the least informed souls," but, surely he could get the Congress to see reason. In this desperate hour, deliberation and calm was what was called for, not demagoguery and special-interest maneuvering.

State to state tariffs strangled their internal trade. That was the good old mercantilist way, to imagine that absolute control of every detail was the only route to economic success.

New rules will determine the nature—and, therefore, the outcome—of the game.

In the Indies, Hamilton had received a providential education, nothing like that of the gentlemen planters. Working in the store of a Dutch-American who did business in a Danish colony, trading with Portugal, Spain, France, Holland, Denmark, and England, he had seen the international machine of business at work.

The international is the only sphere of economic activity which is mostly free of government regulation. This was what I want for American business. While there must be procedures to follow in place, it is never wise to attempt to control the detail.

If the debt can be transformed into a species of paper money, the wheels of industry will turn. A financier's sleight of hand will monetize this debt. If regularly serviced, the value will be stabilized. In Countries where the national debt was properly funded, it answered most of the purposes of money.

266

Brilliant colors swayed in the forest of masts before him, where so many merchantmen rode at anchor, heaving on the swells. The traders were already here: the Dutch, the Portuguese, British and French. The material needed to grow a healthy republic, the first since Rome, was here in the raw wealth of these quarrelsome states, a wealth the rest of the world coveted.

There had to be a way to make both politicians and people see reason, see the plain pragmatism of his ideas! Hadn't the great financier Necker said that laws concerning money ought to be as simple as possible so that everyone, both lettered and unlettered, could understand them? Necker had also said the burden of new taxes should always fall upon "luxury and splendor" rather than upon necessities. A financier must also keep his promises to the public. Otherwise, there would be neither public credit nor justice.

If America's finances are public, it will prevent distrust of government. It will also prevent the use of insider information in the markets, that stimulus to dangerous fluctuations.

Hamilton looked west, into a glowing September sundown, now illuminating the shore. Shafts of light cut through tall clouds to fall upon the green crowns of the trees. Watching such a sky as a child, his mind full of a stew of Calvinism and classical myth, he'd imagined God, as a grave old gentleman, reclining upon a couch of billowing white. Hamilton still believed in The Lord and accompanied his wife to church regularly, but it had always seemed to him that earthly destiny lay in a man's own hands.

The responsibility for the successful founding of this new American Republic lay upon him heavily. Oh, yes, the words were there for the world to see, the brave Declaration of Independence, the much wrangled-over, balanced system of government created by the new Constitution. The ideals were common to Americans, even among the ordinary, semi-literate foot soldiers beside whom he'd fought and frozen.

Still, who would bite the bullet and argue for the funding and assumption, the only honorable way to deal with the debt? No home-state-minded politician, that was for sure.

Perhaps I will always be an outsider. However uncomfortable that is, it leaves me—alone of all of them—free to tell the truth—at least, as much of it as I can see.

Funding: to agree upon and then pay the taxes necessary to extinguish the debt. Assumption: the taking on by the national government of the separate States' war obligations.

Taken together, a distasteful medicine, but essential to irrevocably binding the states together. Debts, contracted in the common cause of the Revolution, would then be shouldered by the whole nation.

Hamilton could not fathom why it was so hard for politicians to understand what any junior clerk knew. Good credit was a necessity for businesses—and for nations. Americans and their representatives had loved liberty dearly, but so far, they seemed unwilling to pay for it.

He paused to watch a man in a small fishing boat toss chum over the stern of his craft. A mob of gulls gathered, wheeling and circling, their wings tinted by the last of the sun. Diving into the sea and squabbling, their raucous cries rose into a golden sky.

Hamilton enjoyed the sight, although he considered gulls little better than winged rats. Scavengers, however, had their place in the world, even in the marketplace.

Speculators are the gulls of finance, now flocking to the feast of America's devalued assets. There were two kinds: the domestic variety, who bought raw land using devalued state securities to make their purchases, and foreigners, who bought domestic securities cheap in America and make a killing by trading them in the now bullish Amsterdam markets. None, naturally, were interested in bringing the securities to par, which was exactly what must be done in order to establish America's credit.

I must find a way to harness that private greed for public ends. I will use their short-sightedness, their hunger

268

for quick profit, as the way to lure them into assisting the nation to long-term goals.

To restore public credit, two things must happen. First, the United States must honor its obligations, and find the money to do so. Second, I must convince the legislature that now is time to pay the price of their liberty.

Though the war had ended five years ago, the process of auditing state accounts had only just begun. The argument about how to do this had been going on since The Treaty of Paris. The dilemma was that each state believed—*or acted as if it believed*—that it had spent more than its share.

The Southerners had not, in their customary above-the-law manner, bothered to keep accounts. Now, they expected the other states to accept "sworn statements" in lieu of actual records.

The notion brought a grim smile to the man who'd once been Nicholas Cruger's clerk.

Little wonder that so many of these planters who look down their noses at me are economic slaves to their European factors, men who are experts at keeping two sets of books.

There was also the overhanging foreign debt, money owed to the French, Spanish, and Dutch. Just the cost of servicing it was enormous: $1 million a year. Because of the devastating interest, this was what he'd have to deal with first.

Hamilton knew which of his creditors he liked best: the shrewd businessmen of the Dutch Republic. They were the most stable of the group, the richest, and most likely to feel goodwill towards another republic.

As soon as he had things in hand, he would begin prompt interest payments. He hoped to eventually be able to refinance the entire foreign debt with Amsterdam. The Dutch, upon publication of the American Constitution in Europe, had turned bullish and bought American domestic securities on a large scale. The price, he'd just learned, had risen to 37.5 cents on the dollar. Pitiful, of course, but far better than under The Articles of Confederation.

Nevertheless, goodwill would not last forever. *I have to get Congress to move, to strike while the iron is hot. Dealing with the foreign debt problem is a now-or-never proposition.*

Virginia and North Carolina had little or nothing to gain from assumption of debts by the federal government, and those two states alone held nearly a fourth of the seats in the house. Hamilton knew that passage of the funding and assumption bill would be difficult.

There were two popular attitudes towards the public debt which only made things worse. First, there were the ideologues who believed the debt could simply be repudiated. Another, less irresponsible, but equally impractical group, into whose camp his one-time ally, James Madison, had gone, believed there should be discrimination between original and current holders.

Hamilton had to refinance on more favorable terms with their overseas lenders, and then—somehow—obtain additional revenues.

And here I run headlong into that fighting word: Taxes!

Direct taxation by the federal government was the only substitute for an inadequate earlier system of quotas and requisitions. The years Hamilton had spent as Washington's aide camp had taught him what didn't work and that a stable government needed to have the power to care for its citizens.

And, of course, we must fund a small, permanent army. It is madness to believe that distance alone will keep European powers away. Let us recollect that peace or war will not always be left to our option....

Hamilton was considering three kinds of taxes: direct taxes, excises, and duties on imports. Duties on imports, when six cities handled 80% of the business, would be the easiest. He planned to lay excises upon only luxury items and liquor, which were not necessities of life, despite the fact that frontiersmen found whiskey as indispensable as cornpone.

270

There is no part of the administration of government that requires extensive information and a thorough knowledge, so much as the business of taxation. The man who understands those principles best will be least likely to resort to oppressive expedients, or to sacrifice any particular class of citizens to the procurement of revenue....

Hamilton paused in his pacing, glancing around to get his bearings again. He'd gone almost blind with thought.

Tonight, in the state I'm in, I'm fortunate not to have fallen over something.

To his south, Staten Island appeared to float, a dark expanse showing only a few lights. Bantering along the wall behind him signaled the first pairings of the night's sin trade.

Time to start home. No doubt they are keeping supper. Probably, at this very moment, Betsy is putting our children to bed.

Alex, who'd been such a stolid, easy baby, had lately become a handful. Since the birth of James, he'd transformed into a bubbling cauldron of resentment. James's incessant demands regularly disturbed household routine, which made it difficult for Betsy to find the time— or the vacant lap—she needed to reassure Alex.

Hamilton turned away from the ocean, and began to walk rapidly uptown, hoping, as he did so that his supper wasn't ruined and his good wife upset. Besides, he wanted to see the children before they went to bed. Hadn't he made a promise to himself long ago that he would be an attentive father?

Although he moved briskly, a driving anxiety pursued him.

Haven't I been pondering all these issues for the last decade?

Hadn't he negotiated and pleaded for supplies, for arms and pay, hadn't he done all this with nothing but his wits and Washington's rage and moral force at his back? Hadn't he fumed when brave men went hungry, went shoeless and unpaid, while the Continental Congress frittered away

271

chance after chance to end the war and the members lined their own pockets?

He'd seen with his own eyes that good government—active government—was essential to freedom. With safety for all citizens, people, through their own efforts, could win a living from this rich land.

Justice, order, and predictability were indispensable if freedom was not to self-destruct.

* * *

Betsy thought Alexander had been busy before, but since the new government had formed it seemed as if weeks passed with little more than a peck on the cheek, or a body which crawled into their bed in the middle of the night and fell into an exhausted sleep.

Happily, Angelica arrived from England for a visit. Her arrival was like a whirlwind. She gathered Betsy beneath her wing and they sailed away from the preoccupied husband up the river to their father's house. Mrs. Church's children were stowed at schools in England, but Betsy's brood came with their mother.

Their parents were delighted to see them and soon it was as if they were girls again. Betsy was relieved of child care. There were servants, doting grandparents, and two aunts young enough to be playmates for the little Hamiltons.

Angelica and Betsy slept together, as they'd done as children. Lying in late at night or early in the morning, they whispered to each other, confidences about husbands. Angelica hinted that in the fast society in which she'd been moving in France and England, she and John had both had lovers. Those tales of amorous hide-and-seek, of midnight entrances and hairbreadth escapes were incredibly wicked, but exciting, too.

Angelica spoke of a world Betsy could hardly imagine, tales of gambling parties with Dukes and Princes where fortunes were won and lost, of operas and night-long balls, of champagne theater parties and trips to the races. Her long-fingered hands, gesturing extravagantly, glittered with jewels. Her conversation was liberally larded with French.

Angelica had got what she'd always wanted, an escape from the dull Dutch Hudson, from the life of a "Provincial." She had seen the French Court, had been presented to the Louis XVI and his queen, Marie Antoinette, at a formal levee. She and John had visited the famous Mr. Jefferson, now ambassador there, had dined and hunted with the Marquis de Lafayette and his wife.

In England, she'd dined and danced in company which often included "Prinny," the Prince of Wales, the Duchess of Devonshire, and the highest society. Nevertheless, her old restlessness seemed undiminished. Somewhat to Betsy's surprise, Angelica often spoke dismissively of her handsome husband and displayed a dissatisfaction which Betsy found hard to understand.

One morning while Angelica slept in, Mrs. Schuyler remarked to Betsy, "Our Angelica hasn't changed a bit."

"Yes, and why is that, Mama? She has everything she has always wanted—and more."

"Unlike us, my dear, she was born restless. She will never change."

After the Schuyler sisters returned to New York, the new government was seated. The city was full of new congressmen and senators, bustling self-importantly as never before. Angelica easily took her place in the new society. She lived in grand style in a house near the Hamiltons', paying visits and receiving callers.

Her visitors, in the natural way of things, were the very cream of society, both wealthy ex-Tories and Patriots. There were also painters, writers, and musicians who flocked to enjoy the conversation of the beautiful and cultured Mrs. Church, and, of course, to acquire introductions. A Republican salon formed, a humming hive, with Angelica as their de facto queen.

To Betsy it was a strange interlude, a flashing time, one in which the order of her ordinary housewife's world was overthrown. She left much of the care of her house to Gussie and Una and spent her days basking in the reflected

273

glow of Angelica, as if she too were wealthy. For years she'd been too busy, finances too strained, to indulge in those twin luxuries: intimate friendship and leisure.

Angelica's presence was thrilling, enchanting. The things she said! The notions she had! There was magic in the air, something very much like the first months after falling in love with Alexander. Until November, Betsy would follow that marvelous leader, the same one who had dominated her childhood.

After a few weeks, there was guilt, too. It came when she arrived home and saw all the things that had not been done, saw Gussie was quarreling with Una, the children cross and anxious.

Why am I wasting my time like this? Drinking tea and gossiping all day about husbands and scandal—and—Dear Lord forgive me—about sex?

There was no other woman in the world with whom she could imagine sharing such talk. Trying to sort it out in the suppertime chaos of her own domain, she felt ashamed, exposed. She couldn't understand why she had done it, yet the very next day, it would all begin again. Without Angelica, life seemed flat and dull.

Her husband was busy, excited, utterly preoccupied, meeting with Washington and fellow officials continuously about the new government. He occasionally remarked upon the unusual disarray of his household, but he was mostly absent or too absorbed in his work to even pretend to notice.

Besides, Hamilton, too, was powerfully drawn to Angelica. He was one of her most faithful visitors. After a time, it seemed that Betsy met Alexander more often in Angelica's rooms than in her own home. When, at a party, Alexander and Angelica began to banter, to play with double entendre, to speak French, Betsy was captivated. It was like watching a play by the worldly Mr. Sheridan.

So sophisticated, so extravagantly flirtatious—so— European!

Alexander would punctuate his sallies with kisses for Angelica's hands. They danced together like a pair of glorious peacocks. Betsy admired their elegant and seductive banter, the play of their wit, the rapier flash of two swift minds.

Then, as she laughed with the other party-goers at their exquisite daring, dread crept near. It was as if while sleighing on the frozen river, the ice had cracked, abruptly sending her into deep, deathly water. Looking around, hoping to regain composure, to reassure herself, she'd be shocked to see expressions on all sides of cruelty, of smug, knowing speculation. Betsy caught the drift, but the notion cut so deeply, she pushed it away.

* * *

When Angelica went back to England, Betsy wept. For more than half the year she'd luxuriated in the presence of a glittering and witty playmate. Now she was solitary; Alexander was totally immersed in politics.

The great battles of funding and assumption, the only cure for their country, had begun. The Secretary of the Treasury wielded his pen like a sword in service of his ideas. When he wasn't writing, he was visiting congressmen, arguing, trying to bend dubious minds toward favoring his "revolutionary" ideas.

Betsy knew that from now on every day would be the same. She would work in her little house, tend children and manage servants, go to church, and scramble endlessly to make ends meet. There would be no one to brighten the day with amusing chatter or their beautiful presence.

Just before Angelica left, Betsy had a series of nightmares full of pirates and storms, of Angelica murdered, Angelica lost at sea. While her sister's ship was still visible in the harbor, she lay prostrate on her bed and wept, literally so full of grief that she was unable to rise. The Baron von Steuben, Alexander and young Phil were the ones who stood on the harbor wall and brought home the tale of how the sail had filled and carried the ship over the horizon.

* * *

Alexander worked hard every day and then long into the night. Betsy quietly returned to her routine, managing house, children and servants, rarely going out or receiving visits unless it was church-related socializing.

Phil attended a day school, run by a Dutch master who would give him his first grounding in Latin as well as the usual studies. Betsy read to Angel, Alex and Fanny. With renewed energy she set the girls to needlework, to arithmetic lessons and penmanship.

The new government developed a social schedule. After supper, Betsy would withdraw with the other wives while the men smoked, drank, and endlessly discussed politics. The women she sat among were her staid counterparts, daughters of old, respectable families. What they discussed was children, marriages, births and deaths. Scandal revolved around other people, the kind who weren't part of their circle.

* * *

"Public credit is earned by good faith, by punctual performance of contracts. The Dutch have been willing to take a chance on us, but they are businessmen. Goodwill will not outlast their native good sense."

Gouverneur Morris was a visitor tonight. His wooden leg extended as he sipped port and cracked walnuts. Hamilton paced back and forth, filling Morris's sympathetic and knowledgeable ear.

"I agree with you, dear fellow, absolutely and utterly. The course we have taken is ruinous. Still, Hamilton, you've been naive. You have no base in Congress. Why, you haven't even tried to make one for yourself."

276

"I have no ax to grind. I'm only interested in doing what's best for the country."

Morris paused and studied his friend with an odd gleam in his eye, as if the sentiment was difficult to credit. "But no one believes that, you know, so you might as well be speculating, like everyone else. Everyone, I say, from those mealy-mouthed Virginians all the way down—and I do mean down—to our roaring buckskin democrats."

Hamilton shrugged, as if the matter was of little interest, but Morris was not about to let it go.

"They all had the good idea of making their fortunes by purchasing state lands using depreciated public securities. If you bring the debt back to par, you'll spoil the fun and make every other man in the country your enemy."

"Bringing the debt to par is the only way to provide stability."

"Putting personal interest first is habitual with mankind, Hamilton. What did our Congressmen do during the war, most of them? Feather their own nests while poor farmers starved and died for the cause. You've been in the Congress and in the state legislature, sir. Please don't tell me you expect this new Constitution to change things."

"I expected some genuine effort at making this Constitution work and some of the Roman virtues to which gentlemen are supposedly bred. I expected talk of duties and obligations rather than rights and privileges."

"Dream away, my friend."

Bob Troup was also a guest. Betsy was sad to see his dark curls on the retreat, making his head appear round as a ball. It seemed impossible that ten years had passed, since those Albany days.

Morris stared with annoyance into the bowl of his pipe. It wasn't drawing properly. He retrieved a knife from his pocket and began to scrape it out onto the hearth. Betsy told herself not to forget to sweep the ashes up before bed, or the whole room would catch the stink of tobacco before morning.

"Did you know those two friends of yours, Madison and Henry Lee, are in a scheme to acquire lands on the falls of the Potomac?"

"Madison's no friend of mine. When we wrote "Publius" together, I believed he was a patriot. It seems, however, that he's first and foremost a Virginian."

"And what about this business of bringing the site of the permanent Capitol into the negotiation?" Troup reached for the port.

"The idea, apparently, is to delay the funding and assumption. All this weeping about original holders, while they're doing more damage by holding up the plan than the plan itself will ever cause," Hamilton said. "Every delay Mr. Madison forces is a godsend to the very speculators he claims to detest. Why, holding up the vote puts more money into their hands than I could do if I invited them to simply help themselves to the Treasury. Continentals have fallen to less than fifty cents again. State securities are down to as low as two cents on the dollar. We're on the brink of ruin—again."

"Oh, yes, well, Madison et al want to be sure that the outcome of the debate is determined in such a way that he and his friends can line their pockets at public expense." Troup paused to sip and then bowed his head toward Betsy.

"Spectacular port, Mrs. Hamilton."

"I'm glad you enjoy it. Mrs. Church said it was the only kind her husband fancied."

There was a brief polite pause in which Betsy's skill as a hostess was acknowledged by the gentlemen, but Alexander quickly returned them to business.

"As my good father-in-law says, 'local interests will not suffer intrigue and management to grow rusty for want of use.'"

"It's called 'politics,' Hamilton." Morris leaned to one side, returning his knife to his pocket. After retrieving a small bag of tobacco, he began to carefully load his pipe, the brown threads held gently between thumb and forefinger.

"It's called damnable faction, sir, and it's been the disgrace—and eventual downfall—of every other Republic in history."

"Faction it may be, but taking sides (and a little nepotism)—is inevitable in any society."

"I suppose you're right. I keep hoping to find a way to get the inevitable greed, selfishness and corruption working *for* my plan, but so far the exact way to do it eludes me."

His friends laughed. Gouverneur Morris fired a reed from the tableside candle.

"You really are a paradox, sir." He drew on the freshened pipe. "On one hand, you've such high expectations of all these senators and congressmen. Then, a few logical twists later, you're declaring that ambition and avarice are the common wellspring of human nature."

Hamilton flushed while Morris stretched his long torso.

"Yes. You are at your most unconvincing when you play cynic, Hamilton."

"I do not play the part. I simply see the world as it is."

"Ah, do you indeed?" Troup grinned. "Mr. Morris knows, as do all your true friends, that you are a hopeless Quixote, the kind who hides his disappointments beneath the cloak of a misanthrope."

"At least the ladies," Hamilton interjected, "will pour balm freely into the bosom of such forlorn fellows."

Morris raised his glass in Betsy's direction and said, "The man damns himself in the hearing of his wife, but if he can save our republic with his funding and assumption, and allows our experiment in government to be one which survives—he will certainly find fame."

Her husband made a depreciating gesture, but Betsy could tell the speech had pleased him.

"Stop, for God's sake, Morris." Troup laughed. "If his head swells further, it will pop. To the Union of all honest men!" He lifted his glass.

* * *

At supper one evening, Hamilton came rushing in to give Betsy a peck on the cheek. He'd been spending a lot of time in the gallery of the House following the debates on his assumption plan, catching up on his work at Treasury during the night. The children hadn't seen him in days.

"Mr. White of Virginia has moved that I give a report on what taxes could be raised to support the state debts if they do pass the assumption."

"Which means that you will be up all night for days."

"For the next two days, at least. The report will be on their desks before they can turn around. Is there some dinner I can have before I begin, Mrs. Hamilton?"

"I'll go fetch it. But, Alexander, how can you have something so complicated ready in two days?"

"I've had it worked out for a long time. I didn't want to send a list of proposed new taxes up to Congress along with the assumption plan. After all, I can only handle one battle at time. And you know how the very word 'tax' throws them all into a panic. Mr. White thinks he's caught me off guard, but he'll soon find out."

* * *

It was late, a sultry June night. Betsy was rocking Jamie when she heard her husband come in. Upon entering the bedroom, Alexander came straight to give his wife a kiss and then to study his son, who was chewing miserably on his fist.

"What's troubling you, Jamie lad?" He brought himself into the baby's line of sight.

"Papa!" Jamie sniffled eloquently. "Hurts! Ma'm put med'cin' on, but hurts!" He had just passed two, but like all of their children, Jamie talked early. Unhappily, what he mostly did was complain. The older children, even, tellingly, Angel, had dubbed him "Cry Baby Jamie."

"More teeth, I think," said Betsy, watching as her husband, with the supremely tender expression he reserved

280

for their children, caressed his son. As he bent close, she noticed a rarity—wine on Alexander's breath.

"Did Mr. Jefferson bring out his French bottles?"

"He did. I'm so excited and so disgusted about what happened, I'm unsure what we drank."

"Was the dinner about what you thought, a deal for passing the assumption?"

"It was. If you have the strength to listen, I'll tell you about it. I was hoping you'd be up, so I could talk for a little. I know I won't be able to sleep—the wine, the company—that unctuous little rat, Madison and that pompous Jefferson. I've made a devil's bargain tonight."

"You did?"

"Heaven help me. I did. The whole thing stinks, of course, a thing to be expected if that chinless turncoat Madison's in it, but at this point I'd sell my eternal soul to get the assumption passed."

"Alexander! What a thing to say! What do they want?"

"Well, the first thing they want is a decorous cloak with which they will cover the actual deal. I don't like doing it this way, but there doesn't seem to be any other way. I'm beginning to believe that public spiritedness is a mere figment of the imagination."

Betsy rocked Jamie, watched her husband pace in his best white linen summer suit. His color was up.

"The site of the new Capitol is a diversion. The Southerners have wanted the capitol in Virginia, and they shall get it. That, however, isn't all they want, and this way no one on the outside will see it. The real deal is hidden behind the Capitol city nonsense. In a nutshell, they want the sum allotted to Virginia increased so that when state accounts are settled, Virginia will come out far ahead of what it is actually owed, somewhere in the neighborhood of $13 million."

"But—but—isn't that extortion?"

"The exact word, my Angel." Hamilton paused to nod approvingly at his wife. "But, of course, the Virginians have their own way of thinking. Tribute, perhaps, is the word lurking in their lordly minds. Madison, for one, will make a fortune out of those swamp lands he's just bought around the falls of the Potomac."

* * *

"Well, Hamilton," said General Schuyler, "You've got some scars, my boy, but you've done it. Funding and assumption has passed and we can refinance the domestic and foreign debts. You even got your import duties through, more or less as proposed."

"It's only the first step," Hamilton replied. "The excise tax failed and now I'm going to have to fight that battle all over again during the next session. And there's that mess with the bonds, too. You were part of that, sir."

Alarmed, Betsy looked up from her sewing. Troup, who'd been sitting quietly in the corner, suppressed a smile. General Schuyler, however, continued to regard his favorite son-in-law with an expression of indulgence.

"How, I ask you, sir," Alexander said, "are we to support the three percent securities and the deferred sixes as firmly as the straight sixes?" He seemed entirely oblivious to the thin ice he trod. "Now the legitimate speculators are deprived of the protection I wanted them to have. Mark my word—it will cause serious destablization in the land offices. People will be ruined."

When the discussion entered this realm, Betsy felt as they'd begun to speak another language. She lowered her head and went on stitching at the child's frock she was making.

Despite her anxiety, a quiet discussion concerning ways to handle the payments on the various government bonds continued.

"Congress will adjourn in a few days and perhaps you'll have a few weeks of peace. You can bring Betsy and the children up river to visit."   ·

Hamilton sighed. "No rest for the wicked, I'm afraid. As you know, I've been instructed to make a further report on public credit, which means plans for taxes and for a national bank. Besides that I've got to manage Treasury, implement the revised tariff, establish a coast guard to cut down on smuggling and supervise that first loan with the Dutch. I can't say how many people that will involve writing orders to, but I do know that about $60 million dollars will eventually be placed in my care."

"And he's not dazed or worried, he's exultant." Troup shook his head.

"Even before all that, sir, I've got to get a letter out to the public creditors which will tell them what to expect from the new laws, so speculators will not run off with all the profits when the securities regain their proper value. I shall send your daughter and grandchildren upriver, of course, sir, but, as for myself, I fear I have enough work for the next year cut out."

* * *

In September of 1790, the Hamiltons followed the government to the new temporary capital at Philadelphia. There was difficulty in finding a house, for it would have to be in the vicinity of the government offices with enough room for a family with four children. It couldn't be too expensive, either. Hamilton's salary as Secretary of the Treasury would be less than a third of his earnings as a successful New York attorney.

* * *

The walls of the fire-lit green parlor were brightened by stencils of suns and moons. During this particular Philadelphia twilight four gentlemen occupied it. Their suits were somber, the navy traditionally worn by businessmen and attorneys. This, along with their white stockings, made sharp relief against the vibrant colors of the room.

"And so the paper money has been effectively transformed into capital." Hamilton was triumphant.

283

"A most effective sleight of hand," Robert Morris noted. Morris, the oldest and richest man in the room, was the only one who still wore a wig.

"The market value of our paper before you took office was around $15 million, now it's estimated to have risen to $45 million. Not bad, sir, not bad! That's $30 million out of thin air. You should speculate."

Hamilton ignored the last remark. He took another walnut carefully with his long fingers and picked up the cracker. His friend, dubbed "Financier to the Revolution," had lately got over his head in land speculation, a circumstance which was beginning to worry Alexander in his official capacity. The gentlemen were having dessert, sitting at a small table in Betsy's parlor on a raw January evening, enjoying the usual sherry and walnuts.

"Well, we're not out of the woods yet." Hamilton paused to brush hair powder from the sleeve of his navy jacket. "In order to put public credit upon an enduring basis, we need a mint, a revision of the tax system and a national bank. Another go around like we had in Congress over Assumption might just kill me."

"Be honest." Bob Troup laughed. "There's nothing in the world you love better than a good fight."

"You won't have the opposition you did last year." Morris extended lace-encircled plump fingers toward the sherry. "Not only have your measures been successful, they've become popular. And so much is now in our favor. Europe is spoiling for war, but as their grain crops have failed, our farmers and merchants will be the ones to fill their pockets. Credit for prosperity, even the most temporary, is always given to the current administration. Lady Luck is with you there, Hamilton."

"Didn't I hear that Patrick Henry and his bawling Democrats have changed sides?" For the first time tall, elegant Rufus King spoke up. "When their land speculations were ruined by Assumption they attacked you, but after their state securities rose to par, they all made a whooping cash profit which changed their minds for good

284

and all. Jefferson is extremely out of humor because of it. He can't goad them to attack you now that their Democratic pockets are well-lined with Federalist gold."

"Well, whatever they think, we need a bank so we can peg our securities to the market. A bank will provide that, as well as a reliable source for short term loans. Private bankers expand or contract their loans in accordance with the needs of the commodity market, but I can't count on them. It's hardly safe to leave public finance at the mercy of private interests. I want a large, stable money supply for future development."

"Operated for the benefit of the stockholders?"

"That's the only way I can see to get it to work properly. It will be prohibited from issuing notes in excess of capitalization and the Secretary of the Treasury will be able to remove the government's deposits. The books must be inspected regularly as well."

"You'll need taxes to service the interest payments."

"Yes, and I've tried to be careful there. Import duties are convenient, but they should never be so high as to curtail business activity or encourage smuggling. The tax base should be as diversified as possible, so that the burdens are shared around with some equity."

"What about a property tax?" Morris asked. "I'm playing Devil's Advocate here, of course. God knows, I, for one, wouldn't be happy about that."

"If we can manage our finances but keep a property tax in reserve, the Dutch will be impressed. No, I'm thinking of asking for some luxury taxes and a way of setting up the revenue collections that doesn't test the virtue of the collectors. One of the first lessons I learned as a merchant's clerk was how and when to offer a bribe."

Morris and the others laughed. "When we get a system in place," said King, "I have a feeling that the shippers are going to have to work out a whole new way of loading their cargo, especially if they want to evade inspectors trained by you, Hamilton."

As the chuckles died away, there was a soft tap. The door opened and Betsy stepped in. One dark curl, her only nod to fashion, trailed from beneath her cap.

"Excuse me, gentlemen." As the men began to get to their feet, she said, "and please, no need to rise. I shall be gone in a moment."

"No need to leave us, Mrs. Hamilton." Alexander rose and came to take her hand. "I know our conversations of late suffer from a distressing sameness."

Betsy cast an uneasy glance around the room. "I am looking for…." She gave her husband a meaningful look.

"Again?"

"I'm afraid so. We've looked everywhere else but the parlor."

Alexander nodded and then said to his companions, "Excuse us for a moment. A small domestic matter." He got up, then went to the floor-length draperies covering the front window and whipped them back. Simultaneously, Betsy opened the long bottom doors of sideboard which occupied most of one wall.

Alexander's search yielded nothing but a blast of chill air. Betsy, however, found what she was looking for. Ducking, she seized a small arm and dragged forth Jamie, a chubby three-year-old cherub with long auburn curls, wearing a flannel frock and knitted slippers. A large rag doll, held in a death grip by the other hand, followed him out.

"Aieeee! No! I'm not sleepy!"

"James Alexander!" Betsy lifted her pudgy, red-faced child unceremoniously onto her hip. "I've found you, so the rules are you must give over at once."

Much to the surprise of the guests, his protests died. Morris and Troup appeared amused, but Rufus King, a Connecticut man, clearly did not know what to make of this display of "infant wickedness."

"My apologies, gentlemen," said Betsy. One arm held Jamie close, while Hamilton walked her to the door and opened it.

"Shall I come up?"

"Unnecessary." Betsy marched into the hall. She looked so small with stocky Jamie riding her hip. His head, with those burnished tresses, was now pressed with sweet docility against his mother's shoulder.

Hamilton closed the door behind his wife and son. "Excuse us." He spoke to the room in general. "Jamie's fondness for hide and seek and his dislike of bedtime have recently united."

Robert Morris was grandfatherly and amused. "Mrs. Hamilton appears to have him well in hand."

"Except for losing him."

"Mrs. Hamilton was busy presiding at our fine supper. She can't be everywhere at once."

* * *

Betsy settled herself into a corner chair, adjusted her fingerless gloves and picked up her knitting. The conversation she'd interrupted a half an hour ago had not altered appreciably.

"What's this about small coinage, a silver and copper penny and half penny? Is that really necessary?"

"I think so," Hamilton said. "Everyone, even the poorest, should get used to handling money. During the war I kept encountering people who had never possessed a coin. Understanding money is fundamental to any modern society."

"Is this airy philosophy?"

"Hamilton's suggestion is eminently practical," Rufus King said.

"Absolutely, and if the congress hadn't—"

Betsy never heard the rest. There was a crash upstairs, accompanied by the unmistakable sound of childish temper. The commotion sent her flying.

By the time she arrived on the scene, Una had got the combatants separated. Of course, it was not Fanny and Angelica, good little girls with toes tucked beneath their nightgowns, dolls hugged close, but Alex and James. The boys were flailing at each other, one on either side, while Una's black strong hands held them apart. Two bowls, one broken, both spilling sup'pawn and molasses, lay on the floor.

"Jamie said he's not "It"!" Angel offered an explanation.

"He's a big fat cheater!" Alex James's thin, pitted face blazed with passion. It was regrettable, but when they'd inoculated him for the smallpox last summer in Albany, poor Alex had suffered 'a pretty good share' of the disease. He would never die of the scourge, but he would carry the scars for the rest of his life.

"Naht-it-Naht-it-Naht-it!"

"Hush your mouth!" Una cried. "Your Papa's got 'portent visitors in de parlor."

Betsy stared questioningly at Alex, who was, after all, the older.

"Mama, Jamie says he's *never* 'it', no matter how many times he gets caught!" Alex pointed furiously, a small prosecutor summing up.

Betsy shifted her gaze to James, who rolled his eyes beneath long lashes and was doing his best to appear innocent. She believed she had begun to catch a certain drift in Jamie's character.

"Alex, please help Una clean up. Then sit by the fire quietly and read a bit more if you like." She kissed the top of the older boy's ruddy head. Alex liked to read, so she hoped this would mollify him, especially because now he'd be staying up past his bedtime. "Jamie and I must talk."

She marched to her room, James on her hip. Once there, she positioned herself upon a wing chair and settled him firmly on her knee.

"Now, James Alexander, tell me why you aren't "it" when you get caught?"

"You caught me, Mama, not them." James was perfectly serene.

"If you are found, you are "it," James. Besides, you *know* you aren't supposed to be in the parlor when Papa has visitors. That was very naughty of you."

For a moment, Betsy imagined she'd made an impression, but James's focus shifted away into the middle distance.

"Yes, Mama." An instant later he turned to smile charmingly, displaying pearly baby teeth. "Alex couldn't go to the parlor, so that's where I hided." He leaned his head against her bosom and smiled sweetly.

* * *

"This time I've got them." Her husband was exultant. "Jefferson and Madison have been confusing Washington, who, God help him, is no lawyer. You should see this opinion on the Bank they sent to him, full of words the poor fellow doesn't understand. The bank, Jefferson says, violates the laws of mortmain, alienage, descents, forfeiture, escheat, monopoly—and the Constitution. When it suits him, I notice Madison feels that the Constitution is quite flexible. This week, however, he's a strict constructionist."

Alexander was agitatedly prowling the green parlor, waving a handful of paper, scarlet with rage. Ever since he'd become Secretary of the Treasury, Betsy felt that he rarely talked to her. Instead, most of what he said was an endless venting about the battles in which he was engaged. Public business, his plans for America, and the obstacles his enemies threw in his way were all she heard. Only after long thought could she remember the last time he'd made love to her.

"Well, what *does* all that mean? Escheat, mortmain— and all those other things? It sounds quite daunting."

"It's meant to be, but, in fact, it's irrelevant. Massa Tom is a mediocre lawyer, but Madison knows better. They're trying to pull the wool over the General's eyes. I intend to explain this nonsense to His Excellency so he can see it for the obfuscation it is. That is, if he wants to understand. He's involved in speculation along the Potomac, too, and the legality of the Bank is entangled with the amendatory bill about placement of the Capitol."

Betsy, who had become an avid reader of newspapers, did know this, although sometimes it was hard to keep the ins and outs straight. "What will you do?" She looked up from her mending.

"I'm going to write a neat little opinion for His Excellency, exactly as he's asked. And I'm going to demolish Jefferson and his empty jacket Attorney General, Randolph. If they have their way in this business of strict interpretation of the Constitution, we'll set a precedent which will strangle the country inside of twenty years. There is no way to foresee the future, and therefore we must begin to use implied powers for dealing with the unpredictable events the government will, over time, encounter."

"Mr. Hamilton, you are preaching to the choir."

His severe, abstracted expression was swiftly replaced by one amused and tender, one which seemed for the first time to acknowledge her hard-won understanding.

"Yes. Forgive me. I shall be in my study until the opinion for his Excellency is written. Don't let me be disturbed unless it's absolutely necessary."

He was already halfway through the door when she called after him.

"May I bring you supper?"

Alexander paused, hand on the door.

"Yes, my dear. But tell me, how are you managing? Is there nothing for a father to settle?"

"Not really, just Alex and James pummeling each other, as usual. I think I've got that sorted. I told them I wasn't going to try to understand whose fault it was anymore, that I was just going to paddle them both if there was any trouble because I want them to get along."

"The judgment of Solomon." Hamilton smiled. "And will you do it?"

"I already have. They got so angry at me they forgot to be mad at each other. It has been a lot quieter since Mama became so horribly unjust."

Hamilton laughed and returned to slip an arm around her waist.

"I think you've got them out-generaled, Queen Bess."

Betsy leaned her head against his chest, rested one hand upon his severe black jacket.

"We do miss you, Alexander."

"I miss you, too." Hamilton raised her small hand to his lips. "Do I smell apples baking? And please bring me vegetables, but no gravy or meat. I'm on McHenry's diet until this is over."

* * *

Betsy heaved a sigh of relief and smoothed her party dress. In the center of the table sat the tea, steaming in a fine English china pot her mother had given her. The surrounding fare was substantial. The guests were obviously enjoying their repast. It was a full-scale affair, a long table covered with savories as well as sweets.

Some, Betsy had made herself, some she had brought in from famous Philadelphia bake shops. From her kitchen had come apple, pumpkin, kidney and pigeon pies, conserves of pears and plums, and loaves of bread.

That wonderful Dutch treat, *oleykoecks* dusted with sugar, those that had escaped the nimble fingers of the children, were not an hour old and wafting fragrance over the table. From the German baker, there were sticky honey cakes and high tortes of nuts, cake and cream. A fine ham sat in state beside the tea pot with slices cut to order by Davie, who had stayed with them. He was resplendent tonight in a fine new wig, coat and pants.

Betsy knew that to the Philadelphians as well as to the rich southerners, her tea was a simple affair. No roast pig, no pheasant, no songbirds stuffed in pigeons stuffed in ducks stuffed in turkeys. Nor any French cook backstage drowning everything in sauce, such as Mr. Jefferson employed.

Betsy didn't have money for such luxuries on the slender salary of her public servant husband. Even if she had had, her Dutch housewife's upbringing wouldn't have allowed her to ever feel easy with a French cook in the kitchen.

After a little time, she overheard the judgment of Philadelphia society upon the table of Mrs. Secretary of the Treasury.

"Pumpkin custard baked in the pumpkin. How quaint!"

"Yes. Good Lord. I haven't been intimate with the dish in years."

"Well, try some. It's delicious. I'd quite forgotten how good it can be."

The first speaker was Mrs. Willing, a tall and fashionably dressed brunette, a member of an old Tory Philadelphia family. The second, Mrs. Bingham, was younger, fair and bejeweled.

"Look at this whipped cream! I must say, this is the first edible Republican tea I've had. The torte is Herr Kumkraker's, certainly, but excellent as usual. The rest, I divine, came from her kitchen. I must confess it's all extremely well prepared."

Betsy, holding her chin high, strode to confront the speakers. Mrs. Willing, she thought, was, as usual, sailing just to the lee of rude, but then, what else could be expected from someone whose father had been a war profiteer? The other lady's maiden days had been spent coquetting it among the red coats during the occupation. One of her bosom friends had been the glamorous, notorious, and now forever banished Peggy Shippen—Mrs. Benedict Arnold.

"Ah, Mrs. Secretary Hamilton, such a marvelous table!"

"Yes, and so perfectly apropos for our Republican Court." Mrs. Willing caught the flash in Betsy's dark eyes and quickly added, "These days, with so many well-trained émigrés to employ, one is liable to overlook one's native diet."

"Such satisfying food! Why, it's the kind of tea my worthy Grandmother Chew often served."

"Your chef…is, ah, from New York?"

292

Betsy was certain they were fishing for an admission that she had "stooped" to cooking. Gazing into those smug, smooth, carefully made-up faces, she was ready to give them something to gossip about— those foolish women, too proud to enter their kitchens.

A man's arm slipped beneath hers, interrupting.

"Ladies!" Hamilton saluted Betsy's antagonists, bowing gracefully. Both women returned his greeting with the responsiveness that Betsy knew usually welcomes a man who is both good looking and powerful.

"Mr. Secretary."

"Mr. Secretary."

"I overheard you ladies discussing our chef." His glorious blue eyes flashed at Mrs. Bingham. The reigning beauty's color rose beneath her rouge.

The secret of his power over all of us, Betsy thought with a deal of irritation, is that he acts as if he's not only been in our bed, but that he's eager to get back in!

"Actually, a mere cook, ladies." Hamilton began smoothly, sending the merest flicker of a wink to his wife. "She is a marvelous Dutch woman from Albany, sent to us by Mrs. Major General Schuyler. If you can believe it, she speaks not a word of English. My wife is the only one who can communicate with her."

While Mrs. Bingham and Mrs. Willing were mulling this astonishing fiction, he added, "Plain fare it is, but, I must confess, 'tis quite rich enough for a man with a delicate constitution."

"You, Mr. Secretary?"

"Ah, yes, unfortunately so. Please excuse me, my dear." He set Betsy's arm free. "It is imperative that the ladies taste the pigeon pie."

Collecting them, one gorgeous belle on each arm, Hamilton began to steer them along the length of the table to where the pigeon pie sat in state, rich brown gravy flowing from a generous cut where the Knoxes had already assailed it. Davie, helpfully attentive, picked up a plate and a server, ready to offer whatever the ladies fancied.

"I confide, of course." Hamilton spoke in lowered tones. "I must trust implicitly in your discretion."

The ladies nodded, curls dripping from their towering hairpieces, eager to have his attention.

"Did I hear you say something about a delicate constitution?" asked Mrs. Bingham. "That you should have any weaknesses at all, Mr. Secretary, is an astonishing notion."

"Ah, Madam, if only I had none. In fact, I have several. A Spartan diet takes care of one." Here he paused, blue eyes tantalizing them. "Marriage, I confess, assuages the other."

The buxom Mrs. Willing leaned closer and tapped his chest with her fan.

"But, surely, if the weakness is still with you, you must occasionally experiment with other cures."

At that moment Betsy became aware of a short wide presence behind her. The woman was heavy, but except for the rustle of silks she had approached as silently as a cat.

"Ah, Mrs. Hamilton, there you are, my dear!"

"Lady Washington." Betsy collected herself and made a graceful curtsy.

"A splendid table you've set. The General and I have been wondering. What do you call these?" Martha's plump hand gestured in the direction of a plate of fat, fragrant oleykoecks. "I can't remember the Dutch name for them, but even after all these years I do remember eating a scandalous quantity at your youngest sister's baptism. They were then—and are now—quite wonderful."

A tall figure, impressive in civilian black velvet filled the vista behind her interrogator. Betsy raised her eyes for what seemed like forever before she met the frosty scrutiny of Washington.

"Your Excellency." She dropped a curtsy.

Always formal, the massive white head came to bow over her hand. "Mrs. Secretary Hamilton."

"Quite delightful and still warm, these little treats." Martha tasted another with a pleasure that lit up her the round face beneath the lace garnish of a cap. Betsy knew that a woman whose kitchen cured four hundred hams a year wouldn't think it shameful that Mrs. Secretary Hamilton had cooked much of what was on the table.

"Thank you, Lady Washington. I made them just before the first guests arrived. You have to be very careful to beat the batter for exactly the right amount of time. Too short, and they're heavy. Too long, and they toughen."

"The oil mustn't be too hot, either, I reckon." Martha regarded the oleykoecks with a practiced eye. "A triumph! Lighter than beaten biscuits."

"Indeed." Washington spoke solemnly, as if delivering an opinion of the greatest import. "I remember enjoying these at Mrs. Schuyler's table." He appeared ready to say more, but instead there followed one of those long pauses which afflicted his conversation. Betsy and Martha stood quite still, as if suspended, alongside His Excellency.

"How," he finally inquired, "did you keep those children of yours out of them?"

"Well, sir, they each got one earlier, but I confess that even that hasn't been sufficient. I had to resort to bribery and promise to make more tomorrow."

"Understandable." The General picked up another sugar-dusted delicacy.

They took places beside the Knoxes. The rotund Secretary of War and his even heavier wife were happily eating from heaped plates. In this ponderous but appreciative company, Betsy managed to savor some of what she'd labored so hard over.

After taking the edge off his appetite, His Excellency asked to see their children. Betsy, not without trepidation, sent Una to collect them.

As she'd hoped, Philip, now a fine boy of eleven and home on a break from school kept the younger ones in order. He even made a nice little speech.

"We're most honored by your interest, Your Excellency." Phil made a polite bow. Although his hair was dark, the closest of all the children to Betsy's, his features were undeniably Alexander's.

295

Martha Washington, smiling, extended a smooth, plump hand, as if he were a man. As Phil gracefully saluted it, she said, "You are certainly every inch your father's son, Master Hamilton."

Phil held his elegant head high.

"And look at our pretty Angelica," said Martha, tipping the girl's chin. "Your Papa says you have learned to play some lovely airs on your London spinet. Some day you must play for us."

Betsy smiled and hoped that James and Alex wouldn't start shoving each other. Phil, bless him, must have been thinking the same thing, because he had positioned himself between them. James seemed innocent and charming in his little boy's skirts, but it was becoming increasingly clear that he was an equivocal character. He and the serious, literal-minded Alex were oil and water.

"They're fine children, so healthy and fit."

Washington gazed at the four young Hamiltons with approval, but Betsy knew he wouldn't say a word directly to them. It was always like that. He'd ask to see them. She'd march them out and then he'd admire them from a distance, as if they were a fine pack of fox hound pups. He was at a complete loss with children.

The General's uneasiness was catching. Alex and James stared upwards at the great Washington with anxious eyes. The red of their father's hair glinted in a range of hues, from Angelica's ginger to the dark chestnut of Phil.

"Your youngest is getting taller, Mrs. Hamilton," the General observed. There was an undeniable breeder's approval in those cold blue eyes. Betsy recognized the expression. The same glinted in her father's eye as he, at home, surveyed his ever-growing mob of grandchildren.

"Yes, James is getting to be quite a big fellow. Soon, perhaps," Washington gravely speculated, "there will be another."

"Not this year, I'm afraid, Your Excellency."

"Certainly not!" Martha cast a merry glance at her husband. "The poor man is far too busy with his bills and reports to trouble Mrs. Hamilton."

The Knoxes laughed. Betsy hoped the embarrassment she felt wouldn't show. Martha, in her earthy way, had hit the nail on the head.

"Say good-afternoon, children."

Following Philip's lead, Alexander bowed and Angelica curtsied. Pudgy James managed a sort of bob and would have gone back to staring skyward at His Excellency, but Phil caught his hand.

"Come on, Jamie. It's time to go upstairs now."

Betsy heaved a sigh of relief when the door closed behind them without incident.

* * *

"How could you tell such a story and keep a straight face?" Betsy asked while she and her husband were undressing for bed.

"Which story?"

"Hamilton! Did you tell so many you can't keep them straight? The one about the Dutch cook."

"It was better than listening to you tell the truth."

"Well, sir, we can't afford a French chef."

"No." Hamilton made a wry face. "Only those fellows who style themselves 'men of the people' like Mr. Jefferson, and clever speculators like old Bob Morris can afford French chefs."

"Well, I wouldn't want a French chef. Gussie, Una and I do quite well by ourselves. I had a hundred compliments."

"Indeed, but we can't have Mrs. Bingham telling Philadelphia society that you do your own cooking."

"Why not? Isn't this a Republic? Lady Washington knows I made most of it and so does His Excellency. They don't look down on us."

"No, they don't, but we don't have to put on airs for them. The old man knows everything about me anyway, warts and all, just as I do about him." He came behind her,

297

began to run his fingers through the dark hair she had been brushing. "Sitting with the mighty Secretary of War and his wife guaranteed that you'd not be troubled any further by those twin vipers of fashion. An excellent strategy, Mrs. Hamilton."

"It wasn't strategy. I enjoy people who relish my cookery. I couldn't have swallowed a bite around the others. And as for you, turncoat! Tell me this minute what you said to the beautiful Mrs. Willing's extremely leading remark?"

"To what do you refer, my darling?"

"The conversation concerning your weaknesses, dear Alexander, and I don't believe you were talking about the digestive ones."

"Ah, the other weakness." He stopped playing with her hair and dropped a kiss on her shoulder.

"Exactly, sir." Betsy drew a deep steadying breath and said what was on her mind. "Do you occasionally try other remedies?"

"What a shocking question from one's wife." Fair lashes lowered themselves demurely over his blue eyes. His response, she noted, was a parry, nothing close to denial.

"Answer the question, sir. And," she continued, trying for lightness she did not feel, "none of your lawyer's talk about self-incrimination, either."

"When do you find time to study law? Don't I give you enough work?"

"No equivocation, Mr. Hamilton."

She was in earnest, but instead of an answer he drew her up from her seat and kissed her, a romantic gesture which sent a reliable thrill. The bed behind them was, for once, empty of feverish or apprehensive children.

"Dear Queen Bess, in spite of the paradoxical strength of the aforesaid weakness, I can barely find time to make love to you. Besides, mistresses take a great deal of time, a commodity which you must admit I do not possess in abundance."

298

Betsy wasn't satisfied. She pouted as he drew her towards the bed.

"Lack of opportunity is your reason for fidelity?"

"Didn't you hear me tell those alarming women that a man would have to be out of his mind to risk the use of other remedies for a weakness as crippling as mine? Especially when he'd found one that assuaged all his plaguey symptoms so entirely."

He ended by pressing her down into the pillows and kissing her again. His intensity left her breathless.

"Now, little Mrs. Hamilton, what about His Excellency's stimulating suggestion that Jamie is old enough for a little brother? It sounded a bit like an Executive Order to me."

A kiss or two later, he was rolling over her in a long-married, matter-of-fact way, when Betsy stopped him.

"I shall only permit the liberty which I divine you are about to take under one condition."

"You, Madam, are hardly in a situation to dictate terms. However...." He nuzzled her neck. "Because I am a gentleman, I shall restrain my base desires until I've heard your plea."

"Promise." Betsy twined her arms around him. "Promise not to get up and go back to your desk afterwards."

"Agreed, sweetheart." He smiled beautifully down at her. "Shall I rock us both to sleep?"

~The End~

Part Two
Glory Passes

~~~

Chapter One
By Passion Undone

Hamilton was busily writing a recommendation to Congress, a proposal for an "industrial policy." It would be his third major report in two years, "The Report on Manufactures." He had seen the riches of his new country, seen the inventiveness and entrepreneurial drive present in the citizens. He had been planning, all the while imagining an almost undreamed of future: America—the richest and most powerful nation on earth. He brimmed with ideas, coming to him so suddenly and quickly that his hand had finally cramped so badly he could barely hold the pen.

At night, after the business of the day, he planned for the future. He wanted government to provide protective tariffs to nurture American manufacturers. It was of great importance to grant bounties and direct subsidies to entrepreneurs and artisans, both to encourage invention and to assist fledgling U. S. businesses.

Hamilton envisioned a system of standards and inspection that would facilitate internal commerce through an extension of the banking system. This, he thought, would get American manufacturing off to a running start.

Why should every new idea or invention be European?

He'd been gathering data for months.

"I request that you will give me as accurate information as it shall be in your Power to obtain, of the Manufactures of every Kind carried on within the Limits of your District,

whether incidentally in the domestic Way, or as regular Trades, of the respective Times of their first Establishment, the Degree of Maturity they have obtained, of the Quantities periodically made, of the Prices at which they are sold—of their respective Qualities, of the impediments, if any, under which they labour, of the Encouragements, if any, which they enjoy under the Laws of the State and whether they are carried on by Societies, Companies, or Individuals...."

He imagined America as a "balanced economy." Here, manufacturers, as well as farmers and the growing class of "artificers," would stimulate every kind of production. His quill scratched furiously. He believed that industrial entrepreneurs could afford to pay better in the United States than they did in the old world. Along with Washington and Franklin, he took a liberal attitude towards emigration of "industrious persons" and favored giving financial assistance to skilled workmen to help them get here.

He understood that Jefferson and most of the southern gentlemen had a vision of their new nation as a slave-owning republic, each local lord overseeing fifty acre kingdoms. They wouldn't encourage change. Hamilton knew quite well that his "Report on Manufactures" was going to be even more suspect and controversial than Funding and Assumption.

He paused, wiped sweat from his forehead, and refreshed his quill. During these blazing Philadelphia summers every other high political functionary was out of town, relaxing in the cool, clean countryside. Washington was at Mt. Vernon. Jefferson, Monroe and Madison were at their hill-top plantations.

Betsy had gone, too. Unaccustomed to the intense heat and humidity, she suffered so much ill-health in summer that they'd agreed she should take the children and go to Albany. It meant a carriage journey across New Jersey to New York City, after which she and her brood embarked upon one of her father's sloops and sailed up the Hudson to The Pastures.

Grueling heat aside, Philadelphia was also dangerously full of fever. Betsy seemed especially vulnerable. She had been ill since early May, and the children had been wearing her down. Not Phil, of course, but Angelica had been going through an exhausting spell of queer black moods and night terrors. And despite her new method of dealing with sibling rivalry, Alexander and James remained locked in what was, apparently, to be an unending battle.

Hamilton knew he was little help. He had the future to plan for, deep into the night, as well as his daily Treasury business and all the rest. During these summers, with every other high official out of town, he *was* the American government.

Tonight—not a breath of air! Alexander had already untied his stock and removed his jacket. The table he at which he sat was covered with paper, but he couldn't tolerate clutter for long and so paused occasionally to order his work.

"*As to the furnishing greater scope for the diversity of talents and dispositions, which discriminate men from each other....*"

He set the pen in the well and then groped along the table for the handkerchief again. Perspiration had come dangerously close to marring his work.

"*...there is, in the genius of the people of this country, a peculiar aptitude for mechanic improvements, it would operate as a forcible reason for giving opportunities....*"

A loud knock sounded. He'd been so deep in thought, he startled.

"Sar." A bare-legged servant stuck his head around the door. "There's a gen'lewoman wantin' to see you. Says she's a cousin of Mr. Livingston of New York. She's got trouble she needs your help about."

"She didn't happen to say *which* Mr. Livingston, did she?" Hamilton sprinkled sand on the paper. He knew at least eight New York "Mr. Livingstons."

"No, Sar, she di'nt."

Hamilton turned over the card the fellow brought, but aside from the name, "Maria Reynolds," there was no other information. A supplicant at his door wasn't unusual. Gentry in trouble were likely to call here, particularly at this time of year, when everyone else prominent was out of town.

"Show the lady in. But—give me a minute to get dressed."

"You'll be glad you saw 'er, Sar." Hamilton noted an unaccountable smirk.

Shaking his head, he stood to slip on his waistcoat. The servant was impudent, but Alexander mostly overlooked it, for this ex-soldier generally had his wits about him.

At the mirror, he folded the stock around his throat and tied a loose knot. Next, he shrugged on a white linen coat. He often wished that he, like the servant, could get by wearing only a shirt and trousers. He mopped his brow again.

Philadelphia is even more like Hell than usual.

The door opened. "Mrs. James Reynolds, Sar." The servant bowed her through.

As the woman approached, Hamilton's eyes widened. She was young, straight-shouldered and tall enough to look him straight in the eye, but utterly female, all voluptuous curves and sway. Her hair was a glossy, rich brunette. Her skin, flushed by the heat, looked soft. Her cheeks were bright, her eyes deep blue.

Celestial Venus!

Hamilton was rarely at a loss for words, but he could barely summon sufficient courtesy to motion this fair creature to the chair the servant brought forward. When she smiled, a nervous, yet confiding smile, everything else in the room vanished.

Hamilton stayed behind his table, but even with this formidable bulk and all those stacks of paper, she was a palpable presence.

With charming diffidence, she explained that the Livingston's she was kin to were the Livingstons of Red Hook. Hamilton had never heard of them.

303

More distant kin to my Betsy?

"How may I be of service to you, Mrs. Reynolds?"

As she replied, her creamy bosom began to rise and fall in agitation. "I know you're a terrible busy man, sar, so I'll come straight to it. I'm sore ashamed to come to you like this—like a—like a beggar—but my husband has left me in such straits I don't know where else to turn."

Her voice was teary, low and soft. An accent far more common than that of her initial speech came creeping in.

Not real gentry, or just clinging to the edge...? Alexander's sympathies were immediately engaged.

"My Mister has found hi'self another woman, ya see, sar, and the night he left me and my little girl—she's just five—and—and—why, sar, 'e—'e beatin' me right in front of my little girl, for 'e's the very devil when 'e's drunk." The blue eyes spilled over, brimming with shame and helpless rage. "I want to go home to my own people in New York, sar, and leave Mr. Reynolds for good—but I—I haven't no means."

What incredible skin—so fair and beaded with sweat! Five year old or no, this young mother was not even out of her teens.

"Please—please—don't be offended, Colonel Hamilton." She turned those luminous eyes sadly towards him and withdrew a handkerchief from the cleft which separated her round breasts. "I'm so ashamed for tellin' you—a perfect stranger—'bout my disgrace, but I've seen you about the city and you always look like such a kind gen'leman. My landlady said to me this very mornin' that you're a good Samaritan for helping out folks in trouble, 'specially New Yorkers. If you could just give me enough for the coach back to New York and—and—to settle with my landlady, I'd be ever so grateful."

She was affectingly nervous, stammering and girlishly wringing the handkerchief.

"Really, Colonel, there's no one else I'd dare ask."

Hamilton removed his own handkerchief and mopped his brow, where sweat poured. Even his palms were perspiring! He wiped them surreptitiously, one at a time, upon his breeches. In this damnable, relentless heat, not even the linen jacket could be long endured.

He had to clear his throat before he could reply. All the time he was intently aware of those eyes fixed upon him, and of the heavy scent—sweating young female and a cheap floral perfume.

"Well, certainly, Mrs. Reynolds, it sounds a good plan. To return to your family, that is. I'll be glad to assist you, but I don't have so much as a dollar here."

The dark eyes stared, incredulous. Her pink lips parted slightly. She looked, he thought, childishly expectant, in breathless suspense.

"Let me see. I will get a bank bill and send it to you. Will tomorrow be soon enough?"

"Oh, yes, Colonel." The tears stopped as quickly as they'd started, and she sprang to her feet, dabbing her eyes. "Oh, thank you, Colonel! Everyone said you was a most kind gentleman, and indeed—indeed—so you are!"

Hamilton, following her lead, also stood.

"Here, sar." She stepped forward and laid a folded bit of paper on the desk. "This is my address." Then she cast her eyes down. "I'd be grateful, too, Colonel, if you would come yourself and—and—not send a servant. I—I shouldn't like for anyone to see what I'm reduced to—me and my little girl."

* * *

"Knew you wouldn't be sorry to see her, Mr. Secretary. Weren't that some fine piece of woman flesh? Her husband must have lost 'is mind. I ask you, where's 'e goin' to find another filly that'll ride like that one?"

"Mr. Donelson," Alexander said, "your eyes are obviously good, but your ears must be even better. I warn you, sir, if you ever listen at my door again, you will find yourself looking for another job."

305

The man tugged his forelock and mumbled, "Yes, sar, Colonel, Mr. Secretary." As he backed out the door, Alexander caught a flash of his mocking grin.

He removed his jacket, the stock and the waistcoat again. He sat and tried to go back to work, but he was no longer able to concentrate. The scent of woman, of her rose perfume, lingered in the room. Hamilton kept trying to bring himself back, to refocus upon his "Report on Manufactures." He swatted at a mosquito that came buzzing by his head, while silently cursing the whole race of women. All he could think about was what he hadn't had since Betsy had gone to Albany, well over a month ago.

What I should be cursing is sex itself.

Alexander leaned back and stretched his arms over his head.

After only a few weeks without a wife, I'm like a bull locked in a barn, smelling cows in the pasture. Here I sit, unable to think about anything but kicking the walls down and finding one of them....

* * *

The meat of the cold supper Donelson brought was iridescent. Alexander pushed it aside and took a bite of the cold potato beside it.

"Pig slop!" Once again he thought ruefully of Betsy, wishing this time not just for her presence in his bed, but in the kitchen. In the end, he ate only the dish of greens dressed with oil and vinegar and a chunk of bread.

As the sun finally lowered, he dismissed Donelson and went for a walk, hoping to clear his head. On his way, he secured a bank bill for thirty dollars. His thoughts were in an unaccustomed state of drift.

Not much refinement or education in that young woman. Still, the cheeky Mr. Donelson was right. She was indeed "some piece of woman flesh."

Hamilton took the paper out of his pocket and looked at the address she'd given, written in a sloping, childish hand.

306

In spite of her request, he considered sending Donelson over with the bill in the morning. Then, thinking about the man's salacious remarks, he decided against it.

It would indeed be kinder, less demeaning, if he did as she had asked and brought the money himself. The address was not a particularly respectable one, but, as she'd said, it was probably all the poor creature could afford. Coincidentally, it was only a few blocks away from where he now stood.

Hamilton approached Skeep's Inn through the hot twilight. One close look at the outside was sufficient to know that the house was the kind where the few empty rooms upstairs were used for assignations. There followed a tug of arousal, for he had experienced some thrilling encounters in places like this. Certain adventurous and sophisticated ladies, ladies of fashion and monumental discretion, had met him in exactly such places.

The blousy landlady greeted him with a sly smile and directed him upstairs. The air of the place so unsettled him he actually forgot what number she'd said.

Just as he stood hesitating in the sweltering corridor, Mrs. Reynolds came out of one of the doors, a candle in hand. Seeing him, her child-like face brightened.

"Oh, thank heaven you came, Colonel. I was so afraid you—you—might not believe me—might not come."

In spite of the relief on her face, her voice suddenly held the same verge-of-tears desperation he'd heard earlier in his office. He came closer, now feeling not only lustful, but protective.

What a world it was where a beautiful young woman could be abused, where she and her small, helpless child could be so casually abandoned!

A blistering memory rushed in—his mother clutching him against her full bosom and bitterly weeping over loss and betrayal.

The bouquet in that dark hallway—*woman, sweat, heat*—was so familiar.

307

Mrs. Reynolds was in a state of undress, a morning gown hastily thrown on—over what? Grateful for the darkness, he experienced a reckless surge of response.

"Please 'scuse my appearance. It's this dreadful heat, Colonel. 'Tis made me 'most faint."

"I've come with the bank bill, Mrs. Reynolds. I hope it will be sufficient to help you home to your family."

He was reaching into his pocket, but she forestalled him, impulsively catching his hand.

How young she is!

"We mustn't stand out here. This ain't really a nice place, you know, Colonel, but it's the only shelter I can get since Mr. Reynolds is run off. Please come in for a minute. Just so's I can say a proper thanks, you know. Mrs. Skeep's brought up some lemonade just now and I'd be so honored if you'd take a little with me."

Feeling like a sleepwalker, Hamilton silently allowed her to lead him through the door.

Inside were two windows through which a hazy twilight appeared. A slight hot breeze made the thin curtains quiver, but otherwise the room was stifling, smelling muskily of young unwashed bodies. By the low light of a single candle, he saw a pair of battered chairs, a small table, a washbasin and the room's centerpiece, a disheveled bed, curtains absent. Under-clothes and the dress she'd worn when she'd visited were tossed across the foot.

Mumbling something, he tried once more to thrust the bank bill into her hand.

"I can't tell you how grateful I am to you, Colonel Hamilton. This is a miracle! Now I can get back to my folks. Philadelphia is a hard city—and much too hot. Hot and hard, and ever so lonely! I don't know a soul."

She poured lemonade from a sweating, lukewarm pitcher. A moment later, the glass of the pale liquid was in his hand.

"Except now, I know you!" Her features were illuminated by a bright smile.

Even her teeth were beautiful! White, even—the perfect ornament for such a tender mouth.

"Just think! Such a busy, 'portant man helping me!" Lovely long hands clasped in a girlish gesture of delight. "Mr. Reynolds said I'd have to sell myself to get the money to go home. I was so afraid, Colonel Hamilton! Not only for me, but for my little girl!"

"Yes, your daughter. Is she here?" Hamilton had half expected to see the child curled in the bed. That was usually the case at his house.

"Oh," said Mrs. Reynolds, turning in an offhand way. "She's there." She gestured at what he now saw was an opening into a small curtained space. Abruptly, he had a queasy feeling.

What is this, anyway? The disreputable boarding house, this purported Livingston cousin who had so impulsively invited him into her room, this tale of a runaway husband? Was Donelson more acute than he knew when he wondered what kind of man would run away from "a filly like that?"

"Take a look at her," said Mrs. Reynolds. "Don't worry about waking her. Sleeps like a stone, she does."

Hamilton followed, all his senses prickling. Mrs. Reynolds lifted the curtain. There, instead of what he'd almost begun to expect—a lurking accomplice bent on violence—was a small truckle bed. On it lay a little girl, quite naked and soundly asleep. A brimming chamber pot sat nearby, filling the air with the acid and sugar smell of child's urine.

"There she is. My poor 'Arietta."

The girl had round fat cheeks, a thumb in her mouth, and a tousled mop of brown curls.

Hamilton felt a pang. Images of his own children arose, little bodies cuddled against the nut-brown flesh of their mother.

"Mrs. Reynolds—" He began a retreat, looking for a place to set down the untouched glass. Suddenly he was stifled—by the heat—by the smell—*by memory....*

"Maria, please."

"I must go. My being here will jeopardize your reputation." He turned, but she caught his arm. A young goddess with plenty of strength, she held him, brought him to a standstill. Cornflower eyes again shone into his, but suddenly the smile wasn't childlike. It was knowing, inviting. Her scent flowed over him like a wave.

"Oh, *please* don't go! Stay and talk to me for just a little. Drink the lemonade. I put gin in it. It's been so long since I've had any company. It would be such a pleasure."

"I doubt that a woman as lovely as you ever lacks for any sort of company she wants." He tried to keep his voice light and quickly set the glass on the table. Hoping that gallantry could be used to gain distance, he caught her hand and raised it to his lips. Mrs. Reynolds accepted the salute, and at the same time allowed her morning gown to slip. As well as the blinding perfection of one full white arm, he saw a series of purple bruises, the kind punched in by brutal fingertips.

"Mr. Reynolds did that before he left." She readjusted the gown as if the slippage had been accidental. "It's not the first time, either. May his new woman have joy of him."

Temptation! Lust! The present and the past, like two enormous ships under full sail, collided.

"I'm beginning to wonder if you ain't an imposter, sir." Mrs. Reynolds stepped forward and abruptly slipped her arms inside his jacket, her voice husky and teasing.

I am always in control with women—always! But this one—he was a sheep having a first encounter with a well-trained herd dog....

"Well, you don't act much like the Colonel Hamilton I've heard tell 'bout."

"What?" He put his hands upon her arms, but could not find the will to push her away.

It is clear what's on offer ....

"Oh, you're pretty enough to be Colonel Hamilton." She ran her hands along his sweating sides, "but I heard 'e was the kind who never shirked an engagement." Her arms locked around his waist. "I had such a dream 'bout you

310

after I left your office. Don't you want to hear 'bout all the wicked things you made me do?"

The morning gown fell, this time completely. There were no stays, nothing but a transparent chemise, raised by the fullest, hardest young breasts he'd ever seen.

The child didn't wake, although he feared it. When she noticed him casting worried looks in the direction of the screen, she just smiled, rocked full hips beneath him encouragingly.

"She won't wake—laudanum."

Taking his face in her hands she pulled him down to sample the delights of rose-tipped breasts.

Maria made love with appetite and determination. In one astounding moment, he found himself pushed off and rolled onto his back.

"I like riding better," she explained. The full hips descended and he was repossessed. After that, there were no more words, just a sweating, panting struggle.

* * *

Hamilton stumbled through the streets after midnight. He was exhausted, ready to sleep the sleep of the dead. When he lay down in his own bed, however, his mind refused to let him rest. His flesh was drenched in the cloying odor of rose; his imagination still ran wild. The memory of things just passed beat a fiery pulse in his mind.

* * *

The next day he threw himself into his work, buried himself in numbers, in flurries of paper. Outside the relentless sun beat down, making a shimmering oven of the streets. Again and again, he wiped the sweat out of his eyes. By afternoon, he had not only removed his jacket, but his stock, his waistcoat, had even opened his shirt.

This morning he had washed and washed, but he could still smell that woman's scent. Whenever he took his eyes away from the columns of figures for a moment, he was

311

haunted by remembered images of her young body, by the memory of female flesh avidly striving against his.

Over and over again he scrubbed his sweating face with his handkerchief, using up one after another. He tried to rub the images away, but all that seemed to do was encourage voluptuous day dreams.

* * *

Alexander worked doggedly, but the fact was he'd been unable to add two numbers together since the blazing sun began to lower. At last it was time to send Donelson and the maid of all work home.

Night came, and with it a hooded figure by the back door. Without hesitation, he threw it open and drew her into his arms. She responded, as hot as he, as wanting. There was no talk. In an instant, they were passionately struggling to mold their bodies together.

"Where?" She urgently fumbled at his drop buttons.

Gussie was upriver with her mistress. Her room was near—and empty. Alexander pushed Maria through the door and onto the narrow bed. He expected to have a long session with buttons and laces in the dark, but under the cloak he found—nothing.

* * *

Betsy reclined on a blanket beneath a great sycamore, and unfolded the letter from her husband, intending to read it again. Jamie, recovering from some sort of summer cold, dozed against her. He was almost asleep, ginger lashes lowered.

The handsome red brick pile of The Pastures overlooked the slope behind her. Above her head the great tree whispered; the cool green Hudson flowed peacefully below. Content, Betsy stretched and sighed, watched as Alex, Angelica, and Fanny romped along the reedy shore with cousins.

They had arrived at the river in pony carts, nurses and children, young Hamiltons, Schuylers and that single precious little van Rensselaer. The sallow pallor of her city-bound children had transformed during the past weeks into a healthy summer glow.

The children threw sticks in the water and then pelted them with pebbles, an occupation which would soon leave them soaking wet. Betsy remembered happily playing exactly the same game with her own sisters and cousins in exactly that spot.

"I will wait with all the patience I can for the time for your return, but you must not precipitate it. I am so anxious for a perfect restoration of your health that I am willing to make a great sacrifice for it."

It was the first time Hamilton had ever written that he didn't mind her long absences in Albany.

This summer too she'd noted something rather odd about his letters. At first he'd sent a lot of them full of medical advice about James, but after she'd written to say that a little bark and a little paregoric at night had put to rest whatever ailment had been plaguing the child, his letters became infrequent. That, in itself, was unlike him—her 'indefatigable penman'! In fact, for the first time ever, she was the more faithful correspondent.

When she'd at last inquired why he hadn't written, he'd answered that his letters to her must have gone astray, "stolen by some very abominable person." She knew that letters were often opened and read, especially those from one politically important man to another, but these were simply personal, a man to his wife.

What real interest would anyone have in what Alexander says to me? Not only did his excuse seem unlikely, but the high drama he'd invoked was uncharacteristic.

Or, even more disturbing, was it fiction?

Rumination ended when a pretty black woman appeared, carrying a light blanket over one arm.

"Here, Mrs. Hamilton." She unfolded the blanket and shook it out. "Your Mama said you should rest. Esther an' I will be right here and Mr. Rensselaer and his lady are down

313

close by the water. Don' you fret. We'll all be watchin' over those babies of yours."

Betsy allowed herself to be covered, carefully keeping James close, warm flesh against hers. The river sent reflections of light upward, into the faded leaves of the sycamore. A gentle breeze arose, dapples chased across the water. In no time, rocked in the languor of her Albany cradle, Mrs. Hamilton was fast asleep, boy child in her arms.

* * *

Betsy came back down river in company with her children, sailing on her father's sloop. Peggy, who wanted to do some visiting and shopping in Philadelphia, traveled with her. Hamilton had written that he was "indisposed," that he couldn't meet her at New Ark as he usually did. A small graying gentleman, a clerk of the Treasury, came in his stead to accompany the sisters to Philadelphia.

Betsy was glad that Peggy had come along, for Alexander was very busy, very abstracted. She sensed, however, that there was something different about his busyness this autumn, something more than his usual anxiety over his important official tasks, over politics, something beyond mere preoccupation.

She had expected him in her bed the first night. She had missed him, after all, and in spite of the risk of conceiving another child, she wanted him badly enough to hazard loving. He, however, rather formally said that he still suffered the indisposition that had prevented him from coming to meet them in New Ark. After she was in their bed, he came and dutifully kissed her, but retreated to the day bed he kept in his study.

He seemed far more at ease with the children. He lay on the floor and let the boys climb all over him. He wrestled with Alex; he kissed and teased Angelica and Fanny into giggling fits. He threw James high into the air. For an hour there were shrieks and delighted squeals, as Papa, all

314

dignity forgotten, in shirt sleeves and waistcoat, played with them.

One night, soon after she'd come home, Jamie awoke crying. Betsy lifted him out of bed and carried him to the rocking chair, but only a few moments later, Hamilton came in the door and insisted upon taking him.

"You go back to sleep, Bess. I know you're exhausted from traveling, and I haven't been able to sleep, anyway. I made the mistake of reading that creature Freneau's newspaper and now I shall be up all night, composing suitably scathing rebuttals to him and his paymaster, Jefferson. It seems like years since I last did this, and," he continued with an odd, forced smile, "I don't want to get out of practice."

* * *

By early November she was sure. There was another woman, somewhere in this terrible city! A woman Alexander loved, but one he loathed, too, a woman he at once desired and feared, a rival who lay like a sullen cloud in his mind.

When he went out in the evening and came back so late, when he went to sleep in his study and didn't come to her, she wept. She didn't know what to do, how to fight back.

There had been other women into whose arms he had gone, and then, just as quickly, returned. From those arms, she had received him as a sinner repentant, ready to rededicate himself to his wedding vow.

This was different, a long-lasting affair, with a woman who was not of their social class, perhaps, even, *a harlot*. It was a kind of threat to their happiness she'd never imagined.

Hamilton, who wore his heart on his sleeve, often looked guilty. Although he was affectionate, the tenderness he bestowed upon her was much the same he gave the children. She tried to ignore what she knew in her gut, to put it aside, to tell herself she was imagining things, but his uneasiness, his new secretiveness, didn't end.

315

They attended a dinner party at the Bingham's. Alexander remained by her side all evening, gallant and attentive. During conversation and wine, while a scattering of Philadelphia snow descended outside the windows, he suddenly started to tease about their wedding night.

"When I finally went upstairs, entirely too full of your father's beef and whiskey, I found you sound asleep, you adorable creature."

Mrs. Knox snapped her fan shut and laughed softly.

"Did you really fall asleep before he came to you, Mrs. Hamilton?"

"Indeed I did. Mr. Hamilton and my papa and Mr. McHenry were downstairs talking about war business for hours."

Her companion shook her head, setting her pink jowls in motion.

"Nothing ever changes with you men, does it?" Lucy Knox made no secret of the fact that she was thoroughly out of patience with 'the political passions.'"

Henry Knox, a genial bear, patted his mate's fleshy hand soothingly.

"Nothing ever changes with anybody, the way I see it. Mrs. Hamilton, as we all know well, is a most commonsensical lady. Getting a little sleep early on in the evening is an example of this, for I believe I also remember hearing Mr. McHenry telling me that even those French counts were impressed with the bridegroom's—energy."

Before this could go farther, Hamilton cut in cheerfully, raising a glass. "To my wife's good sense." While Betsy blushed, Hamilton kissed her check and whispered, "and to her sensibility as well."

At home, as soon as they were out of sight of servants, Alexander swept his wife towards the conjugal bed. When it proved, as usual, to be full of children, he escorted her into his study, sat her down on the sofa and set about undressing her.

316

"The floor is such a discreet place." Hamilton smiled down at her. "I doubt if a single child will even stir in sleep."

"I fear you know all the discreet places."

She'd been trying to tease, but the cloud that crossed his face made her wish she'd never opened her mouth.

"Oh, Eliza!" He knelt and embraced her. "God knows I don't deserve you."

Did he, at last, understand that she knew?

In the shadow her words had cast, his head came to rest against her bosom, a gesture both contrite and humble. Betsy caught the oddest flash of Jamie, acting out repentance after some long-planned misdeed.

They spent the night together on the study floor using the blankets he kept upon the divan to warm his now frequent sojourns. Later, after she made a shy invitation, he made love again. Hungry for him, Betsy discovered abandon. He responded in kind, his slim body eager in a way that wasn't feigned. She would always believe this the night when their Johnny was conceived.

* * *

They awoke to the interested faces of children. There stood Phil, Angelica, Alex, and Jamie, a flannel of which he was particularly fond slung over his shoulder. Fanny Antil peeped around the door. The children all stared, rosy lips agape.

"Why are you sleeping on the floor?" Angelica looked uneasy. Phil, home from school, and looking as if he might have had a notion, quickly captured her hand.

As if on cue, the littler boys threw themselves onto their father like puppies, began rolling happily around atop the heap of blankets.

"Yes, why?" Sitting up, Alex took a long, interested look at his parents. "And why have you got on only your shirts?"

317

"Only shirts?" Hamilton challenged. Grabbing his namesake by the foot, he toppled him and began some serious tickling.

How handsome he was!

Betsy rolled away from the shrieking melee which instantly developed. That slim waist, those strong arms, almost exactly as he'd been in the days when he'd been courting her. She sighed, thinking of the silvery stretch marks on her own breasts and hips.

Hamilton shook his son playfully. "What makes you say that I've taken off my clothes? Can't you see that I have on a fine suit, all of broadcloth? I think I shall go straight out and pay a morning call upon His Excellency."

"No! No!" Alex shrieked, writhing from his father's tickling. "You can't do that! You're naked. You are!"

Jamie hurled himself upon Hamilton's back and wrapped his arms around his neck. His father dragged him over his shoulder and began to tickle him as well. Phil, his budding maturity overpowered by longing, joined in.

Betsy managed to grab her cape from the heap upon the turkey carpet. Wrapping up in it, she got to her feet.

The place where she'd lain with her husband was now a heaving mound of blankets, through which odd flashes of flesh, toes and nightgown showed as husband and boys rolled about, laughing wildly.

"Come with me, Angel." She extended her hands. "And you, too, little Fan." Both girls' eyes were questioning, but they remained silent as they passed along the chilly corridor together.

As they entered the bedroom, Una looked up from her task of setting the fire. Surprise and then amusement overcame her stern features, for her lady's dark hair was loose and tousled and she was barefoot, wearing but a shirt and the cape.

"Is there warm water yet?" Betsy asked, hoping to maintain her dignity.

"Yes, Ma'am." Una, who was the soul of discretion, hid her face behind a blanket she was folding. "I go an' git it now. Why don't you come on wi' me, Fanny darlin'? You left your special doll-baby in the kitchen."

"Did I? Missy Emma?"

"You did, my darlin'. You don't wan' that bad lil' Jamie to hide her away somewhere again."

Fanny's expression said that she definitely did not and she went, without another word, away with Una. It had taken the child most of a day to find her doll the last time Jamie had decided that this would be a fun trick to play. After they had gone, Angelica finally voiced the expected question. "Why were you and Papa naked?"

She'd known it was coming, but when it did, Betsy had a pause. Never in her young life had she seen such a shocking sight. She couldn't imagine her own parents caught lying on the floor, undressed, together. Still, her man had been a-roving and a wife must do what a wife must do. It seemed best to make an honest answer.

"Your papa and I were loving each other, Angel. Husbands and wives sometimes hug and kiss each other—in a—state of nature."

"Well, couldn't you hug and kiss without taking off your clothes? Why did you have to do that?" Angelica positively squirmed with discomfort.

Betsy stilled her, taking that thin little face between her hands. "Because it's nicest to touch that way," she said firmly, giving her daughter's forehead a kiss. "And someday, after you are married, you will want to do that, too."

Angelica studied her mother solemnly. Her blue eyes filled with disgust. "I'm sorry, Mama, but I don't think so!" She spoke with high decision.

* * *

Christmas wasn't the end of the other woman. Betsy knew she was still in her husband's mind—and therefore in hers—a shadowy and unwelcome third party. Alexander was, as usual frantically busy, working late into the night.

He called for more hot water than usual, instructing Davie to bring it straight to him in the study if he'd slept there.

Every now and then, though, in spite of his fastidious precautions, she'd catch the scent of her rival, a musky femaleness mingled with cheap attar of roses, still clinging to his clothes.

* * *

All through winter and into the spring, along with all of that, the ugly warfare of politics went on. His report on manufactures and the subsequent battles over that went on in the newspapers and in Congress. Mr. Jefferson attempted to have her husband censured for mishandling Treasury monies, a move that caused him to live at Treasury for weeks, marshalling his clerks to copy mountains of figures, and sending letters to every port in the country for their records. Accusing him of malfeasance was a lie, of course, the kind a vituperative and inventive enemy would naturally concoct.

"I think the Virginians do it," Oliver Wolcott, a friend who'd signed the Declaration of Independence, observed one night, "because they don't have a ghost of a notion about accounting or handling money themselves."

"You know, perhaps you're right. I've never met a planter—either here or in the Indies—who knew anything about money," Alexander said. "They're land rich, but perennially in debt and it's more than partly because they are too high and mighty to have any truck with mere bookkeeping. They let some other fellow do it, a bailiff, or, worse, a London factor, and then wonder why they are robbed blind."

While Wolcott nodded, Hamilton continued. "Nevertheless, there's more than that going on here. These fellows have a hatred for me the depths of which I'm just beginning to fathom. All I'm trying to do is make this country—my country, too, as well as theirs—strong enough to survive."

320

"It's dead simple, dear fellow. It's their way or no way at all. In a world in which you are surrounded by ignorant poor whites and slaves, it's easy to grow accustomed to having your every caprice looked upon as stone tablets straight down from Sinai. They use the word a great deal, but they really have no interest at all in 'liberty,' except for themselves and their own set. Besides, it's far more politic to attack you than General Washington." Robert Morris had entered the conversation with a grim smile. "See my prescience in not wanting your job, Mr. Secretary?"

* * *

That pink seashell was what he craved, the puss of Venus!

The tears of Maria, her infectious laugh, her pearly white teeth, the flowery lips, her quick, ardent tongue! He knew she was not in the least innocent, but he also understood how impossible it was for a woman alone not to become corrupted, to end by doing things in which, had her circumstances been better, she never would have engaged.

And here I am, despite knowing it all, ready to be man-the-animal and trade money for sex, to take yet another bite from this second-hand juicy apple, savor what has so clearly been put up for sale....

She seemed so hungry for romance, so eager for passion, on the floor, on the bed, this way and that way and any way at all, while his veins ran fire. And why should she not be in love with him, when she was married to such an oaf? He even tried invoking Diana's image to make things – *if not right*—or, at least understandable.

Perhaps, like my first love, Maria is pleased to play the game, for it mirrors her true desire.

Certainly, he meant a great deal more to Maria than just another....

From the shadows, The Reverend Knox stepped forward and pointed a finger of admonition. Whenever this figure from his past materialized, Hamilton felt the cold chill of the Biblical warning: *"the wages of sin is death."* The pox

321

was real, and he had seen its work in his youth, the effects as horrible, at the end, as those of leprosy.

But his fear and his sense of shame didn't last long. In an instant, lustful memories would bloom like flowers, full of images of Maria's voluptuous body and enveloped by all the turgid fragrance of her ocean....

Another summer came. He'd watch the gathering twilight until, finally, all the fantasies died. There was, in the compulsion that drove him out of doors, no poetry. Would he get his hat and coat and go out, through the dark, odorous streets to get there—so late now, because it was May again—hoping all the time not to be recognized, not to be followed?

And then, the boundary crossed, he'd enter some rented room, and soon they would both be blind, only wanting to fall into bed together, to swim-*with touch and taste and sweat*-in the lubricious Element of Water.

* * *

Sir:

I have this preposial to make to you, give me the Sum of thousand dollars and I will leve the town and take my daughter with me and go where my Friend shant here from me and leve her to Yourself to do for her as you think proper....

—James Reynolds

Hamilton lifted his hands, pressed the fingers against his temple. Next, he crumpled the note and let it fall upon the floor.

I should have known this was where it would lead. And yet I—fool—sinner—adulterer—

And even as his thoughts berated, the lawyerly part pursued with the only pertinent question:

How deep is Maria in this blackmail? Has it all—every scene between us—been a game? Have I been but a cock-blind target for a pimp and a clever whore?

322

His legs felt weak.

You will be lucky, my man, if it's only the two of them at this game. Start thinking, you fool!

He did. A few minutes later, he arose, picked up the wadded paper again and then, carefully, smoothed it out. *Repellent, but it should be saved.* Furthermore, as alarming as were the contents, it was suddenly quite clear to him that he had better—*somehow*—extricate himself. The money demanded would empty his purse, but for now, at least, he'd have to pay.

My Betsy must never find out.

* * *

Betsy's world ran in tandem. Sometimes, during this time, she felt as if her beloved husband's life never touched hers. Summer had come again, with its usual discomforts and illnesses for herself and the children. She was heavily pregnant by now as well, but nevertheless, sensing what she did, she refused to leave Philadelphia.

At last, early one muggy August morning, she awoke with the now familiar labor pangs. By noon, she had a new baby in her arms, this one to be christened John Church Hamilton, after her darling sister's husband.

* * *

From the very first, she believed that she and Johnny had a special connection. If this baby woke and cried in the night, she could simply think: *Oh, darling babe, please give me another half hour of sleep...I will nurse you when you ask again; I promise.* And, like the magic, the crying would stop. In half an hour, he'd "ask" again. The second request was always easier to answer. Scooping him from his cradle, soaking wet, she'd awaken to first turn up the lamp and then change the baby into dry diapers and shirt. Next, she'd get herself and the pillows comfortably situated for nursing.

Her nights were as filled as the days, mostly with children. Which child was (or was not) in bed with her changed daily, like face of the moon. Angelica was often there, whispering some fear, and now, little Johnny, too. Their household kept the washerwomen busy with bedding and diapers.

Hamilton was not much around, either to sleep, or about the house one way or the other. Sometimes, it seemed, he lived those few doors down at the building which housed the Treasury. And if it wasn't work, it was to make plans, some sort of late meeting with influential friends or with subordinates from Treasury. These outings could also be social, which she understood was an important ingredient of political life.

Sometimes, she would suspect his absence was actually due to neither, no matter what sort of explanation he made. The reason for disbelief would be something she didn't dare dwell upon. Despite this resolve, the *known-unknown* evil would rear up in the midst of ordinary tasks. For instance, when, as she and a maid sorted laundry for the washerwoman, a handkerchief with a streak of rouge and a hint of that atrocious scent would thrust itself forward from among the innocent daily heap of pee-soaked baby shirts, the grimy cuffs, caps, and stocks.

* * *

Yes, Sir, Rest assured I will never ask you to Call on me again I have kept my Bed those two dayes and now rise from My pillow wich your Neglect has filled with the shorpest thorns...my heart is ready Burst with Greef I can neither eat or sleep I have Been on the point of doing the moast horrid acts as I shudder to think where I might been what will become of me...do something to ease my heart or els I no not what I shall do for so I cannot live....

After a series of such pleading letters, his resolve to stay away from Maria melted, despite the now obvious danger. She had, of course, sworn on her soul that the blackmail was all her husband's doing, that she, herself, was madly in love with him. They found new places in which to meet.

Dear Sir: I shal be miserable till I see you and if my dear freend has the Least Esteeme for the unhappy Maria whos greatest fault is loveing him he will come as soon as he shal get this and till that time My breast will be the seate of pain and woe, adieu Col Hamilton....

* * *

The only good that came of the unspoken trouble was that Hamilton again found time to attend church with his wife. They would go to the small Dutch Reformed church on the east side of town, which stood like a gaunt survivor of more genteel days, close to the river. When the heat rose and they entered the time when she was usually gone away north, he escorted them to an Episcopalian church in a better area, surrounded by trees which staved off the summer heat. It was a good walk to get there. Betsy, though, always liked activity before the hours of sitting. It got the circulation going and helped her stay awake during the long and often uninspired sermons.

Alex, James, Angel and Fanny would trot in their wake, like ducklings. If Phil was home from school, he would head up the group like a little prince and escort his sister on his arm.

If it was too miserably hot and humid to go out, after one of those horrible, sweltering, sleepless Philadelphia nights, Hamilton would assemble the children in the curtain-drawn parlor and read the service, either Episcopalian, or Presbyterian, from books she hadn't known he'd possessed. He read beautifully, with deep feeling. Betsy sensed a new humility in him. When he answered the boys' questions about religion his answers were no longer such a rationalist's pat response.

He repents! He strives against his baser self. And I love him so much; am I not bound to forgive?

During those painful times, she'd often find herself thinking of things he'd told her about his parents' marriage, the revelations that sometimes slipped out— although he'd always be embarrassed, clearly regretting what he'd divulged—stories about screaming and insults, about cruel, bruising blows.

I shall not engage with him, not even over this heartless infidelity in which he persists. Once unleashed, who knows what we might say—or do? After all, I am a Schuyler. Although my heart may break, I shall never be brought so low.

Chapter Two
Honest Men and Knaves

Business had boomed since the United States' credit problems had been resolved. Corporations were chartered at record rates during 1791-92; money came flowing into the country from abroad. Every port was building new docks to accommodate all the new foreign shipping. Taxes in the countryside were much reduced; farmers were getting good prices for their crops.

All seemed well, but suddenly another newspaper appeared in town. It began to publish articles critical of the government and most particularly critical of the Secretary of Treasury. *Such malcontent!* Betsy, now a constant reader of the papers, declared that she had read this claptrap before, from the same people who had opposed the union itself. Some men must always be reaching for political power, aiming to benefit no one but themselves.

When she declared this, her husband smiled, a pleasant moment of affirmation.

"Yes, Hamilton, my dear. I have been paying attention."

"I see that you have. And because you wear your Federal colors so very proudly, I shall this minute deliver a note from Mrs. General Washington that somehow landed on my desk today."

"And you wouldn't have given it to me otherwise?" Betsy shook her head. Sometimes she wished he'd stop playing at gallantry—*or whatever*—when he spoke to her. She much preferred plain dealing. She understood that his verbal fencing delighted the ladies who were not married to him—like her sister. Already more than a little irritated from reading the sniping, hostile newspaper, she unfolded the note and discovered a request for her presence at an official tea party.

"Good heavens! Again? It's tomorrow, too. I do hope Johnny is calmer so I can attend with good conscience."

"You poured tea for important visitors so beautifully during the Revolution that Mrs. General Washington has never forgotten. And you know how taxing all that enforced sociability is on both of them. A day doesn't pass without the President declaring how he longs to be quietly at Mt. Vernon again."

"Oh, I'm certain Mrs. Washington would like my company as much as anything. So many of the other ladies in Philadelphia are—*haut ton,* is the phrase, I think. Sometimes it's entirely daunting to us both."

"Do you feel up to another presidential levee? And do you have another dress you can wear?"

Betsy was pleased by his concern. She could see him wondering if another dress would be required to appear again so soon at their "Republic Court." It was like him to think of that, for good clothing was terribly important to him, perhaps because when he'd been a poor boy, he had often been shamed by his appearance. Unlike her father, her handsome Hamilton liked a French tailor.

"Don't worry about the dress, sir. Lady Washington writes that she has one on hand she thinks will suit me very well. And I do enjoy her company, you know. She reminds me of my own dear Mama. I shall certainly do as she asks and be happy to appear in a borrowed dress. She's the soul of tact, and she understands how tight our domestic budget is."

* * *

Susan Bradford and Betsy had known each other since the Morristown days, those icy nights at Cochran's where they'd roasted chestnuts. Susan, in fact, had a longer acquaintance with Alexander, for he'd lived with her family when he'd first immigrated to America. Her other companion, Sarah Rawle, was fair and freckled, wife to another prominent Philadelphia businessman. This lady was pregnant, but comfortably and fashionably dressed in a yellow *robe volante* with plenty of tucks and vents for

328

expansion. She was a tall, strong woman who remained entirely determined to be in company whenever an occasion presented itself. That night, in good company, the ladies took their leave of their gentlemen with good cheer, intent upon a good chat about servants, babies and households, leaving their men free to talk business as long as they pleased, or, as Susan had said, "till the cock crows."

"I can't possibly stay that long." Betsy spoke as they retreated into a comfortable sitting room where Mrs. Bradford's attentive servants were in the act of lighting candles.

"Never fear, my dear," her hostess said. "We'll call a carriage to carry you both safe home whenever you want. Those men can do as they like." She turned to a gangly servant girl. "Nancy, please fetch these ladies' reticules."

Even as wealthy as these households were, the women would not be comfortable simply sitting without handwork. From the handbags that had accompanied them as a matter of course, each lady withdrew a project. Sarah Rawle's was, naturally, baby clothing. Susan Bradford had her embroidery frame in the room. She settled into a chair already set beside it, containing a half-finished fire screen.

"Would anyone like more wine or anything else?"

"Some fennel tea would be lovely," said Sarah. "After that huge supper and with this baby in the way, I couldn't possibly put another thing into my stomach."

"Yes, I believe I'll join you," said Betsy. The supper, she thought, had been a little rich for her taste. The fennel would certainly settle that. There was a swish as she bent in her pink silk polonaise gown to collect her own handwork, an in-progress stocking with a ball of cotton yarn and five small needles attached.

"Ah, you and your stockings," Susan said, smiling. "Do you know, Sarah, the very first time I met Elizabeth was during the war in Morristown. She was at work on a pair, chatting with her Aunt and knitting away. I remember wondering how she could talk and knit at the same time, but by the end of the war and hundreds of stockings, none of us had a bit of trouble doing it."

In an adjacent wood-paneled room in the Bradford home, William Bradford, Hamilton, and William Rawle, (now serving as a US attorney for Pennsylvania), pursued their own interests. The men were close in age, all three veterans and now engaged in the business of nation building. All were dressed in the dark suits and white silk stockings of the professional class.

Hamilton had been holding forth. As usual, he'd abandoned his seat and begun to pace while he talked.

"A man cannot foretell what fate will overtake his efforts. The whims of the universe or the designs of a determined enemy are sufficient to bring him low. Government should create justice and good order, where men stand in equality under law, and where ingenuity and industry are assisted. I think that is the only possible utopia mere men can devise."

"As you know, Hamilton, that is not going to be easy. 'Justice' is moot where men are involved. As for 'good order,' you describe a smoothly functioning bureaucracy, but not our glorious new republic, whose turbulent businessmen are flush with credit and ready to corner a market, or hunger to speculate themselves to a quick fortune in raw land."

"Indeed! And too much available credit can play hell with honorable intentions." Rawle had spoken of several notable bankruptcy cases which he was litigating.

"And that is why we must be a little devious while we build, so that we can trick the tricksters. I quote Pope: '…self-love in all becomes the cause/Of what restrains him, Government and laws.'"

"One of the prime dangers that I see is the rise of a mass of artificial credit," Bradford said. "The first ill wind that blows will cause all the leveraged businesses to collapse and spread ruin among innocent and guilty alike."

"And I've heard we have exactly such a situation blossoming in New York City with that so-called Million Bank," said Rawle.

"As I am most anxiously aware, sir," Hamilton said. "William Seton, cashier at the Bank of New York, and I are in daily correspondence by express rider. Seton is refusing to accept deposits from speculators which are tendered in bank notes, with my blessing, I might add. Many of those notes, he says, are drawn on the Bank of the United States—which conjures up a host of fears." As Treasury Secretary, Hamilton had been heading off get-rich-quick schemes one after another ever since the Assumption bill had passed.

"The nation's bank in the hands of speculators; what a desperate notion. Do you think they will actually attempt it?" Bradford leaned forward in his seat.

"Apparently, their plan is already in motion. I have approved Seton's course of action which is to pay out only in specie from our ports. Seton knows the Treasury will stand behind all legitimate banks against the attacks of speculators."

"Speculation is a necessary evil," Rawle observed, reaching for his glass, "but disrupting the market in order that a few might benefit to the ruin of the many…that must be opposed by the government at every turn."

"I intend to. There must be rules of conduct and serious consequences for those who abuse the laws to feather their own nests, even in our new Utopia."

Chapter Three
Yellow Fever

Hands busy—this time, embroidering a new pocket—
Betsy overheard a conversation concerning some difficulty
about a man her husband had employed at the Treasury.
One Mr. Reynolds, who'd been using information illegally
obtained there, had been attempting to swindle war
veterans out of their pensions. Betsy couldn't understand
why her husband, usually so astute when it came to his
clerks, had employed the fellow. Hamilton had turned
white when the subject was brought up in her presence by
Oliver Wolcott. It seemed Mr. Jefferson and his friends
intended to make an issue of it, and to pretend that
Hamilton himself was the actual architect of the felonious
scheme. Of course, her husband was mortified by his
apparent failure of judgement in hiring the man and
alarmed, too, by the suspicions that would fall on him. It
would make his work with Congress even more difficult.

* * *

Just after Christmas, there was an inexplicable afternoon
visit by three congressmen. Enemies, all of them, and
accompanying the group came Hamilton's good friend and
assistant, the Controller Oliver Wolcott, with an anxious
furrow creasing his brow.

Encountering the group as they emerged from a long,
low voiced discussion in the good parlor, Betsy saw her
husband white-lipped and silent. Abraham Bendable,
Frederick Muhlenburg and Senator James Monroe—all
antagonists—paused long enough to bow when they
happened upon her in the corridor.

The first two men seemed disconcerted, discomfited.
But foxy-face Mr. Monroe had given her such a penetrating
look that she had lowered her eyes as she curtsied in return,
keeping Johnny hugged tightly to her breast. As the

gentlemen departed, stepping carefully over the toys scattered up and down the hallway, Mr. Vendable's eyes fairly spilled reproof. Hamilton looked so wretched that Betsy didn't think she'd dare to ask him what this *tete-a-tete* was about. When she heard their servant ushering the gentlemen to the door, she knelt and began belatedly collecting blocks, soldiers and wooden horses.

"Just the Anti-Federalists trying to tear my heart out, nothing unusual. Nothing I can't deal with."

Even as he made the explanation, one for which she hadn't asked, his cheeks flamed.

He lies—!

Without meeting her eyes, he retreated to his study, where, after closing the door, he'd talked in hushed tones for another hour with Wolcott. Even after this personal friend had taken his leave, Alexander didn't emerge from behind that closed parlor door for a very long time.

Betsy found her own retreat, the kitchen, where supper was being prepared and the table laid. Sitting down, she rested her head in her hand. Una, knowing better than to speak to her mistress when she looked this upset, continued working without comment.

Betsy swore to herself that this year, no matter how bad it was, no matter how much Papa begged, and no matter what Hamilton said, *no matter what, I shall not leave him.*

* * *

The latest foreign crisis revolved around Citizen Genet, the French Ambassador. The man seemed bent on involving the United States in the war the government of France was apparently intent upon starting with every other nation in the world. Their own popular revolution had devolved into a killing spree and the streets of Paris ran with the blood of innocent and guilty alike. Not only in faraway France, but in America, too, the violence of "Jacobinism" shrieked from the newspapers.

Sailors in Philadelphia, on shore leave from the French fleet, were implicated in a series of robberies and rapes, which pretty quickly turned the mood of the more law-

333

abiding populace. Tension ran high when it became known that the French were using American ports, most notably the temporary capitol, to outfit British ships captured in offshore battles to be used in privateering. Such acts endangered American neutrality, which was the only possible course for a weak new country during a continental war between superpowers.

Washington understood. In spite of the passionate arguments by Jefferson in favor of supporting their old friends, the French, the president issued a proclamation of neutrality. This, in its turn, set off another round of attacks upon the administration in the newspapers as well as verbal fireworks in Congress. Rocks were thrown in the streets, while the rabble tramped about, ominously calling each other "Citizen." Crowds gathered to drink, cheer and light bonfires when they heard that the King of France—who'd helped America win its own revolution—had been beheaded.

The most rebellious, encouraged by Mr. Freneau, the editor of Jefferson's newspaper, started calling President Washington "King George." They even went so far as to publish a cartoon in which he was shown kneeling, waiting his turn at the guillotine. One wild night the grand old man bravely walked out onto his stoop and faced down a mob that had come roaring up the street waving torches and shouting anti-government slogans, apparently ready to do some kind of mischief at his house.

* * *

The Secretary of the Treasury and his friends sat around the dining room table with brandy. Hamilton cautiously sipped. The others outright gulped as they discussed the dangerous mood of the Philadelphia mob. They talked about "the cloven hoof of Jacobinism" and finally agreed that "Jefferson and his friends should take a lesson from our old friend Lafayette," now rotting in a dungeon, that "it is easier to get the genie out of the bottle than to put him back in."

Stories circulated about atrocities, not only in Paris but in the other large cities in France. The children of an entire village, it was said, had been locked into ovens and then roasted in the name of The Glorious Revolution.

Hamilton plunged into the fray, writing pieces for the Federalist newspapers that were signed, "No Jacobin," supporting the Proclamation of Neutrality and attacking Marat and Robespierre as "assassins still reeking with the blood of their fellow citizens."

Summer in Philadelphia was yet another misery. There was plenty of rain, but the heat never retreated. The city steamed and stifled whenever the breeze died. Soon a contagion arose from the riverside, the dreaded yellow fever. People first died of it in Water Street and then it spread to more affluent neighborhoods. Death came after a few days, while the victim suffered blinding headaches, back pain and endless vomiting.

To stem the contagion, people gun-powdered their houses, scrubbed the walls and white-washed them, the same treatment that was used for a bug-infestation. Some drank vinegar, some washed in it. Others chewed garlic, hoping to keep the sickness away. Men and women too pursued daily tasks while holding cigars in their teeth, because tobacco was also said to be a preventative.

For a time the government remained, doing business and keeping up a spate of brave talk, but the disease spread relentlessly and the numbers of dead among the poor mounted. The rich left in an unseemly haste for their country estates. General Schuyler wrote to Betsy, begging her to come north, to bring the children with her. Hamilton agreed that she should, but Betsy refused.

Then the day came when her husband left the building next door—the Secretary of the Treasury's office—and went straight to his bed. His head ached. He was flushed with fever.

"Damn it! I have it. I remember the touch of Yellow Jack only too well."

Still, the next day, Hamilton decided that he was well enough to go to work. There was an important cabinet meeting scheduled.

"There's just too much to do," he said. "If it's merely some nasty summer indisposition, I don't want to humor it. Besides, if I don't get to that meeting, Jefferson will twist His Excellency's head backward on some crucial matter. A good soldier doesn't run home in the middle of a battle."

Holding a vinegar-doused handkerchief to his face, Hamilton left for his meeting. Early in the afternoon, though, he returned. Unusually, a hack carriage brought him to the door and then tore away down the street as soon as his passenger was deposited.

"Oh, my dear Hamilton!" Betsy met him, stumbling in, leaning against the wall to aid his passage. Even in the dim hallway, curtains closed against the heat, she noted the bloodshot whites of his eyes.

He refused her arm, took hold of the back of a chair to support himself.

"Don't touch me, Betsy. Keep the children away. Send for Doctor Stevens at once."

Betsy sent Davie running to the home of their new doctor, Alexander's boyhood friend, Ned Stevens. This gentleman had, fortuitously, recently left the famous medical school at the University of Glasgow and had come to Philadelphia to start a practice.

Next she wrote a note to President Washington, which explained that "Secretary Hamilton is ill with the prevailing fever," and sent their Davy off with that.

Upon meeting Doctor Stevens for the first time, and this only a few months past, Betsy had been surprised, for this slim stranger might have been Hamilton's brother. He had the same long head, the same pronounced furrow between the eyes. Stevens was taller and not as fair as her husband, but the general outline was much alike.

So many tales and rumors! Such coarse things whispered about my husband by men who hate him....

336

Betsy had sat, hands busy as always, today with a frock for herself, and covertly watched them together, these two childhood friends. They'd been long separated, but today it appeared they were, albeit somewhat formally, feeling their way toward a renewed acquaintance. Only briefly did she hear them abandon this mutual caution and reminisce about their shared boyhood. Her husband had remained ever curious about the latest medical notions and ideas, so the conversation easily moved to that.

Edward Stevens had said, after an apology for discussing a distasteful subject so candidly, that dissection of corpses had taught him far more about the workings and purposes of the human body than any other method of study. When Una arrived, peeking around the door with a question about supper, Betsy had only been too happy to quit the room.

Today, after Doctor Stevens arrived for his consultation, Betsy suddenly realized that she felt sick too, dizzy, joints aching, an ever-increasing sense of sheer exhaustion. By evening, everything had grown confused, blurry. Neighbors came and took the children. Later, there wasn't much she would remember of that week, except for some odd scenes, played out like an immodest dream.

At one time she and Hamilton, both dressed only in thin muslin gowns, were helped into a large laundry tub of water in which ice floated. Arms around one another, heads reeling, nauseated, they'd sat near fainting with pain. Betsy remembered shaking, watching saw-dust covered lumps of summer ice bump against her husband's knees.

Only when they were both ready to collapse, teeth chattering, would Stevens order his servants to help them out. Unlike Doctor Rush, the most prominent Philadelphia doctor, Stevens had given up the practices of bleeding or cupping to arrest a fever. Instead, he used the West Indies cure, with ice baths to bring down temperature, lots of bitter quinine water, wine, and a diet of whatever they could keep down.

After a week, both husband and wife began to feel better, well enough to collect the children from the

337

neighbor's houses and begin a retreat to Albany. All along the way they were harassed, denied lodging, and, in some places water, for the fear of contagion was universal. Hamilton was weak as a kitten, but was roused to eloquence on several occasions to talk people around, at least to give them water so that they could proceed. It was a terrible five days for all of them. Betsy was grateful that Johnny was still at the breast, although she could tell from his constant whining that illness had left her with little milk.

General and Mrs. Schuyler greeted them with open arms, but not so the City of Albany, which sent officers to confiscate and burn the Hamilton's clothes. When the General furiously sent them away, an order of quarantine was set upon his house. Alexander wrote a long letter to the council, assuring them that he and his wife had been pronounced cured by Doctor Stevens before they'd left Philadelphia and that they had brought no clothing that hadn't been washed.

As soon as Hamilton recovered from the illness and the exhausting journey, he was in a frenzy of anxiety about the government, for the Capital had simply been abandoned. The President remained at Mount Vernon. Jefferson, after much dinner table sneering at Hamilton's "hypochondria" and "timidity," had not stopped running until he and his retinue of servants and slaves had reached Monticello.

It was early in November, with news that the plague had subsided, when Hamilton, Betsy and the servants drove back to Philadelphia. Papa Schuyler persuaded them to leave the children behind, in case there was any chance of the infection returning.

By December, the fever had disappeared, as mysteriously as it had come. Hamilton corresponded constantly with Betsy's father, trying to coax him to send the children home. The doting grandfather had taken it into his head to keep them until spring. Angelica, whose nervousness was so worrying, was reported to be "perfectly happy." Johnny, they learned, had begun to walk,

338

navigating the long central corridor of the house with ease. Johnny was also, as the General put it with grandfatherly pride, "striving to articulate."

Chapter Four
Nation and Family

Betsy leaned on the window and watched the snow. It was rushing down now, but she knew it would be over before it had covered the ground. It was March, but already, here in Philadelphia, winter was nearly over. The idea was somehow discomforting. Albany winters were gloomy and long, with so much cold, dark and ice, but here in the south she was always left with a curious sorrow for the lack of it.

The January their oldest, Philip, had been born; Hamilton had been tottering around, weak as a kitten after his pneumonia, while she had been suffering the assorted miseries of childbirth. There had been two days of blinding, howling white, the Seneca's "white panther" stalking the land. Through the tall windows of her father's house had come a frigid dawn of staggering beauty, cobalt-blue and rose. The northern trees had been sheathed in robes of silver, limbs like wrists sparkling with diamonds when the first rays struck them.

What did it matter that you could see your breath in the room, or that the wash water had frozen in the basin? She had come through her first childbirth well and with a healthy son. Her husband had fought in and survived the glorious last major battle of the war.

Here in Philadelphia, it was always too warm, too bright. Winter was like autumn. Spring brought great heat, but in the depths of summer, the relief of a thunder storm couldn't be relied upon to come and cleanse the sultry, dead air. Those Philadelphia Julys and Augusts were crushing, steaming and unrelenting, far worse than those she'd endured in New York City.

She watched while her husband worked day and night, but all anyone ever seemed to do was to criticize him and

340

make him into the scapegoat for everything that went wrong. The new government—the country—meant so much to him, and all he ever seemed to get in return was abuse. She thought, listening to him pace for hours in his study, whispering those drafts of documents aloud, that he would soon go quite mad. Betsy tried not to dwell on it, but she'd begun to truly hate Philadelphia and everything about it.

Tonight they were giving a party—a political party, for whatever kind could there be? She had done it in New York, managed it with a larder stocked with what had come down the river from Albany. It was so much more difficult here without Papa's largess smuggled through the kitchen door.

The people were more difficult, too. Hamilton would float among them, glowing and gleaming, talking and talking, all his plans and projects, the gleaming future he saw for his adopted country transporting him through mountains of work and never-ending nights without rest. Friends and enemies alike would smile with him, would laugh with him, unable to help themselves when met by his charm. Even His Excellency would unbend, become frostily playful.

At these parties the president would unfailingly ask Betsy for the first dance. They would tread a minuet, formal and elegant as a pair of cranes, or, perhaps, a great gray crane and a little brown sparrow. Then other gentlemen would politely ask her and she would dance for a little. All the time she'd be waiting for the moment when she could escape to make a supervisory circuit through her kitchen and then sink into a corner where the discussions were housewifery: problems with servants and the maladies of children.

The women of style and fashion, the women who scintillated like her sister Angelica, continued to dance, to stand with the men, sipping wine, bantering and laughing. There was always one to whom her husband was especially attentive, one with whom he danced a time or two more than was exactly proper, one upon whose white arms his fingers lingered.

Betsy would try to ignore it, but finally she would meet someone's eyes, meet a look aimed straight at her. She'd see pity—or worse, a look of cruel curiosity, the "Does she know?" writ plain. Was it true, the thing they hinted at, or was it simply all malicious gossip—because her husband knew how to charm, because he was handsome and debonair?

There were other parties, too, the kind he attended alone, gatherings ostensibly male and political. Still, Betsy knew there would be a few women present, the sparkling kind, ladies whose reputations were supported by the wealth of their husbands. For their part, these very husbands were not averse to swapping domestic product for official preference. It was done this way in every capital of the world. Amour, sweetened with advantage. When he came home from such gatherings, it was often very late.

In the morning, he'd spend a long time in his room, washing fastidiously and dressing. Meanwhile, in the kitchen, Betsy would be busy cutting bread and pouring tea, or spooning out bowls of hot yellow cornmeal and milk, the ubiquitous sup'pawn for the younger children.

Alexander's blue eyes always shone at the sight of the children. He would cheerfully ruffle the head of whatever little one was closest, brush a kiss against Betsy's cheek.

"Good morning, Mrs. Hamilton." They'd greet each other gravely. As they sat drinking tea and eating bread, conserves and butter, she'd occasionally bring whatever household details, those very few, she thought appropriate to his attention. Then there would be talk with the children about school and what was being studied. Alex would enumerate a long list of complaints against James. Pudgy James would offer an ingenuous rebuttal.

"Clearly, both of you fellows are going to law." Hamilton sighed. "How many times do I have to tell you that brothers should stick together and not quarrel?" Once they were settled and quietly eating their breakfast, Angel

342

would come and wind herself around his neck. He'd put back her hair and give her a kiss, brighten at her femaleness. If she was sad, brooding on a bad dream or frightening story, he'd cheer her by talking about her brother Phil, a subject which brought equal joy to them both. They'd practice a little French together. Sometimes, in the evenings when he was at home, he'd sit beside her while she worked at her music. He'd exhort her to be busy and cheerful. With a glance towards Betsy, he'd ask Angelica to help her Mama, "who has so much to do."

The children adored their father and so whatever time he spent with them had a wonderful effect. For a few hours there would be peace between Alex and James; Angelica would play her lovely music and not alarm Betsy with her moods and dark notions. Papa's magic presence, regularly, if sparingly bestowed, could charm them all.

It worked with Betsy, too. On the nights when he would come home, the nights when he wasn't too late, too exhausted from wrestling with politics and finance, Hamilton would come smiling into her room, take the brush from her hand, then draw her up from the seat before the mirror and begin to, very tenderly, kiss her.

In no time, without words, she would believe that he still loved her as a husband should, that whatever he'd done, she should understand and pardon. She'd heard other wives say that they denied their husbands, but Betsy never denied her husband anything. It simply wasn't possible. But afterwards, instead of falling asleep, as an ordinary man might, he'd rise and walk to his study. Late into the night she'd hear his pen scratching, letters, for the newspapers, and correspondence to the friends and allies he had in every bustling port and big city.

Lying alone, she'd wonder if he ever really saw the ordinary world. He was so often abstracted, thinking, planning, studying, his restless mind focused on statecraft, on law, on finance.

So hard for the rest of us to understand, my Hamilton.

Letter from Philip Schuyler to his daughter:

My beloved Eliza: The following anecdote which I learned from Judge Benson may amuse. A gentleman travelling from NY to this place stopped at Kinderhook and made several turns in the street passing to and fro before the store of a Mr. Rodgers. Apparently in deep contemplation and his lips moving as rapidly as if he was in conversation with some person-he entered the store, tendered a fifty-dollar bill to be exchanged. Rodgers refused to change it, the gentleman retired. A person in the store asked Rodgers if the bill was counterfeited. He replied in the negative. Why then did you not oblige the Gentleman by exchanging it? Because said Rodgers the poor Gentleman has lost his reason; but said the other, he appeared perfectly natural. That may be said Rodgers, he probably has his lucid intervals, but I have seen him walk before my door for half an hour, sometimes stopping, but always talking to himself, and if I had changed the money and he had lost it I might have received the blame. Pray ask Hamilton if he can't guess who the gentleman was. My Love to him, in which you participate. Adieu my Beloved Child.

* * *

Johnny was feverish and cranky, refusing everything except milk pudding and only a few bites of that. The heat came on, as bad as last year. She could look out over the yard at night and see lightning flashing in the north, but the rain never seemed to come. Heat bloated, infusing everything she touched.

How I long for the storms of Albany, for the black clouds to bring torrents of rushing, cold rain to wash the dirt and heat away!

After luncheon she and Johnny would lie down together, sweat, toss and doze. She would need all her strength for his night-time crying spells, for Angelica's nightmares, and

344

for whatever other interruptions the darkness brought. Her husband, even, might come home and take whatever children were with her up and put them in their truckle bed before climbing in to embrace her.

Bright beautiful Alexander wanted her! As soon as he kissed her in the way that signaled it, trembling, she'd lift her nightgown like some wanton. She prayed no children would wake up, that she could go, go, get the release she so badly needed, respond as her man's pride required. Since the business with that other woman, she knew she must fight fire with fire, at least as well as she knew how.

What if he fell in love with someone else again?

In this dirty world of politics he insisted upon inhabiting, the other side could use that sin to ruin him.

* * *

Finally, the days began to run together in a blur of baby care, of nausea, of sleeping like the dead, of waking to Johnny's querulous cries, of feeling his sweaty little body stuck to hers as she rocked and sang, rocked and sang. He was losing weight, subsisting on air, not on the custards and sago puddings that Una cooked especially for him.

In the middle of this downward spiral, Alexander suddenly pulled back from his work and noticed.

"In three days I'm taking us to the country, out towards Trenton. It will do us all good. Darling Johnny, and you, too, my angel."

His fingers traced the damp side of her face. Betsy was in bed, head on the pillow, dark hair tangled. Johnny was, for the moment, asleep beside her.

"I'll write to Washington. Damn it, he can do without me for a week or two. If the roses don't come back to both your cheeks, I'm packing you off to your papa's." Thoughtfully, he stroked the toddler's curls.

"No! Absolutely not! I won't leave you."

So many things she couldn't, wouldn't, say....

Hamilton studied her for a long moment and then kissed her, very softly.

"Mrs. Hamilton, I'm far too busy to misbehave."

When Betsy was silent, contemplating the warm touch of his lips, he repeated, "We'll go out to the country and see if Johnny improves. The heat this summer is enough to kill a strong man, much less a child."

"But what about the others?" Her hand moved to touch his sleeve. "Fanny is on an even keel, but Angelica has been having nervous spells again. Why, before you got home the other night she woke up screaming that Philip had died. It was over three hours before I could get her back to sleep."

"You know, Mrs. Morris has often said that she would be pleased to have Angelica and Fanny any time. They have a genteel Santo Domingo maid who can pet the girls and speak French to them. Phil and Alex can stay at school with Doctor Frazer in Trenton. Jamie and Johnny can go with you."

Betsy's eyes filled. It all seemed so pat. Was he taking her out of the way of something? Something that had already begun, something that she, isolated in the house with her pregnancy, her sick baby, wouldn't suspect?

Then she thought, nevertheless, for a few days anyway, she'd have him to herself, away from politics, away from his work, away from whom or whatever! There would be only two children, a manageable number, and her dearest husband.

* * *

Hamilton was frantically busy until they left, trying to get everything in order. Washington, in his icy way, gave him leave to go, but insisted on several long written opinions about "the Kentucky business" before their departure. At last they left Philadelphia, children safely stowed here and there. Mrs. Morris told Betsy not to worry about Angelica, but to "try to keep that husband away from work for as long as possible."

346

And then they were off, driving towards New York. Jamie was full of high spirits and chat inside the rocking coach. His father held him and laughed at his son's gab.

How I wish that Hamilton could be like this more often!

As for Johnny, he rested quietly in her arms. The long carriage ride, the rocking and the fresh air, sent him into a sound sleep. She looked down at the sleep-twitches of his violet eyelids.

That night, though, Johnny seemed sicker than ever, his lips almost gray. Alexander took his pulse, felt his head and then offered him drops mixed with water.

"Ugh! No, Papa! No!" Johnny protested and made a face, but in the end he accepted it. He had learned to vomit things he didn't like, but from his father's hand the bitter draught stayed down.

When sleep came to both boys, Betsy and Alexander undressed to their shirts and sat on the edge of the bed together, watching their small dreamers curled together like baby mice.

"I'm so tired." Betsy leaned against her husband's shoulder.

"I know." Tenderly, he stroked her back. "I know."

It had been a long drive in the heat. Betsy's face felt singed from the hot wind that had blown into the carriage all day.

"I think you should go on to Albany."

She stretched out beside the children, sighing.

"I'm just so tired, Hamilton. There's another baby coming."

"I thought so."

Lying behind her, he rested a hand on her hip. Then, although she was exhausted, it was impossible to fall asleep right away. It was bliss to have him with her, to have his breath against her hair, to know that for a few brief days he'd be hers and hers alone.

* * *

In New York they stayed with Bob Troup and his wife and family, who were delighted to entertain them. He and Alexander, now both grave men of state, grew giddy and boyish together.

They made arrangements for Betsy to go up river on one of her papa's sloops with the little ones. Alexander sailed up river with them for one day and then disembarked at Fishkill. From there, he would return to Philadelphia.

"Promise me." She took his hand. "Promise me...."

"Promise what?" *Oh, how those blue eyes flashed!* People were on every side, farmers, sailors, travelers rich and poor alike. Johnny was in her arms. For a two year old there wasn't much to carry, a thing which frightened both parents. Betsy tried to hold back, but tears fell, first one hot splash and then another.

"No tears, my angel. I promise I'll behave myself; I never want to make you unhappy like that again—or to ever again break faith with you. Now, you must make me a promise too. Promise you'll get your roses back." His long fingers collected the tears.

"Yes. I'll certainly try."

"I will be miserable without you, Eliza, and without my little ones. God bless you and our sweet angels."

He kissed Johnny's damp forehead. Jamie had been swinging on the new little nursemaid's arm, but Alexander caught him and lifted him up high before setting him on his feet again.

"Now, Jamie Hamilton, listen! Your brother and your Mama are sick. You must help by being good. No arguing, no complaining, and you are to obey Miss Charity," he indicated the solemn nursemaid, "just as you would Miss Gussie. No, that's not right. Far, far better than you mind Miss Gussie! Your word of honor, James."

"I'll be good, Papa." James locked his arms around his father's leg and clung like a monkey.

Just like me, thought Betsy, *once you've got his attention, you're in no hurry to let go.*

348

"Papa?" Jamie asked, "Will Angelica be all right without Mama?"

"Yes." Hamilton clearly was a little surprised by an expression of concern from James, the most self-interested of his children. "I'm sure she and Fanny will be perfectly happy with Mrs. Morris, who declared herself entirely ready to spoil them."

When Jamie didn't look convinced, his father said, "If there are any problems, Philip can come home from Trenton."

Jamie nodded his auburn head. Everyone knew that for Angelica, Philip's presence made the whole world right. James kissed his father twice.

"The first is kiss is for you, Papa," he said, "and the second is for Angelica."

* * *

Above the joining of Fishkill and Hudson, the Catskills appeared. Betsy's spirits lifted at the sight. Bearing the sloop on its back, the Hudson poured green water against the bow. Farms, orchards, forests, all were lush and green, high summer all around. Along the shores, people bathed and boated. In the early morning, deer drank. Betsy saw it all as she walked back and forth, carrying Johnny, querulous and delicate, in her arms.

It was cooler now. Betsy felt better at once in spite of the strain of traveling with a sick child. The nursemaid had all she could do to keep track of Jamie, who raced up and down the deck, in constant danger of falling overboard. The wind blew from the north, so they tacked back and forth, slowly making their way upriver.

Cool at last and fresh, cold mornings! The cabin was close, but once on deck, it was another world. The shimmering, stinking streets of Philadelphia were only a dreary memory.

At the first sight of the red brick house up the bank, of green lawn and orchards spilling toward the water, Betsy felt her heart leap, in spite of the ache of missing Alexander.

As they tied up at the quay, she saw dark towers crowding ominously in the west. Maybe there would be a storm this evening, a big one.

It is a paradox to be so domesticated and yet crave sky fire as I do!

Mrs. Schuyler was there, shaded by a parasol held by a servant and leaning on a cane. She was relieved that they had arrived before the threatening weather. Cornelia, seventeen now, and the last of her siblings, Kitty, now twelve, was there, too, the latter bouncing like a puppy. In a minute Kitty had Jamie's hand and the two of them went romping off together.

"Such energy!" Mama sighed as Betsy embraced her. "After three days up that river, all I'd want to do is wash and go to sleep."

Johnny's gray eyes goggled when they entered the spacious interior of The Pastures. When he began to fuss, one of the house slaves was dispatched to show them to the room they would all share.

"It's time for his medicine."

"Well, dear, I'll come with you, but you must help me up these stairs. I'll stay up once I'm there. These days one trip up and down is plenty. And don't worry about Jamie," her mother said. "Maggie is in the kitchen and she'll keep an eye on him. All you'll have to do is nurse Johnny."

Slowly, mother and daughter made their way from the parlor to the narrow staircase.

So many memories! Betsy's hand slid over the gash in the banister where the tomahawk had struck. It had been painted over, but never filled in.

Happier memories came, too: merry games of chase, romping and laughing with a bevy of cousins. The winter day when she'd come down with such hesitant dignity to greet Alexander. There he'd stood in his blue and buff, a golden beard glinting on his thin cheeks after all those days on the road.

When he had ridden to her all those years ago, she had uncovered a fear of giving her heart to him. And it had proved real, that fear. The dark shadow that followed her Hamilton, that lay behind the brilliance of his mind, was a real presence. Only a few days gone by and how she missed him, ached for him!

It's a bad old joke. I can't live with him and I can't live without him.

So much time gone! Now here she was home again, pregnant for the sixth time, her husband still obsessed by his desire to wear fame's laurels. Time had changed the whole world, had changed everything except Hamilton's Herculean striving.

And, oh, look at Mama!

Once she had been Albany's "Morning Star," now transfigured by *Inexorable Time* to a fat, aging Dutch housewife. Nearly wide as she was high, her mother was barely able to climb her own staircase.

Betsy sighed as she followed. So much in her world hung from by merest thread, that about as substantial as spider web.

Would Johnny live? Would her husband be faithful? Would Angelica be all right without her?

Life only grew harder as one grew older. As much as she missed Phil and Alex, it was a blessing, just at this moment, that they were in school.

"We'll have Dr. Stringer in for Johnny tomorrow. I suppose Mr. Hamilton's given full instructions, though," said Mama. "Maybe, after how well he and his friend Doctor Stevens did with the yellow fever last year, we'd be better off heeding him than our doctors."

As Betsy had hoped, there was a storm that night, a satisfying, world-rocking one. Betsy, with Johnny making a hot small bundle against her breast, sat close by an upstairs window and watched. In flashes of light, she could see her roommates. The nursemaid huddled on a corn-stalk mattress, asleep like the dead. In the big bed were the shapes of her sister Kitty, and of Jamie, too, all unconscious despite the rolling thunder.

351

* * *

The next day awoke gray and chilly, one of those surprises to which the north is prone. Johnny seemed a little more animated, but his color was bad. Easily frustrated, he cried often. Betsy and the nurse carried him; Kitty and every woman servant in the place held him. They took turns singing and rocking.

What a relief it was to be cool at last and to have so much help!

Still, Betsy worried. Her baby was feverish and hot, weeping and achy.

She and Doctor Stringer consulted, settling on doses of lime water and bark tincture for the daytime and feverfew tea with a tiny drop of laudanum at night. Papa ordered up a carriage and daily she would wrap Johnny in blankets and drive out with him.

Jamie went running everywhere, ate constantly, played at the edge of the river, fell in, and romped in the sun until his pale face turned pink. He gave Betsy a kiss good morning and a kiss good night, and for the rest of day stayed as far away from her and Johnny as possible. He went about his own business, cheerful, full of jokes and utterly intent upon his own good time. While Betsy thought that again Jamie showed an unpleasant lack of sympathy, at least he'd wasn't demanding her attention.

In the night she sat and rocked querulous Johnny, fed him sips of feverfew tea and wiping his hot forehead with vinegar and water. All her attention ought to have been on the child in her arms, but her husband's image would sometimes interpose itself.

Was his beloved body wrestling love with someone else in the steamy heat of Philadelphia?

By day she drove out with Johnny to "exercise" him. Peggy visited with her boy Stephan, and the little boys played while the sisters caught up on Albany news. Occasionally, Jamie, sun-burnt and cheerful, remembering that he needed her, would come crawling into her lap for a hug or a kiss, his mouth smeared with black raspberries or sticky-fingered, a honey cake in hand.

* * *

It had been warm for the past few days, an unpleasant echo of the city from which she'd fled, but today those welcome cloud castles were once more prowling the horizon. Under the shade of an elder apple, red cows ruminated, flopping their tails against the flies. Betsy walked quickly, but as she passed beneath the original decrepit denizens of the orchard, with their thick trunks, a childhood memory intruded.

Pausing to look up, she knew she'd passed beneath the same tree she'd climbed into all those long years ago, when she and her sisters had played at being frightened. It had lost limbs, but still stood, looking much as she remembered. She thought of the terror she'd felt imagining more Indians lurking in the woods behind the potato patch, scalping knives sharp.

Gone forever!

No more would brown half-brothers arrive from the forest to collect manhood presents. At Albany there were hardly any Indians anymore, the great tribes shriveled to almost nothing by war, by white man's farming and diseases. Their cruelty and their kindness, their knowledge, their mystery—all vanished from the land along with their totem brothers—the beaver, the bear and the wolf.

A gust of wind whipped at her shirt. Aroused by the sight of black clouds west, Betsy lifted her arms to the sky. The sleeves fell back and there was her own brown skin, the green veins, and below that, the pulse and whisper of the new life in her belly.

Is this love of place, the compulsion that always drives me home, come from an unknown ancestress, a woodland woman whose child some Dutch ancestor brought home?

Or is just that I was born and bred here and the food which made me grow came from this earth, the essence sucked through the roots of native grain fields and fruit trees? This land, by broad, green river—I too have been nurtured here, same as any Mohawk.

* * *

A letter came to Betsy from Philadelphia, one not from Hamilton. She took one look at it, at the unfamiliar, sprawling awkward hand on the cover and then, leaving Johnny with the nurse, took the letter and went rapidly down stairs. Without as much as a glance at anyone, ignoring the cook and her helpers as if they were invisible, she passed through the house and then into the kitchen wing. From there, she walked outside and then up the hill, into the orchard. As soon as she knew no one could see her, Betsy lifted her arms to the sky. Her sleeves fell back and there was her own brown skin and green veins. Lower down, she felt the pulse and whisper of the new life in her body.

When she arrived at the split rails that kept the cows in, she gathered her skirts to ease her passage. The motion wasn't executed as gracefully as when she'd been a girl. At last, she reached a small cluster of young beech.

Branches moved, the tops tossed by restless wind. Clouds spilling over the hill behind were livid, gray and green. Betsy noted a distant rumble with rising excitement. *Thunder!*

Completely hidden now, she took the letter from her pocket. After reading it again, she methodically tore it into tiny pieces. Soon, she'd go back to Hamilton, to the ever growing, dirty city, trailing his red-headed children, but right now she was safe in her home place, standing alone between sky and earth.

At the first flash and strike, she let the pieces go, let them fly with the dead leaves that swirled up into the air. A bolt of white blazed down, momentarily blinding her. Rain came roaring, but Betsy didn't move. Instead she stood, arms raised like a madwoman. Water streamed down her cheeks.

"He's mine! He solemnly promised; you're a liar!" Betsy shouted into the treetops. As if in agreement, the Thunderbird shrieked before sending claws of fire through the western sky.

* * *

These days Papa was almost always ill. When the gout wasn't troubling him, the gravel was. Mama, too, was far from well. Just to ascend the stairs after supper was in the nature of a pilgrimage for both of them.

After changing from her wet clothes and coming downstairs, she met Prince emerging from the study wing.

The tray in old slave's hand shook as if it had a life of its own. Since the last time Betsy had visited, Mr. Prince had suffered a seizure. Now his hands trembled all the time. His master had offered him retirement, but Prince said that would kill him "quicker den poison."

"You got dose wet clothes off, Mizz Hamlt'n?" Prince peered from beneath white brows as she approached. "Mr. General was fit to be tied when he heard you was in dat rain."

"Yes, but I'm dry now, Prince."

"Well, that's good, Mrs. Hamilton, but you're not a chile anymore. Even chickens got 'nough sense to come out o' de rain."

"You are right. I shouldn't have gone so far from the house when I could plainly see there was a storm coming." She understood the well-meaning behind his scolding.

Both Prince and Mama's trusted Judik had always enjoyed a great deal of freedom of speech when it came to straightening out children on the place—white or black— who seemed to need it.

"Well, the General's been askin' for you. I just put a fresh pot o' tea and a good fire in the study. I've got this cup for you, so you can get warm and keep the General comp'ny."

Betsy thanked him and then went to tap at the study door. Rain jangled overhead as she put her head in.

"Ah, there you are, Mrs. Hamilton." Her father's cloudy eyes must have been fixed on the door.

"Prince said you were expecting me, Papa."

"Yes, my dear."

Her father had been at his desk, working a long mathematical calculation. The sketches that accompanied this were the General's newest hobby-horse, plans for a canal system that would join the Hudson River to Lake Erie. On a long ago visit to England he'd seen canals all over, and had been impressed by the amount of freight and grain that could be transported in that way.

"What's this wandering around in a rain storm? Prince says you came in soaked to the skin."

"Oh, Papa, you know I love a good rain." As she spoke, she handed him his cane and helped him navigate to the big wing chair by the fire.

"Damn!" He groaned as he settled in. "Pardon me, Bess. I've had some of Doctor Stringer's tincture, but nothing these days is quite enough to slap down the misery."

He nodded, slumped forward in the chair, attention seemingly drawn to the flickering fire. Betsy moved a low table close, carried the teapot and cups to it and drew up a stool for herself, all the time enjoying warmth. She waited patiently for her father to collect himself, to pitch his thoughts over the pain and the oncoming tide of opium.

"It's not prudent, child, either to allow oneself to be soaked, nor to tempt the thunderbolts, especially now that you're carrying again."

Betsy shifted uncomfortably. She hadn't spoken of it, but her mother, with maternal perception, had somehow divined it and informed the rest of the family.

"Mr. Prince has already given me a scolding, Papa. He said that even chickens have enough sense to get out of the rain."

Her father nodded. "He's right, you know. He's always been a man of high common sense, our Prince."

356

Betsy smiled and began to pour tea.

"I'm fine, Papa, really. The lightning and I have a peace treaty. And a little rain won't give me a cold."

"Now, love, be honest. When you were a girl that business of standing in the rain meant you were upset. Didn't you once tell Mama that you were letting it wash away your trouble?"

"Do you want sugar, Papa?"

"You know I do. And milk." His black eyes met hers, suddenly focused and shrewd. "It's Mr. Hamilton that's troubling you, isn't it?"

Betsy sipped her tea and tried to order her thoughts. This conversation was inevitable.

"Well, you can tell me. I may be an old fellow, long out of the fray, but maybe I can shed some light upon the vagaries of mankind." He appeared to know what the trouble was, so Betsy spoke plainly.

"There are other women, Papa. It's been going on for years, even while we were first in New York. It never lasts long, but something happened the last summer I visited that was different. I think he still sees her sometimes. A dreadfully common creature, I believe."

It was the General's turn to sigh.

"That he has admirers among your sex is nothing new, Eliza."

"Admirers? Papa, Alexander stood in the parlor of this house and promised Dominie Westerlo that he'd be faithful to me just as I promised to obey him. I keep my part of the bargain. I'm a good wife." Fiercely, Betsy held her father's eyes. "In *every* way."

"No one doubts it, Eliza. Everyone knows you have as much merit as his housekeeper and treasurer as he has as Treasurer of the United States. More than that, everyone believes that your union continues as it began, one of enamored love." The old-fashioned phrase imperfectly covered his rising discomfort. "As for the rest, well…" He waved a gnarled hand dismissively. "Flirtation and even an occasional—intrigue—is necessary to certain masculine temperaments."

357

"You know I haven't a jealous nature. I think I understand Hamilton very well, but I'm not enough for him and I never have been. And that hurts me, Papa, hurts me very much."

"How do you know this, Eliza? Has he told you?"

"No, of course not. He doesn't want to injure me. Besides, these—*amours*—are the one thing in life he's a coward about."

"May I suggest, Eliza, you might be only supposing?"

"Yesterday I had a letter, Papa."

"Letter? Oh. The unsigned sort, I'd imagine."

"Yes."

"Eliza, you should never read such things. The fire is the proper place for the words of someone who makes accusations and doesn't admit to a name. I would like to suggest that a woman who has been rejected is the one most likely to write such letters."

"Oh, Papa! Stop defending him." Betsy leapt to her feet and began to pace back and forth in front of the fire. "I should have known you would. You adore Hamilton. You always have. Everything he does—or has ever done—is no less than perfection in your eyes. And you men always stick together. It's so horrible, the way every one of you pretends infidelity is your natural right."

"I do not approve of infidelity, Eliza. But, even with the best will in the world, men do have lapses, especially in a wife's absence or illness. And a man of such high intelligence is simply more restless than simpler ones. That, combined with Hamilton's physical energy and passionate temperament make it—not—unexpected."

"How far you have retreated, Papa, from defending his innocence to describing a prize stallion!"

Betsy sat down beside her father on the stool, put her head against his good knee and sobbed.

"Men are so horrible. Even you, Papa! My heart is broken and still you take his side."

Slowly, the general laid knotted fingers on his daughter's neck.

"Hamilton is as he is, my child, always brilliant and sometimes unkind. But, no matter what, Elizabeth Schuyler, remember who you are—one of the first ladies in America. Rely upon it. Hamilton's sense of honor will always return him to your side. If it's any comfort, dear child, I believe that you are always first in his heart."

Betsy sobbed, sobbed as if she'd never stop, and simply took what comfort her father's stroking brought. It was useless. No matter how much her father loved her—*well, men were men and women were women*—always and forever on opposite sides of that mysterious divide. The new life her husband had caused, begun in a firestorm of midnight kisses, fluttered.

* * *

"Now we're going to wrap this around your head, Johnny." Betsy spoke to the wondering gray eyes of her youngest.

"What are you going to do to him?" Jamie asked. He watched with cold-blooded interest while she swathed his brother's head in a towel.

The kitchen was full of onlookers. One of Mr. Hamilton's strange West Indian cures was about to be implemented. Johnny pulled at the towel and whined apprehensively. Pompey, Prince's oldest son, would perform the actual business.

"Now, pick him up, Pompey," Betsy said, "and we'll duck him headfirst in the water and draw him through. Then pull his head out and leave his body in, just as I explained."

"Yes, ma'am." Pompey was dubious. "I'm not gonna keep his head under water for long, Miss Betsy. He'll flat drown."

The tub of water had stood over night in the kitchen and was cold as it could be. Johnny began to flail like a mad man as he was held by the feet and lowered headfirst. Pompey did just as he'd been told and brought Johnny's

359

dripping, swaddled head up quickly. There were a series of muffled shrieks.

"Hold him in!"

Pompey grimaced. He didn't like being the one to terrify this sick child, but he did as she ordered. As soon as Betsy unwrapped Johnny's head, the kitchen rang with screams and sobs.

"Properly stimulated!" General Schuyler declared over the noise, shifting his attention from his purple-faced grandson to the instructional letter in hand. "That's done it, Mr. Pompey. Colonel Hamilton says we're to take him out, rub him hard and give him brandy and water."

The towels were ready and so was the medicinal mixture. Johnny was set on the kitchen table and dried. Though his skinny shoulders heaved with distress, he took his dose of brandy like a man from the hand of his grandfather.

* * *

Betsy kept up the practice of daily drives with Johnny. When he seemed better, she had herself rowed across the river to Peggy's waiting carriage and conveyed to Rensselaerwyck. The sisters hugged and kissed and visited around Johnny. Time was proving Peggy more like Mama than any of them. Her chestnut hair was still beautiful, but she had become very much the full-figured, serene Dutch house wife.

"Johnny certainly looks better," Peggy said as they settled themselves comfortably into seats inside the gazebo overlooking the river. She'd managed to persuade Betsy to let her maids carry off her small nephew so they could talk.

"Well, yes, I think so." As always, when Johnny wasn't clinging to her, Betsy experienced a wave of sleepiness. "It was terrible when I did as Hamilton asked and stopped the laudanum. Every day I made the tinctures weaker, but it got so he was hardly sleeping at all. He cried and complained of aches all the time. I swear I almost started it again. If I'd

360

been home, I'd have been up for five days straight rocking him. Thank heaven for Mama, Cornelia, Kitty, my Charity and all the housemaids! And Johnny hasn't been easy to hold, hot one moment, cold the next, and so terribly restless. I think it's passing, though, at last. He's eating again and he's falling asleep naturally again."

"He looks much better, I think. *You* need to take care of yourself now, take advantage of the help you have while you're here. In fact, I'm going to give you a lecture right now. You know you can't save him if it isn't God's will that he live." Tears filled Peggy's clear blue eyes. Except for her first born, she'd lost all her children.

"Well, dear, you know we were both raised to be good mothers."

"That's so, and by the very best mama that ever was. Still, darling, please think of yourself once in a while and rest. And Mama has told me you're expecting again."

"Yes," Betsy said. "And, heaven help me, it hasn't even been two years since Johnny." She wasn't, in truth, particularly happy about the coming "blessed event," but that was nothing to say to her less fortunate sister. Instead, she changed the subject.

"Every letter I get from my Hamilton is full of medical advice. He loves them all, but Johnny is the apple of his eye."

"As busy as he is, that man of yours does treasure his babies. And he keeps you almost as busy as Papa kept Mama. Just think of it, the three of us born in the first three years they were married."

"I can't imagine how she got through it. At least when Papa went to England she had a few years rest, although, of course, she was left all alone with the house to build, and all of us, as well as a frontier plantation to manage."

The conversation paused, as they pondered those adventurous old days and then Peggy asked, "When will you be going back to Philadelphia? Not until cool weather, I hope."

"Well, sadly, I'm going back soon."

361

"Why? Stephen writes he's quite certain that General Washington is going to send Hamilton with the army to quell the rebellion in western Pennsylvania. Wouldn't it be easier for you to stay here?"

"I need to get back to Angelica. She's so anxious all the time, and she's been bounced between Mrs. Morris' house and Mrs. Bradford's all summer. Hamilton's so busy—you know what a taskmaster our president is and of course those spiteful congressmen and their horrible newspapers never let up for a minute. My little girl probably wonders if her father even knows she exists. Right now, he probably doesn't."

There was another reason she'd go south, however.

If I don't, my husband will ride off to fight the rebels, and maybe get killed. I'll never see him again.

The tender kiss they'd shared in the cabin of the river sloop might be the last she'd ever taste. Betsy shook her head, trying to get rid of the notion, but knew that one of those unwashed, whiskey-breathing animals would like nothing more than to put a bullet through Hamilton's head.

* * *

Betsy was now inclined to believe that the laudanum had been the last part of Johnny's troubles. After some days without it, his appetite came back and he began to climb out of her arms, to sit on the floor and play. One afternoon she had gone to take a nap and left Johnny sleeping in the truckle bed.

She'd heard him rouse, but had rolled over and fallen back into a deep sleep when Kitty had come in and scooped him up. Later, after a satisfying nap, she learned that Johnny and Jamie had been taken by their grandfather down to the Hudson to fish.

Papa too must be having a good day!

She dressed, tied on a bonnet, picked up a parasol against the sun and then took the path down to the river. At the bottom, she came upon the pony and cart, the pony unhitched and quietly grazing. Her sons played happily in the sandy shallows, floating sticks, chasing fingerlings with an old china cup and soaking themselves. At first Betsy wanted to scold her father, for both children were wet and muddy, but then she didn't.

They all look so completely happy.

The old general sat in a chair his servants had brought down, taking in his line. Tall, black Pompey lifted a nice string of five good-sized fish out of the water.

"Look at this, Mrs. Betsy."

Her father smiled. "Your boys have been asking for a fish dinner. They were watching these coming out of the water with eyes so round you'd think we had pulled in old Leviathan himself. Ever since Pompey told him they were for supper, Johnny's been saying that he's going to eat a whole one."

"A whole fish! Pompey says I can't eat it, but I can!" Johnny, barefoot and damp, came running to her.

"We'll have to share," Jamie said. "There aren't enough for everyone and you can't eat a whole one, anyway. And what about Grandma? And Cornelia and Kitty? And what about Pompey? He should have one, for he has helped us fish all afternoon."

Pompey, like Prince, his father, was usually grave, but when Jamie championed him so emphatically, he allowed himself a smile.

"Why, of course, Jamie," said Grandpa Schuyler. "Mr. Pompey must certainly have a nice big fish."

"Well, there must be washing up before there is any supper." Betsy studied her sons' muddy arms and legs.

Not much later they were all in the pony cart, going back up to the house together. Betsy walked beside them, pleased to see that Johnny was so lively.

"Pompey, take those fish to Cook and have her fry one for Master Johnny right away. I don't want him to wait," said her father. "The mood may leave him. And tell her to choose one we can get the bones out of. Now that he's feeling so much better, it's no time to choke him."

He ruffled the child's auburn curls.

"And don't forget that one's for Pompey!" Betsy was pleased when Jamie said it again. She knew Pompey had been riding herd on her boy almost every day.

"Yes," Grandpa Schuyler agreed. "Mr. Pompey will have biggest one—that mean old croaking catfish, who fought so hard and near broke my line."

Pompey was pleased. White folks didn't much like catfish, which, to his mind, was well and good. That particular monster would make an enormous feast, and, after all that watching out for Jamie he'd done, he was definitely owed some special treatment.

That afternoon Johnny delighted them all simply by sitting on a cushion on a kitchen chair and eating bite after bite of fish. He followed supper with a dish of baked plum custard.

The whole family rejoiced. They would not lose their darling Johnny! Shortly thereafter, Dr. Stringer pronounced the child cured and Betsy knew she could go home to her husband with a clear conscience.

Chapter Five
The Whiskey Rebellion

She sailed down river to New York, where she stayed with their old friend, Colonel Nicholas Fish. The following day he escorted her and the boys to New Ark to the house of Elias Boudinot. There they remained until, a few days later, Alexander came to collect them.

Philip and Alex were in school in Trenton, so on the return journey they had stopped so Betsy could visit with them. How her heart yearned over those boys!

My Philip's big dark eyes! And how Alex has grown!

What a perfect gentleman her oldest was, kissing her hand and calling her *"ma chere mere"*! He was charming, probably very much like his father at that age. Then there was Alex, with his scarred face and a tinge of red in his hair. This had been his first term at the boarding school. At home, he was a whirlwind of discontent, often at odds with the others, but in the great world of bigger boys, of hard study and hard switching, he'd grown dignified fast. Nevertheless, she was delighted to find that once the closing of a door left them private, he was more than ready to hug her and kiss her cheek.

After collecting Angelica and Fanny from Mrs. Morris, they'd at last settled into the Philadelphia house again.

The rebellion in the western counties and down into Kentucky was on every tongue. It infuriated Alexander. Whenever he returned from a cabinet meeting he'd speak of the threat this lawlessness posed to the union. Any sort of popular uprising would certainly be noted with alarm by America's foreign creditors. They might even threaten the carefully arranged series of borrowing he'd just concluded with the Dutch.

To make more difficulty, Henry Knox had gone on private business to land in Maine. This meant Hamilton had to manage two departments, War and Treasury, with Jefferson and his pack of hounds forever at his heels in Congress and in the papers. Days passed when Betsy hardly saw her husband. In the morning he'd gulp tea and bread while not even seeing her and half the time muttering to himself as he always did when sunk in work.

Bad news came daily. In western Pennsylvania, there were attacks upon tax collectors and their families, followed by awful scenes of tarring and feathering. There were robberies, and the barns and homes of people who spoke up for the government were burnt in what seemed to be a wide spread breakdown of law and order.

The state government appeared paralyzed. Too many powerful factions in Pennsylvania sympathized with the rebels. President Washington, after giving the local authorities almost a year in which to sort it out for themselves, had at last determined that the army would have to be brought in to restore order. In the absence of Secretary of War Knox, the Secretary of the Treasury, whose whiskey tax was the subject of unrest, must be the one to ride at the head of it.

"If you make a policy, you should be the one who goes to enforce it, but I'd rather deal with the Iroquois any day, for they are men of their word," Hamilton said. "Some of those backwoodsmen's only claim to be called human is that they walk upright—and drink whiskey."

* * *

Back in Philadelphia, in another of those late September heat waves, Johnny began to decline again. He whined, his skin was hot, his appetite sank. Every afternoon, the fever returned. All day and half the night Betsy and Gussie and Angelica, too, rocked him until they were ready to drop.

Jamie had been quarreling over marbles with Fanny for what seemed like days; the new puppy had peed on the Turkey carpet again. Angelica was in one of her moods, crying and brooding over some tragic tale she'd read.

366

"Only Philip can make me feel better. Only Philip, and he can't come home from school."

One night when Betsy had finally got Johnny down, she went, wearing her nightgown and carrying a lamp, to check the rest of her lambs. They were all sleeping on the first floor tonight. It was simply too hot upstairs.

Jamie had stretched out with the puppy on one of his father's old cloaks in front of a window. Betsy wondered if he would catch a chill if a breeze sprang up later. The little dog looked up at her with eager, bright eyes, and thumped his tail. Betsy knew to her core that she didn't want to get him started again!

Now where is Angelica? Gussie said she'd put her to sleep here, but the mattress on the floor was empty. Betsy had an idea, though, and she made her way as quietly as the squeaks in the wide-board floor would allow toward her husband's study.

Sure enough, inside that room was a glow from a candle. An amber circle wavered around it, but the light did not encompass Angelica, who was tucked into the window seat, hugging her knees.

"Why aren't you in the parlor?" Betsy joined her daughter. "Gussie put you there, didn't she?" The child's narrow face was wet.

"She did, but I couldn't sleep 'cause Jamie snores. Besides it's too hot. I'm waiting for Papa."

Gussie had braided Angelica's flaming hair and pinned it up in order to keep her cooler, which gave a most mature look. The night outside was thick, palpitating with heat and cicada chant. Betsy gathered Angelica close, and stroked her daughter's damp cheek.

"My heart, why do you read sad stories when you know they will make you feel so bad?"

There was a pause and she felt a quiver in the thin little body.

"I can't tell if books will be sad when I start them. And, Mama, you *know* sad things are true. They happen. Good children swell up and die from horrid contagions. Innocent people get murdered—like poor, golden-haired Jeanie

367

McCrea that the cruel Indian scalped, or the poor settler girl who ran back into the fire so the wicked men couldn't be able to hurt her anymore."

Betsy hugged Angelica close, inwardly cursing whatever Albany servant had told her daughter those choice tales of frontier war. Betsy rocked the delicate body in the fine white chemise, praying that Angelica wouldn't wake Johnny.

"God took them to heaven, Angelica, just like Reverend Cuyler says. And, besides," she said, "we're far away from Indians here. Now hush, baby, hush! Mama is tired, so tired."

From earliest years Angelica had been so very anxious, the first of the children to ask the fraught question: "what happens after you are dead?" She'd always weep for hours after if they chanced on some roughneck beating a horse in the street.

Tonight, in response to her mother's soothing, she stopped crying, but the next topic she hit upon was even more disturbing.

"Why is Papa always so late? He creeps in here and sleeps on the day bed. I'm worried about all these things and he's not here to talk to."

"I know." Betsy hugged her daughter tight.

A thin wail arose from down the hall.

Not again! Betsy's heart sank to her toes.

"Oh, heaven!" Unable to stop herself, she began to cry, too. "Oh, Heaven! I hope he hasn't fallen out of his cradle. Could you help me, sweetheart? When we get Johnny to sleep again, you must get in bed with me."

She wiped her eyes fiercely, half expecting Angelica to refuse, to prefer brooding and waiting for her beloved Papa. This time, however, her daughter surprised her. Soft fingers came to touch her mother's face.

"Are *you* crying?" Angelica seemed incredulous.

"Yes, Angel, I am."

There was a pause, the child's bright eyes upon her, clearly caught up in the astonishing revelation that an indestructible grown-up could weep. Betsy feared that this knowledge would be yet another frightening discovery.

"It's just because I'm so tired." Betsy wiped her eyes on a corner of her nightgown, feeling guilty.

Had she ever seen her mother cry from sheer exhaustion and helplessness?

There was a pause. The wail from the next room hiccupped, expanded.

"Well, I'm wide awake." Suddenly brisk, Angelica swung her thin legs down from the window seat. A small and ghostly white figure, she crouched to pick up the candle.

"You rest, Mama. I'll bet I can get Johnny back to sleep."

Without another word she padded away on her narrow bare feet. Betsy had to follow quickly to catch up to her.

* * *

When Hamilton rode away at the head of the army, it was the end of September. Betsy worried about him, not only because of the danger, but because he didn't seem to be feeling well. Since the yellow fever, he'd been vulnerable, complaining of gut pain and back pain. His ability to concentrate was noticeably down, perhaps, at last, to the level of an ordinary man's.

"Please don't worry, Eliza." He'd assured her for the last time as he swung up into the saddle. "This business will be over soon, I'm sure. It will probably amount to nothing more than an agreeable ride in good fall weather."

Betsy wasn't soothed. She knew Hamilton was despised by many, certainly by those whiskey rebels. She tried to bury her worry in traveling to Trenton to collect Philip and Alexander. At once, with two big boys at home, there was more activity. At first, she rejoiced in it.

Philip, bless him, kept everyone in order. Now that he was home, Angelica was calmer, too. Betsy often found them curled up together studying. They practiced reading

French with one another, their two shiny heads, red and ruddy brown, almost touching as they leaned over a book.

Betsy worked at straightening her household accounts. Over the summer, things had been neglected, for Hamilton hardly ever had time to tend to personal business and they had both been ill off and on. There was the nurse, the maid, and the cook to pay, as well as the brought-in help for the heavy autumn tasks of scrubbing the windows and the porch. The curtains had to be changed from summer to the heavy winter ones. Rugs needed beating. Blankets had to be taken from the cedar trunks and examined for moth damage. The wainscot had to be rubbed with turpentine to ward off the autumnal invasion of Philadelphia bugs.

Now, in this time of plenty, food was laid in. Root vegetables of all kinds must be chosen and bought, then dug into sand boxes in the coolest part of the cellar. Even with a great deal of care, the hot climate here made keeping food more difficult. Preserves had to be made and laid away, apples, pears, and peppers must be sliced and hung on thread in the kitchen.

Days filled with housewife's cares hurried past. Angel's music master took employment with a Virginian and went south, leaving her disconsolate. Another had to be speedily found. Jamie ate too many sweets and grew round as a ball.

During all this, Betsy would read about the march of the federal army to the western counties. There were invitations to tea with Mrs. Bradford and Mrs. Washington, which she made time to accept. She hoped that a condition of absolute busyness would keep her fears away. She tried not to indulge in dark thoughts, but there were signs it was a losing battle. One night she had a terrible nightmare, dreaming that Washington had come to tell her that Hamilton was dead, bushwhacked by some backwoods sharpshooter.

"It's all right, Mama. It's all right." She awoke with Angel's skinny arms around her, bravely attempting to play a mother's part.

"I'm roused now. Thank you, darling!" The tremor she'd heard in her daughter's voice forced her to reach for control. She soothed them both by stroking Angelica's fine hair.

"What did you dream, Mama?"

"Just a nightmare, darling."

The image rushed back—the Commander-in-Chief's monumental ivory face, the flat delivery of a tale that could bear no rhetoric. In a dark pine forest, her Hamilton white and still, his high forehead surrounded by blood....

"Let's be very quiet, Angel, or we'll wake up Johnny."

There was the clink of flint on steel in the next room. Soon the gentle flair of candlelight advanced through the door.

"Is everything all right?" It was Philip, his young face full of concern.

"I had a bad dream," said Betsy, "and Angel woke me out of it. She is a wonderful comfort."

Philip shone the candle around the room, every bit the man of the family.

"Look, Mama. We're safe. There are no Schagticokes, no Tories, no Jacobins, nor any other kind of villain in this house!"

This was what Grandpa Schuyler had taken to telling his grandchildren when they were frightened by night shadows or by nightmares. The familiar quote made Betsy smile.

"No pirates, no sharks with sharp teeth, and no hurricanes neither!" Angel chimed in with the nightmares her father spoke of, her sudden bravado no doubt encouraged by Philip's presence.

* * *

Despite the support from the older children, a mist hemmed her in. Even with the children, no matter how close she held them, how much she tried to find firm ground in caring for them, in brushing their silky hair, in bathing, feeding, and snuggling. Inch by inch, Betsy felt herself sliding away from everyone, down into a hole with

371

only her fears for company. She walked through the days by rote, isolated and alone.

Something else was wrong, too, something not in the phantom world of the mind, but something real. Soon after the nightmare, there were cramps and a dull ache, one that settled in her lower back. Examining her petticoats, she found spotting. This had happened before. She knew what it meant.

The time had come to send the boys back to Dr. Frazer's school, but she was torn between needing Philip's help and getting him away from what was coming. Phil was only thirteen, but he seemed to understand that something was wrong with his mother.

"Alex should go back," he said, "but I think I should stay. You aren't well, Mama. Gussie keeps saying so, and she's always right. And Angel says you're having more bad dreams than she is."

"No. I can't keep you from school. What would your father say if you fell behind?"

"I'm tops of my class. It won't be hard to catch up. Shouldn't I stay? At least until Papa returns?"

Betsy's heart swelled with love, but she said, "No, you and Alex will go to Doctor Frazer's just as planned. It's only Alexander's second term, and he's not as good with people as you are. He needs his big brother."

Philip looked sad and uncertain, so much so that Betsy put her arms around him.

"Phil, dear, I love you so much. What a help you've been with the little ones, and you make Angel so happy! She and I both wish we could always keep you here."

"I love you, too, Mama," Philip said, hugging back, "but if you need me, please send for me. Someone we know will come and bring me home. I know it's hard for you by yourself."

How blessed I am, Betsy thought, as she saw off the boys in a carriage with an attorney friend now on his way to Trenton. *And how particularly in that son!*

372

How many boys of his age would take any interest at all in younger brothers and sisters or in the cares of his mother?

* * *

Rain fell and when the sun returned. Philadelphia steamed. Betsy drove to the market with Davie and busied herself laying in a winter stock of apples and squash. She made more conserves from grape and pear. She chose and bought a couple of tongues, one to cure and the other to pickle. She kept up with the maids and the cook, but all the time she could feel terror right behind her.

Hamilton! My Hamilton! Will I ever see him again?

His face rose before her, floated between the world and her eyes. For the spotting and cramps she suffered daily, Betsy took raspberry tea. She also joined Angel in a daily dose of tincture of hops and valerian, hoping this would make her calmer.

One morning, half-asleep and still deep in the overnight fog, she arose from washing in the basin to find bright red streaks in the water. Nothing was left to do now but to get rags from the shelf, call for Gussie, and climb back into bed.

Doctor Stevens was sent for.

"Is the baby moving?"

"Yes."

"Well, Mrs. Hamilton, all I can do is tell you is to stay off your feet. Preferably, don't get up at all. I'll have a prescription sent from the apothecary. Hawthorne is stronger than raspberry, and may help in other ways. Take the medicine and rest. Send if you have an increase in bleeding or pain. Nature will take its course. If the child is meant to live, it will, otherwise you mustn't blame yourself."

In a departure from his usual undemonstrative bedside manner, Doctor Stevens, his long face a colder, less animated version of her husband's, patted her hand before taking his leave.

Betsy drank her medicine and managed as well as she could from bed. Gussie reported that Angel was helpful with Jamie and Johnny. She marched off every morning to the little school she and Jamie attended, holding him tightly by the hand and keeping him out of mischief. In the afternoons she rocked Johnny and played with him.

It was curious, but as Betsy sank, Angel seemed stronger. Betsy petted her and praised.

"What a grown-up lady you are, helping Mama and Gussie every day! Papa will be so proud of you when he comes."

Oh, but would be come home? Would he?

It was only a momentary distraction to observe Angel's happy glow. Betsy felt as if she'd been swimming for years now, seeking dry land in a world that had turned to restless ocean. It was November again, the light going earlier every day, longer hours of the brooding darkness with which to contend. Hamilton hadn't returned, although his letters and the news that Mrs. Knox brought every day assured her that the Pennsylvania rebellion had collapsed.

Hamilton was busy dealing justice in the west when the baby stopped moving. In the past, carrying a child, Betsy had experienced occasional flashes of panic, as if the fetus was draining the life out of her, but now, after a few hours without those companionable kicks, came the onset of panic. There was not enough strength to say anything to Gussie or send for Doctor Stevens.

What was the use? Betsy, certain of her loss, lay in bed and wept.

Lucy Knox arrived to visit around eleven. The sight of that fat, extravagantly dressed figure sweeping into the darkened room—for one stunning instant—reminded Betsy of her mother on a party day.

"Oh, Lucy!" She spoke before her visitor had even closed the door. "My baby has stopped moving and I'm in labor!"

Mrs. Knox's fair bulk approached the bed with astonishing speed.

"Have you called for Stevens?"

"Oh, but what can he do?" Betsy sobbed. "I've lost my baby and my Hamilton's not here. And both Jamie and Angel have started coughs and Johnny fell on the stairs yesterday and hit his head and—oh, God! I can't bear it!"

"There, there, my dear. Don't fret. Your husband will be home soon, and, now, right this minute we'll call Stevens and my doctor, too, Doctor Kuhn." In an amazing burst of speed, her wide body bustled away to the door.

The doctors came, examined, and consulted, however, it was Doctor Stevens who took Betsy's hand and said firmly, "Mrs. Hamilton, you're correct. Your baby is still. Let me remind you that so far you've been a very lucky woman, bearing and raising five healthy children. Doctor Kuhn and I agree that your labor is proceeding quite normally. If the loss is clean, there will be no danger to you."

This cold comfort was almost worse than none at all.

"I want my husband. I need him. I need him! And he's not here. He's never here! Never! Oh, God! Hamilton! Oh, my Hamilton!"

Doctor Stevens administered a calmative. Lucy Knox did her best to soothe, and then sent off a rather confused note to her husband, Henry. In it, she asked that he send a message west.

"This stupid rebellion!" After the doctors had left, Mrs. Knox returned to Betsy, weeping against the pillow. "This barbaric, unending politics! Haven't we all managed without our men for years? Gone through a long war and all that worry with little compensation—and worse, no thanks? And now to be abused by those dirty Jacobins and that pusillanimous Jefferson, who spent the war in hiding! Why, you're simply worn out, my dear. We all are. Sick and tired of all of it. But you must be brave now, just a little longer. I won't leave, not until you tell me to go."

Betsy tried to be comforted, but now that she'd started, she couldn't stop the crying. An experienced commander, Lucy Knox sent orders and requests in all directions. As a result, Angelica and Jamie were collected as they left school by Mrs. Morris and were not in the house to hear their mother's cries.

Brief and violent, labor was soon over. Doctor Stevens quickly wrapped the small blue body in an old pillowcase and handed it straightaway to the slave woman who always assisted him, signaling her to take the child away.

"About five months." He spoke softly, as if to himself. "Now don't you worry, Mrs. Hamilton. You will be fine. You'll have to bind and use ice to get rid of the milk, but at least at this time of year you shouldn't be too uncomfortable. Everything looks normal, but you aren't to wait a minute if you suspect a fever, but send for me at once. I'm sure that won't happen, however. I believe that this will be the end of your trouble."

"My baby!" Betsy keened. "My baby! And those wicked rebels may still kill my husband!"

Lucy Knox sat beside her and held Betsy's hand and talked on, hoping to give comfort.

"The poor little fellow was quite still. He's gone straight to heaven without all the trouble in between the rest of us have. Oh, my dear, I know what you feel, better than that cold-fish doctor. I've lost babies, too, and, Elizabeth, do you think I'll ever forget burying my darling Julia in that frozen churchyard at Morristown? Ah, me!"

She heaved a great sigh at this bitter war-time memory and continued, "Your heart is broken, yes, but you must think of the lovely angels you already have. Just as the doctor says, you are lucky to have so many beautiful children. Oh, Elizabeth, my dear; do stop. It won't do any good and you know that we poor women have to be sensible, for the men never are. Always on about honor and duty while everything day to day goes to the devil. Lie back now—that's a good girl—and try to rest."

That afternoon a letter under presidential cover went west to Secretary Hamilton, saying that Mrs. Hamilton was *"in danger of, or has had a miscarriage"* and was in dire need of her husband's return *"to tranquilize her."*

* * *

Early the next year Hamilton resigned from the cabinet, but he was still busy politicking, working for the acceptance of a treaty with the British. It wasn't a popular stance among the common folk or even among some better educated people, people of property like Jefferson, who found it politically expedient to speak highly of the French, no matter how many atrocities their new revolutionary government perpetuated. When John Jay negotiated a treaty that guaranteed the safety of United States shipping in return for neutrality in the coming war between Britain and the French Directory, he was burned in effigy by mobs in every city.

Chapter Six
Battles Lost and a New Horse

Hamilton slumped forward, sitting on the sofa in the parlor, holding a cloth to his forehead. Despite this, blood dripped onto the gleaming floor.

Bob Troup, tall and plumper than ever, his forehead appearing even higher than before as his hair receded, knelt next to the sofa. Rufus King sat beside Hamilton. Their clothes were filthy and torn and they all had bruises. Clearly, they'd come from more than a hard ride.

"Are you sure you're all right, Ham?" Troup was solicitous.

"Yes. It throbs, but I don't feel dizzy or as if I'm going to vomit, so it can't be serious."

"Spare us your usual imitation of a physician, Hamilton," said King. "I think we ought to call Hosack. You were unconscious for a time and there's a lot of blood."

"Scalp wounds always bleed most handsomely. Remember?"

"Yes, I recall the glorious days of our revolutionary youth, but this is more than a scalp wound, my friend."

377

"Yes," said King. "I saw the piece of pavement that sturdy Irishman lobbed. You don't have to be a hero for us, sir."

"Hamilton!" Betsy rushed into the room. "Whatever…?"

"Democracy in action," King explained. "He tried to speak in favor of Mr. Jay's treaty with the British, but Jefferson's drunken partisans aren't interested in listening to reason—and they certainly don't believe in any freedom of speech except their own."

"Well, not if it doesn't echo their opinions. Lacking any brains of their own, they attempted to reduce your husband to their own level by knocking his out with a paving stone and then dragging him into the gutter."

Betsy knelt beside Troup and put her hands on the bloody cloth.

"Oh, my dear! Why did you even try to talk to that rabble?"

"Someone should tell them the truth. They're being lied to—used! We have to trade with England and we must stay out of this war if we want to survive. We can't get tangled up in the chaos that's taken over France—"

"Do be quiet, sir, and let me look."

"I haven't got any blood on the upholstery, have I?"

"No, my darling." Betsy replied without taking her eyes, or the fresh handkerchief she was applying, away from the wound.

Mud, she thought, for certain, but she thought she could coax that out.

"Haven't you yet learned?" scolded King. "Lying and flattering, using their ignorance and playing upon their emotions are the proven ways to win popular elections. Successful politics has nothing to do with Reason, or—God Help Us—with the Truth."

The maid poked her round, white-capped head in the door to see what all the commotion was.

"Anneke, dear, please fetch a basin of water and the vinegar," Betsy said. "And my sewing kit." She dabbed at the wound, trying to see how large it was.

Beneath his fine gold freckles, Hamilton went an entire shade paler.

"Must you stitch?"

"Yes. It's deep and long." Betsy drew a breath, worked at getting some mental distance from the fact that this was her husband. "I see bone."

"Well, if that's the case," said Bob, "we need whiskey." He stood and went to the walnut highboy and retrieved a bottle. "At least, I need some." He poured himself a shot. "Frankly, we're lucky we got away from that mob with our heads still attached."

"No, thank you," Hamilton said, when Bob offered a glass. "But please, gentlemen, do have some."

"Don't be ridiculous. Have this right now, and then we'll splash some directly on that wound, no reason to wait."

"An excellent notion, as always, Mr. Troup." Betsy said.

"Here, on this handkerchief." Bob began to pour.

"And where, Mrs. Hamilton, did you learn surgery?" King inquired as Hamilton, at her insistence, lay back upon Betsy's lap.

"My Aunt Cochran taught me the winter I stayed at Morristown during the war."

Rufus King expressed astonishment that a daughter of the Schuylers should have dirtied her hands in the hospital, but Hamilton smiled and said proudly, "Oh, yes, Nick! She did her family proud, and—Ow!"

And after that, he didn't say anymore, for Betsy had begun, without preamble, to apply the whiskey soaked handkerchief to the wound. Soon after, his sandy head cradled, he closed his eyes and gritted his teeth, while his wife swiftly plied her finest needle.

* * *

"But you're not in the government anymore."

"Washington needs me."

"He was always on the fence when you were fighting with Jefferson in the cabinet and it made you furious."

"Yes, and that, I'm afraid, was his job. But, you see, McHenry's written to tell me that since they caught Randolph taking a bribe from the French, they're without a Secretary of State. There's no one competent who is willing to do it. His Excellency has asked for my help. He needs instructions for his minister in London."

And that was the beginning of a most curious time. Public life, Washington said, had "grown so vile that no decent man wanted any part of it." He'd asked Hamilton to prepare his seventh annual message to Congress and sent along the relevant official documents.

Once again heeding the call of his Chief, Hamilton, continued to work for the government. The department heads, his old friends, Thomas Pickering and James McHenry, sent information and questions. He wrote back, detailing his thoughts about what ought to be done.

* * *

Looking up from papers neatly laid upon his desk of bird's eye maple, Hamilton told Betsy that he'd just finished writing to an old comrade in arms, Henry Lee, about acquiring a new horse.

"Won't one of those blooded horses be dreadfully expensive? You know Papa would gladly give you one."

"Well, dear, your father has given me entirely too many fine things. You were a particularly precious gift."

"Desist, sir! Am I a girl to be deflected by such flattery? You know Papa would be delighted to give you a colt. The last time I was up, he groused that he couldn't make any money on horses these days, that he had too many to feed, and that an old man simply didn't need a barn full of frisky horses."

"The plain truth is that your papa's colts are too frisky. I spent all the time I ever cared to at a gallop during the war. I'll leave your papa's wild horses to the honorable Stephen

380

van R and your sporting brothers. My old friend Colonel Henry Lee has some plantation walkers with easy tempers and gaits, just the thing for a preoccupied lawyer on his way to Poughkeepsie, Philadelphia or Hartford for a trial. Now that I'm in the way of earning some decent money, I can afford a handsome horse."

"Oh, can you? When did you last examine your household accounts, Mr. ex-Secretary of the Treasury?"

"Well, I have my own peculiar requirements in a mount, which, by the way, are rather like my requirements in a wife."

"Mr. Hamilton, what is about to come out of your mouth?"

"I was about to say that a wife must have looks and be able to go the distance. Whether she goes fast or slow is immaterial. In fact, I'd far rather she were slow."

"Be careful, sir."

His laugh today had a cheerful sound. "Let me tell you all about Colonel Lee's horse. The last time he and I corresponded, he told me about a fine animal that one of his boys had ridden too hard. The horse was quite beautiful, but ruined for hunting. He's still got a smooth, fast walk and can go all day, though for tearing around the country as his sons insist, he is useless. Doesn't that sound like the perfect horse for me? I'm always riding and working up a brief in my head. I don't want a naughty horse who decides to run me under a branch because I'm not paying close attention. And because Lee's horse is less than perfect, I shall even be able to afford him."

"So! I'm a less than perfect horse?"

"No. Just reliable, willing, good tempered—and good looking, like Colonel Lee's gray."

"You are getting in deeper with every word, sir. I think I shall be bad tempered and unwilling for a month, just to show you that to compare your wife to a horse is supremely tactless."

Here the conversation ended, at least the coherent part of it, for Hamilton set about the only strategy now open to him. Pulling his wife onto the sofa, he began to press an argument which wasn't remotely verbal.

* * *

The horse arrived from the south about eight weeks later.

"What a beauty!"

"Sure is!" Their man of all work, forgetting himself, interjected his own estimation, but no one present could argue with it.

Betsy, with Johnny eagerly alongside, had gone out to see the new arrival at their small backyard stabling. The horse was silver-dappled, rather than simply gray, with dark eyes and muzzle and elegant conformation. He stood, Betsy guessed, barely 15 hands high, but not so big as to make his not-so-tall rider look even smaller on his back. She produced an apple from her pocket and handed it to Johnny, so that he, who was currently mad for horses, could be the one to give it.

"What's he called again?"

"Riddle."

The horse stretched his neck over the stall door and took the apple from Johnny's small fingers with surprising gentleness. Johnny looked up wide-eyed—absolutely in love—as the crunching began above him.

Riddle proved calm, gentle, and capable of an endless, fast, rocking walk, exactly as her husband's old comrade in arms Colonel Lee had promised. Hamilton often boasted that "Riddle is the most sensible, easy-going horse I've ever owned."

Hamilton spent so much time corresponding with remaining members of the cabinet and advising them on policy that he might just as well have been one of them. When Washington was ready to resign his office, the General did as he'd done during the war, asking Hamilton to play the part of secretary, to take the words out of his head and write him a farewell address. And just as he'd done for so many years, Hamilton obliged and wrote a powerful and healing speech for the retiring father of his country. Good secretary that he was, no one ever heard the tale from his lips.

Chapter Seven
Another Elopement

Betsy's little sister, Cornelia, had grown from a pudgy little girl to a blooming eighteen. She'd attended a society wedding in New Jersey during the spring of 1794, the wedding of Eliza Morton to Josiah Quincy of Boston. It was a union of Quaker and Puritan, unthinkable a generation before, but money and breeding were more important these days than religion. The young celebrants were drawn from the best families of New Jersey, New York, Connecticut and Massachusetts.

Here Cornelia Schuyler had a fateful encounter with Washington Morton, brother of the bride. This young brave, one of the first generation christened in honor of the great general, was handsome and athletic. He'd walked to Philadelphia from New York on a wager, a feat that made a loud noise in the privileged young bloods who were his friends. When Cornelia came back up river from the wedding in New Ark, she was escorted by Morton, a dashing chestnut-haired gentleman who rode in upon a magnificent horse.

Washington Morton was light-hearted, rejoicing in his strength and high spirits. He showed the young Schuylers and Hamilton cousins how he could do handsprings and cartwheels. He swam across the Hudson and back several times without a breather. He caught horses loose in pasture by their manes and rode them around, aided only by his hands and feet, like an Indian. He romped and tussled with the Schuyler mastiffs and made a boon companion of the meanest one. The Hamilton boys, Phil, Alex and Jamie, as well as their cousins, the older Philip Jeremiah and Rennselaer Schuyler, followed Mr. Morton about like the pied piper. When Washington was done playing with the boys, he was off in a pony trap with Cornelia, sparking her without an ounce of prudence. Betsy warned her sister, but discretion had never been Cornelia's long suit.

General Schuyler was not pleased. Although from a wealthy family, Washington as yet had no idea of what career he would pursue, nor did he show much evidence of book learning. He was drifting into life, indulging himself with the sizable allowance his father provided.

Betsy was not surprised when one morning her father and young Washington retired to the study. In the broad downstairs corridor, on her way to fetch something for Mama, she heard the rumble of her father's voice, that deep authoritarian tone, and knew, without catching a word, that a suitor was being rejected.

Soon, Papa banged his cane on the floor and ordered the carriage. From upstairs came the sounds of bags being packed, of doors slamming, of Cornelia sobbing. The old general accompanied the young man to the wharf and stayed until he'd seen both the unwanted suitor and his baggage on board the noon sloop to New York. Back at the house, Cornelia wailed and smashed china, much as her eldest sister Angelica had done twenty years before.

"I'd just as soon marry you to some unlettered frontiersman." The general roared back. "This Mr. Morton has no idea of responsibility, has done nothing yet except peacock about upon the foolish generosity of his father! Now, Cornelia, promise me you will have nothing further to do with him—either by word—or by letter."

"I cannot do that." Cornelia's dark eyes were full of fire. All too clearly, here was another Schuyler daughter imagining she was the beleaguered heroine of a romance.

"What?! Do you mean to disobey me?"

"I cannot bind myself, Papa. I will not promise."

"Disobedient girl! Great God! What have I done to deserve this? Go to your room at once and stay there!"

Head high, Cornelia swept up the stairs.

"Where does she get this language? This defiant deportment? It's those damned British novels, isn't it? I swear to God—if I find any in this house they shall be burnt."

385

Betsy thought it far more likely that the earlier elopements had been the corrupting influence. As she watched the scene from the window seat, chair back embroidery in hand, she again wondered how it was that she—Elizabeth—was the only Schuyler girl who hadn't had to climb out of a second story window for a husband. Watching her father stamp upstairs after Cornelia, his cane and boots loud, she also had a strong sense the grand finale would be played out before she went back to Philadelphia.

As with Angelica and Peggy before her, Cornelia was locked in her bedroom. Here, she, too, languished attractively at the window. Her particular friend, Miss Westerlo, the Patroon's half-sister, came to visit her almost every day. As word got out, various young male cousins, van Corlear, De Lancey and Cuyler, too, came on horseback and then climbed into an ancient tree beside the house. As their horses crunched fallen apples, they carried on long, amusing conversations with the beautiful and ever so attractive prisoner.

"Are you going to obey Papa?"

"Would you?"

The sisters were sewing together, sharing a broad window seat. The fourth Hamilton son, Johnny, crawled along the floor, contentedly muttering to himself and playing with his Uncle Rensselaer's long ago abandoned wooden coach and four painted horses.

"You know I was always obedient, so I'm hardly the one to ask. When I was your age, my cousins called me 'the little Saint.'"

Cornelia smiled condescendingly at her matronly sister, a full nineteen years older. "If Papa had told you that you couldn't marry Brother Hamilton, you would certainly have run away with him. Don't tell me you wouldn't have."

"Papa only wants the best for you, Cornelia. Mr. Morton is a very dashing fellow, I'm sure, but he isn't settled yet. Perhaps if he began to study for the bar, it would change Papa's mind."

Cornelia tossed a dark shiny head—her hair and eyes were almost as dark as Betsy's—and fiercely stabbed the needle into a pin cushion.

"What is more," Betsy continued, "the truth is that *I* would have been willing to elope, but Mr. Hamilton would have none it. If Papa had refused him my hand, it would have been the last I'd seen of my dear Alexander."

"I don't believe that for a minute. Angelica says that Mr. Hamilton can be quite impetuous."

It was with difficulty that Betsy resisted a sisterly urge to smack her.

* * *

A few mornings later, Cornelia was missing. It wasn't a mystery, because a sturdy ladder lay abandoned beneath her bedroom window.

"Damned useless dogs!" Mr. Schuyler bellowed at the pair of sad-eyed mastiffs who crouched nervously, tails sagging, at their master's approach. "And these people of mine whom I feed and clothe at such great expense! I'll have all of you skinned!" The slaves, unsure of whether it was them or the dogs he was talking about, cowered too.

"Not a bark, not a whimper! No one vigilant! Their pockets lined by that young rake! I shall sell you all down to South Carolina, every damned lazy one!"

Dogs and slaves made themselves scarce, while Betsy tried to get her father to sit down and her mother tried to get him to drink the calmative she'd hastily prepared. His face was scarlet; his breathing came so hard that they feared apoplexy.

The morning was spent with both parents imagining dreadful outcomes, each more dire than the last. Around one o'clock a messenger came trotting up the hill. He bore a note sent by Judge Theodore Sedgwick of Stockbridge, a town about thirty miles east of the Hudson.

Mr. Washington Morton, the son of a dear friend, and Miss Schuyler, the daughter of another, had appeared in a fine coach and six at his door around dawn. Distressed by

387

the impropriety, he'd been compelled to call a minister and see them married. Otherwise, he said, Miss Schuyler would have been compromised.

Betsy found herself staying on longer than she'd meant in order to soothe her parents. The upset caused her father to suffer another violent attack of gout and the resultant pain made him impossible to deal with. The more details he discovered about the elopement—Rensselaer learned much by drinking one night with one of the young van Corlears, cousins who had been Washington Morton's partners in crime—the more he roared and shouted.

"To plot against a prudent father! Worse, to *borrow* the plot out of some accursed, trashy English novel!" He growled and thumped the floor with his cane, red-faced with rage. "Laudanum in the dog's water and in the slaves' beer, a ladder, row boats across the river, then coach and six *white* horses to Stockbridge...."

"Now, Papa." Betsy tried to get him settled into his chair.

"A muscle-headed dandy-prat! He'd better not set a foot on my property again, with or without your sister! I give it a year, just a year, and then she'll be down on that landing, yes she will, just you wait and see, a baby in her arms, no doubt, mistreated and penniless! And then, by God! Then I'll tell her she can just go away and starve with that spoiled, inconsequential, ignorant, pudding head!"

Chapter Eight
Fortitude

"Arm yourself with resignation. We live in a world full of evil. In the later period of life misfortunes thicken round us. Our duty and our peace both require that we should accustom ourselves to meet disasters with Christian fortitude...."

* * *

Philip Schuyler was sick with gout and gravel and every other thing aged flesh is heir to. Hamilton had been in Albany on litigation and had seen how poorly his father-in-law was.

Betsy and Cornelia traveled up river together to tend and cosset him. Betsy was six months pregnant again, but this time had been feeling tolerably well. A journey to Albany, even to care for an aging parent, was always a pleasure. She thought it would be pleasant to spend time with Cornelia, too.

Her sister's wild young husband had settled down quite nicely, using his inheritance to provide for them while he applied himself to his books. In due time, he came to the bar and was off to a good start as an attorney. Of course, there was a Morton baby, too. The grandchild and the father's going to the bar had once more combined to reconcile Papa Schuyler. Cornelia was welcome at *The Pastures* again, although her father remained fabulously stiff with her tall, good-natured husband.

* * *

Betsy lay in bed, her thin back towards the door, the great ball of her belly before her. She never seemed to gain

389

any weight, even while pregnant. This year silver strands mingled with her dark hair.

At the sound of Hamilton's entrance, she turned, one arm thrown protectively over her bosom in a modest gesture, one which had never changed since their first night together. Observing, he felt a flash of irritation.

Seventeen years married! How can she still be so shy?

"Hamilton?"

"Yes, angel, I'm home."

"Is your business in Philadelphia done?"

"Yes—at least until after the baby's born."

"How soon will you return?"

"I don't really know. It could be quite soon, I'm afraid."

Thinking about the pamphlet he was organizing, the one which would detail his connection with Mrs. Reynolds and put an end to the rumors that he had used government resources for speculation, Hamilton experienced a rising heartbeat. The thought of the damage he'd done to his reputation, to his marriage—and the blackmail he'd paid—far more than he could afford over the years—was agonizing.

When he'd at last refused, Mr. Reynolds had gone to James Monroe, claiming to have proof Hamilton had stolen from the Treasury, a lie which his political enemies had now fanned into a spectacular fire. Hamilton could bear this no longer. He intended to end those aspersions upon his public self by confessing that his sin was adultery, and not peculation.

What would his Betsy do when all his dirty linen was dumped out for the world to see?

Sitting on the edge of the bed he tried to soothe himself by petting her, but she pushed his hand away and laboriously sat up.

"You've challenged Monroe to a duel, haven't you?" Her dark, shadowed eyes rose to his. "That despicable lying snake-in-the-grass!"

Hamilton was so astonished, both by her vehemence and by what she already knew, he could find no words.

Stunned, he stared at his wife. The lump that was his adored Johnny shifted behind her at the sound of his voice. Just beyond the light of his candle, he'd noted the gangly length of Angelica, sleeping down in the trundle bed.

In spite of all my care, she knows about the duel! The look in her eyes told him that lying would be useless.

"Well, yes. It's true. Monroe will never make my honor as cheap as his. But—oh, Eliza, my angel! How did you...?"

"John Church, who, I gather, is your second, let it slip to his wife. Why you men all think Angelica's so clever I'm sure I don't know. She's never been in the least discreet."

Hamilton stared, once again speechless. He'd never heard her say anything remotely disapproving about her adored sister.

"You, Mr. Hamilton, seem to be caught in a trap you set for yourself, but I don't see why there is any need to compound the sins already committed with a duel."

His head rang as if she'd slapped him.

"I've committed no—um...." The unwelcome image of Maria Reynold's sumptuous body interposed, an unwelcome, libidinous specter, so he amended quickly. "None against the public trust, at any rate. Damn Church, anyway, and your sister, into the bargain. You weren't supposed to be upset, especially now."

"Never mind 'especially now.' You didn't worry much about me during that summer, I gather, and it's far too late to change that. I want to know the truth—for once—Mr. Hamilton."

It didn't happen often, but when it did it was a force to be reckoned with.

My loyal, loving wife is very, very angry!

"Please, Mrs. Hamilton, surely you can see I had to challenge Monroe. Back in Philadelphia, just before Johnny was born, I explained to him what this Reynolds business actually was. He, Venable and Muhlenburg came to see me, asking about a man called James Reynolds who had made accusations. I told them the truth that day and they promised to remain silent on their honor as gentlemen, for

391

the Reynolds business was a private matter. What Monroe's notion of honor is shown by the contents of the newspaper published by his creature Callender. That contemptible Monroe! To think, we crossed the Delaware together as comrades! He apparently believes he can go on insinuating forever that I'm guilty of stealing from the Treasury because I'll never dare throw the lie back in his face. At the very least, I have to *offer* to put a bullet into him."

"I think it's gone quite far enough without a duel. You are the one who gave the challenge, aren't you?"

"Yes. I called him a liar—that he plainly is—and then, of course, the scoundrel had no other choice than to go through with it."

She had meant to be hard, meant not to cry, cry the abandoned way she had in her sister's parlor when Angelica had finally confirmed her worst suspicions.

Oh, the pain of resurrecting all that disgusting business about the low woman! She'd never forgotten the pain she'd felt when Hamilton had finally confessed.

As was to be expected with so much talk and tension, the children were waking up. Johnny rubbed his eyes and peeked out from under the blanket. Angelica turned over. She looked a little wild, as if she had caught the drift of what was being said.

To forestall any trouble there, he got up, went around to the other side, crouched to sit on the truckle bed beside her.

"Wake up, Angel." He patted her back. "It's Papa. I'm home, sweetheart."

There was a scramble in the bed, and then not only the soft maidenly arms of his thirteen year old daughter, but the chubby ones of Johnny, clasped their adored father.

"Papa!" They joyfully embraced him. "Papa!"

Betsy kept her back to them and tucked herself up around her belly. Inside, whatever Hamilton child this was flailed and kicked. She was furious, but the tears, a combination of grief, frustration, rage and advanced pregnancy, were unstoppable. The restless creature inside

392

her belly stretched, kicked impatiently, bringing her hand to her side.

In a few minutes, they'd all be embracing her. Hamilton would be in the role he played so well—tender, caring father, loving husband.

Oh, and all these things he is, but he is also a madman who constantly menaces our peace. Old wounds force him, time and again, to prove that he is a man of honor. He must adhere to every stricture of the code....

* * *

Elizabeth's pains started just at bedtime, but it was simple to get the children together and pack them off to her sister's for the night. As Hamilton emerged from the study where he had been putting the finishing touches on a brief he would deliver in a Poughkeepsie Courtroom, he noted how Phil handled the task of getting the younger ones ready. They obeyed without question or quarreling, even the stiff-necked Alex. The oldest boy had smoothly managed him, sending him off to tell Aunt Church that Mama's time had come and that the others would be soon at her door. Alex had relished the drama of playing messenger. As soon as he was gone, Phil marshaled the others.

It was only a few blocks to the Church's elegant townhouse, so his children set off on foot. Alexander watched from the study window as they set off into the warm summer sunset.

A fine gaggle of young geese!

Phil had set Johnny on his back. Angelica carried the music that went with her everywhere, especially to Aunt Angelica's, who loved to hear her play. Her crinkly ginger hair was tucked into modest cap. Chubby James showed off, rolling a hoop ahead of them all.

Only a few hours later, just after midnight, Hamilton held the swaddled, squirming form of his newest son. Sturdy and compact, the child was born gray-eyed and sporting a fine fuzz of pink hair. The pattern for young

Hamiltons was to start like this, although all but Angelica had, after a few years, darkened to brown tinted with varying amounts of their father's copper.

The new baby was christened William Stephen. Stephen in honor of his uncle, Stephen van Rensselaer, but the William was something of a mystery, even to Betsy.

Was it for that Scots relative with whom Alexander had lately been in correspondence, a British diplomat, William Hamilton? For the financier William Bingham whose advice he'd sought while setting up the Bank of the U.S.? Or was it for Colonel William Jackson, a doughty federalist backer whom Betsy knew only slightly?

Hamilton cryptically explained his relationship with Jackson as "a man to whom I've recently become very close." Betsy suspected that because her brother-in-law John Church had been called to Boston on business, Jackson had stepped in as second in the prospective duel with Monroe.

* * *

The third day after Billy's arrival was her fortieth birthday. Betsy sat nursing, bolstered by pillows, the baby in the crook of an arm. She held a scrap of flannel in the hand of the other, stemming the sympathetic leaking. Hamilton, from the other side, admired her motherly expertise.

Billy drank furiously, arms and legs thrashing inside his swaddling. Alexander sat down beside his wife, and announced he'd hired more help.

"Now, before you start telling me that she'll be useless and that you will have to get out of childbed and show her everything, I want you to know that Mrs. van R trained her."

"Peggy?" Betsy looked away from the baby, surprised.

"Yes. Once the girl understands our routine and the cantankerous ways of Gussie, it should go well. Her name

394

is Anneke and she arrived from Rensselaerwyck today. I'll send her in whenever you're able to see her."

Betsy removed Baby Billy from the empty breast, an action that immediately produced a wail. With one hand supporting his chin, she began to expertly bring up the burp, patting his back. No easy task, for Billy alternately protested, sagged, and lurched.

"Peggy trained her? A girl from Albany?"

"Peggy trained her, but she's not from Albany. She's from some little valley town, Hoosic, I think. Maybe she won't run off straightaway to get married." Alexander paused to kiss his wife's thin cheek. "Besides the new helper, there's a beautiful dress for Mrs. Hamilton at Mrs. Sayler's shop. Both are much deserved birthday presents for you, my darling."

The gifts did please. He never paid much attention to the household, but here he'd gone to a lot of trouble, probably exerting every ounce of his formidable charm in order to get a well-trained and docile servant away from Peggy.

Billy interrupted her expressions of gratitude by suddenly producing a series of noisy, booming burps. His parents began to laugh—so much sound from that tiny body! Abruptly a cup of curdy liquid followed the rude noises out.

After all that action the baby goggled, apparently bewildered by his own body. Betsy seized the flannel and tried to soak up the spillage. Hamilton arose and returned with a towel from the washbasin and another baby wrap.

Betsy managed a "thank you" after they'd got the baby, the bed, and herself somewhat dried.

"What a wonderful notion to get more help."

"I'm glad it makes you happy. I haven't been much good at that lately."

She sighed, unwilling to deny it, and busied herself rewrapping their kicking, squirming fifth son in the dry cloth his father had located.

As he'd been before his birth, Billy was active. Even prone, he somehow managed to propel himself from one end of his cradle to the other and back again, driven by a furious urge to control his body. Almost at once he tried to hold his head up, to find and suck a still recalcitrant and wandering thumb. Frustrated in these feats of endeavor by a newborn body, he spent a lot of time squalling. Movement, in the form of rocking, walking, or bouncing seemed to be the only things that quieted him.

His father sat down again to watch this newest Hamilton charge at the other breast. Billy attached himself like a bulldog and then choked as the milk, so rudely summoned, came in a rush and gushed out his nose.

"Haven't I heard that the older you are, the calmer your babies?"

"That's what Mama always said." Betsy adjusted Billy into a more upright position. Even her expertise wasn't always sufficient to master him. His arms and legs churned vigorously, even while nursing, so much so that even in the August heat it was easiest to make a flannel cocoon out of him.

"Look at him. He's frantic, as if I've been ignoring him for the last hour instead of picking him up at the first squawk."

"Yes. He always starts with a roar. I've never seen a baby go from a deep, peaceful sleep straight into howling without as much as a note of prelude. Clearly, this is a fellow of the most ardent and resolute opinions."

"Just like his father, I'd say."

Hamilton responded by leaning to drop a contrite kiss upon the top of his wife's head.

* * *

Betsy was grateful for Hamilton's attorney's salary that allowed her to have more help here than she'd ever had before. With this energetic and demanding new baby, she'd need all the assistance she could get.

Her husband took his turn rocking the cradle, as he'd always done. He even encouraged Phil to try his hand at soothing this new baby brother.

"It's good practice." Hamilton watched as Philip carried his tiny, complaining sibling back and forth across the Turkish carpet. "You don't want to be as nervous as I was with you, do you? Why, I'd hardly ever touched a baby before your grandmother handed you to me. Mama could tell some funny stories about how awkward I was. It was fortunate that you liked to be cradle rocked. It felt safe doing that."

"The truth of it is that cradle rocking can be done with a foot while reading law." Betsy smiled at the memory. "Phil, dear, you always were such an amiable fellow, you took to whatever your father did."

"And you were a much easier baby than this wild boy. A little rocking, a little supper, and you quite reasonably went off to sleep."

Phil's dark brows pinched with alarm as Billy groaned, wiggled and banged his head against his brother's shoulder. Every grunt, every head bang, seemed to signal either one of his now well-known fits of spitting up or of relieving himself with such a vengeance that the mess usually shot out one leg of the diaper.

"Don't worry, Phil." Angelica advised, watching her brother's apprehensive face. "Just jiggle him while you walk." She shared a woman-to-woman glance with her mother. "And," she added, "Whatever you do, don't stop."

It was very domestic, a warm time together, but Betsy knew Hamilton was writing, up till late every night. He said it was a political pamphlet, but she feared it was about that shameful business with Mrs. Reynolds.

Letters passed between Hamilton and Colonel Jackson almost every day. Just as ominous, a servant carried in a copy of Mr. Callender's incendiary, libel-filled newspaper. Hamilton read that, too, and then paced and raved.

Finally, when Billy was barely a month old, the other shoe, the one on which Betsy had been waiting, dropped.

"You're going to publish this?"

Betsy already knew the answer to the question. She let the papers fall onto the table, unable to continue reading. First, it was long, and second, the embarrassing and confounding content was like some cheap novel. Was all that scene by scene recounting necessary? Did it not make the unfaithful husband—and his betrayed wife—into a laughing stock? The little she'd read left her feeling as if he'd emptied a pail of filthy water over her head.

They were alone in his study, a summer storm threatening. Phil, Alex and James were now gone back to school. Johnny was at her sister's. Angel was sitting in the parlor rocking Billy, whose whirlwind body had just found repose.

"Yes, and I'm ashamed to my soul. I'd give anything to live that year over again. But they've forced my hand by suggesting I've stolen public money. Because Monroe and Jefferson are habitual liars, they can't imagine I'd dare tell the truth, especially about something like this. Well, I'm going to surprise them. After this, it will be known that I'm a damned fool and a damned sinner, but no damned thief."

Her husband apparently thought the speech very fine, but the look in Elizabeth's eyes showed him otherwise.

"Oh, Eliza."

He reached for her small hands, wanting very badly to cover them with kisses, but, steeling herself, she turned away.

"You will do what you see as your duty, Mr. Hamilton, of that I have no doubt. Thank you for the courtesy of preparing me."

There she stood, at a not-to-be-crossed distance, diminutive and erect, daughter of van Rensselaers and Schuylers. She knew that he desperately wanted to throw his arms around her, but the way she'd spoken let him know he'd better not.

Turning her back on him, she went to lean against the sill, to stare through the wobbly six over six glass. Appropriately, a late summer downpour began. The street streamed with people: vendors, merchants, children, sailors, chickens, horsemen, dogs and drivers, all rushing for cover. The rain was so loud that for once the din of the city was nearly drowned.

398

"Monroe's slanders have forced you to it." Slowly, she turned to face him again. "Does Philip know? Do Alex? James? They'll be endlessly tormented, you know."

Hamilton, one hand resting on the table, stood beside the table where she'd sat and studied the interminable pamphlet. His face had gone scarlet to the hair-line.

"I talked to the boys the day before they went off to school. I explained to them that my unforgivable sin is justly punished, not only by this humiliating trap devised by my enemies, but every day in witnessing the pain I've given the best of women, their mother."

"And the duel?" Betsy lifted her chin, brushing his apology aside. "What about that?"

She knew he was weak now, that he would not be able to tell a gallant lie.

"Please don't worry. Colonel Jackson seems to have the matter well in hand."

Betsy understood from this remark that the seconds were negotiating, attempting to avoid the actual confrontation.

"But I shan't settle for less than an apology. Either that, or Monroe will rest under the fine and much deserved title of liar."

There was a pause. Rain and wind rattled the windows.

"Mr. Hamilton, may I ask who Mr. Monroe's second is?"

Alexander removed his handkerchief and wiped his eyes.

"Colonel Burr is Monroe's second, Ma'am."

Betsy felt a chill. The brilliant and able Mr. Burr was now a dangerous player for the other political side.

She knew that Hamilton had grown to detest his old comrade-in-arms, to believe that he was a public man operating without principles. As such, he'd be a great danger to their new Republic. Burr seemed interested for the most part in gaining power and not very particular about how he got it. She knew her husband feared Burr as an "embryo Caesar," a man who talked "liberty" but whose true aim was to line his own pockets at public expense.

The dislike Betsy had learned to feel for their always charming, witty, high-living neighbor had become visceral lately, but for her own reasons. Colonel Burr's manners were impeccable, his presence pleasing, his New England pedigree distinguished, his dark eyes come-hither and his conversation always amusing. Nevertheless, Betsy had heard far too many stories about ladies who had lost their peace of mind to Aaron Burr. Yielding to him ended in heart-break and scandal.

Colonel Burr treats everything like a game....

"Please don't worry, my dear. Burr won't let it come to the interview. The dexterous counselor will find a way to slide Monroe out of it."

* * *

Hamilton was traveling again. Trials took him out of town, but Betsy knew that politics, of course, was mixed up in it too. Then Philip fell sick with a persistent fever and was sent home from school. Betsy had him to care for as well as the new baby.

Any threat to Phil, Angelica took personally. She was, much to everyone's surprise, a constant in the sickroom. Betsy was happy for her help, and Phil seemed much easier with his sister present. The almost physical connection that had existed between them for so many years had never really broken.

During Phil's illness, Angelica seemed perennially weary, but she didn't fall apart under the strain, although Betsy feared it. Sitting in bed at night, talking with her wakeful daughter and nursing William Stephen, Betsy felt a deeper closeness with Angelica than ever before. Together they were sharing the burdens and cares of the household.

In spite of all vigilance, Phil's fever rose to a great pitch. He tossed and babbled crazily. From his trial in Hartford, Hamilton wrote letters full of medical advice. When the fever grew very high, their New York doctor, Doctor Hosack, agreed to try the West Indian treatment. Bark was administered and every occurrence of high fever was met by immersion in a cold bath.

By the time Hamilton came home, their treasured eldest was on the mend, sitting up in bed. Angelica was a constant companion, reading to him and seeing that the kitchen produced whatever her brother craved.

"You'd never believe how grown-up Angelica was," Betsy told her husband. "She took such good care of Phil. I don't know how I would have managed without her."

Together they shared a surge of relief and happiness. Perhaps their anxious, fearful daughter would mature normally after all.

* * *

Angel, wearing a white high-waist dress of fine muslin, played the fortepiano, the one sent from London by her namesake Aunt. It was, they understood, by a famous maker, a musician himself, an Italian called Clementi. It had been clear to Betsy that her sister had meant to impress with that bit of information. Knowing a little of the world her sister inhabited, it was beyond a doubt, a *very good thing* to be a fortepiano made by Clementi. However, on this side of the water, that could only be conveyed by tone and delivery, not by an appeal to some widely known celebrity.

They'd recently begun subscribing to concerts given in the City by the Haydn society, which Angel adored. At home husband and daughter often made a very fine picture playing together, which they did in the evenings when Phil was gone. Hamilton sang well, Betsy thought, and Angel loved to accompany him. Very often now, in the excellent illumination provided by a pair of attached oil lamps—*so much better than the flickering vagary of candlelight*—they sat happily side by side. They were both fair and fine-drawn, and both had elegant long fingers. Similarities between father and daughter were ever more remarked upon as time passed.

On this evening, Phil was at his sister's side. Company had come for supper, her sister and her husband, John Church, and their oldest son, another Philip. (Calling "Phil!" among a group of this generation of cousins always led to the turning of a great many heads.) Everyone had dressed for the special occasion and the younger Angelica's hair had been specially arranged. Two fine braids had been looped about her head to form a classical crown. One ringlet, the kinks smoothed by a careful application of a curling iron, trailed over her shawled shoulder, a ribbon of red. The older Angelica looked on approvingly, for after a life in Paris and London among high society, even in daytime, fine clothes and careful makeup were not optional. She and her husband were always beautifully attired.

Hamilton and her older sister had already indulged themselves in their usual bout of banter and flirtation at dinner, Church and Betsy looking on and occasionally sharing a look. As always, it was like watching a play, watching those two—risqué and worldly. John always seemed to find it amusing, watching men fall all over themselves to flirt with his wife. He, a fine-looking man in his own right, apparently didn't feel in the least threatened. Betsy knew how much Angelica adored being the center of attention. She was fluent, almost as daring in her remarks as the men she loved to provoke and lead on. It was, she'd often thought, as if her sister was a rare native species that John had collected during his initial flight to America those many years ago, a treasure he could display at the extravagant parties they still gave. John, like his wife, had an apparently limitless store of energy, for he conducted business all day and then gambled at cards all night, a practice to which he was addicted. In so many ways, they were well-matched.

Betsy set down her sewing in order to watch as well as listen, for her daughter at the piano was a being transfigured. Hamilton had early recognized her passion for music. To some extent, he shared it. Their daughter's face was rapt, almost beautiful while she played. Hamilton sat beside Betsy, his eyes closed, his handsome stockinged legs crossed. He'd even leaned back against the pillows.

Betsy thought he was truly listening, for his lips did not move, as they so often did when he was pretending to pay attention while actually thinking about something else. Lately, it might be a brief that occupied him—or a searing indictment of a political rival intended for the newspapers. "Relax" was something her husband never did. It had been an uncommon sight in the days before Angel had become so adept, but, here, *music does serve to calm the savage beast*. The misquote brought a reflexive smile to her lips, but she lifted a hand to conceal it. A smirk at the end of such a lovely musical moment was not even to be contemplated.

"Whatever was that music, my little Angel?" Her sister spoke as soon as it seemed decent to do so, long after the last winged chord quavered out of existence. "It made me feel elated. Gay, like dancing, but sad, too, like a sweet old memory. And how your fingers flew! There were a great many notes."

"That song was composed by a German professor, Herr von Mozart," said Phil. "And you're right, Aunt Angelica, it is most difficult music to play, as is the stuff of all those German professors. I've heard some people say that Herr Mozart's works are even finer than Herr Haydn's."

"I most heartily agree!" Angel was an eager partisan. "Herr Mozart's is the most perfect of all the music I know." Her transparent gray eyes grew dreamy. "I imagine him as a beautiful young man with flowing blonde hair. I see Orpheus—only with a fortepiano, instead of a lyre."

"Oh, indeed?" Philip broke into a rude grin. "I'll wager, Sis, that your Herr Mozart is short, plump, sweaty, and pale as a boiled dumpling, just like all those Pennsylvania Germans."

For the last half-hour they had floated in a world of music and rarified feeling, perhaps a trifle too long for Phil, who prided himself upon his no-nonsense view of life. Although he was tolerant of his sister's flights of fancy, he was not above teasing her, believing, just as the rest of the family did, that she should occasionally descend to earth.

Her husband, suppressing a smile, shook his head at Phil. Angel, unlike her Aunt, did not have a sense of humor with which to defend herself. At the age of seventeen, it seemed unlikely that this necessary buffer would ever develop.

Predictably, Angel protested. "What a piggish thing to say!" Instead of tears, however, Phil found himself on the receiving end of a punch.

"Ow! My arm...I didn't mean— Wait!" Phil, laughing, tried to catch her hands. "Did you learn that from Jamie?"

"You are a boor and an idiot." Angel, precious score pressed close to her flat chest, was on her feet now.

"Philip—"

"Angel—" Betsy cautioned.

"Angelica, dear, come to me, sweetheart!" Her aunt, a little anxious at the outburst, had stretched out her sparkling fingers. "Don't let him upset you!"

"In one way I think Herr Mozart's quite like Orpheus." Having gained a pause by pretending he was about to retract, Philip wickedly ended, "Herr Mozart has also entered the underworld."

Angel turned pale, her body rigid. For a moment, the adults feared what would come next. Angelica's emotions were always passionate. She still wept for days when the latest of her long succession of canaries died. Even fictional characters could summon the most abandoned grief. Reading Shakespeare's tragedies had ended with her being sent home after only a brief stay at that fashionable girl's boarding school. Her grief for Romeo and Juliet, for Lear and Cordelia, had simply been too all-consuming for her instructors to understand.

"You mustn't ever joke about death! It's dangerous!" She sat down again and seized her brother's hands. Gazing deep into his eyes, she spoke intensely. "Some people are just too perfect for this horrid, horrid world. Herr Mozart's music declares to me that he was one of them!"

404

After this stern pronouncement, there was a pause in which Angel closed her eyes and lifted her chin. A shiver went straight through her sparse frame. Betsy, like the other adults in the room, held her breath.

"Well, perhaps your Herr Mozart *was* as handsome as his music is beautiful." Phil, knowing he'd gone too far, contritely bowed his auburn head over his sister's freckled fingers, bestowing a comforting kiss. "I leave it entirely to your splendid imagination, Sis."

"Not imagination!" Angel's eyes flashed open; she stamped her foot. "I know what I know!"

* * *

Hamilton—and Church too—sent warning looks in the young man's direction. The flights of a woman's fancy, her whims and caprices should be—*ought to be*—by the gallant, courteous and always-in-control male—guided and indulged.

"I'm so sorry, dear sister. I confess I am jealous of anyone who can arouse such a passion. His music is absolutely sublime." Phil, being Phil, had picked up the hint.

"Well, you don't deserve it, but because you have apologized, I shall play another one of Herr Mozart's sonatas. If you listen properly, you will hear the sound of true genius." Angel, two red spots blazing on her cheeks, returned to the fortepiano.

"Wait, Sis. Let's try the duet I saw." Phil had a pleasant tenor voice, every bit as good as his father's. He enjoyed showing it off.

The girl beamed; a rare and heart-warming sight. Her moods, Hamilton knew, were powerful, mercurial. He'd caught a disturbing glimpse of his own intense passions in the fragile mirror of his daughter.

"You just want to make sure that you impress Kitty King at her party, naughty fellow!" Angel protested, plucking at Phil's sleeve. Smiling now, her disposition might never have been otherwise.

Swiftly settling in to play again, she began with her customary precise touch. Hamilton indulged in a fleeting fantasy of the notes as butterflies dancing over a sunlit, flower-filled meadow.

Voices of brother and sister joined. Their father prayed that neither of them would ever experience anything as sad as the words:

> *Now you are leaving,*
> *Going far, far away,*
> *And I shall be here alone.*
> *How shall I live,*
> *Beloved,*
> *Always in anguish?*
> *I shall never be happy again;*
> *And you, who knows if you'll*
> *Ever think of me again?*

Hamilton watched the pair with pleasure. Perhaps he hadn't had his daughter's head stuffed with Greek and Hebrew like her dauntingly brilliant neighbor, Theodosia Burr. Still, his musical Angelica was every bit as cultivated as the bluest bloods of the City. Pride in her was followed by a fleeting fear as he pondered the fact that their Angel was of marriageable age. For her, so sensitive, not just anyone would do.

Colonel Burr seemed to be in the process of marrying his adored, highly-educated Theodosia off to a doughy Carolina planter of great wealth and tiny intellect, simply for the sake of the political advantage to be gained by the alliance. Spinning around the apparent paradox, Hamilton imagined he'd at last unraveled it.

Here, once again, was proof of Machiavellian intent, the hallmark of Burr's every action. The ruthlessness of dispatching his elegant, clever, bookish daughter to a boorish planter had another advantage, one not material. As proudly possessive as Burr had always been about his Theodosia, such a match—one guaranteed to leave the girl cold—would ensure that her adoration of her father would remain intact. *Nay, in southern exile, it might even grow!*

His own daughter was not sufficiently sturdy to be traded for advantage. Her anxieties, her absorption in music and her absolute disregard for mundane things like cookery and sewing, would require a husband who was not only well off, but indulgent. Perhaps, he sighed, thinking of the active and unimaginative young men of their circle, she'll never find a husband. It was easier to think with uninterrupted happiness about his son.

Imagine the boy taking the time to know about something as inconsequential and ornamental as music, in addition to the languages, mathematics, history and rhetoric he'd soaked up! My first born will certainly carry on my own service to this country....

Intellectually and physically gifted, his son was certainly destined for great things. Moreover, he was already a long step ahead of his father, for he wouldn't have to overcome poverty and the stigma of a base birth. Alexander Hamilton had lavished love, attention, and the finest education upon Philip, everything for which he himself had had to struggle.

Chapter Nine
Peggy

It was horrible to discover that Betsy's bright, happy sister Peggy had started a decline. Peggy and Stephen had been regular visitors to their home in New York for years, but that spring Stephen came down river alone.

"Peg's extremely sick. I don't want to alarm you, Mrs. Hamilton, but, perhaps you could visit—soon."

Alarmed, Betsy returned to Rensselaerwyck with Stephen. What she saw shocked her. Plump rosy Peggy was now gaunt and listless. She lay in bed or upon a sofa all day, trying to endure a terrible pain that had settled in her abdomen.

The ugly sallow color of her once beautiful skin reminded Betsy of sicknesses she had seen before, the kind she wouldn't wish on anyone. Aaron Burr's only true love, his long dead wife, had turned that awful yellow during her cancer-tortured last year.

Betsy brought Angelica along when she made her first visit to Peggy, but wished, as soon as she saw how it was, that she hadn't. Exactly as she had feared, that same night, the girl's imagination erupted.

Sitting up in bed, holding her sobbing daughter in her arms, Betsy assured the servants who had come running at the sound of those heartfelt, piercing screams, that "it's only one of Miss Angelica's nightmares."

"Aunt Peg was saying good-bye to me." Angel paused to clutch at her mother with fierce desperation. "I bent to kiss her, but—oh, Mama!" A huge shiver arose straight from her core. "Under the nightgown, I saw she was nothing but a skeleton, with a few shreds of flesh. There was a great big worm inside—and it was eating her!" Angel sucked in a panicked breath and rolled her pale eyes toward her mother. "A nasty, huge rose worm!"

Betsy gathered her close, inwardly flinching at the horrible vision, but the nightmare proved to be literally true. The Doctors agreed that Peggy did indeed have a cancer. Her abdomen swelled and she became very weak and languid, unable to get up at all and subsisting mostly upon larger and larger doses of laudanum. Nurses were engaged to tend her.

Her only child, Stephen van Rensselaer IV, was sent to New York City, to the school the younger Hamilton boys attended. Betsy played mother to him. When Stephen van R. wondered how she could manage so many children, Betsy assured him that "I have always found boys easy to have about the house. One more hardly makes any difference."

Of course, she knew that her nephew would be in for a shock. Sharing a bed with his cousins would be just one of the accommodations this pampered only child would have to learn to make.

* * *

Hamilton was again closeted in his study, spending most days there, writing, writing, writing. That closed door was how it had been for as long as she could remember. Betsy, sewing a button onto one of his jackets, sighed. She wondered if it was her imagination, or if he really was busier than when he'd been Secretary of the Treasury. Once Washington had retired, she had hoped he, too, would completely retire from public life and be plain Attorney Hamilton.

Certainly, he had declared that this was his intention, but she should never have believed it. Back in 1783, he'd promised her that after one term in the Congress, he would be done with politics. Thinking of how long ago he'd made that promise, her lips twisted into a wry smile.

These days, John Adams was President. He, a proud New Englander, loathed her husband, had called him "bastard brat of a Scots peddler." Still, from what she knew, her husband was not only head of the Federalist Party, but pulling the strings of Adams's cabinet. Before, no matter how hard her husband and Mr. Jefferson had fought, the ultimate decision had remained with George

Washington. Now, from the tenor of things Hamilton said, as well as the amount of time he spent closeted in his study—not to mention those express riders who carried his letters straight to Washington City—Hamilton, though now behind the scenes, was still attempting to run the government.

He also kept up his law practice and acted as chief party pamphleteer. He churned out pieces for the New York Federalist newspapers. He read ceaselessly: newspapers, briefs, legal decisions, the texts of bills pending in legislatures, both state and national. He didn't seem to sleep at all, and when he did rest, it was mostly on the day bed in his study.

After testing the button for sufficient give, Betsy made a strong the knot and then snipped. The needle returned to the cushion. She soothed the fine material of his navy jacket, taking stock of her work. She had her dear children, had good and trusted maids and the ladies of her church circle, but sometimes she missed younger, gayer days.

When, very occasionally, she and Hamilton went to dinner together at the house of some mutual friend, he'd take her arm and smile, then tease and flirt with her and the other ladies at table, she had the odd feeling that her husband had just returned from a long absence.

Since she knew how hard he toiled to make the government function and how much time he took from his family, the cruel things printed daily in the Republican papers tore her heart. He hid that from her as much as he could, especially because the story about the Reynolds woman was still dredged up again and again.

On the way by ferry to Staten Island to see an end of term exhibition at which James was to give a speech, Betsy had picked up one of those Republican papers, just abandoned and not yet flown into the water. Livie, a new maid, stood forward, leaning on the rail and fighting off the intense motion sickness she suffered. Though knowing what she would find, Betsy had begun, with horrified fascination, to read.

"Alexander Hamilton is a thief who battens upon public monies."

Why, then, do I feed my children bread and butter, stew and fish pies? Why do we live in a little rented house in town, with not enough rooms for all of them—or even enough beds? Why, instead of buying new, do I spend my days mending and patching?

"Alexander Hamilton is an adulterer."

Why should that matter to anyone other than me? If I can go on loving him and bearing his children, then he has forgiveness from the only pertinent judge in this world. And isn't it said that the "noble" Mr. Jefferson uses his slave women in a way my father never did?

"Alexander Hamilton is a low-born foreigner."

He is also a man who has done more and given more than most of America's born first citizens. From the Revolution onwards, this country is all he's cared about. He's given it his passion—his life!

Betsy, jaw clenched, let the paper slip. The last sentence she'd read was straight-out insanity: *Satanic black blood swirls around the monarchial Hamilton's heart."*

The paper, caught by a freshening wind, leapt to take rattling flight into the bay.

Why do they hate him so much, when near every breath he takes is in their service? America is his true mistress, and who should know that better than I?

* * *

The following March, Peggy's torment ended. Hamilton had been in Albany trying a case and had stayed on at the general's house when it became clear how near to death his sister-in-law was. Peggy wasn't always conscious, and her struggles with the pain drew her deeper and deeper into herself. Before she passed away, Betsy came upriver, too. Seeing her sister's wasted form, she again recalled her daughter's horrible nightmare.

"A rose worm, indeed." Hamilton sighed when she'd reminded him. "For a rose was what our Peg always was."

411

At the funeral Betsy was distressed by the behavior of one Miss van Cuyler. The way she and Stephen van Rensselaer were comforting each other left no doubt that as soon as a decent spell of mourning had passed, there'd be a wedding.

"Poor Peg is hardly cold in her grave. Mrs. Church remarked she thought that Anna van Cuyler was awfully prominent, awfully solicitous and awfully—present. And so it seems she's been—the little buzzard."

Surprised by his wife's unusual vehemence, Hamilton opened his mouth and then, just as quickly, shut it. His face showed that he couldn't even begin to think of a reply to this, the most unkind speech he'd ever heard come from his wife's mouth.

Chapter Ten
An Unexplained Absence

Betsy stood on the rise behind her father's house, looking down at the handsome brickwork. The place was quiet these days, and a little down at the heels. Blue sprays of chicory and goldenrod grew at edges of the garden between the kitchen and study wing. Not only the master's children, but most of the servants and their families were gone. The boarded windows of outbuildings and the surrounding nettle-and-wildflower wilderness made mute testament to the fact that these cabins hadn't been tenanted in years.

Where there had been armies of fowl, now a mere dozen red chickens roamed, muttering and scratching in the yard. The barn was in the same state. What had once been bursting with stock, with teams of plowing oxen, with horses for harness and pleasure, with red and white cattle, was now three-quarters empty. There were two carriage horses in the nearby pasture, both handsome fellows, but gray at the muzzle.

In the orchard, the trees seemed ever more crooked and thick. It had been a good year for fruit and the trees were loaded. Betsy had gone with the children of the cook to pick the last apples. They had climbed into the trees and Betsy sorted what they dropped. The most perfect were for eating, the next best for butter, pies and sauce, the rest, worms, scab and all, for the press.

A violent, cold weather change had arrived that afternoon, sending flurries out of the gray western sky. Betsy sent the children and a pony cart loaded with baskets back to the house. She didn't go with them.

Above her head, the clouds lowered and the Hudson below changed from green to gray. In the distance, she could see a small boat diving for the shore. Great oaks and chestnuts higher up groaned. Shivering, even inside a

413

woolen cloak, Betsy sat down behind a tree and wrapped her arms around her knees. The wind was freezing, but she was determined to stay and see the weather come.

She didn't have long to wait. A sudden bitter blast sent sleet and snow into the shriveled leaves. Johnny and Billy were safely in the house. Phil was at Columbia, Alex and James were at Doctor Frazer's school in Trenton. Even Angelica, who hadn't had a bad spell in well over a year, was again in that same finishing school for young ladies which her glamorous aunt had so long ago attended.

Billy was fourteen months old now, but not a bit calmer. An ability to walk and to climb had appeared simultaneously. Unlike the other children, who'd been fairly resigned to the time when they'd been tied to apron strings, from the start, he'd roared like a bull at any attempt made to restrain him.

The poor little nursemaid spent her days chasing him as he toddled indefatigably through her father's house. Her mother complained that Billy had toppled one of her treasured tea sets to messy and tragic ruin on the parlor floor.

"I swear that child could pull the whole house down around his ears if left solitary for five minutes."

While Hamilton was on business in Philadelphia, without so much as a letter or a by-your-leave, Betsy had boarded one of her papa's schooners and sailed to Albany. Hamilton had spent the past year rushing between New York and Philadelphia, politicking day and night for his newest cause, reorganization and proper funding for the army.

The terrible finale he'd prophesied had come in France, which had passed from moderate reform to revolution to orgies of head-chopping, into anarchy, and then onward to Napoleon's aggressive militarism. France was making war war on the world—her old ally, the United States, included.

Against President Adams' will, Hamilton had been made Inspector General of a newly mustered army. As usual, he pursued the task with the determination of a Fury.

414

To support his position, he wrote pamphlets by the score under various *nom de plume*.

Betsy, sitting under the apple trees, hoped he'd be surprised when he'd finally returned home to find only servants in residence. She had not explained to anyone why she had, so suddenly, taken the little ones and sailed upriver.

Bob Troup had instigated her flight. At one of those hard, fashionable New York parties, which, since the Reynolds business, didn't do much except give her a headache, Betsy had been fanning herself and pretending to look out the window as if she were watching for someone to come in from the torch and carriage-crowded courtyard.

She'd tried to ignore the knots of gossip, which, as usual, seemed to have something to do with her husband. In the middle of the room a flock of belles, presided over by her sister Angelica, besieged Hamilton, now resplendent in his new Major General's uniform. Philip Church, her sister's oldest and now Alexander's secretary, looked on with undisguised, youthful amusement at the folly of old men.

Dearly as she loved her older sister, Angelica's behavior often stretched her patience to the breaking point. What on earth was she supposed to make of the letter her sister had recently sent, saying of Hamilton: "I love him very much and if you were as generous as the old Romans, you would lend him to me for a little while."

Betsy was thoroughly sick of "old Romans," and even sicker of contemporaries who attempted to dress up their immorality with these—supposedly joking—appeals to ancient customs.

A tall shadow cast itself over her. "And who is this hiding here? Not Mrs. General Hamilton?"

It was Bob Troup, rounder than ever. Although the lines in his face showed his age, his hair—at least, what was left—was full of playful curls.

"May I ask what Beauty is doing, lingering alone here, unattended?"

He affectionately captured and kissed her hand.

415

"I'm not in the mood tonight. And, you, dreadful flatterer! As you well know, I never was a Belle."

"None of your false modesty, my lady. How else do you suppose you ever caught the roving eye of Alexander Hamilton?"

"I didn't need to be a belle. I was a Schuyler, sir."

As soon as it came out, Betsy frowned. Through the Philadelphia years, through the pain of the other woman, she'd schooled herself to wear a dignity which never allowed anything remotely disloyal to slip.

"Well, Mrs. General, I've come to chat. I thought you looked rather lonely." When he leaned close, she smelled brandy.

"Thank you, Bob, but I'd better stay by myself." She was thoroughly annoyed that he'd slipped through her defenses and that a thimbleful of sympathy from an old friend had been sufficient. "And please disregard what I just said. I am not myself tonight."

"I won't forget, Mrs. Hamilton, although you may have my assurance that I shall never repeat it. But come, Ma'am. Let's walk."

To her surprise, he peremptorily laid a hand on her waist.

"You may have solitude after I speak my piece, but first you and I," he said in a gruff, brotherly fashion, "must have a *tête-à-tête*." Betsy felt her jaw drop when he added, "Aren't you and I the oldest of old friends? Except, perhaps, for our dear strutting Major General."

By the door, Troup turned to take a look at the rout. Hamilton, a little plump these days and at his most animated, was the radiant center of a stellar group of ladies. All the great hoops and panniers of the old regime were gone, and their dresses were now diaphanous folds of sheer white muslin. Low-cut and high-waisted, they turned every young woman into a classical goddess. Hamilton had waxed lyrical about this new fashion.

No getting a pig in a poke these days!

416

It annoyed her every time he, with an irritating male gleam in his eye, repeated it.

Bob steered Betsy into an adjacent parlor. Here they discovered a foursome, young men and their ladies, chattering happily. They looked up for an instant, but neither Attorney Troup nor Mrs. Hamilton was of sufficient interest to hold their attention.

Betsy decided to overlook her companion's odd behavior. Of course, as the closest thing to a brother her husband possessed, he'd always held special privileges. He, after all, shared intimate memories, of college, of the three of them living in that old, drafty Albany house.

"May I ask what this is about?"

"In his youth," Troup intoned, displaying the comic gravity that afflicts a certain level of inebriation, "your husband's single-minded pursuit of fame was a virtue. That boyish flash was a charming means to attain an end. Now, we're all older. Most of us have become dour citizens who approach goals with the subtle treachery of middle age. Hamilton, on the other hand, continues to race about exhaustingly, the same comet he was at eighteen. He's without a doubt the most brilliant person I've ever known, but also the most exasperating. Frankly, everyone marvels at how you endure so patiently his heroic and unflagging public persona, the self-centered eye of every political storm."

"Colonel, I believe you have drunk far too much. Tomorrow, you will most certainly regret it."

"Well, yes, I have drunk too much, Mrs. Major General, but there shall be no regrets." Bob laughed, and then as if to emphasize what he'd said, one big hand came to brush her cheek. "And you know you must never argue with a drunk—it only maddens 'em. So, patiently hear me to the end. It makes me damned cross to see you standing in the corner, that beautiful hair of yours full of silver threads, looking so forlorn."

"Colonel Troup, if you don't stop this minute, I warn you, I shall be forced to discipline you. And I don't want to do that, especially not in front of those children." She indicated the group upon the settee.

"I know you despise drama, but do you think our dear Hamilton would even notice? At this very moment, I believe, he's busy adding to his already excessive reputation for gallantry. The Field of Mars is not yet available to the conqueror, so the Field of Venus will have to do."

He nodded towards the open door, where for an instant Hamilton became visible, dancing by with an elegant society wife on his arm. At the same time, Troup caught her hand and kissed it. For some reason she allowed it, even though the caress was warm, far from the brush of polite formality.

"My advice, dear Eliza, is to make a small scandal yourself. Don't suffer in silence. It only allows him to go frolicking off without a thought in his head except more of his endless quest for glory."

"You are absolutely astonishing!" Betsy drew herself up to every inch of her five feet and tried fixing him with her severest daughter-of-the-Patroons stare. "That you should say such things! You, his oldest friend! You know Hamilton, how brave he is, how gifted—and how great! In spite of the lies that wicked Jefferson spreads about him, there's no one who has sacrificed more to preserve this country—no one—with the exception of General Washington."

"Absolutely. I'd never dispute that. The fact that you still have to pinch and scrape to feed and clothe your brood should be sufficient proof to all doubters of his high-minded probity in office. I don't deny any of what you've just said, but tonight I'm not interested in the deserved glory of our friend. A fine woman like you shouldn't be standing alone on the edge of a party like someone's jilted sweetheart."

As he'd been speaking, the young people arose as one and romped past them, on their way to the ballroom. Only one, a slender girl, probably the youngest, cast a backward, curious glance in their direction.

"Does it really look that bad?"

Bob kept hold of her hand.

Everything conspires to unhinge me! All at once, she'd felt a powerful need for her handkerchief. Bob released her hand just long enough to present his.

"Well, it's not quite that bad, but I do hate the sight of women in tears—unlike your husband who usually finds it an opportune moment to make love to them."

Without a moment's hesitation, Betsy smacked him. She intended to follow this with flight, but Troup's long arms simply gathered her close.

"That's right, Eliza. Show your spirit!"

"Colonel Troup!"

"Ah, Madame, restrain your wrath 'till your old friend has given counsel. The next time Hamilton goes trotting off to Washington City to have a wonderful big brawl with John Adams or Jefferson's minions, you take your babies and go to Albany. Don't say a word. Just go. It'll throw a good scare into him."

Betsy was so astonished that she made no further attempt to escape.

"Go away? And not tell my husband?"

"Yes. He'd be the only person in our circle who would be amazed if you went home to your father and stayed there."

"How dare you, sir?"

"In my humble opinion, you took all those lectures he used to give about noble Roman wives far too seriously. The truth is you're a far greater Stoic than he is."

Betsy wanted to weep. Troup, relentless, pursued.

"Why do you let him run wild?"

"No one can keep Alexander from what he wants. I've enough problems of my own without starting a domestic war."

"There's talk, you know."

"There's always talk. He's never had a reputation for— for—"

419

"Chastity." Troup filled in the blank.

The well he'd tapped was so deep and so full that Betsy couldn't fight anymore. Now that there were no witnesses in the room, so she rested her head upon his chest and released a few tears.

"I love him so much. You—you, of all people—should know."

"Oh, my dear! All his friends love him. He dazzles us with his mind, charms us with his wit, astonishes us with his passion and his genius, and then, when we're on our knees before him, he kicks dirt all over us. Nevertheless, you've kept your dignity. There isn't a man I know, who doesn't call you the quintessence of what a wife should be, but even after all these years you still haven't learned the best way to deal with him."

Betsy raised her eyes, stinging with tears and full of questions.

"Punish him for his disregard. Don't you understand? You're the only person in the world he's truly afraid of. As it stands now, he thinks he can always come back."

"But, Bob, he <u>can</u> always come back. I need him. I love him."

"And you are absolutely essential to him. You may rely upon it."

"I'm no coquette. I never have been." Betsy blew her nose.

"Just go to Albany."

"But, that's wrong! That's what I did before and it led to all those—awful problems. He was alone and it isn't safe to leave a man—of his temperament—alone."

What she couldn't say was that she had sworn, after the business with that low slut and her criminal husband, never to leave her husband's side again.

"I'm not talking about an expedition for the health of the children. Go home to your papa and stay there until he comes and begs you to come home. He needs you, but he forgets that he does."

Footsteps approached, so Bob stepped back. As a flushed couple came through the door and then looked disappointed to find the room occupied, he whispered, "May I have the next dance, Mrs. Hamilton?"

His long face was solemn, but those dark eyes of his were full of laughter.

"I'm out of humor, Colonel." All at once, she was furious with him.

"Never mind, my darling. A dance will set you right."

Before she could escape, he'd appropriated her hand firmly and refused to let it go. To forestall any gossip, she was forced to accompany him onto the floor and tread a measure.

* * *

She had been angry with Bob, but the seed of rebellion had been successfully planted. Now, here she sat at Papa's, on the cold ground, back against an apple tree, watching just the smallest bit of sleet fall while dry leaves whirled aimlessly.

Betsy missed Peggy more than ever. As much as she loved Angelica, she had lately been driven to admit that Angelica was part of her problem. While John Church worked hard at his insurance by day and his gambling by night ("two closely related enterprises," Hamilton had wittily observed), Angelica held court in her gilded parlor. Hamilton gaily paid respects to his Church sister-in-law almost every day and flirted with her outrageously whenever they met.

Gossip, *naturally*, was rampant. Dearly as she loved both of them – well, sometimes, it was too much. Most likely, Betsy thought bitterly, all I've done by coming here is get out of their way….

It had been a month since she'd come up river. Although Hamilton had written the usual "dearest Eliza" letter, she was still waiting to see if he could tear himself away long enough to present himself in Albany. At the beginning of the week just passed, she'd had a letter from Troup.

"Stick to your guns, Mrs. Major General. Stay in the fort! No running to New York to surrender, before the dense fellow even understands that this is war. Stiffen your resolve! If you do not, I swear my wife and I shall have no further truck with you, dear and long-time friend though you are."

* * *

"May I ask what this means? Just one of your little scratchings propped on my desk when I return from Philadelphia?"

This very morning she had been thinking that he would never come, but he'd arrived in the afternoon, blowing in on that same flurry of early cold. Gray silvered his foxy hair, although his blue eyes were as brilliant as ever. At this moment they were flashing wonderfully, but the intent was not to charm.

The venue was her papa's study. Betsy had chosen it for this discussion, much preferable to the bedroom. There, he always had her at a disadvantage.

"You don't have to be nasty about my letter. It's no secret that I've never been much of a writer."

"Well, it didn't tell me anything. I've worried."

"Not much, it seems. It took you over a month to get here."

Her tone surprised him. With a rush of satisfaction, she noted that he was on the verge of losing his temper.

"Well, I didn't know I was supposed to come after you. Did you say anything about that? All you said was that you were going to Albany with the little ones. What was I supposed to make of that? That you enjoy being here is no secret. I supposed you wanted to spend some time with your parents. Then Troup starts needling me, saying that I'm such a clever fellow, but apparently not clever enough to see that my wife's run off." He stopped pacing and swung around to face her. "Have you run off?"

"Yes. I believe I have." Betsy ran her fingers slowly across the satiny surface of a maple table which had stood in this room ever since she could remember.

"Well…what?" He sputtered to a halt. Clearly, he hadn't expected that. "You must come back. The boys will be home from school soon and—and—I—I need you. You know I'm involved in all this business, this ungodly mess with the army, the newspaper correspondence, pulling McHenry's strings at War, advising Wolcott at Treasury and Pickering at State, all of us hoping that self-righteous lunatic Adams doesn't blow everything up in our faces. Some of the New England Federalists are talking secession. I'm writing to Christopher Gore, hoping they can put a stop to it. I don't have time for—whatever this is."

"Yes, you do, Mr. Hamilton, unless you want me to remain here."

He looked astonished and then, swiftly, angry.

"Mrs. Hamilton, I thought it has been determined that your absences have been the cause of much trouble."

"Are we speaking of that low Reynolds woman?"

The name brought him toward her, splendid eyes flashing. He looked as if he wanted to chastise her, perhaps not actually to strike her, but give her a shaking.

"Yes! Yes! Fool, dupe, and unshriven sinner that I am." Before he got to her, he dropped into a chair, where he passed a hand across his face. "I'm not a monk, as I'm sure our long association has taught you. It's most difficult not to get into some scrape while you're gone."

Betsy continued to trace the burls in the grain of the table with a finger.

"I believe," she said severely, "that you manage all sorts of adventures even while I'm at home. And what you say hurts me, Hamilton. Am I just a convenience to you? A wife, so you don't need to risk your health at a brothel?"

"Elizabeth! Good heavens…."

"Don't lie. Are you really so different from the other men in our circle? 'Rarely' is perhaps a truer word than never, sir. And why only rarely? Because the finest drawing rooms in New York are open to you?"

Hamilton blinked, momentarily stunned. He was not the kind of man, however, to shirk a challenge.

"Is it to be the unvarnished truth, then, Mrs. Hamilton?"

"Why not, sir? We've been married for a good many years."

"Every time you are pregnant, Elizabeth, I'm afraid. Afraid I'll lose you."

"And so you restrain yourself."

When he nodded, with a fleeting expression of self-pity, she countered, "Your restraint, however, seems only to extend to me."

Once more I've scored.

Shame coursed over his mobile features.

"That's the way it's done, Eliza. Men have needs."

"Women have needs, too, or there would be no one to commit the sin of adultery with."

For a heart-beat he gaped. Then, he threw back his head and laughed.

"Dear Heaven! The unvarnished truth, indeed."

He sprang to his feet and caught her in his arms. She thumped his chest twice with both fists, but he held her tight.

"Don't! Don't you dare laugh at me and then kiss me!"

"I'm not laughing at you, Eliza. What you just said is God's honest truth, something which no one, for some reason or other, ever says."

Betsy wasn't mollified. She struggled, tried to get a hand free for a slap. "I hate you when you are unfaithful. I try to remain above it, but I always know when it happens and I'm sick with jealousy and anger. Why can't you be chaste? I am, and I'm certain it's just as hard for me."

She succeeded in pushing him away, or, perhaps, he simply let her go. At any rate, they stood quite still now, staring at each other, a little out of breath.

"Quite an unconventional conversation for a man and wife, but the truth *is* refreshing."

"I understand your work for the army is necessary for the safety of the country." Betsy continued the attempt to maintain her distance, her dignity. "I just want you to remember who truly loves you, has always loved you, Alexander Hamilton. You should know how deeply you have hurt me."

"You're right, dear one. Although I don't deserve it, I here and now beg that you forgive me and, further, that you will allow me to accompany you home to New York with our children."

In an elegant gesture, Hamilton bowed his head before lifting his wife's fingers to his lips. Those blue eyes sought her gaze, but Betsy thought she recognized his oratorical persona taking hold.

I distrust you most in that mode.

"I love you. I can't live without you. You are the best of women. It's been wrong and cruel of me to take advantage of the nobility and patience which you so reliably display."

"So!" She stamped her foot and firmly backed away. "The reward of the good and dutiful Aquilaea is disregard and infidelity! I say *damn you*, Mr. Hamilton."

* * *

They spent the dark afternoon in this fashion. Hamilton was gallantly understanding, apologetic, tender, and finally, when all else failed, seductive. Only a few days later, the couple were on their way down the river, pushed along by a ferocious north wind which had brought the first snow to Albany.

Betsy stood on the deck of the sloop as they rounded craggy West Point and watched the clouds, a dark line to the north. She feared that nothing had really changed.

How I wish I was back in Albany, watching the snow! Oh, to be buried, trapped, surrounded by that clean glittering white, to not be going back to the city, that place where intrigues boil, where the press of events will carry my husband away.

* * *

425

In the warmth of his renewed attentiveness, another child came. To everyone's surprise after the long string of sons, Betsy gave birth to a daughter. Unlike Angelica, this little girl was like her mother, born with slate-colored eyes and dark hair.

"A Catherine for my dear Mama." Betsy's lips brushed the fuzzy head of her baby.

"At the risk of seeming a domineering brute, I wish to—respectfully—disagree." Hamilton gazed tenderly at the two of them.

"What?" Not an hour beyond childbirth, Betsy's dark eyes flashed.

How dare he argue, when, at last, I have a daughter to name?

"There are already Catherines aplenty among the cousins. I want to name this little nut-brown maid after her mother, the finest woman God ever fashioned." Hamilton bent close, his smile encompassing mother and child in a radiant circle. "Why, look at her, so dainty and dark. She must look exactly as you did when you were newborn."

"But...."

"No, no, my dear wife, I absolutely insist."

Despite her best effort, annoyance was soon overcome by something like pleasure.

"But not another 'Elizabeth'. That wouldn't feel right."

"We shall christen her 'Eliza'." Alexander stooped to kiss the top of the baby's downy damp head. "And she shall grow to be as beautiful, as generous, as courageous and strong, as her mother."

Chapter Eleven
A Country House

"I beg you, as you love your country, your friends, and yourself, to reconsider dispassionately the opinion you have expressed in favor of Burr...."—To Theodore Sedgwick, January 21, 1801

* * *

The election of 1802 was a losing, rear-guard action for the Federalists. The popular party, the Democratic-Republicans, carried the day. However, before the outcome of the race for President could be decided, a constitutional crisis had to be unraveled. As it was then written, the man who garnered the most votes would be president, and the second place finisher would become the Vice President.

There were four candidates, President John Adams, Aaron Burr, Thomas Jefferson, and Charles Pinckney. Jefferson out-polled all the others, but after the Electoral College vote, he and Aaron Burr were tied, throwing the decision to the House. It took thirty-six ballots in the House of Representatives to decide the issue. Hamilton, when consulted by his party, wrote that although he disliked them both, he did not trust Burr, a man whose only aim appeared to be personal power, "a la Bonaparte." In the end, a single congressman changed his vote, and Thomas Jefferson became third President of the United States.

* * *

"Truly, my dear sir, the prospects of our country are not brilliant. The mass is far from sound. At headquarters a most visionary theory presides. ... No army, no navy, no active commerce; national defense not by arms but by embargoes, prohibition of trade, etc.; as little government

as possible within; —these are the pernicious dreams which, as far and as fast as possible, will be attempted.... Mr. Jefferson is distressed at the codfish having latterly emigrated to the southern coast, lest the people there be tempted to catch them, and commerce, of which we have 'already too much,' receive an accession. Be assured this is no pleasantry, but a very sober anecdote."— To Rufus King

* * *

"Come quick, Ma'am! Come quick!" cried the Anneke. "Miss Angel is havin' a fit!"

Betsy dropped her mending and raced down the hall after Anneke's flying skirts. In the good parlor they found Angel running in circles, cap gone, hair loose and streaming. The white muslin dress fluttered as she ran. Grim-faced, Johnny begged her to stop.

A knot tied in Betsy's stomach. She'd seen this too many times recently not to know how it would end.

"Angel! Angelica! Stop now!"

Her daughter paid no attention, just continued to circle wildly. She laughed, only it wasn't really a laugh. Harsh, loud, the sound was just a hair's breadth from a scream.

"Angelica! I said stop!"

Angel began to spin like a top, arms extended, hair and skirts flying.

Betsy might have grabbed her, but she was afraid. If thwarted in this state, Angelica was liable to hit, and hit hard, too. Everyone in the family had taken bruises from her.

"Johnny! Come here! Let her be!" With a lunge, Betsy removed him from his sister's orbit. For a moment she and Anneke stood, helplessly watching as Angel spun faster and faster.

Abruptly, as Betsy had known it would, the whirling stopped. The girl staggered, swayed, and pressed hands to her high white forehead.

428

"Oh, no! I tried. I tried. It's still here! It's too light—light and right, light and tight-fight-smite, bite-bite-bite!"

She sank to her knees, wrapped her arms around her body and panted. Once down, she rocked, hard and rhythmically.

Betsy came cautiously, knelt and put her arms around the rigid, swaying body. Once before, during a protracted spell of this, Angel had suddenly lashed out and hit her mother. Despite Betsy's embrace, the rocking went on. The thin body in her arms was now hard and unyielding as stone.

"Heavy! Too heavy! It's all light and heavy, light and heavy, light and heavy, light and heavy! Crushing me...."

"Hush, darling. Mama's here."

Angel continued to rock. Her words died to a mutter. After a few minutes of this, Betsy spoke to the maid. "Anneke, take Johnny away and bring me Miss Angel's medicine."

"Not that!" Angel screamed. "Not medicine! It sinks me! Drowns me in ditch water! I won't! You don't want me in slime, do you? Not with them! **Not with them!**"

"No medicine." Betsy tried to maintain her hold. "Just come to bed, my Angel. I'll stay with you and you can rest."

"Rest?! I can't! You know I can't! You can hold me. Papa can hold me—no help anywhere. Phil! Phil! They are in my head, won't go away. Right here! Here! Dear! Fear! Peer! Leer! Queer! Mere! Here! Here! *Here!*"

The girl hit Betsy with such force that she fell at full length onto the floor. With a bound Angel's long, coltish form sprang away. There were pounding feet, and then the door crashed as she went storming out of the room.

"Gussie!" Betsy cried at the top of her lungs. "Anneke! Help!"

As she struggled to her feet, Betsy heard a commotion in the corridor. Anneke shouted, "No, Missy! No! Stop, now!" Next came the sound of breaking glass along with a crash as the front door was flung wide.

Angel, flying through the corridor, had met Anneke with the medicine. Like a runaway horse, she'd plunged into her, knocking the bottle out of her hand. Anneke outweighed Angelica by a good forty pounds, but the force of the collision staggered her.

Johnny had gone manfully charging after his sister, but what this slight little fellow could have done except follow was questionable. Fortunately, among the young men who were just turning onto the Broadway was Phil, returning in company with his cousins, Philip Church and John Schuyler.

"Phil!" Angel cried. She leapt against her beloved big brother's chest like a large, mannerless dog. "Phil!"

Philip took one look at his sister's loosened hair, at Johnny and Anneke in pursuit, and knew what had happened. He threw his arms around her.

"Come on, Sis. Hush now. Let's go home."

To the questioning eyes of his cousins, he sent a warning shake of his dark head. With an arm firmly around her waist, he set off toward home. Angel, as docile now as she had been wild an instant before, went with him. She pressed against him close, like a lover.

* * *

"I don't know what would have happened if Phil hadn't come home. She just threw me off."

"Have these spells been coming with more frequency?" The doctor peered over his spectacles.

"Yes."

"And the hysterical laughter is followed by wild activity and then depression?"

"Yes, always. As you see, she's in bed sleeping. She'll sleep all day and prowl the house at night. Nothing we do or say seems to help. Sometimes I'll find her huddled behind a chair like a stray cat. When she's like that, nothing she says makes sense and she won't eat. You can see how thin she is. In a week or so she comes out of it, although

430

she's quiet for a long time and practices her music very hard, sometimes for twenty hours at a stretch. Thank heaven she plays well, for sometimes she gets stuck on a passage and repeats it until we're all ready to go and shake her teeth out."

"Of course," Hamilton said, taking his wife's shoulders firmly in hand, "we don't. She seems to be soothing herself with the music, and, frankly, almost anything is better than the times when she's frightened or starving herself, but the spells when she's—when she's—herself—are briefer."

Hamilton stopped and looked at his wife for confirmation. A little guiltily, Betsy thought.

Her husband had spent all spring up river in a fruitless campaign effort for his brother-in-law, Stephen van Rensselaer, who, despite everything he said or wrote, had lost to George Clinton (in landslide) the Governorship of New York. With these blows at the ballot box, the once mighty Federalist Party's power had evaporated, her husband's influence along with it. Hamilton was still writing furious editorials for the newspapers. It was now, suddenly, a last ditch rearguard political action, but he wouldn't—or couldn't—give up.

"Normally, our Angelica's very docile, very affectionate," Hamilton said. "She reads a great deal, practices her music assiduously—she's very talented—but she's always been sensitive, easily frightened by things she saw or read. Lately, there has been a change, though. She's not usually loud or wild, but if she is, we know that within a few hours she'll be in tears and buried in that terrible depression. This is the first time she's run away. Is there something we should be giving her that would help? Especially if we think we see a fit coming?"

"The medicine we have been using frightens her, Doctor," Betsy said. "I think she ran because Anneke was bringing it."

"Yes, she used to take it without question if Fanny brought it to her, but since our Fanny's married young Arthur Tappan and left us...."

431

Hamilton nodded. Then he explained what the medicine contained. Dr. Hosack agreed that something less powerful might be in order. Two tinctures were prescribed. The first, compounded of hops, lettuce and valerian was for her insomnia. The second, of Jersey tea, passion flower and fit-root was for the times when the strange restlessness came on. He recommended that the old mixture, heavy with laudanum, not be used unless Angel was in danger of harming herself or others.

* * *

I am always happy My Dear Eliza when I can steal a few moments to sit down and write to you. You are my good genius; of that kind which the ancient Philosophers called a familiar; and you know very well that I am glad to be in every way as familiar as possible with you. I have formed a sweet project, of which I will make you my confident when I come to NY, and in which I rely that you will cooperate with me cheerfully. "You may guess and guess and guess again; Your guessing will be still in vain." But you will not be the less pleased when you come to understand and realize the scheme. Adieu best of wives & best of mothers, Heaven ever bless you and me in you....

During a restful retreat north into Harlem heights to escape the fever and the worst of the summer, they'd shared a farmhouse with the Churches. Here, Hamilton was seized with a notion to build for himself. Betsy, after a survey of from her own household accounts, would now see her ordinarily frugal husband at his standing desk with house plans spread before him, or taking time to visit architects he knew through business, or old friends who had built. Whenever he'd travel up river or ride into Connecticut on legal business, he'd return with drawings of homes that he'd visited. Now that the world of politics had turned and cast him out, she hoped his boundless energy might finally turn toward some quieter field of endeavor.

Doctor Hosack, who also served as a professor of Botany at Columbia, had begun a botanical garden, with greenhouses and tropical plants about three miles from the city limits. The family visited with the younger children, for the doctor, who was also a family friend, had sent a note to say that he had acquired some new plants and would welcome a visit.

William and John came with them in the carriage, while Betsy sat contentedly. At the moment, Hamilton's attorney's salary made domestic matters easier. Baby Eliza was today in care at the house of a friend. She was not yet two, a tiny little creature with dark eyes. Betsy wouldn't ordinarily have left her, but otherwise it would have been too long a day out for a toddler. Betsy knew she'd pay the price later in milk discomfort. She had been in no hurry to wean her youngest, but this outing was to be an unaccustomed break from child care.

"And what do you see over there, Johnny?" Hamilton engaged the boys with conversation along the way. Billy sat on his right, Johnny on the left. Both leaned against their father.

"An old Dutch windmill, Papa, lifting water. You took us to see it."

The road came sufficiently close to the structure that they could hear the gears creaking and squealing. Patched sails rotated sluggishly; the wind was slight. Even above the sounds of carriage and hooves, there came the faint splash as intermittent gushes of water entered a holding pond.

"See? It's almost full." Her husband pointed to a place where water lapped high on a ring of cattails.

Billy, craned and gazed, jaw-dropped at the size of the building with its great sails. He'd been precariously transferring from her side to Hamilton's, requiring attention from one or the other of them, but now he stopped. A few months ago, on their last trip out, the family had gone inside, so the boys could observe it working. Billy, though so young, still talked about the experience. Father and sons stared back for a time as if loathe to let the great machine recede from sight.

Dust banged up from the hooves and floated along beside them. It might be spring, but there'd been a dry spell. Today had dawned clear again, which made it perfect for a drive. Sunlight poured down, shining on her husband and sons, there in the front of the calash.

Their friend, Doctor Hosack, was a busy man. He taught at the old King's College, now rechristened Columbia. He maintained a private practice and was raising a large and growing family—he had more children at home than did the Hamiltons—even with the three upstate cousins the family had taken in so they could attend good city schools. As both the men were habitually engaged, this visit had been carefully arranged. "Spontaneous" only happened when her sister Angelica and her husband arrived on the scene, and, Betsy thought, most of the time, that was the way she preferred things.

Soon, they drew up to the tall central building flanked by single-story extension with slanting glass roofs. Around the grounds, men were digging, apparently at work on creating a tulip garden. The doctor's carriage was visible at the end of the drive, so their coachman made for that.

"Ah, here you are, my dear friends! Punctual as always."

The doctor, tall, long-headed and rather portly for such a young man, came forward to greet them. Between them, he and Hamilton helped Betsy and the children down and then ushered them through the door of the nearest hot house.

Every time she visited, Betsy was amazed by the odd sensation—the humidity, the softness and fragrance of the air—at whatever season. And this building was full of tropical plants, palms and other unfamiliar vegetation, all set about in tubs and planters. Alexander was at once intrigued by something about the way the glass was supported. His friend, William, seemed primed for the subject too, but occasionally, they'd stop talking construction and remark upon a plant.

434

Some of the palms were actually getting quite tall. Johnnie thought so too.

"They will have to use a ladder to top it or it will hit the roof."

"I don't believe you can do that to a palm tree, so I'm not sure what they'll do when it grows so high. You'll have to ask your father or Doctor Hosack."

The men were ahead, pointing to the cast iron ceiling joints, apparently the latest thing. She followed, breathing deeply as she moved through the strange damp atmosphere.

"Oh look! Here are the lemon trees." Johnny, having made the trip before, could show off what he'd learned. She smiled down at his thin, bright face. The blade shaped bright leaves were lovely to view, especially this early in spring when color outside were still sparse.

"Yes, young man, those are the lemons and close by, the limes, both just now setting fruit." Hosack stopped and turned. He, like her husband, was frank and open with children, and ready to encourage Johnny's interest. Billy, however, tugged at her hand like a puppy on a leash. It was as if he had an imaginary goal in mind, even though he'd never been inside the place.

Betsy paused and bent down to him. "Be a good boy, Bill, and stop pulling at me. Walk properly."

All Hamilton had to do was to turn and send a single look to complete the small discipline. *Billy might sass the maids,* Betsy thought, *but he never even considers acting up around his father.* It was good, she'd decided, that Hamilton would be at home more as this son grew.

"And here we are, just over here." Hosack indicated a group of large earth-filled tubs. "My newest acquisitions. I wonder if you can recognize any of them?"

The plants were barely more than sticks, though they all were bravely sprouting leaves.

"For instance, is this one familiar?"

"Well!" Hamilton said, studying the tub's occupant, "I never thought to see one of those again."

"They are easy to transport of course. No beautiful flowers, but I thought the plant itself, and the way its fruit is used for food, most interesting."

* * *

Hamilton took a deep breath as he recognized it. He heard himself speak, distantly: *This is breadfruit.* The taste came back abruptly, as if it was only yesterday. Breadfruit could be tasty, yes, with plenty of pepper, salt and oil—or, even rarer, topped with a treat like butter or cheese. But well-cooked, mashed and mixed with a small helping of fresh fried fish and grease hot from the pan, it was still excellent. It was the food, like the north's potatoes, which filled a poor man's empty stomach.

It was a past that didn't trouble him much anymore, but there the little plant sat in the tub, proof that his island— *beautiful—accursed*—even so far away, still existed. He heard himself responding to the doctor's questions, asking about the shipping and care, about what island it had come from. Apparently, Barbados. He smiled and nodded, but all the time the glass ceiling glowed as the sun beat down upon it, and that moist, tender heat enveloped him. For an instant, gazing at those bright pinnate leaves was like gazing at the world through a telescope turned the wrong way. Everything around him became small and bright, impossibly far away.

They shared a pleasant picnic dinner set on trestles inside the main building. The doctor's wife, her maid, and three of their children had come out too. They were joined for the meal by the head gardener, who also knew his botany. Billy was engaged by one of the doctor's sons and they both sat down to play with tin soldiers that had come riding along in jacket pockets. Hamilton summoned himself from the past to be a good guest, to ask the expected questions and be attentive to the answers, to be charming to the ladies and to keep a sometimes amused parental eye on the children, who hadn't yet decided what they felt about one another.

Soon, they'd depart and drive north quickly, to take a look at the land and old farmhouse they now owned. He hoped to oversee the site where the cellar would be dug for the one and only extravagance of his life, the new house he'd decided to build. The idea had come to him soon after Eliza's birth, the idea of a country retreat. He knew it would please Betsy immensely to place her in the kind of setting her upbringing had given her the right to expect. Hamilton earned a great deal these days with his law practice—more than four times what he'd made working twenty-four hour days for the government.

Why not afford them this single indulgence?

In the fever-ridden summers, she could stay there with the more vulnerable younger children and their sadly afflicted Angel. As her own mother had done at *The Pastures* long ago, she'd supervise the building and landscaping of a house. He'd stay in town with the older boys and work.

Hamilton had been pleased to be able to employ John McComb, Jr., a prominent NYC architect who'd also designed and overseen construction of the newest City mansion, just completed. Overlooking the East River's Hell's Gate, that house belonged to a mutual friend, the merchant Archibald Gracie. McComb had also drawn plans for the many serviceable new lighthouses constructed by the Washington administration. Hamilton appreciated Mccomb's professionalism and was willing to undertake the debts he'd be forced to assume. Although he had never done such an extravagant thing before, it didn't seem an unreasonable risk. Besides, he knew how happy it would make his wife. Philip Schuyler, also delighted by his favorite son-in-law's project, had already promised his own fine northern hardwood.

The house would have tall windows and porticos, be in many ways a smaller version of McComb's original creation. Hamilton had been attracted to the design as soon as he'd driven out to see it, for it had reminded him of the

437

plantation houses of the West Indies, the kind that he'd longed to be the master of in those long ago days when he'd been a merchant's humble clerk.

Now he could do as he wished, create a house full of natural light, a house perfect for entertaining their many friends and business associates. He'd designed the first floor with joined octagonal rooms, like a crystal. When the doors between were opened, there would be a large, gracious space with a view of country-side. The green leaves of the trees would reflect in mirrors on the patio doors, bringing an illusion of the outside within their dining room, more lovely and changing than any wallpaper. From one porch you would have a handsome view of the East River; from the other, the mighty Hudson.

* * *

At last, after much traveling back and forth, they all were here, even Phil, his studies temporarily left behind, as well as Alexander, James, Angelica and the younger ones, too: Johnny, Billy and little Eliza, toddling in her little cap and dress, busily prattling as she walked across the sheep-cropped lawn. Betsy held Hamilton's arm. Her lovely dark eyes sparkled. She was flushed, like a girl again, utterly enchanted.

Their new house was finished at last, yellow with a white trim. The interior, too, was painted an even brighter shade. Betsy had chosen the color. In a way, the intensity had at first seemed to him old-fashioned, but as soon as the painting was completed, and they'd stood at the pocket doors and surveyed the room, he knew she'd been correct.

"I thought it might be too bright, but I see that I was incorrect. The green you've used for my study has dried in a handsome fashion, too. It will certainly provide rest for my eyes after a long day."

"I am so very happy that you like it, my dear. And now we must put on the finishing touches. My sister writes that she has a beautiful silver *girondole* she purchased in Paris

438

that she will give us for our dining table. It should look most elegant at dinner parties and it will cast so much more light than single candles."

"Ah! Like those Mrs. Morris had in Philadelphia? The crystals always make the scene appear so very gay."

"This one is for the table's center, so the reflective plate is the stand and the crystals all hang from branches above. My sister says it will give us stars on the ceiling, which will be delightful."

"Our Angelica is so very generous to us, her poor relations." Hamilton winked at his wife, though as their lawyer he knew that John Church's finances were far more precariously balanced than even his own. "Have we ever seen this marvelous object?"

"I don't think she's ever had it out of the box. You know how many splendid things they brought back with them."

"Neither of them ever do anything by halves, do they? Church has often said that he'd need a house at least twice as big as the one they have to display all the fine things Angelica purchased in London."

Hamilton smiled down at his wife. Of late, he was beyond certain he had married the right Schuyler sister.

My faithful Aquilea....

"And, my dear, before I go off tomorrow and forget to take it out of my pocket as I did yesterday, here is a plan for a garden I've drawn up. I hope you approve, Mrs. Hamilton."

Betsy smiled. She and her father had shared some thoughts on that subject already. "I believe that with Papa's advice and the help of Mr. Dumphy and his boys, it should not be difficult. We've just today received bundles of berry bushes and pair of fine plum trees from Papa. Mr. Dumphy has already dug them in—'twill keep the roots fresh until we decide exactly where they should be set."

"And your father writes that he has sent to Holland for bulbs, red and white tulips and yellow narcissus. By next spring, this lawn cannot fail to please the eye."

Betsy smiled at him, heart-shaped face shining with pleasure. Hamilton knew she hoped they were at last

439

embarked upon a calm sea, one which would carry them into a peaceful, ordinary world, one brimful of respectability and comfort. He was now a busy lawyer, one whose brilliance and attention to detail made him much sought after.

They had already made arrangements for the older boys to stay with him during the week and attend their day schools and college. The younger ones and Angel could remain in the healthful, peaceful country with Betsy. She would continue to be his able household treasurer, and he would work as no other man she'd ever known could. Personally, Hamilton might be disappointed with the path his country had chosen, but, as a family, it appeared they would prosper at last. He and his Betsy would grow old together, here in this cheerful, elegant, modern house.

Chapter Twelve
Fortune's Fool

Philip lay on a bare bed, eyes rolled up, only the white showing. His fingers twitched. Sometimes he panted, laboring after breath. Betsy lay on one side, Hamilton on the other. They kissed his hands and wept. Philip groaned at the movement of the mattress when they joined him, but otherwise gave no sign he knew they were there.

He is dying—in agony. My baby!

Dark blood and internal fluids soaked the bandages about his waist. The smell of ruptured gut was in her nostrils. Stricken boyish faces gathered around the bed— Phil's friends.

Children! Only children. Their bodies grown, their opinions formed, but still so young, so rash, so rude, so proud, so foolish!

Philip and his college friend, George Price, had invaded Mr. Eacker's box during a play. Young Mr. Eacker had published an inflamatory piece in the newspapers, highly critical of Hamilton. Both boys were more than a little drunk; they'd caused a commotion with name-calling, pushing and shoving. Eacker, one of Aaron Burr's party, had ended by challenging both young men to a duel. Price had gone first to the dueling ground, and Eacker had spared him by throwing his shot away, the honorable *deloupe*. Philip, it seemed, had started the brawl and so he was counseled by his father to be a man of virtue and throw away his shot as well. This duel, though, had gone differently. Phil Hamilton shot into the air; George Eacker took aim and put a bullet into his opposite.

My reckless child, so proud of his father, publicly challenging Eacker's slanders! Now these men of party have sunk so far as to kill the oldest son of their great antagonist when they couldn't injure him in any other way.

441

As they wept, lying on that bare bed beside him, they told their son again and again how very much they loved him. By dawn, Phil's eyes clouded. His brief, shining twenty years had ended with a long sigh.

Beside her bloodied, motionless boy, Betsy sat and prayed, prayed to the God everyone said was merciful.

Surely this nightmare upon a bare, curtain-less bed in the house of stranger...I will wake up now, and it will not be true.

Twenty years ago, on a freezing Albany morning, in the last surge of her labor, he had come into the world. Upon the window, a glittering tree of frost that had grown during the night. Her mother had been there, Doctor Stringer, and that wise, gentle-handed Dutch midwife.

A perfect man child laid in my arms, wet, eyes wondering. I can still call up a memory of that first sharp tug at my breast.

Hamilton sat on the other side of the bed, his eyes fixed on the body of his "eldest and highest hope." His skin seemed to have turned gray, shriveled. His eyes were desolation.

Betsy knew she couldn't give way to her own grief.

My husband needs me, needs me now as he has never needed me before.

She thought of another face, too, now no doubt as agony-seared, as bleached and aged as that of the man beside her. Home was many miles away, but, somehow, Betsy heard the sound of Angel screaming.

* * *

Betsy leaned on her sister and watched as Hamilton, supported on either side by John Church and Bob Troup, attempted to cast the handful of dirt onto the coffin. Instead, he swayed, nearly fell. Troup caught him or he would have fallen onto the snow-limned pile by the grave. Accompanying the rasping sobs of the black-clothed mourners came a long low moan as raw November winds blew from the ocean.

Hamilton's head dangled. His grief had found the bliss of unconsciousness. Troup supported his friend in his arms, his own round face contorted. Releasing her sister's arm and stepping forward, Betsy did what had to be done. She put her hand into the clay and performed the last necessary task. An icy clod fell with a terrible thump onto the coffin.

"For dust thou art and to dust thou shalt return...."

She couldn't imagine her gay, beautiful Philip under the ground, as cold now as the earth into which she'd put her hand. All her concentration moved to how she must walk back to their carriage, how she must get her husband home.

Thank God for all their friends, for the Churches and faithful Bob Troup!

Oh, God, my darling Phil! Bright laughing face beneath dark hair, now gone, gone forever.

Her sister's arm slipped around her. Bob Troup, Nicholas Fish, and John Church supported Hamilton. Everywhere tears flowed, accompanied by a surging chorus of sobs. People passed in a blur, the drawn faces of family and friends. Phil's college chums and his Schuyler and Church cousins were all present.

There stood Philip's good friend, George Price, who had faced Eacker four days ago on those same Weehawken Heights. He hadn't been worth the bother of killing, unlike the first born of the great Hamilton. Price's rosy, handsome face was gray, lined, at least a decade older.

For Betsy, there were no more tears. She was hollow now, empty as a winter gourd. Her eldest daughter had been left at home in the care of a nurse. Just as Betsy had divined, at the moment of Phil's passing Angel had known. Shrieking, she'd thrown herself upon the floor and pounded her head until blood ran. Gussie, terrified, had, in desperation called for help from the other servants. It had taken all of them to tie her with sheets to the bed post. Only a huge dose of laudanum had finally extinguished her screams.

Betsy knew that their other children, too, were in various stages of fear and grief.

How can I tend so much needing? And my dear Hamilton, the man of action, the fearless warrior, beaten at last by this, the lowest and cruelest blow of his enemies. When will I be able to quietly remember the first tug at my breast on that ice blue morning?

Oh, how the sunlight had sparkled on the frosty windows of *The Pastures* as Alexander, so young, sat beside her, bursting with wonder and reverence at the miracle their love had created.

Shining Philip! Cut down before his life had even begun. He'd been the perfect sacrifice.

* * *

Hamilton lay on their bed and sobbed. The sound was like one of the children now that he'd been crying for such a long time. All the adult stiffness was gone. She'd just closed the door upon Angel, drugged into quiescence. Her daughter's forehead was blackened and swollen as if some thug had beaten her. She was speechless, her gray eyes utterly blank.

She's hiding now, somewhere deep inside.

The younger Alex was caring for his brothers. The scars stood out angrily on his thin, serious face. Now, tonight, he looked almost as prematurely old as had Phil's friend, young Price. It was bearing down on this sixteen-year old that he must now assume the burden of being Alexander Hamilton's oldest son.

It will all have to wait for tomorrow.

Tonight the children must minister to each other. Right now, her husband needed her desperately.

Betsy sat in front of the mirror, blindly following a night ritual of brushing her hair, but her arm could barely move under the weight of loss. Finally giving up, she, in chemise and petticoat, pulled a blanket over Hamilton and climbed in beside him. The November darkness was deep, the cold creeping in, but it didn't blot out the sound of a house full of weeping.

"It's my fault. I should have forbidden it, but I let him go. I trusted them to understand he was only a boy. I as good as killed him—my precious, my darling son."

She held her husband close, stroked his high forehead.

"The evil of this world killed him. That wicked little man killed him."

Even as she spoke, she knew it was only half true.

Hatred for her husband had killed Philip. That, and the antique ceremony of gentlemen, one her husband revered, one in which he'd taught his son to believe. It was pure murder, this "Honor."

* * *

They were at last living full time in their beautiful new house, eight miles out of the city, set on a height with that glorious view. He had named it 'The Grange,' after the Ayreshire seat of the lordly Scots Hamiltons. Now, with Phil gone—Phil who had taken a large part in the planning, who had ridden out so many days to oversee the workmen—there could be no perfect happiness. Hamilton returned on the weekends without joy. In the octagonal parlor before supper, the family clad in black, they knelt for prayers.

Angelica's battered face healed. Her mind did not. Young Alexander surprised his parents with a new concern for her. He tried repeatedly to engage his sister in life again, to take her driving in the shay or ramble in the woods as she'd once loved, but most of the time she refused, preferring to hide in her room.

Johnny, a fine little boy who often found his attempts at things manly undermined by an almost feminine sensitivity, was the only sibling to whom she'd freely talk. Most days she stayed in her room, tending her caged birds and reading works of devotion. She wept and prayed for hours on end.

445

The beloved fortepiano, once a warm family center where songs were sung, was forsaken, silent.

* * *

"Philip's death is the cruelest blow anyone could imagine, but she's grieving too hard." The elder Angelica shook her head sadly.

"It's as if we were all too proud. We faced so much danger during the War. We raised these children through contagions and thought it was our due. Now, for whatever reason, God has seen fit to take away our precious Phil."

"Oh, Eliza!" Angelica slapped her hand impatiently upon the arm of the sofa. "If the old monster were anywhere around, he wouldn't have permitted the duel!" Her sister's years in various European courts had left her a skeptic. "God had no part in this. Philip was murdered by a despicable Burrite creature. And now we're all so worried about our darling Angel, too. Why won't she come down to the City to visit? She always used to love to play her piano, no matter how bad she was." Angelica leaned closer, rested an elegant hand over her sister's. "Oh, Eliza, dear, tell me the truth. When I had the other children to tea last week, I'm afraid I persuaded Johnny to confide a few family secrets. He said that Angelica talks to Phil as if he were still here, that she—she's—not right—for days at a time."

Elizabeth heaved a sigh. She didn't blame Johnny.

Few grown men could resist the stratagems of Mrs. Church, so what defense could a twelve year old muster?

"It's true. Hamilton and I have tried to reason with her. If we say that Philip is dead, she becomes hysterical. She says that God lets her talk to Philip because she can't live without him. If we ask why we can't speak to him, too, she says it's because we aren't good Christians, because we don't truly believe in God and in eternal life. Hamilton is at his wit's end. If we do get close to making her admit he's gone, she goes into a frenzy. And I haven't told you the worst. Just last week Hamilton insisted that she admit that

446

Phil was dead. As soon as she said it, she screamed that her father was killing her, that she couldn't live without Philip. Then, before we knew what was happening, she dashed away and put an arm through a windowpane."

"Dear God!"

"The doctor said we were lucky she didn't sever an artery. He thinks time may heal the trouble in her mind, that perhaps the best thing to do for now is to leave the delusion alone."

"Oh, I'm so terribly, terribly sorry! Why haven't you told me?"

Betsy shook her head. "We've endured so much sorrow this winter. I'm starting to fear she's not going to get any better, that my dear child has lost her reason for good and all."

"I hate this." Furiously, Angelica pulled a handkerchief out of her sleeve, and blew her nose. "That such monstrous things should be happening to the best, the dearest people in the whole world!"

Her sister's arms were around her, but it was hard to take comfort from the heartfelt embrace. Elizabeth shifted uneasily. Not only was the May afternoon warm, but she was close to another delivery. The baby inside swept a limb in a slow passage across her belly.

"I'm sorry, dear." She disengaged herself. "It's just that I'm getting too old for this baby business." She leaned back and rubbed the throbbing spot on her side. "My back aches most horribly today."

A squeeze of Angelica's long fingers came to substitute for the hug.

"And what do you think your astonishingly virile husband has given you this time? Another boy?"

"If I survive it."

"Hush, Bess! There's always suffering in childbed, but you were made for bearing. You have the quickest, tidiest births of anyone I've ever known. Have you," Angelica speedily rushed on, hoping to draw her sister's attention away from the trial before her to the happier time afterward, "decided upon names?"

447

"Well, it's time to go back to tradition, don't you think? I wanted to call Eliza 'Catherine' for Mama, but Hamilton absolutely insisted upon naming her for me. If this little one is a girl, she shall certainly be a Kitty—for dear Mama at last, just as you have done with your oldest girl. If it's a boy," Elizabeth said, tears spilling from her dark eyes, "he shall—he must—be another Philip."

* * *

"Mine is an odd destiny. Perhaps no man in the United States has sacrificed or done more for the present Constitution than myself; and contrary to all my anticipations of its fate, as you know from the very beginning, I am still laboring to prop the frail and worthless fabric. Yet I have the murmurs of its friends no less than the curses of its foes for my reward. What can I do better than withdraw from the scene? Every day proves to me more and more that this American world was not made for me."—To Rufus King

* * *

It was bitter March when Mama Schuyler died. Just as she'd lived, it was done without fuss. The death of Philip Hamilton the year before had started her on a downward spiral from which she never recovered. Hamilton had been in Albany on business. When his mother-in-law's end seemed probable, he wrote to Betsy, asking that she visit and cheer her father who had been plunged into yet another terrible time of mourning.

Betsy came quickly, but not soon enough to see her mother. She brought with her the two youngest children. There was the four-year-old dark-eyed charmer, Eliza, and the newest baby, Little Philip, now nine months old.

As soon as she'd arrived, it was apparent that the events of the last year had been particularly hard on her youngest sister, Catherine. Without all this unending train of tragedy, Kitty would have been in the city, flirting and dancing at

448

winter balls. The family had barely stopped wearing black for Peggy when Philip had been killed—and now, Mama was gone.

Papa was absolutely insistent that Kitty care for him. She dutifully spent her days reading to her father or taking dictation, for he still kept up a large correspondence. At night, she carefully measured out the hundred drops of opiate he took at ten o'clock and then read him to sleep.

It was no life for a young girl, locked up in the house with an ancient, sickly father. Poor white-headed Prince wasn't much better off than his master. For years the general had been trying to retire Prince, but the slave always wept and refused to give up "taking care of things in your house, General." This, after all, had been the business of his life. The titular heads of the household were the venerable master and slave, but neither could walk unassisted. Betsy was relieved to see that her brother John had found a sensible, able-bodied black couple to take care of things. They had all they could do every day, looking out for two doddering autocrats.

Elizabeth wasn't sure what to do to help Kitty, who was yearning to start a life of her own. She was like a ray of sunshine in the empty, silent house. Her father seemed to draw strength from watching Kitty speed up the stairs or dashing down the hall on an errand.

Returning one day from some time with the kitchen staff, she'd heard baby Philip distantly roaring. The sound sent her running. In the study wing, she found her father, gouty foot propped, seated but leaning forward on one of his elaborately carved walking sticks. He was apparently speaking to the baby. Philip sat, red-faced and with a deeply aggrieved expression on his fat, teary face.

"I can't get up, young fellow, and believe me, I'm heartily sorry for it. So, we'll just have to discover another way. Come on now, man to man, tell me why you can't crawl over and fetch your toy?"

Philip sat back and goggled at the ancient bundle in the chair. When his mother had appeared, he'd stopped yelling, but his pink lower lip quivered and he heaved a pathetic bubbly sigh. Transfixed, silent, he gazed at his grandfather.

"Where's that Sally?" Elizabeth asked. "She shouldn't have left you alone with him."

"Don't fuss. Sally took your rascal 'Liza along after she went out to answer the call of nature. A good thing too, because that little squirrel was all set to climb onto my leg. But this fellow and I, well, we've about got the trouble all worked through, haven't we, young Phil?"

Philip hiccupped solemnly. Large dark Schuyler eyes swung back and forth between his grandfather and mother. He was ten months old, a stolid, determined block of a child, who evidenced nothing, either in appearance or temperament, of the first Philip. So far he'd shown absolutely no interest in moving on his own.

"Mama!" He yelled imperiously, raising his chubby arms.

Betsy bent and lifted both Philip and the desired, out–of-reach toy, a wooden horse with a floppy hair mane. Philip grabbed it and let out a squeal of triumph, one plainly directed as his grandfather.

"Got you jumping, hasn't he?" The old man chuckled and then shifted uncomfortably in his chair. "He wanted that, and he wanted it handed to him. I told him he'd have to crawl and get it himself and he didn't like that. Not one bit." Papa Schuyler paused to clear his throat. "He understood everything I said, but he isn't too interested in doing for himself, is he?"

"Oh, I suppose it's because we all wait on him." Betsy smiled indulgently at her baby. He, with grave satisfaction, held the horse's head with both hands and then thrust it into his mouth.

"Well, yes, that's part of it, but not all. We certainly pampered Kitty when she was a baby, but she still crawled early and got into everything. Now, Eliza, I'm going to tell you a thing or two I've learned today about this fellow. I believe he's the first one of yours who might be called a real Dutchman. The plain fact is that he can't see it's to his

450

advantage to crawl. He doesn't have to spend any energy with everyone dancing attendance, so he doesn't. My advice is that you stop rushing to get him everything he wants. There'll be some roaring and then, after a time, he'll start to do for himself."

Her father's knotted hands reached to pinch the toes inside the nearest knit bootie.

"Crafty Dutchman."

"No." Phil yanked his foot away then buried a rosy face against his mother's neck.

Her father grinned, an ancient, gummy smile. "See? The rascal understands every word." He chuckled and tickled the foot again. "Listen here, little lad. I've got you pegged."

It warmed Elizabeth's heart to see how the little ones always stirred her father up.

"Well, I've wondered if I should make him work a bit harder, because all the others were crawling and some even walking by his age, but I don't want him screaming and upsetting you, Papa."

"That bothers you more than it does me. One of the few benefits of old age is going deaf."

Her father sighed, and settled back into his chair.

* * *

Almost at once Kitty confided she had a beau.

"It's Mr. Sam Malcolm. I met him last year in New York at Angelica's. He's asked Papa for my hand, but Papa did what he always does. He put Sam off and then told me he wasn't good enough." She sniffled, put her hand urgently on her sister's arm.

"Who is good enough, I ask you? The only man who got one of us Schuyler girls just by asking was Mr. Hamilton. Papa seems to think we should all marry paragons, that ordinary gentlemen aren't good enough, even if they're rich like Mr. Church or Mr. Morton. How often does a man like yours come along, for heaven's sake? Papa 'bout had a fit over Nelia's choice, and look at how well that's turned out. Washington's made such a success at the bar and they're so

451

happy and gay and have the most wonderful parties. Oh, Bess, you must help me! Papa's so sick and sad and I don't want to hurt him, especially now that Mama's gone, but I'm going crazy. I cry my eyes out every night for my Sam. We've been apart for months now. He's been writing—he sends to one of my girlfriends. He says he loves me, but what if he grows tired of waiting, finds someone else? Oh, Betsy," she wailed, collapsing dramatically into her sister's arms. "Soon it'll be too late. After all, I'm—I'm—so old! Twenty-two!"

Smiling over her sister's shoulder, Betsy stroked the long, dark hair and listened patiently. It was hard to take Kitty's problems seriously. She found herself, as she often did, thinking of Phil, who would have been twenty-one this winter. Just as clearly as if it were yesterday, she remembered Kitty squatting beside Phil and giving him those companionable thumps on the head the day after Peggy had eloped with Stephen. In those days, it had been all elopements and births.

Now there is nothing but death.

Perhaps, though, after their Papa got accustomed to the idea, a marriage and some new grandchildren would make him feel better.

"Write and tell Sam to come to Albany. Do you think he can?" Betsy was familiar with young Mr. Malcolm and his family and knew that he was an entirely suitable match for a Schuyler girl. He wasn't rich, but he belonged to a respectable old New York family. Sam Malcolm was a surveyor, a profession where fortunes could still be made on the opening frontier.

"Sam's already here." Kitty blushed. "Don't tell Papa, though! He was out west surveying for Colonel van Schaick in the Genesee valley until a couple of weeks ago."

"I wondered why you were taking the pony out every day. I never knew you to be so passionately fond of riding."

"If you weren't here, I wouldn't be able to get away even for an hour. Sam says I should marry him right now, but I'm afraid." Kitty shook her head. "Papa will be so

452

angry! If he bursts a blood vessel and dies, it'll be my fault."

"Well, don't do anything rash. See if Sam can wait a little more. My Hamilton is finishing up a trial at Poughkeepsie. I'll send for him to come here after his business is done. If anyone can talk Papa around, he can."

Kitty seemed content with the idea. She went about her business every day with a lighter heart, especially after Betsy told her that Hamilton had written back, promising to come up as soon as the session was done.

Then, the very day he was expected, the old pony that Kitty had been riding returned without her. Knowing what was in the wind made Elizabeth nervous long before anyone else. Making a quick trip to Kitty's room, she found the note propped in front of the mirror.

* * *

Dearest Papa and Sister Betsy:
Please don't worry about me. I've gone to marry Sam Malcolm. We'll send again after we're man and wife. Please forgive us my dearest darling Papa and give us your kind blessing."

* * *

"Oh, Kitty! You naughty, naughty girl, to leave me with this! Thank God Hamilton's on his way. I'll never be able to stem the tide alone."

She went downstairs to prepare Papa's decoctions of marshmallow and nettle, (for the gravel) and burdock (for his gout). "And," she thought, "I'd better make sure we've got laudanum. He'll fly into a rage and that will just aggravate everything. Then Prince and I will be up all night with him, which neither of us are up to."

As she'd expected, there were floods and floods of tears as well as roars from the general when the note was, a few minutes later, discovered by one of the housemaids.

"By God, the selfish hussy couldn't stay! She couldn't! I'll never forgive her! No, I won't! She couldn't wait a little while, stay with me until I die. How long could that be? A year? But it doesn't matter anymore, Eliza, for this will certainly kill me. All the world will be glad to be rid of this useless old hulk. I'll be glad to go, yes, I will! It's no world these days for anyone but filthy levelers, murdering Jacobins, and those thrice-damned southerners!"

"I'll stay with you, Papa."

"You can't stay! You've got a houseful of children! Your Angelica's sick and then there's that husband of yours, whom you'd better keep your eye on!"

That, she thought, was probably the closest to a critical remark she'd ever heard Papa make about Hamilton.

"Well, I'll stay for a little longer."

"For a few weeks! And then what? Who will read to me, write my letters, now that my eyes are so full of cotton? I shall be all alone here—all alone!"

"Prince is still here. John and Elizabeth are close, and so are Phil and Sally and Rensselaer and Eliza. They can get some good genteel people in to stay with you and they'll bring the children to visit."

"Prince is as useless as I am, and, as for the others, they're busy. They've got their own lives to lead. I need someone here!"

Like reinforcements coming over the hill during an Indian attack, Alexander appeared, striding in, booted and spurred, banging the dust from his hat. He found wife and father-in-law in the study. Prince, too, was now in attendance. Whenever Betsy ran out of breath, the old servant had been trying to fill the gap, to convince his master "to be easy 'bout Miss Kitty" and "to take a little medicine now, Mr. General, sir."

After a time, though, Prince had begun to weep in sympathy with his master. Now both of them were sitting side by side, one in a wing chair, the other on the matching stool, gray heads bowed over their handkerchiefs, sobbing about the miseries of old age and the heart-breaking

454

ingratitude of one's children. Betsy exasperated and tired, had been about to join them.

Prince staggered to his feet and wobbled over to take Hamilton's hat.

"Thank you, Mr. Prince." Hamilton let the hat go. "Why don't you take that into the kitchen and see if we may have some tea? But you should just stay there and rest by the fire. Someone else can certainly bring tea up to us."

"I don't want any tea."

"Well, Papa, perhaps Mr. Hamilton does."

"Yes, indeed General Schuyler, I believe I would like tea. I also believe, sir, that there's been some excitement...?"

"If that's what you think a daughter's betrayal constitutes, sir."

"Papa...."

"Give me a kiss, Eliza, love." Alexander slipped an arm around her waist and saluted her cheek. "Why don't you go and make sure Mr. Prince remembers what he's in the kitchen for? The General and I have some talking to do. You know, just two generals together, discussing strategies with which to combat the vagaries of life."

"Hmph!" Her father growled. Using his stick, he angled himself away. His black eyes, the most alive part these days, shifted to a close study of the fire. He looked exactly like a dignified old Mohawk chief, with his craggy features, black eyes, and snow white hair.

As Elizabeth closed the door behind her and walked towards the kitchen wing, she felt somewhat miffed by the way her husband had simply taken over.

After all, I've been coping with Papa for the last month! But does he ever listen to me?

Still, the rushing sense of relief she felt soon overrode resentment.

If anyone can talk Papa into a draught of medicine and then into acceptance of what Kitty and Mr. Malcolm have done, it will be my eloquent, persuasive and oh-so-much-by-Papa-beloved-Hamilton!

455

Chapter Thirteen
Colonel Burr

In the spring of 1804, Hamilton's influence and politicking had kept Aaron Burr from high office once again, this time from the governorship of New York. A cloud hung over the entire affair. At a dinner party at Judge John Tayler's house, Federalist rancor towards Jefferson and Burr was openly and virulently expressed.

There was wine, far too much, more than Hamilton had drunk in years. What he'd said that night he believed to be true. Nevertheless, this hardly excused it. Rage sprang the words before an audience of roaring Federalists, but his insults did nothing to alter the past, or to shift the burden of his loss and grief. And someone had been listening, someone who was not really a friend to Hamilton or to his party, and he reported on the shocking thing he'd heard.

* * *

It was a clear New York evening, after a day spent in a stuffy, noisy office on Wall Street with his law clerks and ever so many clients. Hamilton had been barely able to keep his mind focused on the sometimes subtle, sometimes flamboyant practice of law.

Now the day was over. Instead of returning to his townhouse, he wandered from street to street, along the familiar paths. With Burr's formal demand for an explanation lying like a cold stone in his pocket, he hardly knew where his feet took him. He felt like a ghost, wandering through old haunts while the usual good weather evening crowd of hawkers, carters, and laughing youths— their evening pleasures just begun—passed him by without so much as a tip of a hat. Every aspect of his life for the last few years had been like sinking in quicksand. Inside and

456

out, he felt a ruin, a relic of some now fabulous, near-mythical age.

There was no refuge in the long hours of work he kept, no refuge anywhere. It tore at his heart when the Republican newspapers called him "monarchist," "embezzler," or "tool of oligarchs."

They still, in their heart of hearts, believe I am not a real American.

Not even sterling service in the military and at the nation's founding, where he'd labored with his whole heart and mind, not marriage to Elizabeth, daughter of General Philip Schuyler, had carried him into their sphere. No matter what he did, no matter what feats of daring or intellect he performed in service to America—nothing made any difference. To these hereditary gentlemen, men like John Adams or Thomas Jefferson, Hamilton would always be "the bastard brat of a Scots peddler," a jumped-up little Creole clerk.

Worse, because he understood economics, because he believed trade and sound finances alone would preserve this unique American experiment in liberty, he was tarred as a "money man." The planters, always at odds with their factors and bankers—as well as Jefferson's ever-growing unwashed constituency—mocked his knowledge. No one, except for a few financiers, appeared to comprehend the intricate perfection of the great machine he had built to serve them.

Men close to him had been speculators in land and paper, some embezzlers, some swindlers, men who wanted to rig the odds, this Hamilton knew, although he'd never been part of it. The fact that his family would lose nearly everything if he died tomorrow was singular proof that he had never feathered his nest with public money.

That political meeting, he remembered as delirium. He'd felt safe among men who thought as he did, had been urged on by their roars of assent. He had gone too far, as he had done all his life when rage overcame his reason and swept common sense away. Hamilton wished he could call those words back, those words spoken in supreme contempt for Burr.

"Les grandes ames se soucient peu des petits moraux."

It was Burr's favorite phrase. The lengths to which he may have carried that belief! Even, perhaps, with his adored and adoring Theodosia. The memory of what Angelica had confided, just a few years ago, of what her pale, girlish lips had whispered, had haunted him.

Colonel Burr has made Theodosia his forever.

Shocked, the spy at Judge Taylor's ostensibly Federalist gathering had written down what Hamilton had said. Eventually, in the unerring way of such things, those words returned to haunt him.

And, by this, I arrive at the poisoned now.

Standing in his office earlier, the bustle of the city outside, Hamilton knew, as he'd studied Burr's letter, that it would probably be the death of him.

He returned from his inner dialogue when a gray, stolid presence appeared in his path, bringing him to a halt. There stood Trinity Church, the graveyard gate open. People strolled within, enjoying a bright summer evening beneath the elms, more walkers in search of green and a bit of quiet than sorrowing visitors to the dead.

Heaviness weighed him down, like a great stone. It was no accident he had come here. It was so clear tonight, the circle of his life—the ordained end.

Discretion, that's what everything came down to. Exactly as that monster Cruger had advised.

He walked the slate path around the squat gray structure, his feet taking him to the ground where his Philip lay. Tears sprang as he reached the headstone, as they did so easily these days. The hollow spot within his chest throbbed, a vacancy where once had beaten a heart of warmth and fire. The wound left by his boy's death had aged, perhaps, but he knew it would never heal.

As much as Eliza loves me—and needs me—what right have I to go on living after sending our splendid boy to die, after advising him to play the man of honor, while all the time, knowing what I do about human nature?

The eager, obedient son had paid homage to his father's precepts. He'd given his life.

For the past two years, since burying his first born, Hamilton had tried to go on, to care for his wife and his children, to embrace life again. He'd striven to excel at his practice, had kept his hand in politics, had kept a candle burning to guide his wayward and faithless mistress, Lady America, home.

Yet none of it mattered as it once had. Nothing he said or did appeared to have any effect. The world had moved on. He walked; he breathed; joy had fled. Standing among the graves, studying his son's headstone, Hamilton tucked his hat under his arm and pondered.

My body aches all the time. My bowels purge blood and leave me weak as a kitten. Every old wound, every past illness, revisits. Dying by inches is no good way for an old soldier. Burr has always been an excellent marksman. He'll be delighted to put down this old war horse.

Hadn't he written long ago—so very long ago—to his childhood friend, Ned Stevens: *"I would risk my life, 'tho not my Character, to exalt my Station."*?

The New England Federalists were again toying with Burr's secession idea, although the spring elections had wrenched New York from their grasp. Didn't he now have a way, right here in his pocket, to put an end to Burr's political career? To put an end to his emptiness—to his failure? Perhaps, one last time, he could make a difference.

I will heed the text upon which I have so relentlessly preached. I will offer my life in service to this country. I shall end a True Roman.

Hamilton paused, studied the tender green carpet that covered his son. There was at once terror and relief, as if he'd just floated safely over a mountainous St. Croix wave.

Interrupting this crescendo of feeling, a weary, heart-shaped face, a dear image, formed among the lacy arms of the elms. Her appearance staggered his resolve.

Eliza...my sweet Queen Bess....

For love of her, and for plain paternal duty, I've gone on this long. It's a cruel decision, but Betsy and the children will survive—all except for my Angel with the broken wings, already lost in the abyss—

I will leave my family deep in debt, a thing I'd sworn I'd never do. Single-minded public service had seen to that. He hoped Betsy's family and his loyal friends would see she did not sink into financial or emotional ruin, although their splendid home, shining with light, would almost certainly be forfeit.

So many times I've broken her faithful heart. But she will go on because of our children and because she is truly strong, far stronger than I am. I hope she will do better once all her worst fears are realized, for when I am gone, that particular torment will end. God help me, I've caused her so much suffering and may yet do more....

Taking out a fine lawn handkerchief, Hamilton wiped his high forehead. He lifted his gaze beyond the churchyard, to the thriving red brick world beyond. There were more shops and merchants than ever before. Hawkers were packing for the night. Tired apprentices called out to one another as they were released for an hour or two from their toils. The last knot of traders from the exchange would be noisily heading to their tavern—the aptly named Bull & Bear. All this activity would survive him, the man whose plans had created a haven where enterprise could grow and prosper.

I will return to my office and answer Colonel Burr's demand in an equivocating, windy manner—me at my worst.

Hamilton's lips twisted with grim self-mockery. After years of arguing cases, both with and against Burr, he knew the man well. He understood exactly what would drive the Colonel—*past comrade in arms, present foe*—to implacable fury.

The simple fact of the case: What he'd said on that drunken night *was* unpardonable. True or not, Colonel Burr had every right in the world to call him out.

So, let him. Perhaps, after all these defeats, after so many mistakes, after so much indignity, 'twas simply time to be a soldier again, to roll the dice and let Fate decide.

* * *

After a north wind night it was chilly in the study, for the warmth of the day had not yet penetrated. Hamilton, used to economy, had not set a fire in the hearth. He stood, stretched, and went through the adjacent room to open the porch doors. Now, late morning, it would be just as easy to bring in some warmth from the out-of-doors.

His papers were neatly laid on the desk, but Hamilton was no longer in the mood to ponder them. Instead, he gazed into spring, moving and glimmering in the garden. All his plans had come together in a gratifying fashion. Last spring, Betsy and the old gnarl-handed farmer, Dumphy, had had a congenial meeting of the minds over the laying out of the tulips, fruit trees and dogwoods. Today, the grounds were ablaze with color and form.

Elizabeth and little Phil were visible. His youngest wandered in a white dress, a solid two-year old with a deliberate air. Four year old Eliza with a cap covering her shiny little girl curls, followed. She was, as usual, attached to her mother's dress by a knotted fist. She was not much happier about her little brother than Alex had been about James. She, however, expressed her distress mostly by clinging, as her mother said, "Like a burdock."

As he watched the domestic scene in the garden, he felt a stab of anguish.

What have I done?

Swallowing hard, he paused to draw a deep breath of country air, all scented with grass and flowers. He struggled after calm.

If I live—well and good for me and my family and for what's left of the Federalist party—perhaps, once again, I shall stand at the center of events.

His youngest stumbled, fell full length in the grass. Betsy bent to set him on his feet; the sturdy toddler didn't cry.

If he kills me, Burr will certainly be discredited.

Moreover, I, Alexander Hamilton—bastard, upstart, foreigner—will end my life in an affair of honor, proving, once and for all, that I am a gentleman, an equal.

No one could ever tarnish that. He must hold his nerve, follow the course he'd set.

There was a distant echo, like tearing fabric, as he watched Betsy and the children enjoying the bright garden. Since Phil's death, he'd lived at a remove from his nearest and dearest, the ones who should matter the most. Every day it was harder and harder to read the news, to hear all he'd stood for mocked and misinterpreted, to watch the once bright banner dragged in the mud.

He knew the *Code Duello*. When the day came, the moment when he and his enemy stood upon the heights at Weehawken and faced one another, the both longed for and feared *"brilliant exit"* he'd written to Laurens about, so many years ago, would, almost certainly, take place.

Chapter Fourteen
The Last Secret

Betsy witnessed a spring rush of giddiness when Hamilton, with much behind the scenes letter writing, had assisted with the defeat of his old enemy, Aaron Burr, running for governor. Hamilton insisted that working against Burr wasn't personal, but only because Burr was at the center of the secessionists who wanted to take New England out of the Union. As always, he distrusted much that Jefferson said, but he thought it imperative that the Union be preserved.

"Jefferson is president now, and clearly enjoying the exercise of his executive powers. Any 'free speech' that isn't to his liking is labelled sedition. Power changes everything."

This was all she knew, but since April, Elizabeth sensed something wrong. Her husband was preoccupied, but not in the usual way. It wasn't that he was inattentive, for he was very affectionate. How careful of her feelings he was, how tender and playful with the children!

She couldn't quite put her finger on it. Hamilton had never been what anyone would call relaxed, so it wasn't his intensity that was unusual. Now, sometimes even on week nights, he'd leave work early and ride the eight miles out to The Grange, declining invitations to the sort of business gatherings that would have ordinarily kept him in town. Of course, he still spent hours in his study on weekends, but at least as much time was spent with the family.

He took long walks with Alex and Jamie, listening to their youthful philosophizing and giving advice on school and life. He wrote a fatherly treatise on "Discretion" and presented it to Jamie.

Now, sometimes, Betsy discovered him sitting in the garden swing, watching Johnny conduct a battle in the grass with those toy soldiers he couldn't bring himself to abandon, while Eliza, now an adorable brunette coquette of five, cozied and flirted in his lap.

Sometimes, he sat with Angelica, watching her tend her caged birds. If she was, as they now put it, "herself," he always asked if she would play for him. Then he was all attention, lost in the loveliness she could still draw from the keyboard. If Billy was particularly rambunctious, he'd renounce paternal dignity and chase his "wild Indian" all over the house, then bombard him into submission with pillows.

Naturally, the children were delighted by so much attention from their beloved father. When he returned from the City, those beautiful young faces turned towards him like sunflowers.

There was bounty for her, too. If she came into his study to consult about some household expense, Hamilton was likely to draw her down onto his lap for kisses, to pull off her cap and playfully loosen her hair, as if it were long years ago, as if he were still a young officer stealing kisses from someone's pretty daughter.

These caresses were warm but chaste, often in the presence of children whom he'd just left off petting. At night, he'd come without fail to say good-night, a gaunt, handsome shadow that would suddenly materialize behind her in the dressing table mirror. Happy, she'd turn and lift her chin for his kisses, the whole time wondering if he wanted her as much as she wanted him. No matter how tender his caresses, however, he always ended by retreating to his own room.

Elizabeth's bed was never empty, of course. When she blew out the candle and climbed in, it was as it had been for years, shared with children, these days little Phil and Eliza. Sometimes Angelica would be there, too, oppressed by the dark feelers of an on-coming bad spell. Johnny and Billy were her husband's most frequent nighttime companions.

Behind his loving, tired eyes, she understood there lurked a terrible new sorrow, one he refused to share. More disturbing than the fact that he had not done so was the

464

existence of something she'd observed for years in Angel, but never before in her husband—*remoteness*—as if he daily went through the motions in a world of shadows.

* * *

It was early in July, during a fragrant summer night at The Grange, when she woke to the familiar sound of a night terror.

Angelica!

Rousing herself, she slipped out of bed and walked, in the hobbling gait of the middle-aged who have too quickly arisen, to the adjoining room. This was a nursery, one which would perhaps be forever occupied, if not by babies, then by this child whose mind continually strove against a crippling sensitivity.

"Mama! Mama!"

Betsy hurried through the door, rushed to clasp the sparse body in her arms.

"Oh, no! Mama! Tell me it's not true!"

"Angelica, dear. Wake up. Wake up now."

Betsy dreaded these dreams, dreaded the content almost as much as the depression they heralded. Since Philip had been killed, Angelica suffered at least one debilitating night terror every week.

"Oh, Mama! Papa was in a duel—just like my dearest Phil!"

Elizabeth held her daughter, felt racking sobs shake the too-thin flat-chested body. In spite of the heat of the night, she felt terror, one that went to the marrow. Her belief in premonition was unwilling, but since the train of deaths that had afflicted them, the destruction of gay Peggy, the sudden death of her mother, the brutal annihilation of their beloved Philip, Betsy had been forced toward an unwilling conviction that what seemed to be a nervous disorder might actually be, in her daughter's case, the unbearable curse of prescience.

In her arms, Angelica shivered fiercely and recounted the dream, much as she always did.

465

"They fired at the same time, but Papa fired his gun into the air. The other man smiled when Papa rose up on his toes, spun around and fell." Her daughter's voice was steadily rising. "Like Philip! Just like Philip!"

"Angelica, hush!" She hoped to push down her own fear by drawing her eldest daughter close. "Please don't wake the little ones. Now, now, my darling, it's only a dream, a terrible bad dream. Come to my bed."

"Is Papa here?"

"You know he's in town tonight, at his dinner with the Society of Cincinnati. And after all those old war stories they have to tell each other, you know he'll sleep at Colonel and Mrs. Troup's. Mr. Troup certainly won't let your father get into any trouble. Besides, there will be no more duels, no matter what. Your father has solemnly promised."

Elizabeth's gaze traveled across her daughter's shoulder into the darkness. Outside were night sounds, a shivery rising and falling chorus of tree toads. As she rocked Angelica against her shoulder and made soothing noises, her mind turned over the other "bad dreams" she had listened to, the one about Peggy and the worm, the one about Phil—that one, the culmination of a whole lifetime of night terrors.

She thought of how tender but restrained her ordinarily sensual husband had been. An icy finger touched her heart, cutting through the sticky summer heat. Dawn came and neither mother or daughter had again found sleep.

* * *

Hamilton, who'd been out for an early morning ride, urged Riddle forward. Betsy, just from the herb garden with sprays of sage, tarragon and rosemary for today's chicken stuffing in her hands, smiled up at him.

How young he appeared today! His hair, the ginger now well mingled with silver, glinted in the sun as he halted the horse beside her.

466

"Come on, my Betsy, step up."

He gave her no time to refuse. In the next instant, he'd leaned down and slipped an arm around her waist, a middle-aged marauder.

"Hamilton! No! Ow! What are you doing?"

Once he had her in the crook of his arm, there was nothing else to do but find his boot with her slipper, to push up onto the front of the saddle. The ease with which he conducted the maneuver was quite breathtaking, even though neither was as spry as they'd once been.

"What about the children?" He was trotting them away, across the sunlit yard.

"What children? I seem to remember some responsible young adults, as well as four reasonably intelligent servants in the house. I believe your well-organized home is competent to shift for itself for an hour or so."

His arm tightened around her waist. Then he gave Riddle a little tap with his heels which sent the horse into that wonderful, smooth, rocking-chair gait. Soon they were beneath the dappled canopy that shielded the road which led down to the Hudson.

"Remember that hot afternoon in Morristown? The one where I collected you at Aunt Cochran's gate just before you went back to Albany?"

"What?"

"Don't tell me you've forgotten. That afternoon haunted me 'till December. Your appeal to honor nearly killed me, you know. After leaving you off again at Cochrans', I was wretched. I felt sure that after I'd set you boiling, some New York cousin would come along and get the benefit."

"Alexander Hamilton! What a shocking thing to say! And why were you so unsure? After you, cousins only looked duller than ever. Was that why you sent me all those awful letters? You scared me to death with all your scolding and fretting."

He didn't answer, just pressed his lips against the nape of her neck. The horse beneath them, a true miracle of horseflesh, moved them along with barely a jostle.

"This horse is a wonder."

Riddle proved his worth again at once when, out of the bracken beside the road, two woodcocks doodled across their path. His smooth stride broke only for an instant.

"Look at them!" Hamilton noted the birds' slow motion passage. "A pair, too! Why, I was afraid the poor devils were all gone. Perhaps if Farmer Vandervoort and I can keep the poachers out, we'll have a few for ourselves. It's sad to remember how it used to be, how much game there was, when I first came to Manhattan."

"I visited the city in autumn the year I turned sixteen," Elizabeth said. "One morning the sun disappeared because the geese and ducks were flying, leaving us quite in the dark. Now, with such floods of people arriving, everything has changed."

The Hudson sparkled into view. At a place with a good view of the far shore, they rode off the road into fallow land. Under a shady cluster of poplars, Hamilton halted Riddle.

Slipping down, he helped his wife dismount. The reins were left to trail on the grass. Hamilton removed his coat and spread it in the shade close to the tree. Betsy looked at the coat and then at her husband's expression with surprise.

"I have pies and a roast in the oven, Mr. Hamilton."

"Livie will deal with them. Come and sit with me." Getting down first, he caught her hand. "Old memories should be revived from time to time."

The locusts chanted a weather forecast. Today would end hot. The brightness, the humidity, did rather remind her of a certain long ago day.

"Easier for you to sit now than in the laced and whalebone fortifications you ladies used to wear. All young rakes early learned dexterity."

"You are extremely wicked today."

"There was one padded pair of stays I remember quite well."

"Mr. Hamilton!"

Arms encircled her. She was drawn close, kissed and lowered onto the jacket. The wifely cap was removed. As she lay back, smiling up at him, a sweet scent rose from nearby wildflowers.

"What are you doing?"

"Why, being entirely too familiar with your eternally modest self."

As Elizabeth shivered with excitement, he leaned on his elbow, smiled one of his beautiful smiles and said, "Would you let me do what you wouldn't in Morristown?"

"What? Goodness! No! I'm a respectable woman. I make love only in my own bed."

For a moment he looked cross. Then, suddenly, with one of his volatile changes of mood, he laughed. "Exactly the same girl I married. But, did you know," he teased, blue eyes flashing, "there were many young ladies of good family who lost their innocence, if not their virginity, in sylvan trysts with young officers?"

"What—you wicked man—is the difference?"

"That you have borne eight children and still do not know the difference is not much of a tribute to me as a lover. Let's play that you are one of those virgin belles, and I, the irresistible young officer, shall demonstrate."

Light cut through the leaves and rippled across them. Nearby, Riddle contentedly swished his silver tail and tugged at the grass. Locusts buzzed. Fat clouds rode like moving castles across the blue vault.

"Goodness me! What are you doing, sir? What if Mr. Vandervoort drives his cows down the lane?"

* * *

Later, he leaned back against the yellow and beige mottling of the tree and stroked his wife's loosened hair. Betsy kept her face pressed against his shirt. She was embarrassed to the core.

What I, an upright matron, have just done....

He took her face in his hands, gazed seriously into her eyes.

"I've been wanting something very wicked for a long time, wanting to show you how much I've loved you."

469

He kissed her again, very tenderly, so she ignored his curious use of the past tense. The sun, now high in the sky, poured honey-gold through the leaves.

Elizabeth was abashed at the idea of returning home so disheveled. At the same time there was a languorous desire to go all the way into irresponsibility, to do as her satisfied body wanted and fall asleep in his arms. All those hours they might have spent together, all those months and years of absence on this or that duty to America, the country he'd rescued by the sheer force of his wit and energy, this ungrateful land where so many reviled him. Were those lost hours to be recovered here at last, at this elegant house he'd built to make her happy?

For a blazing instant her heart flew, winging over the green pasture, the shining gray-green river. Perhaps, despite all her fears, all would be well—at last.

"I do love you, my darling."

They passed a perfect hour dozing in one another's arms. For a span beneath the shade of whispering trees, Hamilton and his lady enacted the part of youthful, trespassing lovers.

* * *

The next weekend was also happy, if more formal. They gave a dinner party for the Trumbulls. On Sunday, she and Hamilton spent the morning surveying the garden together. They'd been enriching the sandy soil with straw and manure ever since they'd bought. This year, their cabbages were thriving, although Dumphy had been kept busy with an early attack by an army of looper worms.

Before dinner, as he always did, Hamilton read the Episcopal service aloud to the family. They sang hymns and prayed together. Angelica, always so grim these days, seemed almost cheerful. The family shared a merry meal together. The older boys had just come up from the City with books by the score. Although Alex Junior was on the verge of graduating from Columbia, he would soon continue on into the study of law.

Like all happy times, the day passed swiftly. After a light summer supper, they went outside again. Hamilton lay on the grass and talked with his children until long after the fireflies had gone to bed and the stars come out.

"Tell us about the time you had to swim for it." Johnny loved this story. He and Billy, arms around their knees, sat on the lawn close by.

"Yes, please, Papa," said Billy. He had not had nearly enough of this one.

James, who'd been lounging in the grass with a book and affecting a measure of teen boredom, sat up and smiled. All of Hamilton's sons relished this story. It didn't really seem possible to them that their father, usually so grave and tied to his desk, could once have been a daring soldier in George Washington's hard-pressed army.

"James has heard it too far many times, I think," their father said.

"Not at all, sir."

And so Hamilton, imperfectly hiding his satisfaction, obliged by beginning the story of the skirmish at Daverser's Mill.

"We were camped near Valley Forge, which we'd all get to know much more intimately in a few months. General Howe had just beaten us at Brandywine, though I must say that we Americans were getting better organized. The British army had begun its march upon Philadelphia, coming up the road above the Schuykill River. I was sent out by General Washington with a troop of horsemen under Henry Lee to destroy the stores of flour at Daverser's Mill and reconnoiter a little, to see if we could find the exact location of the enemy. I'd posted lookouts at the top of the road that went down to the mill to give us warning, and we'd taken possession of a flat-bottom boat, in case we needed to retreat. Lee's men got busy and fired the mill directly. The poor mill owner was distracted, but he knew that it would be either us or the British, the way things were. I gave him our surety from the Continental Congress,

471

but, of course, in those days, it was not worth the paper it was written upon and he and I both knew it. I had my orders, but I truly felt for the poor man. It was a terrible sight, with the fire leaping through the windows, the end of all his enterprise...."

"And then the British came!" Billy leaned against his father, bright-eyed.

"And so they did. We were down by the river near the boat when we heard shots from above. It was our sentries, warning us by getting off a few shots at the British dragoons who'd just arrived, flying down the road. Our fellows did their job and then they ran, while the redcoats came clattering down the incline toward the mill. They fired, a great volley, which killed one of Colonel Lee's dragoons and wounded another of our men as well as one of the boatmen, just as they were trying to push off."

"And then they shot your horse." Billy was breathless.

James prodded his smaller brother. "Stop interrupting!"

Billy tightened his grip on his knees, hoping to suppress himself. His father smiled at the "Wildman," but also touched a cautionary finger to his lips.

"Yes, they shot my horse, and it was a shame, too, for he was a brave fellow and had served me well. When he dropped, he dumped me on the road, but one of my men, McCready, pulled me up and we jumped into the boat, just as the others cast off. Not all of us had weapons—mine were still on the saddle—and the British were pouring shot into the boat, volley after volley. The boatmen didn't dare try to steer because of the shooting, and we just floated on down the river, which was in flood after a days of heavy rain."

"And Colonel Lee galloped safe away." Billy had already forgotten his brother's earlier rebuke.

"So he did. And then the boat began taking on water. McCready couldn't swim, but he grabbed one of the oars. We decided one way or another we were for it, with the bullets still hailing in, so I went over the side into the water. The current was swift, but it was carrying the boat back

472

into the shore, just beyond the mill. I knew I didn't want to end up a prisoner—which is what happened to poor McCready—but I thought I'd made a mistake as soon as I hit the water. It was all I could do to keep my head above it. Finally, there was a bend and the current carried me against a snag, a big tree that had fallen in from the other side. I managed to hang onto that and then climb along it, back to shore."

"And then you climbed up the bank and a man on a mule came along and doubled you back to General Washington's headquarters where they were all very glad to see you."

James grabbed Billy, and began to tickle.

"Stop! Don't!"

"It's time for you to stop being a baby and get sent to boarding school to learn some manners, don't you think?"

"James; let him be."

Jamie disengaged and then put distance between himself and now his stunned little brother.

"Boarding School?" Billy's jaw had dropped. The shock of the notion was sufficient to render him motionless, incapable of pursuit.

"Yes. You will be going to Reverend Branford's. In the autumn, though, William," his father said.

At the news, Billy dropped onto the ground and leaned, as if for protection, against Hamilton, any desire to chase James obliterated. All at once, he seemed much smaller.

* * *

The day had been spent as if Hamilton hadn't a care in the world, as if he hadn't a stroke of work to do after the summer legal recess ended. Betsy enjoyed the lazy day, but soon after supper, she suffered an attack of aches and shivers which sent her to bed early, while the rest of the family stayed out to star gaze. This sort of malady had begun to happen regularly and she was beginning to wonder if it was—*at last*—the change.

473

"I hope you feel better tomorrow, love." She was half asleep by the time Hamilton entered her room, candle in hand. "Don't get up tomorrow if you feel poorly. I have to leave around sunrise for an early appointment in town. Unfortunately, I may not be home again until next weekend."

"We'll miss you." She turned over to sleepily regard him, his trim form and those still startling blue eyes.

"And I shall miss my Queen Bess and my little ones. Perhaps things will go along swimmingly and I'll be able to get home earlier."

Carefully, slowly, drinking her in with his eyes, he bent and kissed her.

Good as his word, he was out of the house before dawn. When Betsy asked at breakfast if anyone had seen him off, Johnny said that he had slept with his father overnight.

"He said he'd like me to keep him company overnight, then he got up ever so early. Before he rode away, he asked me to say the Lord's Prayer with him."

Chapter Fifteen
Opus Sit
***

Out of a boom like hurricane surf, Hamilton returned.

The sun, a devil blazing in blue—too bright, too hot....

In the boat again, lying in the sloppy bottom. Oars splashed urgently; cold water struck his face. For a moment, he imagined he was back at Saint Croix.

Then, he remembered Burr's eyes, remembered the cascade of anguish.

God be merciful, for Aaron Burr will not.

A column of light had entered the glade, the ledge above the serene river, the place where duelists customarily met.

I will preserve the Union. I will, once and for all, claim my honor.

He'd excused himself and put on his glasses, more to steady himself than anything else.

Philip died to avenge me, right on this spot.

At the signal, in control at last, he raised his weapon, but as he began to lower it, the pistol went off.

At the same instant, he felt the white-hot passage of a .54 caliber ball.

Impaled! A stake of fire...

Damp green moss upon his cheek....Sometime later, he and the ferocious pain rocked upon water. Hamilton heard sobs, saw a face.

Doctor Hosack? Pendleton?

When the roaring black door opened again, he gratefully fell through it.

* * *

It was on Wednesday, mid-morning, when the men arrived at The Grange. Their horses were lathered, the men grim-faced. They hurried Elizabeth into a carriage, saying that General Hamilton had been taken ill in town. "Very

475

ill," they said. She was terrified, but they wouldn't answer her questions.

"Spasms. The general is sick with spasms."

"Good God! Do you all think I'm feeble-minded?"

She whirled away from Doctor Hosack, back to her husband, stretched upon the bed. They had taken great care to swaddle his abdomen, but her nose told her the truth.

Blood, gut! The foul, dark odor assailed her as soon as she'd entered the room.

Before Hosack could stop her, she'd lifted the sheet, recoiled at what she saw. Hamilton was very weak, but he felt the movement. Drained blue eyes opened, met hers.

"Dearest Eliza. I'm sorry."

Speechless, she nodded.

In spite of all those promises made since Philip had died, he'd fought a duel.

Her knees buckled.

Angelica's dream.

"I've sent for gunshot specialists from the French and British frigates...."

Over the doctor's words, drowning them out, she heard dirt strike the coffin.

"Who did this?"

"Colonel Burr, Ma'am." Pendleton was behind her.

She turned to stare. *Friends!* Hamilton called these men friends: her sister's husband, John Church, William Bayard, whose Greenwich house this was, Colonel Pendleton, Doctor Hosack. These men had let it come to this with Burr, known to be crack shot. These men with all their talk, talk, talk of politics—of—right and wrong—of honor.

"He didn't intend to fire, Ma'am," said Pendleton. "But his gun went off. The shot went into the air."

As if it mattered.

"Colonel Burr aimed to kill?"

"His choice, Mrs. Hamilton."

There was a sound—Hamilton grinding his teeth. His hand clutched the mattress. A single thin, high sound—a note of pure agony—escaped.

476

The monster, the one that Angelica knew so intimately, seized Betsy.

"Hamilton!" She fell to her knees. "Oh, God! Oh, God! Why?" Wailing, she pressed her head against the side of the bed.

His answer came at last, haltingly, and only through immense effort.

"What use would I be if—if he could—call me—coward?" He wrestled for sufficient mastery to continue. "If he said—I was—no—gentleman."

Her hands flew to her breast, the heart within shattered. Hamilton, thin frame shuddering, clenched his jaw and strove against another excruciating wave.

Betsy bent her head to the bloody mattress. Nothing could stop her, no voices scolding that she was a daughter of the Dutch Patroons, that her husband, great as any Roman hero, had made the supreme sacrifice. All she knew was the body grief of a woman losing her man, losing the touch of him forever.

"My son—and now my husband—murdered! Oh God! No justice! No mercy! No pity, not on this earth! Oh my dearest husband! How shall I live without you?"

"Remember, Eliza, you are a Christian." Somehow, he'd whispered a reply.

* * *

Hamilton was sometimes conscious, sometimes not. When awake, he asked for a clergyman. Elizabeth sat beside him. Even in William Bayard's tree-shaded house by the river it was terribly hot, a hell on earth. She fanned him, wiped his brow and carried water to his lips.

Bishop Moore from the Episcopal Church in New York came and Hamilton asked for communion. At first the bishop refused. Proprieties must be observed. Hamilton had participated in a duel; he was not formally a member of the church.

Doctor Mason, Betsy's own pastor at the Dutch Reformed Church came, but refused to give the sacrament because he was not permitted to give private communion. After a few hours, Bishop Moore relented. He returned, heard Hamilton forgive his enemies—among them Colonel Burr—and gave him wafer and wine.

The children arrived. There they stood, Alexander, just in his first year at Columbia, James, John, Angelica, Billy, Eliza and little Phil. In the scarred face of oldest boy, fear and shock mingled. Just eighteen, he was about to become the man of the family.

Angelica held baby Phil, seemingly absorbed in his prattle. She refused to give him up to Doctor Hosack and barely glanced at her prone and suffering father. Betsy could not fathom her tearless control.

Not ten days ago the child dreamed this, a thing she and I know well. Could her Angel's tenuous sanity endure another nightmare come true?

James held restive Billy firmly by the hand. Eliza at once attached to her mother's skirt. She stared up at the prostrate figure on the bed with eyes that by the minute grew rounder and rounder.

"Papa?" Her high voice piped. "Papa?"

* * *

Hamilton opened his eyes and looked at his children, a long look. He'd hoped to speak, but now, contemplating what he'd lost, words were impossible. He closed his eyes and pinched his fair brows together.

* * *

Clutching Philip, Angelica turned, bolted through the door. Her mad dash galvanized the adult witnesses.

"Out! All of you!" Bob Troup, who'd just arrived, seized Jamie's arm and propelled him after Angelica. The boys were white, shivering. They knew what they'd seen.

Papa was dying. Their Papa! The most vital, voluble, energetic man on earth, reduced to that pitiful, speechless sufferer. Outside of the room, sobs tore from them, even as

478

they were being admonished "to be brave." Johnny didn't make it through the door. He fainted upon the sill.

* * *

Day passed into night. The river murmured below, lapping the Greenwich docks. On these grounds, the same where the celebration of the ratification of the Constitution had taken place sixteen years earlier, a somber crowd gathered.

Betsy spent the night beside her husband, wiping away the sweat, offering sips of water. Blood dripped gently through the mattress, forming a puddle beneath the bed. Old friends, like Gouverneur Morris, came one after another, looked in and then went out again, faces inflexible with grief. Doctor Hosack was present. He made repeated, unsuccessful efforts to quell her husband's pain with laudanum.

Her sister Angelica arrived and took charge of the children. The dueling pistols, Betsy now knew, belonged to her husband John.

Had he been willing to countenance this, secretly hoping to rid himself forever of the man who so perennially enchanted his wife?

From the depths of her misery and a thousand fears, Betsy considered the handsome full face of her brother-in-law.

No. This was Hamilton's decision. I must put all that away.

There were constant watchers about the door. Mr. Bayard, of course, Bob Troup and Oliver Wolcott and the haggard, guilt-ridden second, Pendleton, came and went.

Despite the laudanum, in spite of his discipline, Hamilton, although quieter, still suffered. About two o'clock of the following afternoon, while Betsy fanned him gently, his jagged breathing ceased.

* * *

479

"Mama, I want to be there when Papa is buried. Alexander says I'll just shame us if I come."

Betsy rolled over in the bed where she lay beside her daughter. After a long strange spell of calm, and just as she had when Phil had died, last night Angel had suddenly dropped to her knees and beaten her head on the floor until it was bloody.

"I knew it! Oh, Papa! Papa! No! No! Just like Phil! Just like Phil! Oh, God help us! It's only a dream, isn't it? Please! Tell me it's a dream!"

They'd slapped her, dosed her, but nothing stopped it. In the end Betsy had simply joined her, arms wrapped around Angelica so her child couldn't do any further damage to herself. Together, they'd keened their loss.

At last they'd fallen asleep together, overmastered by exhaustion and large doses of powders administered by Mrs. Church's physician.

"Mama." The small voice persisted. "I must be there when Papa is buried. I'm old enough."

She tugged the lids of her swollen eyes apart and recognized the petitioner at the bedside as Billy. As the opiate shroud lifted, she wondered where he had come from. She knew that her sister had locked them inside the room, a precaution against Angelica escaping.

"Billy, how did you get here?"

"Through the window, Mama."

For a moment, she hesitated. "Up the wall?"

"Yes, Mama, on the wisteria. It was easy. They said you were sleeping, but I had to talk to you."

William Stephen fixed her with his beautiful hazel eyes, a wild, haunting echo of her murdered Philip. He sat down gingerly on the edge of the bed.

"Oh, Billy! What if you'd fallen? You could have been...." She hugged him, began to weep, helplessly.

"Don't cry, Mama. Please! You know I can climb like a squirrel."

She took the opportunity to thoroughly kiss him. Billy had rejected cuddling almost as soon as he could walk, but today it was allowed.

"Please, Mama! Alex and James say I have to stay home. It's not fair! I'm not a baby. I want to be there. I won't disgrace us. I promise!"

Betsy tried to collect herself, putting back his tangled auburn hair.

"You may go, William Stephen, but understand that you will have to sit still for a very long time. Mr. Morris will make a long speech about Papa. It will be worse than," she paused, searching for the thing which Billy found most unendurable. "Worse than all morning in church."

"Yes, I know, but this will be for Papa. I'll sit still. I promise."

"All right, Billy, but you must keep your promise. Papa will look down from Heaven. We want to make him proud."

"Mama, when I grow up, I shall challenge Colonel Burr and I shall kill him."

"No! No! Don't you dare say that! Papa doesn't want that. No duels! I forbid it. No duels! Never again! No matter what! Not ever! Don't you dare even think it!"

Frantically, she caught his thin shoulders and shook. Beside her, Angelica stirred and moaned.

At once Betsy released him and turned to examine her oldest child. Purple bruises mottled her forehead. Glinting tears emerged from beneath her red lashes.

Soon—too soon!—She'll awake.... Please God, don't let my daughter be mad.

"Angelica's awake. Run and get help! And Billy!" She cried as he obediently sprang to do her bidding, "Go down the stairs, please. There's a key in the bottom drawer."

* * *

Ships in the harbor, British, French and American, fired till the houses shook. Church bells tolled. For two hours the funeral procession wound from her sister's house towards

481

Trinity. French and British frigates peaked their yards and fired their guns; the forts answered. Everywhere colors flew at half-mast. The society of Cincinnati turned out, as did the students of Columbia, the attorneys, physicians, officers of the army and navy, as well as bankers and merchants by the score.

Betsy saw it all through her veil, holding Billy's hand. Whether it was the small dose of fit-root she'd given or plain will-power, for once Billy's behavior was exemplary. The only sign of restlessness was that one small foot swung rhythmically during the long, long eulogy.

The younger Alexander was a statue, but held his head high. Not a tear did he shed. Yesterday she'd seen him walking back and forth talking with Bob Troup, who was privy to the contents of the will. The boy would had only recently entered Columbia, but Betsy knew he would have to work as hard as he could in order to finish, and go to the bar, to help provide.

All those younger brothers and sisters! The lovely Grange, now a millstone around their necks, with so much left owing. Their father's high ideals and untarnished honesty had left them with few resources, perhaps, even insolvent. Betsy could see grim consciousness of the awful burden in Alexander's rigid stance.

Jamie strove manfully with his grief, attempting to copy his older brother's control, but Johnny, sensitive and adoring, unashamedly wept. The boys looked so much alike: fine, mobile features, that reddish hair the hot wind lifted—the treasure of twenty-three years of marriage.

Gouverneur Morris, imposing, portly, his eyes red and his voice thick, was just finishing his eulogy.

"Although he was compelled to abandon public life, never for a moment did he abandon the public service. He never lost sight of your interests. For himself he feared nothing, but he feared that bad men might, by false professions, acquire your confidence and abuse it to your ruin. He was ambitious only of glory, but he was deeply solicitous for you...."

* * *

The two littlest ones and Angelica were at her sister's in the care of servants, her eldest girl now drugged to unconsciousness. As soon as she'd awakened this morning, she'd torn herself out of her mother's restraining arms, jumped out of bed and pushed her arms through the bedroom window, adding yet another set of scars to those thin white arms.

"Papa?" She'd stood, dazed and barefoot in the broken glass, streaming blood. "Papa? Papa, where are you?"

She fixed wild gray eyes on her mother.

"Write him to come back from Washington. I need him! Need him! Philip! Get Philip! He can make them all go away and leave me alone. Why is he always at college? Why doesn't he ever come home? I must see Philip! I must! I must! I can't live without Philip!"

Betsy tried to stem the tide. She hardly dared to think about Angelica.

The coffin covered with ornate tracery was lowered, lowered into a pit that had been dug beside Philip's grave. The words of burial were spoken. Strong and powerful men, the masters of the richest city in America, wept. Betsy trembled as she bent for the handful of earth.

July makes it warm this time.

As the family withdrew, troops fired three volleys over the grave. Tremendous booms from the harbor echoed the salute.

Sons beside her, a small, upright woman dressed in the black she'd wear for the next fifty years walked from the graveyard, out of the shadow of Trinity Church.

"Hamilton did his duty to the end. Now, my duty is to devote the rest of my life to him, to his memory, but, dear Heaven—this world of disastrous event! After Phil—Oh, God—that I should have to bear another such trial...."

Angelica Church, speechless for once, embraced her sister. Betsy whispered, "Would that I could fly to my

483

Blessed Redeemer, and, in His House, be permitted to once again view my Hamilton."

Epilogue
There's Rosemary...

In November of that year, Elizabeth also buried her father. She'd been at his bedside while he'd wept and apologized even as he'd faded away, sorrowing that he was leaving her and his grandchildren. He'd wanted so much to be a help to her, after "their" Hamilton had been taken from them.

She managed to stay on at The Grange for some years, through the offices of good friends who had raised money to pay Hamilton's construction debts. People rallied around, but there was only so much they could do. After a time, Betsy had to sell the beautiful home where she'd hoped to grow old. Once again she found herself in a rented house in the bustling, dirty City with her younger children, Johnnie, Billy, Eliza, and Little Phil.

It was difficult for Betsy to be poor again, hard to be raising young children alone. Years ago, in a grand gesture, Hamilton had renounced his army pension. Small though it would have been, in these desperate straits Betsy would have been glad of anything, no matter how little. She petitioned Congress to have it restored.

The two older boys applied themselves. With the help of friends like Nicholas Fish and Bob Troup, they went early to the bar. Alexander Jr. quickly established an independent practice in the City.

The younger Alexander Hamilton became a meticulous, stern, reliable and rather humorless man. He tried soldiering, as well, and fought with the Duke of Wellington's army against Napoleon. Later, he returned to fight for his country in the War of 1812. He looked like his father, but somehow it wasn't often remarked upon. Occasionally a flash of joy or good humor, like something seen in an old mirror, would illuminate his features, and Betsy would catch a momentary glimpse of her husband. Alex was a careful attorney if not a great one, who won his cases by dint of hard work and clear presentation rather than brilliance. He was a devoted son to Elizabeth, though sometimes at odds with his brothers—all of whom, in one way or another, he judged "irresponsible" and "selfish." He ended his career as a U.S. Attorney.

Jamie also became an attorney, until, as had often been predicted, he became a politician—successful, glib, and slippery—leaping from party to party with an ease that would have incensed his father. Good looking and smooth-talking, James liked to hold forth about "these changing times which call for men who can see which way the wind is blowing." In New York politics, this meant allying himself with the Clintonian Democrats, whose party—and whose leader—had become over the years an abomination to his father.

As a member of Tammany Hall, that powerful machine founded by Aaron Burr in the last days of his power, James prospered. Continuing the quarrel begun in childhood, every one of James' friends was politically and professionally abhorrent to his elder brother, from Martin van Buren, to the violent, perfidious frontier brawler, Andrew Jackson. James met General Jackson during a trip down the Mississippi to visit the newly acquired Louisiana territories. He'd immediately ingratiated himself with the general, an act that paid off handsomely after Jackson became president. Jamie had the finest career of all the boys, with judgeships and as a US Attorney for the Southern District of New York. He was bright, suave and knew how to be charming, but that was where resemblance to his father ended.

After some years of desperate struggle with her oldest daughter, Betsy relinquished Angelica to the care of a Long Island physician, Doctor McDonald, who kept a country asylum. There, in her room, under a skylight she couldn't reach, Angelica prayed and talked to herself for days at a time. Sometimes, when calmer, she played a fortepiano, those pieces by Mozart, Haydn and Scarlatti she'd loved so much. There were times, however, often weeks, in which she'd do nothing but sit on the floor and weep while rocking a ragged cloth doll which she addressed as "Phil."

When she was calm enough to walk in the high-walled garden, she'd go to a spot near the lilacs and sit on a stone bench, her ginger braid trailing. Angelica's connection with the human race had dissolved, but not the one she'd always had with the birds. Soon, mysteriously, doves, sparrows, and finches would arrive. They'd light on her fingers, her shoulders, even her head and take thistle and crumbs from her open hands. If allowed, for an entire day Angelica would sit, unmoving, neither eating nor drinking, visiting and whispering to her beloved feathered friends.

Johnny also became an attorney, but didn't make much of a mark. He remained close to his mother, and retreated into the world of letters, writing histories and helping his mother to catalogue Hamilton's letters. The sensitivity he'd shown as a boy did not help him to make his way in a harsh world.

For years, Betsy searched to find someone to write a biography of her husband, the one she believed his greatness and self-sacrifice deserved. One by one prospective authors were summarily dismissed or fell by the wayside. In the end, John took up the task, producing a large, two-volume history filled with high-minded sentiments and many tender family anecdotes.

After Angelica, it was William Stephen who caused his mother the most heartache, for he was the child who was most like his father. Billy had an uncontrollable mad streak. He was always riding James's horses without permission and getting whipped for it, or skipping school, or getting into fights with boys on the streets.

Although Billy could hardly sit still, somehow he read every book in the family library. He also learned French from some old émigrés around the City who'd befriended him during his truant days. He was bright and quick, but his restless nature got him thrown out of school after school.

487

Finally, in a crowning act of defiance, he left prestigious West Point, "borrowed" a horse from James and rode off with a saddlebag stuffed with his father's books. Years later, he resurfaced as a successful lead miner, boss of a town called Hamilton's Diggings, way out in Illinois.

He maintained order in that barbarous frontier place, wielding a bullwhip and a gun. Rogues—Indian and White—feared Billy Hamilton's fiery temper. Gentlefolk traveling through the wilderness had the astonishing experience of meeting a man who could summon Eastern polish, a man who could speak French and could quote Pope and Shakespeare, while living among illiterate miners in a rough, one room log cabin.

Billy eventually served a term in Congress, where inactivity and a high collar combined to drive him mad. Finally, when the California Gold Rush began, Bill, then in his fifties, sold his lead mine and went west. It was said he'd made a fortune again, this time in gold. Then, suddenly, he'd died. Murder, cholera—no one in those days of claim jumping and epidemics—really knew.

Alexander Hamilton's grave lay in downtown New York, but William Stephen's lay in Sacramento. In one short generation his father's dream—The United States of America—had bridged a continent.

* * *

The youngest children grew up in far more straightened surroundings than their older siblings. Eliza and her mother remained close, even after Eliza married and began a quiet life. Phil the Younger went into the law through the office of his elder brother. He was well respected in the City as an attorney, although he never grew rich. His specialty was the maritime law in which his father's cases had set so much of the precedent, but "Little Phil" was more inclined to argue on behalf of poor sailors than rich captains.

And even while raising her brood, Widow Hamilton set about doing charitable works, using her influence among her husband's associates to help establish orphanages and schools for poor children. She was just as likely to take the money her brothers sent her and use it to supply the New York orphanage she had helped to found, the first in the City. This organization gave special pleasure to Betsy, for she never forgot how her beloved and brilliant husband had been left as a friendless child, cast upon the world. Beggars and poor widows alike knew that there would always be, not only a hand-out, but a help-out, after a knock upon her door.

* * *

"...When blessed memory shows her gentle countenance and her untiring spirit before me, in this one great and beautiful aspiration after duty, I feel the same spark ignite and bid me...to seek the fulfillment of her words: 'Justice shall be done to the memory of my Hamilton.'"— Eliza Hamilton Holly

* * *

In the bitter November of 1854, as Eliza began the task of laying out the body of her ninety-seven year old mother, she discovered, beneath all her clothes, a little bag pinned to her inner shirt. Inside, folded and unfolded a thousand times, apparently much wept upon, were the last two letters Papa had ever written, letters which explained why he'd gone to meet Aaron Burr. One had been written the night before the duel:

The Scruples of a Christian have determined me to expose my own life to any extent rather than subject myself to the guilt of taking the life of another. This must increase my hazards & redoubles my pangs for you. But you had rather I should die innocent than live guilty. Heaven can preserve me and I humbly hope will, but in the contrary event, I charge you to remember that you are a Christian. God's Will Be Done! The will of a merciful God must be good.

Once More Adieu My Darling, Darling Wife
— New York, July 10, 1804, Tuesday Evening 10 o'clock

Eliza Holly was a small woman with a stoic Schuyler set to her jaw. Today, she sighed deeply, trying to keep tears at bay. The story she'd heard many times, but the faded, familiar handwriting brought the past—and her mother's sorrows—to life again.

Oh, this tiny pale shell is all that remains of our proud mama who has lived for so long—so long! A whole other lifetime—fifty long years after losing Papa.

Sometimes Eliza wondered about the notion of Honor that had compelled her father to abandon them. His absence had haunted her life. Behind her mother's daily good cheer, behind her charming recollections offered to interested visitors, behind her endless acts of charity, her busy hands, or her work for the orphanage, even behind her daily early morning walks, lay that loss.

Pausing, Eliza turned to study her own reflection in the mirror. She'd inherited her mother's coloring, but her once beautiful dark hair had long since turned silver. As she stood, lost in her own reflection, out of the blue, came a memory of the afternoon when that atrocious James Monroe had come calling, had sent in his card.

They had been enjoying fine weather in the garden. Mama, after examining the card the maid had brought, spoke in a low voice, one she used only when she was very angry.

"What has *that man* come to see me for?"

A young and feckless visiting cousin had spoken up before Eliza could find her tongue.

"Why, Aunt Hamilton, don't you know, it's Mr. Monroe, and he's been President, and he is visiting here now in the neighborhood, and has been very much made of, and

490

invited everywhere. He says he has come to pay his respects."

Eliza had been shocked to speechlessness that this enemy, ex-president or not, would have had the gall to set foot inside her mother's house! There had been a long, uncomfortable silence, and then:

"I will see him."

When Mother entered the parlor where he waited, Mr. Monroe stood. He looked unwell and was wrapped in a rather shabby black coat some years out of fashion, a top hat in hand. Mother had stopped in the middle of the room, straight as a ramrod, facing him, with her hands folded and pressed against her bosom. She did not approach and she did not ask the ex-president to have a seat.

President Monroe had bowed, and then made what he imagined was a conciliatory speech. He said it was many years since they had met, that lapse of time brought its softening influences, and that they both were nearing the grave, a time when past political differences could be forgiven at last.

Mother's answer was delivered in a strong, clear voice.

"Mr. Monroe, if you have come to tell me that you repent, that you are sorry, very sorry, for the misrepresentations and the slanders, the stories you circulated against my dear husband, if you have come to say this—I understand it. But, otherwise, no lapse of time, no nearness to the grave makes any difference."

She had stood, small and fierce as only Elizabeth Hamilton, a haughty descendant of van Rensselaers and Schuylers, could, unassailable in her widow's black, facing down an ex-president. After an endless, motionless moment, Monroe had had no other recourse than to retreat.

Father, alive or dead, was Mama's true God. And, how dare that odious man attempt to draw a parallel between them...

Mrs. Holly had hoped to perform the final intimate service for her mother calmly, but she wept in earnest now, recalling her mother's long, lonely devotion. Eliza remembered her father not at all, but she believed she saw

491

him in dreams sometimes. He, the man in mother's locket portrait, would smile, a smile that shone through his eyes, and, somehow, whatever was bothering her would find a solution. Mama reminisced about Papa's "beautiful eyes" and Eliza knew—absolutely—that, somehow or other, she recollected them.

So many grandchildren now…

Eliza herself had not been blessed with children, but Johnny, James and the younger Phil had passed the illustrious family name along. Poor, lost-to-herself Angelica had only recently been released from her sorrows. Eliza had known about her brother Bill's death for the last four years, but better Mama should think that her darling Billy was neglecting her, than that he had died before her.

Hadn't Mother, in her eighties and much against *everyone's* wishes, gone on a grueling journey, a succession of rickety, dirty flatboats and coaches all the way from Albany to that filthy Illinois mining town to see him? Upon her return, she'd remarked that the famous western frontier she'd seen wasn't so different from the Albany of her girlhood, full of white rascals and poor, drunken Indians.

Eliza wondered if Mama had somehow learned that Billy was dead and had simply played along with the family's deception. Lately, the old lady had been doing things like that.

The door creaked as an elderly midwife entered carrying a basin. Together they would begin the sad, distasteful task of bathing the shrunken limbs and washing away the last residues of earthly life. Sighing, eyes blurry, Eliza bent to her task.

* * *

The small bag on a chain seemed to have something more inside. After the corpse was redressed and the candles lit, Eliza retrieved and opened it again. The bit of paper she found was so thin, so worn, so cracked and creased, she

492

hadn't at first seen it. Carrying it to the better light of a window, with trembling fingers, Eliza with great care, unfolded it.

It proved to be a partially obliterated bit of verse. With a sudden chill, she understood that what she held was astonishingly old—*a relic*.

In her father's beautiful copperplate hand, this little verse had been penned during those now practically mythical days of the Revolution, from the time when Alexander Hamilton, a poor, unknown aide de camp to General Washington, had dared to court the daughter of a Colonial aristocrat.

Answer to the Inquiry Why I Sighed

Before no mortal ever knew
A love like mine so tender, true,
Completely wretched-you away
And but half-blessed e'en while you stay
If present love turn a...

Decades of her mother's tears had blotted out some of the words. Eliza fought back renewed tears of her own as she read the lines which remained.

...Deny you to my fond embrace
No joy unmixed my bosom warms
But when my angel's in my arms.

~The End~

I acknowledge a special debt to Forrest McDonald, professor of Economics and Law, who pointed out in his pithy "Hamilton" (1988) that his was the only biography written by a scholar versed in the two disciplines through which his subject made his monumental, lasting contributions to the United States. My characterization of Alexander Hamilton owes much to Professor McDonald's work, as well as to Mr. Chernow's monumental 2004 work. The dialogue is sometimes drawn directly from primary source, those twenty-one volumes of Hamilton's letters organized and published by Columbia University.

~~Juliet V. Waldron

Other Novels by Juliet Waldron
From Books We Love

The American Revolution Series
Genesee
Angel's Flight
The Master Passion, Book 1
* * *

The Mozart Series
Nightingale
My Mozart
Mozart's Wife
* * *

The Magic Series (historical fantasy/adventure)
Red Magic
Black Magic
~Coming soon: Green Magic~
* * *

Pennsylvania Romance
Hand-me-Down Bride
* * *

Richard III:
Roan Rose

About The Author

"Not all who wander are lost." Juliet Waldron earned a B. A. in English Literature, but has worked at jobs ranging from artist's model and scrub tech to brokerage. Thirty years ago, after the boys left home, she dropped out of 9-5 and began to write, hoping to create a genuine time travel experience for herself as well as for her readers. She loves her grandkids, kitties, and hikes, bicycles and gardens. She reads mostly non-fiction history and archeology. For over a decade, she's reviewed for The Historical Novel Society as well as presenting writers' workshops at two HNS conventions. When she was eleven, her mother took her to Nevis to see the island where her hero was born. Now, on 21st Century summer mini-adventures, she rides behind her husband of 50+ years on his black, and ridiculously fast, Hayabusa motorcycle.

Bibliography

Alexander Hamilton by Ron Chernow ISBN: 1594200092 Penguin, 2005

The Papers of Alexander Hamilton, 21 volumes, Harold C. Syrett, Ed., Columbia University, 1987

Founding Brothers by Joseph L. Ellis, ISBN: 9780375405440, Knopf, 2000

Alexander Hamilton, Richard Brookheiser, ISBN: 9780684839196, Free Press,1999

The Rise & Fall of Alexander Hamilton, Vols. 1&2, by Robert A. Hendrickson, 9780884051398, Mason/Charter 1976

Memoirs of an American Lady by Anne McVicar Grant, 1987 reprint of first ed., circa 1808

Catherine Schuyler by Mary Gay Humphreys, Charles Scribner, reprint of first ed., circa 1897

Hamilton by Forrest McDonald, ISBN: 9780393300482, W.W. Norton, 1988

Major General Schuyler, Bayard Tuckerman, ISBN: 9780836950311, Reprint, 1969

The Founding Fathers, a biography of Alexander Hamilton in his own words, Vol. 1&2, ed. by Mary Jo Kline, Newsweek Publishers, 1973

Women of the House by Jean Zimmerman, Houghton Mifflin, ISBN 9780151010653, 2006

Alexander Hamilton and the Constitution, by Clinton L. Rossiter, Harcourt, Brace, ISBN: 9780151042159, 1964

Alexander Hamilton's Pioneer Son, by Sylvan J. Muldoon, 1932

His Excellency, George Washington by Joseph Ellis, ISBN: 9781419307270, Knopf, 2006

American Creation by Joseph Ellis, ISBN: 9780307263698, Knopf, 2007

Aaron Burr, Alexander Hamilton and Thomas Jefferson, a Study in Character by Roger G. Kennedy, ISBN: 9780195140552, 2000

Washington' Spies by Alexander Rose, ISBN: 9780553383294, Bantam, 2007

The Young Hamilton by Thomas J. Flexner, ISBN: 9780823217892, Fordham University, 1997

Jefferson and Hamilton by John Ferling, ISBN: 9781608195282, Bloomsbury Press, 2013

Alexander Hamilton, by Broadus Mitchell, ISBN: 9780195019797, Oxford University Press, 1964

Fire of Liberty by Esmond Wright, ISBN: 9780312292010, Folio Society, 1983

Alexander Hamilton, Writings, ed. Joanne Freeman, ISBN: 9781931082044, Library of America

The Empire State (New York, Settlement Through 1875) by John Benson Lessing, The Reprint Company, Library of Congress # 68-57492, 1888

The Treason Trial of Aaron Burr, by R. Kent Newmyer, ISBN: 978-1-107-60661-6. Cambridge University Press, 2012

The Life of Alexander Hamilton, Vols. 1 & 2 by John Church Hamilton. ISBN: 9781276674782, Nabu Press 2010

Alexander Hamilton by Ron Chernow ISBN: 1594200092 Penguin, 2005

The Papers of Alexander Hamilton, 21 volumes, Harold C. Syrett, Ed., Columbia University, 1987

Founding Brothers by Joseph L. Ellis, ISBN: 9780375405440, Knopf, 2000

Alexander Hamilton, Richard Brookheiser, ISBN: 9780684839196, Free Press,1999

The Rise & Fall of Alexander Hamilton, Vols. 1&2, by Robert A. Hendrickson, 9780884051398, Mason/Charter 1976

Memoirs of an American Lady by Anne McVicar Grant, 1987 reprint of first ed., circa 1808

Catherine Schuyler by Mary Gay Humphreys, Charles Scribner, reprint of first ed., circa 1897

Hamilton by Forrest McDonald, ISBN: 9780393300482, W.W. Norton, 1988

Major General Schuyler, Tuckerman, 978-1417967292

The Founding Fathers, a biography of Alexander Hamilton in his own words, Vol. 1&2, ed. by Mary Jo Kline, Newsweek Publishers, 1973

Women of the House by Jean Zimmerman, Houghton Mifflin, ISBN 9780151010653, 2006

Alexander Hamilton and the Constitution, by Clinton L. Rossiter, Harcourt, Brace, ISBN: 9780151042159, 1964

Alexander Hamilton's Pioneer Son, by Sylvan J. Muldoon, 1932

His Excellency, George Washington by Joseph Ellis, ISBN: 9781419307270, Knopf, 2006

American Creation by Joseph Ellis, ISBN: 9780307263698, Knopf, 2007

Aaron Burr, Alexander Hamilton and Thomas Jefferson, a Study in Character by Roger G. Kennedy, ISBN: 9780195140552, 2000

Washington' Spies by Alexander Rose, ISBN: 9780553383294, Bantam, 2007

The Young Hamilton by Thomas J. Flexner, ISBN: 9780823217892, Fordham University, 1997

Jefferson and Hamilton by John Ferling, ISBN: 9781608195282, Bloomsbury Press, 2013

Alexander Hamilton, by Broadus Mitchell, ISBN: 9780195019797, Oxford University Press, 1964

Fire of Liberty by Esmond Wright, ISBN: 9780312292010, Folio Society, 1983

Alexander Hamilton, Writings, ed. Joanne Freeman, ISBN: 9781931082044, Library of America

The Empire State (New York, Settlement Through 1875) by John Benson Lessing, The Reprint Company, Library of Congress # 68-57492, 1888

The Treason Trial of Aaron Burr, by R. Kent Newmyer, ISBN: 978-1-107-60661-6. Cambridge University Press, 2012

The Life of Alexander Hamilton, Vols. 1 & 2 by John Church Hamilton. ISBN: 9781276674782, Nabu Press 2010

CPSIA information can be obtained
at www.ICGtesting.com
Printed in the USA
LVOW12s0151040117

519652LV00004B/232/P